The Rew

KATE STEWART

Copyright © 2018 by Kate Stewart

ISBN-13: 978-1987593419
ISBN-10: 1987593413

All rights reserved. Without limiting the rights under copyright reserved above, no part of this publication may be reproduced, stored in or introduced into retrieval system, or transmitted, in any form, or by any means (electronic, mechanical, photocopying, recording, or otherwise) without the prior written permission of both the copyright owner and the above publisher of this book.

This is a work of fiction. Names, characters, places, brands, media, and incidents are either the products of the author's imagination or are used fictitiously. The author acknowledges the trademarked status and trademark owners of various products referenced in this work of fiction, which have been used without permission. The publication/use of these trademarks is not authorized, associated with, or sponsored by the trademark owners.

Draft editing by Edee M. Fallon, Donna Cooksley Sanderson and Bex Kettner.
Cover by Amy Queau of Qdesign
Formatting by Champagne Book Design

For my readers, thank you will never be enough. And for those who don't believe love is a fictional character.

Abbie

THE CAR CAME OUT OF NOWHERE.

Actually, it was a cab, and it slammed on its brakes, skidding long black tire tracks on the asphalt while laying on the horn.

I bounded through the intersection in my yoga pants and Nikes and turned to give the driver the one-finger salute. He saluted right back and then continued on his way.

I did, too.

This time, I made sure to look both ways before crossing any streets because Chicago was a fricking hazard to my health. I loved it, though.

I loved the buildings scraping the sky, the murky smog that lingered close to the horizon, and the near-constant noise and activity. It made me feel alive.

In a world where I was constantly jeopardizing that status, I guess that was pretty important.

As I stepped onto the curb, I noticed the man huddled between twin shops on the corner. My heart squeezed a little in relief.

"Bennie," I chastised, as I bent to give him a twenty-dollar bill. "Where were you last week?"

He smiled up at me, his clothes reeking of stale cigarettes and a life of street-dwelling.

"Hey Abbie, I got things to do. You know that." He took the money and thanked me. "You're good to me."

"I worry about you," I told him. "Don't disappear on me. And don't go spending that on your girlfriends, Bennie."

He nodded, eyeing the money and I opened the door to my favorite café with a jingle of the bells. Though downtown Chicago had plenty to offer, I was perfectly happy spending half of my Saturday morning in my neighborhood just outside the city. Sunny Side was a local gem that sat a few streets over from my three-flat in Wicker Park. Nestled in my favorite plush and overstuffed pleather chair, I worked on a kitschy macaroni-topped table. I found I got more done on that wobbly table than I ever could in the three-story townhouse I'd spent a fortune remodeling. I could have saved thousands and ordered three gourmet lattes a day, but when winter set in, I knew that office could be a refuge. For the moment, I was perched in the homey surroundings of the café.

Large white bulbs hung from the ceiling while below, abandoned books and crates acted as makeshift partitions between the varied sized tables. The interior walls were lined with endless rows of chipped and overused coffee cups with a catchphrase to match every mood.

I inhaled the smell of freshly-ground coffee beans wafting through the cafe as I sipped on my much-needed latte in my borrowed mug. It read *I Do What I Want* with a pencil sketch of a cat stretching its middle fingers. I hadn't slept much last night; instead, I freaked myself out with every strange noise or inkling, just like I had done every night for the past year. I envisioned every neighbor in a thirty-mile radius as being a serial killer or rapist, and then I watched *Snapped* to distract myself, which instead, only perpetuated my obsessive paranoid cycle.

It was a problem.

My paranoia and my suspicions that everyone had a motive that included deception or worse.

And Sunny Side, with its never-ending fountain of caffeine, had become my refuge every Saturday. The place I could come to and pretend I was a functioning part of society where my issues didn't exist.

I dove into my Saturday routine, sticking an earbud into my ear and immersing myself in the safety of the public place and my private world of music.

It was hard to say how much later it was when I felt like I was being watched.

My ability to leave reality behind the door of the café was absolute. It very well could've been hours.

I felt it, though.

The stare.

Hesitantly, I looked up.

Then froze.

The Bible states that God created the world in six days. So, when it came to time relevance and divine creation, it stood to reason that the Creator took an extra millisecond on the man watching me sip my third latte.

Now, I'm not that kind of woman—the kind who trips over herself and fumbles through her words when a handsome man glances her way. I learned that lesson in a very hard way, and I hadn't forgotten.

To the frustration of everyone close to me and with the stubbornness that any mule would be proud of, I had refused to notice any specimen of the opposite sex ever since.

Forget that he had rugged, supremely masculine features—chiseled, etched, sculpted, and surreal. Add that to unmistakable height and broad stature, apparent by the way he dwarfed the small, round table that sat in front of him. Mix that with full lips and an impressive set of white teeth. All of this confirmed on the seventh day, God rested, and it was *good.*

But what elicited a storm in my soul and calm in my heart were his ocean-green eyes.

He smiled. Grinned, actually.

Dear Lord. That smile...

I looked away. *Focus. You have work to do.* You don't know him. He could be a psycho.

I sipped at my latte, but the cup was now empty.

Internally, I compiled a mental list of flaws so I wouldn't look up at him again.

Neither of us could look away. Then he flashed that all-knowing smile again. Shit!

Abbie. God. Get a grip. He's probably a skirt-chaser and nothing more.

He wiped the top of his nose. Twice. Subconsciously, I did the same and came away with the remnants of my caramel latte.

Damn it!

It was all over my nose and chin, and I knew that my hair was a wreck. And that was a kind assessment of my appearance. It was slob day—my Saturday ritual—and slob days were non-negotiable.

I deserved them, and so did every other woman on the planet. No makeup, no calorie counting, no responsibility. It was my this-is-the-face-I-was-born-with day. All of that, and the fact that I'd nabbed my favorite table was the whipped cream on top. The guy sitting across from me seemed like the possibility of a cherry. Too bad I'd transferred from the risk-taking department a year ago and into self-preservation. It was a pretty boring department.

Even so, his smile was almost enough to make me want to play roulette.

My own thoughts were whoring me out as if I needed to be rump ready.

Get a grip, girl. It's possible that he's a crazy person. He could sew women's flesh into blankets as souvenirs of his kill list. He could be imagining a new skin quilt with your name all over it.

What the fuck was wrong with me?

I had been so careful for three-hundred and sixty-five long days. Annoyingly, no one else in my life had issues and they were moving forward in leaps and bounds. Then there was me, afraid to even say hello to anyone new, and then all of a sudden, BAM!

One look from that fine-ass man in a room full of caffeine fiends and I was ready to abort my morals and any internal warning that kept me at a distance.

All of them, poof, gone because of that damned smile. It stretched wide, enhancing the most alluring and deeply etched dimples I'd ever seen. They were the real thing, nestled in the corners of his perfect mouth. They didn't make him boyishly handsome. They were dead sexy. Few men could pull that off.

He wasn't testing the waters, either; he was drinking me in with zero hesitation.

Bold.

Bold quiltmaker!

With a kicking pulse, I met his stare, and we appreciated each other, though I wasn't sure what he saw when he looked at me. It was too late to wipe the chin goo off without being obvious. I was positive my lime green nightly face mask still tinted my skin. Heat crept up my neck as he took in my Northwestern hoodie, black leggings, and Nikes. I hadn't run a mile, but I looked like I had, and that was a bonus. Though if he saw me run, well, that would be the real tragedy.

I have a kind of running affliction. It's like some spastic part of me can't believe my body is doing it for exercise, rather than running for my life. From the way my friend, Bree explained it, my run looked like the way Julia Louis-Dreyfus danced on *Seinfeld*, except . . . worse. She said when I run, my arms look like they're giving my body a vigorous pep talk.

I'm a bit bow-legged too, so there was that. But this man knew none of that. His smile told me he didn't mind my lazy appearance, caramel-covered chin, or alien colored skin. From looks alone, he was the type of man you dressed up for. And if Old Jade Eyes and I had a future, he was staring at worst case scenario *and* smiling at it.

He was dressed in knee-length, black mesh sports shorts and a gray hoodie. His Nikes looked new.

He lifted an eyebrow, as my Mac pinged with an invitation for AirDrop. His name was no longer a mystery, and I felt a little panic creep in.

Cameron's Mac: Hi.

I looked above my laptop and took a deep breath before I accepted his invitation.

Abbie's Mac: Hi.

Abbie, he's going to wear your skin! I tried to ignore my inner voice.

Cameron's Mac: I saw you with the homeless guy.

Abbie's Mac: Ok?

He took a sip out of his *Real Men Love Pomeranians* mug and shrugged before he typed.

Cameron's Mac: So, that was nice of you. Most people in the city just walk on by.

Abbie's Mac: Oh. Most people do walk past Bennie. But he's different and I'm not most people.

He lifted a brow and bit his lip.

Cameron's Mac: I see that.

Cameron's Mac: Want to have your next cup with me?

Say yes, say yes! It's only coffee!

Abbie's Mac: No, thank you.

You idiot.
His brows drew tight with his frown.

Cameron's Mac: Sure? How about some breakfast?

My pulse raced with the memory of my last reaction to

that type of attention and the consequences, and I answered without another thought.

Abbie's Mac: No, thanks.

His chuckle was deep and covered me, even across the space between us. He bit his full bottom lip as he typed, his smirk still intact.
Fuck. Me. Damn it, Abbie!

Cameron's Mac: Well, I guess today is not my day.

Abbie's Mac: That's all you've got?

I had no clue why I sent that message . . . why I was bothered that he didn't try harder. Just that fucking smirk. It was sexy as hell.
He read my message and shrugged as he typed.

Cameron's Mac: You seem to enjoy coffee. I don't have an agenda. You're beautiful, I noticed. I wanted to drink coffee with you. You said no. I'm going to scrape up the rest of my pride now and head out.

He closed his laptop and stood while I deflated. Damn it. He was being nice. Since when are guys just . . . nice?
Am I a man hater? Have I become that woman?
I spoke up as he slipped his computer into a worn leather bag.
"I'm sorry," I offered in quick apology. "I was expecting some horrible line or screwed up proposition. The web, messaging, anything that has to do with technology has been

hazardous for me. I've seen enough unsolicited dick pics for a lifetime. I was just being cautious." And that was the truth. But I'd said it aloud in verbal vomit. *Did I really say "dick pics" out loud?*

He chuckled again as he looked down at me from where he stood, then grinned.

"Today isn't the right day." The husky baritone of his voice matched the silky hue of his eyes, which seemed to darken as he looked me over.

"No?" I asked in a whisper as I sized up his six-foot-plus frame and imagined the possibilities.

"No," he said. "Maybe we can *not* have coffee again sometime?"

He'd tapped out with a simple 'no' from me. He couldn't have been that interested in the first place.

I couldn't deny the disappointment welling up in my ovaries.

"O*kay*." I lifted the last syllable when he didn't press further.

Cameron pulled out his wallet and set some money on his table then walked over to mine and did the same.

"At least let me buy your next cup."

After setting the bills down, he stood over me briefly and I caught his scent—purely masculine. I inhaled as much as I could without being obvious. He didn't *smell* like a psycho.

Cameron picked up his man–bag while I pictured running my fingers through his messy, inches thick, dark-brown hair.

Don't let him leave. Tell him you aren't that big of a bitch. But that would seem desperate. You aren't desperate. But you are *horny. Omg, are you horny??*

As if reading my thoughts, I caught another flash of his teeth and had to bite my cheek to keep my reaction in check.

"I'll see you."

"Yeah, see you. And thanks," I said to his retreating back, an octave louder than necessary. "For the coffee," I added. Outside the window, Cameron bent and exchanged words with Bennie before sticking some cash in his hand.

Well, Abbie. Guess you'll just have to wait until the next time you roll out of bed and a beautiful man hits on you. Should happen again, you IDIOT!

Once again, my hesitance had cost me. And I couldn't help but feel like this time it cost me big.

Sagging into my seat, I continued to stare in his direction, watching those broad shoulders walk out of my life.

Abbie

A SHARP FINGER POKED ME IN THE SHOULDER, AND I looked up from my seat on the L to see a woman in a bright pink, bubble-covered trench coat hovering over me. Her face was marred with unforgiving age and her teeth the color of a raincloud. I pulled out an earbud playing "Youth" by the *Glass Animals* before she spoke.

"Do you have a cigarette?"

I shook my head as I inched back, retrieving some of the personal space she'd invaded. "No, sorry, I don't smoke."

"Too many non-smokers in this city," she snapped, as she ogled me closely to see if there was anything else on my person she could ask for. I quickly put my earbud back in and looked out the window at the fly-by houses and trees covered in the fading amber sun.

The woman hovered a little longer before she moved on. I ignored the twinge of guilt. I gave to the needy, not the rude and expectant. It's a skill you acquire when you live in the city.

When I stepped off the train at my stop, the brisk air

slapped me in the face. Wicker Park wasn't exactly riddled with crime, but it was a melting pot and always bustling, which still made it necessary to stay alert. With my tote hanging on my arm, I slid my hands into my coat as I walked past the familiar side street cafés, bookstores, shops, restaurants, and pubs. The neighborhood had an intimate charm and a small radius, but on any given day, you would find it hard to spot the same neighbor in a sea of unfamiliar faces.

I thought of Cameron as I walked through the iron gate and up the steps to my three-flat. I'd stopped by Sunny Side that morning in hopes of seeing him and had worked for hours longer than usual in an off chance to steal another glance. It was pathetic, but true.

My love-life had been a train-wreck for the past few years, to put it mildly, and he seemed like a bright spot, an opportunity. And then . . . he'd left.

I shrugged to myself. *His loss.*

After waiting in vain, I'd taken the train into the city to meet my brother, Oliver, for a late lunch. Turned out I waited for two men that day who never showed. Oliver had texted me last minute, saying he couldn't get away from the hospital, but I knew better. He kept a full schedule, both personally and professionally. Even if he was a womanizer, he was rarely alone. I cursed the fact that I envied him for that, because I never thought I'd see the day.

Flipping through my mail I counted my blessings.

I still had my health, a career I loved that afforded me every comfort, including my oversized home. I made the decision to buy despite my marital status. I was pushing thirty-one and still wasn't part of a *we*, so I lifted both middle fingers to Cupid and invested in a love nest of my own.

The top two floors were mine, but I rented out the

basement floor to a little old lady, Mrs. Zingaro, who'd become my second job. Though she was sugarcoated, she creeped me out sometimes. I swore she was dead or dying every time I saw her perched on the bench in her garden. She was one of those people who would stare off into space and scare the shit out of you when they snapped out of it.

My first experience with this last summer had scarred me for life. I'd found her standing statue-still in the middle of her garden—the garden she dug up after I'd paid a fortune for new sod—with a watering can in hand. She was frozen for several moments as I approached her, gently calling her name. I wasn't sure if a corpse could stand, but in broad daylight, I was certain I was witnessing it.

In retrospect, the decision to approach her in her stupor was about as smart as sneaking up on a cat, and I'd gone down like the lightweight I was when she clocked me in surprise with the watering can.

Not many people could say they got their ass kicked with a watering can. I'm one of the lucky ones.

Because of my tenant's need for company, I'd learned how to pretend to fix many things that weren't broken. And because I was lonely most nights, I indulged her.

Tonight, I was thankful the downstairs lights were off when I unlocked my door.

Cautious, as always, I scanned the living room of the home I'd spent two years remodeling, just to make sure I was alone.

Dark original hardwood floors, two-toned gray walls, and bleached furniture with lemon and navy accents. It was exactly what I'd dreamed up when I'd started the renovation project and was now my reality. It was, in fact, perfect, and I was, in fact, alone.

All alone.

Suddenly I wanted to be anywhere else.

"What in the hell is *wrong* with me?" I asked the empty space.

Restless life syndrome.

My phone rattled in my coat just as I threw my purse on the couch.

Looking at my screen, I thanked God when I saw Bree's name. She'd been gone far too long this time. I slid to answer and launched into her.

"You can't leave me alone like this, Bree! Not for this length of time. I'm putting my foot down. I'm going through something close to a mid-life crisis because of your extended absences, and my imagination is in overdrive. I'm pretty sure my new neighbor started killing small animals in his youth. Seriously, he's creepy. How was Scotland? Wait, don't tell me. You and Anthony had sex in obscene places and you're still glowing in the aftermath. I hate you right now, but I missed you so much, I'm willing to forgive you."

"Wow." Bree laughed in response to my breathless monologue. "Talk about passive-aggressive. You're just bored, and you need to get laid. Your new neighbor's name is Simon, and I already met him when I was waiting for you at your place when you lost your keys. He's harmless and teaches Sunday school. Scotland was amazing, I have so much to tell you!"

To tell me?

"Anthony and I . . . "

"No," I shook my head, interrupting her. "Please, babe, no. You are my last partner in crime! Please, *please* tell me I'm not about to buy another bridesmaid dress!"

"You would be maid of *honor* at this one. And I was thinking silky jumpers?"

It was official. *Always a bridesmaid, never the bride. I was seriously going to be alone now. All alone.* I hung my head. "I love you. Congratulations."

"Meet me at our place in twenty?" she asked hopefully.

"Of course," I said, with a teary smile.

"Abbie, can you believe it?"

"Of course I can," I said as I unbuttoned my coat. "You two are perfect for each other. That's why I set you up."

"I know. I never thought I would say this, but I'm saying it. I'm getting married!" She was choking on emotion, and I couldn't wait to see it on her. I was sure she wore it well.

"I know, I know," I said, pushing a tear away from my eyes. *Suck it up and be happy for her.*

"I'll see you in twenty."

Thirty minutes later, I walked into The Violet Hour, a posh but hidden speakeasy on North Damen. The place looked like a wooden fortress on the outside with a graffiti block on the lower half of the building. You wouldn't know it existed if you didn't look for the gold door handle and the line outside of it.

Bree and I had been regulars since we moved to Wicker Park, and it was no easy feat to get a seat on the weekends. But because it was a dreary and wet Sunday night, I slipped right in. I'd changed into my most revealing dress, a long-sleeved crepe V-neck that exposed just enough cleavage to make it sexy. I'd let down my long, auburn hair and tamed it with a few curls. I felt stylish in my new knee-high black boots. I went heavy on the liner over my light blue eyes and colored my lips in a raspberry tinted gloss.

A single chandelier hung from the ceiling, dripping

elegance but leaving the bar dim enough to be shrouded in mystery. Outrageously tall wingback chairs were arranged around the room and clustered together in pairs of two or four, intended for privacy, but close enough that you had little. Candlelight glowed upon the intimate, white granite tables between the seats. I approached Bree at the bar, and she waved when she spotted me.

"Holy shit, you look hot," she said as she stood from her chair as I slipped off my coat.

"Thanks, babe. I haven't had much reason to dress up lately. I needed the practice." I pulled back from her tight embrace with the most genuine smile I could muster before we followed the host to be seated. I slipped into the green leather chair, and the tension in my shoulders relaxed a little. The sexy and forbidden atmosphere put me at ease. The Violet Hour had the feel of pure seduction, as if the interior itself was saying: *Hey, it's okay to be bad here. Take a souvenir home with you.*

"Okay, let me see it," I demanded, gripping her left hand only to see her finger was bare.

"He didn't plan it," she said with a serene smile as she squeezed my hand and let go. "And *that's* why I said yes. He didn't even ask me."

That earned an eye roll.

"God, that's just like you two. 'Hey, let's go to the movies sometime.' 'Hey, let's move in together.' 'Hey, let's quit our jobs and travel the world for three months.'" I shook my head with a grin, but I secretly thanked God that their three-month walkabout this past summer was over. That separation nearly cost me my sanity. This last trip had only been a little over a week long. Her life seemed glamorous, and I envied her for that, but I was happy she'd finally found someone to keep her grounded in Chicago. At least, that was my selfish hope. It was obvious I was too dependent on her, but she had been my one constant since my first month at Northwestern.

Bree lowered her face and gave me a pointed brown gaze. "Hey, all of those ideas were awesome! And not all *mine*. Anthony came up with a few."

"God save him. Anthony is in for it with you as his wife."

"And he knows it. Jealous?" she asked playfully.

"Absolutely. He's so lucky," I said with a wink. "You'd make a perfect wife for me."

"It's a shame I'm not a lesbian. With the way you look in that dress, I may have folded."

"Ew," I said with a laugh. "If I were going to go that direction, it wouldn't be with you. I've seen where your mouth has been."

"We made out once," she said unabashedly. "Don't you forget it."

"You licked my lips because I ate all your nana's homemade butterscotch pudding. That's hardly making out. And I never did it again."

"It counts," she insisted, running her fingers through her blond ponytail before retrieving a small box from her purse. "I brought you a present."

"Oh, you definitely *should* have. But this can wait. Tell me everything."

"Well," she started without taking a breath, "we'd just had the best sex of our lives."

"Wait," I said as the cocktail waitress approached, and I ordered us two Pimm's Cups.

Bree quirked a brow. "Are you sure you want to hear this? You sounded pissed on the phone."

"Jesus, Bree," I whispered defensively. "Of course, I want to know everything. You're my person. And jealousy aside, which I am admitting to, you look so happy. I'm fucking over the moon about this. I love you and Anthony together."

It was obvious she was chomping at the bit to tell me more. Bree was a big personality in a tiny package at a little over five feet and a few inches. But when she spoke, you instantly knew she was the most dominant female in the room. With her honey blond hair, expressive brown eyes, and mouth like a sailor, she could be intimidating to those who had just met her. But beneath her brash exterior lay an amazing and loyal heart.

"Abbie, he was so open to *everything* on this trip. It was like I was seeing a new side of him. I can't even explain it. I mean, we've traveled all over now, but this was different. So different."

I listened as she spoke about the start of their trip. Bree was known to push boundaries for the greater good. And her fiancé, though mostly conservative, had stepped up to the challenge of courting my best friend, which was no easy feat.

After a few minutes of Bree's chatter, my demeanor changed because her excitement was infectious, and I fed off it until my spirits lifted.

Why worry about a man when you're lucky enough to have a friend like Bree? I no longer felt guilty for being a little dependant on her because Bree was the shit.

"Okay, okay, get to the good stuff."

"Well," she began with a devilish grin. "We were at the fairy pools."

"And?" I said, taking my glass from the waitress with a "thank you."

I took a healthy sip and toasted with my best friend. "Congrats, baby. Drinks are on me."

"They are always on you," she said with an eye roll.

"Say thank you," I said dryly.

"Thank you. Anyway, we were going at it like rabbits, in broad daylight. Oh," she said with a hand to her chest like a coquettish southern belle, which was apt. She was Georgia bred and hadn't dropped her accent since we met at Northwestern. "I can't even. He was everywhere, and I mean everywhere." Her lips twisted into a wry smile. "I've never had it so good. I need him. I have to be with him. I just knew, so I told him so."

"This was postcoital, right?"

"Yes and no. This was between round one and two."

"Aren't the fairy pools a major tourist spot?"

"We had one close call and then took it on the road," she said with a wink. "We christened the whole of Scotland."

"Sweet Anthony, he was so innocent," I muttered, taking another mind-numbing sip of my drink. "Poor guy. You ruined his virtue."

"I've told you this once, and I'm telling you again, anal is how you get them to propose."

I barked out a laugh as she waggled her brows. "Hey, this is my third proposal by a different man. Numbers don't lie. I just decided to accept this one."

"Your ass is tired, huh?"

"Don't be crude," she scolded playfully.

"God, I love you," I admitted truthfully. "Please continue."

"It was so beautiful. You *know* me, Abbie, and you know I'm a total sucker for scenery, but Scotland really is *magical*. And it wasn't just the sex. It was being with him and just *knowing*. It was so . . . seamless. Like kismet or fate or destiny, all that shit you don't believe in. I'd just had his perfect penis, and we were so disgusting, but he just looked at me and I said yes. He didn't even have to ask. That's how on another level we were."

She was so happy; her eyes were literally shining.

"You know you can count on me for whatever you need, right? I'm so happy for you."

She hooked an elated tear away with her finger. "I can't do this life without him," she swore. "I mean, I can, but I don't want to. I'm marrying that man, Abbie."

"Then let's plan a wedding," I said, as I clinked glasses with her. I had the sweet concoction halfway to my mouth when I saw *him* two chairs over.

I froze and looked again.

It couldn't be him.

We were sitting close enough to where I could see his threatening dimples.

His dark hair styled back neatly, so debonair, and it looked like he was born for it. Old Hollywood was the perfect way to describe him.

Cameron wore a black tailored suit and wine-colored tie that closely matched the color of my dress. His presence in the bar had to be a coincidence; it was evident in the surprise that shone in his features when he saw me.

His lips twitched, and his eyes drank me in from hair to boots. His fingers tapped lightly on the armrest of his chair before he trailed a single finger down the leather as if he were tracing it over where his eyes roamed along my neck and chest. It was a seconds-long seduction that had my lips parting and my thighs squeezing together.

"God damn," I whispered under my breath while a blush crept up my neck.

Staggering effect.

Too bad he liked to clip his victim's toenails and make necklaces out of them.

My phobia jolted me back to attention.

Thanks to my ex, it was a new character flaw that had led to some scary nights alone at home. Nights where Bree met me at my front door, teeth bared, at two in the morning because I'd made myself a little paranoid. Okay, a lot paranoid. I'd gotten better. And I hadn't watched that creepy Ted Bundy movie in six months. But for the record, that slow-motion scene with the beachy music where he goes from nice guy to *you're next* . . . well, if you haven't seen it, don't watch it. I'm convinced that actor killed someone to get into character.

See? Paranoid.

Not all serial killers had the looks and charm of our fair Ted, but the man staring at me now with illicit promise in his eyes could easily seduce any woman. Case in point, *me*.

Cameron was speaking to someone I couldn't see. It was definitely another man because I could see slacks and black dress shoes. I might have let out a tiny breath of relief.

"Who are you staring at?" Bree asked, twisting in her seat to look in Cameron's direction.

Discreetly, I held my palms up in my lap. "Don't look . . . You're looking and that's exactly what I told you *not* to do," I whisper-yelled. "Stop looking. You're still looking. Damn it, Bree. And now he sees you looking, and do you see those damned dimples?"

"Damn," she said as she looked over at me. "You know him?"

I shrugged. "Kind of. His name's Cameron and he AirDropped me at Sunny Side on Saturday."

"AirDropped?"

"When you have a Mac, you can find and message other Macs around you and share files and stuff."

"Oh," she said with her typical indifference to technology. She wasn't much of a fan. I was sure if she wasn't a nurse, her wanderlust would have her living in a treetop somewhere.

"Anyway, he asked me if I wanted to have coffee and I said no."

Her eyes bulged. "You snubbed that hot-ass man?"

"Yeah," I said as I glanced his way again. He was engaged in conversation as I held my glass close to me like it would shield me.

"Nuh-uh, sister, you need to put that down and let him enjoy the view."

"Would you keep your voice down?" I snapped. "Yes, I turned him down. You know what happens when I hook up with strange men."

Bree paused. "Not everyone is Luke," she said softly, for what was probably the hundredth time. I shrugged.

"Besides. He's not a very hard worker. He took my 'no' for an answer the first time."

"That's because you're scary," she said with a grin, back to her playful self. I curled my lip at her. "You are. Your resting bitch face is pretty but *scary*. And in the last year, it's gotten worse. Your bitch face reads 'Abandon all hope. You can't stick your penis here.' But, by the way, he just looked at you. I think it's safe to say he gives no shits. He wants to put his penis into your vagina."

"Bree," I scolded through gritted teeth.

"It's been a year. A *year*," she stressed in a whisper. "That's too long, Abbie. I know what happened with Luke freaked you out, but you can't let him win."

I shook my head to keep the conversation short. It was the last thing I wanted to think about right now.

"I'm good. I promise. I even told him—Cameron," I whispered, "that I was sorry for turning him down."

She looked up at the ceiling—her version of an eye roll.

"Well, I guess that's a start. And he's not deterred. He must be new to the neighborhood. If I weren't madly in love and set on forever with Anthony, I'd rock the shit out of that."

"You can't do things like that anymore," I said in a sing-song voice as I lifted my drink and wrinkled my nose.

She narrowed her eyes. "You've been dying to say that."

Shrugging, I glanced Cameron's way, and his eyes were already fixed on me. A spark ignited flames that began to race through my veins, my whole body gravitating in his direction. I mouthed a "Hi" and he winked.

How long had he been there?

"Damn, girl, he looks good on you," Bree said with enthusiasm, picking up her drink and twisting back to speak to Cameron.

Oh, my God. My body tensed with dread, although I should've expected nothing less from her.

"She likes caramel lattes, men who know the clitoris isn't a fictional character, and real Christmas trees," she informed him as if he was suffering from hearing loss.

Cameron's hot gaze remained on me, his grin lifting with each word she spoke.

"I'll keep that in mind," he replied, unfazed by her directness, his stare lingering before he gave her his full attention. "Congrats, I've always wanted to go to the fairy pools."

"Thanks," Bree said as my breath hitched. Had he heard every word? Probably not, but I was sure that he'd heard Bree's words because she didn't know how to talk without yelling. I'd grown used to it over the years, but The Violet Hour wasn't the best place to catch up with a tone-deaf southerner. My face flooded with embarrassment as more drinks were delivered and our waitress leaned in.

"The gentlemen wanted me to ask about *not* having

coffee on Saturday?"

"Did he?" Bree mused slyly before she turned back to Cameron. "She'll be there at eleven. The girl is a night owl and is fond of her sleep."

Cameron's lips twitched in amusement at Bree's candor. "Noted, and thank you . . ."

"I'm Bree," she said, tipping her cup his way.

"Thank you, Bree."

He stood, shaking hands with his tablemate, just as a tall brunette approached him. I continued to stare as she took Cameron's hand in greeting and then let out another breath of relief when she made herself comfortable in his newly abandoned seat.

Not with her. He's not with her.

And neither was his attention. He made it a point to catch my eyes before he disappeared behind the curtain.

"That was some serious eye fucking," Bree said. "He's huge, like . . . damn. I bet he played football or something sexier. Ooohhh, rugby." She waggled her brows as I sank into my chair. "Bree," I hissed. "Why, woman? Why would you do that? I just told you I turned him down."

"Now listen here, heifer," she said, as I rubbed my temples in an attempt to keep my hands from circling her neck. Bree loved calling me a cow when she had a point to make. She claimed it was a southern thing. "That horse there is the one you are going to climb on to get back into the big parade. Call it what you will, 'Abbie got her groove back' or 'Abbie got her back broke.' I don't care. But you will be at the coffee shop this Saturday, and you will be receptive to that fine-ass man. Do you hear me?"

A collective "yes" was hissed in all directions at us. I had no choice but to brush it off because it was the norm. Bree had been told to quiet down at a concert. Who in the hell gets told to quiet down at a concert? Bree, that was who. She sat back, satisfied with her spectacle, as she pitched her voice toward the chairs around us. "Good, then you can each buy me a drink to celebrate my upcoming nuptials."

Abbie

"**H**EY, ABBIE, HOW WAS YOUR WEEKEND?" Kat called out as I walked past her office door and set down my soaked tote next to my desk. I went to greet her and found her thumbing through a folder. I looked like a wet mutt, but she didn't have a hair out of place. I studied her carefully to test the waters. Kat was beautiful, very *Snow White* in appearance with dark hair, pale skin, and red lips, but at times she had an odd temperament. She was one of those women whose mood you had to gauge to decide if she was having *one of those days*.

When I began consulting at the firm she worked for a month ago, I was met with expected and underlying hostility at our introduction. It had been tumultuous for a time, but since then we'd become chummy.

Kat and I were always the first two to arrive at the silver tower at Preston Corp. On the twenty-second floor, Preston was losing money, and that's where I came in. Kat headed up the Finance division and her job was the one on the line. We worked closely together and each day, I gave her assurances that the redlining of the department wasn't due to any mismanagement on her part.

She looked up now and gave me a sincere smile, which was a green flag.

I exhaled and smiled back.

"Well, my weekend started out great and then it got a little weird," I answered. "I had a flirtation with a gorgeous man, but for some godforsaken reason I rejected him, and then I bumped into him again the next day. I don't really believe in fate or kismet but it was as if we were being pushed together. I'm supposed to meet him for coffee and I'm pretty sure if I don't—I'll end up adopting cats. I'm the last of my friends to pair off."

"Ha!" She scoffed harshly, making me jump in my seat. "Run the other way. Trust me, marriage isn't all it's cracked up to be." She slipped her purse into her desk drawer, while the two-carat evidence of her marital status glistened on her finger. "Seriously, it's no *picnic*."

"Tell me how you really feel," I chuckled as she joined me at her door before we made our way to the breakroom for a much-needed caffeine jolt.

Kat's face contorted in disgust as she grabbed two mugs and set them on the counter, her lithe figure wrapped in a new designer dress. She'd been a gymnast when she was younger and a bit of a celebrity. She'd revealed that to me over stale sushi when we had one of many late nights.

Though she did show concern for her position, I had a feeling through our conversations that money wasn't one of her worries. I often wondered if her main concern had to do with the husband she was always ranting about.

"Lately, he's worthless," she fumed as she tapped the artificial sweetener into her cup with perfectly manicured nails. Her phone buzzed on the counter as she stirred in her sugar. "Speak of the devil," she said before she picked up the call. "Hi, Jefferson. It's not a good time." A short pause. "Can we discuss this later? I'm at work."

I stood by the machine as she listened then her eyes went cold as she spewed venom.

"I told you I didn't want it. No, no, it's not all up to *you*. Why are we talking about this again? Seriously, why? The hell you are! Jesus Christ, I'm at work," she whisper-yelled. "I don't have time to talk about this. Go play with your toys." She looked up at me and rolled her eyes. "No, no, no. NO! Listen to me. Listen. To. The. Words. Coming. Out. Of. My. Mouth. I'm done with this. It's not up for discussion and it's ridiculous." She sighed as she ended the call. "See? *So* much fun."

I didn't ask any questions. I'd heard more than one of those conversations and felt bad for the poor man. She was horrible to him. And though I hated to admit it, I felt better about myself at that moment. I wouldn't talk to my worst enemy the way she talked to him, let alone the man I promised forever to. In fact, I'd been on the receiving end of similar insults. I knew all too well how it felt.

Maybe I really was better off alone.

Kat picked up her cup and sighed. "I'm hard on him, I know. But I can't handle when he gets all needy."

"Hey, I'm not judging," I lied.

She shrugged, and I could see little to no remorse in her eyes for the way she just spoke to her husband. "I'm just over it lately. Maybe I'll just go home and screw his brains out to keep the peace for a while."

"Now, *this* is coffee talk." We both turned to see Avery—a

newly hired temp—in the doorway wearing a Cheshire smile.

"What did you hear?" Kat said with a giggle unfit for a woman in her late thirties.

"Something about screwing brains. And if it weren't against company policy to have this conversation, I would correct you. That's not how the anatomy part of it works."

Kat giggled again, smitten, while I rolled my eyes. She fell for his ass-kissing antics daily. I was over it after the first ten minutes I'd spent with him, but it wasn't my ass he kept kissing. Java in hand, Kat and I set out on our day, working through lunch, and purging the majority of our to-do list.

After hours of tireless number crunching, I sat kicked back at her desk and spoke through a mouthful of Shrimp Lo Mein. My mind drifted back to Cameron. I'd been thinking about his smile for the past two days. Although I was mentally kicking myself in the ass, I didn't know if I was ready for anything more than flirtation. But it had been some time since I daydreamed about anyone.

Kat was absently typing up a list of notes. She always preferred working to eating. I envied her for her figure, though she was a little too thin.

I set my noodles down and pushed the day away from underneath my exhausted eyes. "What time is it?"

"Six-thirty."

"Six-thirty?!"

I couldn't believe we'd been at it for so long. I was wiped, but Kat looked like she'd gotten her second wind. I hated riding the train from the city at night. I made quick work of packing up, but Kat hadn't moved.

"Don't you want to get home?"

Kat glanced away. "Not really. But I guess I'll go have sex." She sighed tiredly, standing up to stretch, and I grinned.

"You're a real jerk, you know that? Some of us don't have the luxury of convenient sex," I reminded her as we threw out the trash and grabbed our purses. "Maybe you should just try and enjoy it."

"You don't know him," she rolled her eyes.

"Do you love him?" I asked.

She looked at me pensively as we stepped into the elevator.

"I've been married four years but *in love* only a few of them. That's the most honest answer I can give you. My marriage is a shitty example. Don't let my stance on it sway you. And by the way, I was your age when I got married. He's younger."

"Cougar, huh?" I chimed happily, waggling my brows.

She shook her head with a wry smile. "I shouldn't have told you."

"Oh, you definitely *should* have," I disagreed with a laugh. She rolled her eyes as we walked through the double doors of the lobby.

"Just be careful. You never really know someone unless they want you to," she said absently. "See you tomorrow."

She'd unknowingly struck a nerve.

My hidden fear.

That no man could be trusted.

That every man might hurt me.

I managed to muster a "goodnight" as I grabbed the rattling phone in my pocket and saw the incoming text.

Rhonda: What are your plans for June of next year?

Soon after, she sent a wedding bell emoji. I looked heavenward and shook my head. My guardian angel must have taken the year off or decided I was equally pathetic and resigned.

Probably after I passed on coffee with Cameron.

I stared down at the text. Rhonda knew I'd seen the message. If I didn't respond I'd look jealous, guilty or both.

Me: Congratulations! June is all yours! I'm in a meeting. I'll call you after!

I hit send just before my phone buzzed in my hand with an incoming call. Thankful it wasn't Rhonda calling me on my bullshit, I sighed and slid to answer.

"Hi, Mom. I can't talk now." I watched Kat disappear into the parking garage and started making my way toward the train.

"What a way to greet the woman who grew you in her body for nine months. I have stretch marks, you can give me five minutes."

I sighed.

"Am I really that bad?" she asked playfully, though I knew I'd hurt her feelings.

"No. I'm sorry. I'm just distracted. This insanely handsome man asked me to join him for coffee on Saturday, and I'm not sure I want to show."

"Why in the hell not? It's been long enough. Go have some fun."

I was being consoled by my mother and could feel the blood of an old maid start to circulate through my veins. "Yeah, well, here's the truth. I'm sick of this whole shit show. I'm seriously over it. And working all the time. I mean I don't want to be alone forever, but I'm not sure now is the time, either. I'm at some weird crossroads. They say it happens when you least expect it, right? I'm trying really hard not to expect anything."

"Speaking of expecting, any idea where your brother is?

He promised me dinner this week."

"He's such a shit. He ditched me yesterday for lunch."

"He's probably out at his fort," she said, referring to his cabin in the woods. A place I wouldn't dare visit.

"He's an idiot."

"You watch too much crap," she scorned.

"Mom, Ted Kaczynski lived in the woods. Okay? The Unabomber. People only go to the woods to make moonshine, cook meth, inbreed, plot murder, execute it, and bury the bodies."

"Or hunt, fish, relax, and enjoy nature."

"Or in Oliver's case, hide from the newly-jaded wench of last week." My brother was a playboy who often created his own drama. Growing up, he was a handful and caused enough trouble for both of us. And so, my mother decided to place all her lofty expectations on me. She loved him unconditionally because she had no choice.

"He's probably impregnating," I added.

"I hope so. I'm honestly to the point I don't care as long as he gets a baby momma, so I get a baby."

"Mom!" I admonished with a laugh. "You don't really want him to reproduce, do you? I mean, the ego on that punk."

"You two are taking forever," she scolded. "I thought you and—"

"Did you call for any other reason?" I interrupted. She was going to go on about my ex, Xavier, like she always did. We broke up years ago. And I think her heart broke more than mine had. I didn't have the patience to relive that conversation.

"Yes," she piped happily. "Come over, I'm making you lasagna."

"No. Mom, I know you're trying to cheer me up, but I just want to chill at home."

"Okay, baby, but the invitation is always open." I could hear the disappointment in her tone. I was being a shit to my own mother.

I pulled out my card and tapped it for entrance before I headed toward the train. "Am I mean?"

"Mean?" She laughed. "No, honey, you have a heart of gold and a mouth like no other. You are no bullshit and refuse to give false compliments. A lot of people love the bullshit, but they especially love the false compliments."

"So, I'm bitter?"

"A little, but who isn't? That comes with living, and you aren't fresh-faced anymore. You're no spring chicken."

"Gee, thanks," I said as I walked the long corridor glancing around to see I was alone.

"I just mean that you're no dummy. We raised you to be picky, Abigail. We didn't want you settling. And aside from that idiot you almost handed yourself to last year—what was his name?"

"Exactly, let's not," I said as my spine pricked in awareness. All she knew was that I was dating Luke. And the scary part was she wouldn't have remembered his name. But Bree would have.

"Enjoy the lull, baby girl. I promise it will pick up, and when it does, it might not set you back down. Listen to your elders."

"I listen to you. I always listen to you," I said proudly. My mother was a Pulitzer Prize-winning photojournalist and humanitarian. Her pictures had earned numerous awards across the globe and had changed countless lives. She was healthy at sixty-three, was still married to the love of her life—my father—and still fulfilling every dream she could fit into her enormous life. And though it was full, she refused to stop stuffing it with more of whatever her heart desired. I had one hell of an example set for me.

"You are something else, you know that? You're probably researching your next trip while you stir the sauce. Only my mother would try to save the world while making me a lasagna."

"You put too much faith in me. My lasagna isn't that good."

"Yes, it is, and so are you."

"Flattery, huh?" She laughed over the line.

"I'm trying to be more personable. How does it sound on me?"

"Like you're trying too hard. And you *are* nice. You're a bleeding heart, you know that? Listen, honey, I know you want everything *now*. It's been that way since you were little, but you need to want what you *have* now."

"This is becoming a little lecture-ish. And I'm trying, finally trying to stick my neck out there." If she only knew what an understatement that was.

"Abbie, you're beautiful, successful, and totally independent. I'd say my work is done, but I hope you never really stop needing me."

My heart broke a little with her words. Maybe I was those things before I met Luke, but I was still struggling to get that girl back. So many times, I'd wanted to tell her what happened, and at every single opportunity, I choked. It was no different as I stood mute with the phone in my hand waiting on the subway. She took that silence as confirmation I needed more encouragement.

"Abbie, you worked hard for all that success, and you need to remember that when you get invited to watch another wedding."

She knew. Of course, she knew. "How did you know?"

"I can hear it in your bitter voice." She laughed. "Who is it this time?"

"Rhonda Ziglar, and she's thirty-two, so it gives me hope. Another bridesmaid dress. Another partner in crime gone. Mom, all my rowdy friends are settling down."

"Abbie, look at it this way, if you were a shitty person, no one would want you in their wedding."

"I'm going to give a terrible toast. Maybe it will scare the others away," I said with a sigh. "I'll have a closet full of dresses like that chick in that movie."

"I don't watch movies and you know it. Come over. We'll eat lasagna, plot your speech, and drink too much of your father's expensive scotch."

Shoulders slumped, I nodded though she couldn't see. I didn't know how it was possible, but my mother was cooler than me. "I'll be there in a few hours."

Abbie

THE FOLLOWING SATURDAY—DECIDING TO POSTPONE slob day for Sunday—I sat at my favorite table at Sunny Side wearing a cream sweater dress, skin-tight jeans, and comfortable slip-on Uggs. I'd powdered my freckles and used my favorite shimmering lip gloss. With my tresses stacked neatly and tied up, I sipped my caramel latte—extra foam—and powered up my Mac, *just in case*. I hadn't seen Cameron waiting when I walked in and ignored the slight sting of disappointment. Maybe he'd found someone in that suit he wore who'd said yes to a drink and seemed less complicated than me. I had to brush it off. If it wasn't Cameron, maybe it was someone else.

Abigail, today you will be open to possibilities. You'll leave your cynical and bitter bitch face at the door. You will visualize what you want and go for it with eyes wide open and a clear mind. You are crazy. You've lost your damn mind and you sound like a self-help book. Help yourself by realizing you are crazy.

I buried my face in my hands and sighed before I killed the pessimist for the moment. Two cups into my workload, it happened.

Cameron's Mac: Hi. Sorry I'm late.

I peeked over my screen to see a waiting smirk. The man looked like a cologne ad. I wanted to rip him open, scratch, and sniff, but not in that order. My belly dropped as the soft buzz of his presence drifted over my skin. He was wearing a thin sweater over a button-down, dark jeans cuffed at the bottom—which I found sexy—and brown leather boots.

Amused eyes studied me as his black lashes flitted over his cheeks and he tilted his head in admiration. His expression was as alluring as his threatening dimples. I had to rip my eyes away to respond.

Abbie's Mac: Hi. It's okay, I was just catching up on some work.

Cameron's Mac: What do you do?

Abbie's Mac: I'm a corporate financial consultant. It's a pretty boring conversation starter. But I've got a thing for numbers.

Cameron's Mac: Nothing boring about it if it's your thing. You look like you're in a better mood today.

I gave him a cheeky grin.

Abbie's Mac: Opposed to?

Cameron's Mac: The witchy one you were in last time we were here.

I opened my mouth in mock shock and pointed at myself.

Abbie's Mac: How rude!

Cameron's Mac: Yes, you were. Even so, I bought your coffee.

Abbie's Mac: I did say no. I was polite about it.

Cameron lifted his mug that read *Surely Not Everybody Was Kung-Fu Fighting*. I laughed and shook my head. The air shifted. I let myself sink into the small amount of comfortable playfulness between us. I could do this.
This could be easy. And dare I hope, fun?

Abbie's Mac: I'll let you buy me a cup today, but there are rules.

He frowned.

Cameron's Mac: Already?

Abbie's Mac: Yep. This is how we, meaning you and me, coffee. Just like this, behind our keyboards.

Cameron's Mac: Coffee as a verb? I like it. But no talking?

I lifted my finger in a plea to have him hear me out as it came to me.

Abbie's Mac: Here's the way I see it. First, I don't know if you are interested in . . . more than coffee.

Cameron's Mac: I'm very interested in . . . more than coffee. But I'm okay if it's just coffee too.

Abbie's Mac: I'm old school. And I'm pretty pissed off about this whole technology hookup crap being the new standard. I'm no prude, but it's like I woke up from a monogamous nap and romance died. What happened to getting to know a person before you showed your pink parts? I was serious when I told you I'd been blasted with dick pics. I have proof.

Cameron's Mac: So, you saved the dick pics? You little pervert.

My mouth dropped. "No, that's—"
"Shhh," Cameron pointed to the keyboard.

Abbie's Mac: Like I said, I'm not looking for romance in the ankles-covered, Pride and Prejudice sense, though Mr. Darcy did set the standard for me when I was twelve. I don't have to have Mr. Darcy, but at the very least a cheesy 90s rom-com, overt type of gesture. I just think this whole digital age has ruined romance. I don't have the millennial mindset. Think about it, when's the last time you saw a couple holding hands, or for that matter, some inappropriate PDA? Aside from my friends, Bree and Anthony, I can't remember the last time I saw a couple and envied their connection. It's so fucking sad.

Cameron's Mac: I get what you're saying. It's cool. And your maiden virtue is safe with me for the moment. I'm a little bit jaded too. And by the looks of your cup, I'm already in over my head.

I lifted my mug proudly that read *Man Tears* and took a sip.

He shook his head with a chuckle as we tried to speak around our connection. The force was strong with this one, and I knew he felt it too.

Cameron's Mac: But you do have to admit for someone so adamant about old school, this arrangement makes your point a bit moot.

Abbie's Mac: Touché. But, you see, I'm using it to our advantage.

Cameron's Mac: Your advantage.

Abbie's Mac: Fine my advantage. Mixing old school with new. I look at it this way. We get all the perks of seeing each other, knowing what the other looks like. We get clear visual reception, but we keep it like this.

Cameron's Mac: Until?

Abbie's Mac: Until we're both less jaded. And let's not get ahead of ourselves, it's only coffee. I mean, today it's only coffee. Tomorrow . . .

I shrugged to bring the point home. I was being completely

honest, and I gave myself a mental pat on the back.

Cameron's Mac: Suits me. You could have a voodoo doll in your purse.

This time I held nothing back as I gave him my smile. We exchanged them for several seconds before I got a message.

Cameron's Mac: Are we allowed to give compliments?

I didn't get a chance to answer.

Cameron's Mac: Because if I was standing, that smile would have knocked me on my ass. What's the next rule?

Despite my newly speeding heartbeat, I pressed on. If I had any shot of moving forward, I didn't want to look back. And I didn't want my fears hindering anything new.

Abbie's Mac: We leave our relationship baggage at the door.

He studied me for a moment before he typed.

Cameron's Mac: Nothing but who we are now, at this moment, and where we're going, or where we want to go.

Abbie's Mac: Exactly. No dead weight.

Cameron's Mac: Sounds perfect, but if we do it this way, we do it with one condition.

Abbie's Mac: Shoot.

Cameron's Mac: We won't deal in perfection and absolutes.

Abbie's Mac: And no promises we can't realistically keep.

His slow nod was confirmation we were onto something.

Cameron's Mac: I'm just going to point out now I hate that I have to stare at the forbidden fruit instead of what's behind it.

Abbie's Mac: That's kind of a two-sided thing.

Cameron's Mac: Lend me that dress you wore the other night so I can make it as hard on you.

I grinned and shook my head.

Abbie's Mac: Sense of humor, I like it. My mom thinks I'm a world class smart ass.

He picked up another cup hidden behind his Mac and took a sip as if he were ready for me. It read *Only the Sarcastic Survive*.

Abbie's Mac: I should make that my first tattoo. How many cups do you have over there?

I leaned to the side and peeked behind his Mac to see

several more.

Cameron's Mac: I'm prepared today.

Abbie's Mac: Okay, let's see them.

He slowly lifted the first cup. *Good Morning, Beautiful.* I gave him a lopsided grin that quickly turned into a scowl when he lifted another that read *Show Me Your Kitties.* I palmed my mouth to hide my smile.

His third cup came up. *I love Clit.*

Abbie's Mac: Really?

Cameron's Mac: Too crass, I agree. But I was taking your friend Bree's advice. And for the record, I know the clit is not a fictional character.

I threw his word back at him from the night at the bar.

Abbie's Mac: Noted.

He held up a wait-for-it finger and gave me remorseful puppy dog eyes as he showed me his next cup that read *I Love Your Face.*

Abbie's Mac: Much better.

Thick, sculpted brows double tapped his forehead as he lifted the last cup. *Call Me El Jefe Grande.* I rolled my eyes as he shrugged.

Abbie's Mac: You're somewhere between perfect and a pervert at this point.

"I was in a hurry," he said across the space. I pressed a librarian's finger to my lips.

Cameron's Mac: Really? No talking at all?

Abbie's Mac: Plenty of talking. Just like this.

He sat back briefly with a devastating smirk before he leaned in and typed.

Cameron's Mac: Okay, Abbie. Where do we start?

I was trying so hard to think of something clever, witty, something . . . *more*, but words failed me as we stared each other down. It was perfect. Better than perfect. I had no reason to be afraid. We had every advantage of dating except for the physical aspect, which I knew I wasn't ready for, despite my raging libido. And I needed that distance to be able to get close. It could work. Another stretch of my lips over my teeth had him biting his lip and shaking his head. God, he was gorgeous. Just outside the window behind him, a single gold maple leaf drifted at his back before it floated toward the brightly lit sky. And from that moment on, I knew I would be measuring my Saturdays in cups.

Abbie

Nine Cups

It was our third Saturday, and I had to admit I'd been daydreaming through my week until I got to meet up with Cameron. When he'd asked for another date, I didn't hesitate to accept. A set coffee date every Saturday with no expectations, what could be better?

That morning when I showed up, he was waiting. I walked past him, giving him my best smile, a steaming cup in hand that read *Dear Karma, I have a list of people you missed.* I glanced at his cup and saw it read *I'm here. What are your other two wishes?* and caught his eyes as they swept over me before I took my seat. Though the café was bustling, I was tickled to see the handwritten sign that said *Reserved* before I picked up the fresh daisy he'd placed on it and opened my Mac.

Abbie's Mac: Thank you.

Cameron's Mac: They were fresh out of bloodroots and oleander.

Abbie's Mac: I'm all stocked up on deadly poison at home. But thanks, I'll practice my dark magic on your daisy.

I gave him a knowing grin. Our rapport was building into something . . . familiar. He still gave me hell about my witchy attitude the day we'd met, and I had no issues giving him hell about his crass cup choice. Unwrapping from my coat, a rush of blood crept up my face. I didn't have to look his way to know he was checking me out. Once I got comfortable, Cameron's first question was waiting for me. It was like he was anxious to find out what I would type, which only made me more eager to answer.

Cameron's Mac: Tell me something no one knows about you. That you never tell anyone.

Abbie's Mac: I've got nothing.

Cameron sat back in his seat, hands at his sides, his thick fingers sprinkled with dark hair and spread on the two-seater booth he sat on. Eyes fixed on him, I took my time with my perusal. He hadn't disappointed thus far. He was always impressively dressed, which I'd learned was his typical, no matter the attire. Today, he was sporty chic in silky sweatpants and a zipped up, long-sleeved athletic shirt. A solid black beanie covered his coffee-colored hair and outlined his sculpted face.

Once I'd had my fill, though it was never enough, I noticed the challenge in his green depths as he sat scanning my face.

He narrowed his eyes before he typed.

Cameron's Mac: Too quick to answer. What are you hiding?

I looked up at the ceiling as if I was pondering what to give away but hit him with the only thing I could think of since he asked the question.

Abbie's Mac: Fine. I was born in a sanitarium.

Laughter burst from him as he looked over our screens and mouthed "Really?"

I let him get away with readable whispers despite our no talking rule. Well, *my* no talking rule. Still, he was working hard to keep our agreement.

Abbie's Mac: Yep. Hinsdale Sanitarium and Hospital. The minute I was born, they changed the name. You don't seem too surprised.

Cameron's Mac: I'm not. You're a wonderful kind of crazy. You're all fire, you know that? And you look fucking beautiful.

It was those types of sentiments that kept me glued to that chair for a few hours every Saturday. He wasn't incessant with his compliments. He gave them when he felt like it. The conversation flowed, but he surprised me every so often, and my reaction was always the same. My chest tightened, my throat filled as I stared over at him and mouthed "Thank you." I came away from those moments knowing he wanted it clear that he was interested in more than having coffee with me.

Cameron's Mac: Did you grow up in Chicago?

I nodded.

Abbie's Mac: Mostly. Until I was thirteen when my parents bought a place in Naperville. I love our home there, but I always wanted to move back to the city. I'm a city girl at heart. You?

Cameron's Mac: Same, I came here for college, but I was born and raised in Niagara Falls. I used to live in the city, but I moved here not too long ago.

Cameron owned a small chain of sporting goods stores. He'd told me his dream was to coach in the NBA, and though it never happened for him, he still coached high school part-time.

Abbie's Mac: Welcome to the neighborhood.

Cameron's Mac: You're one hell of a welcoming committee.

He winked, and I felt it to my toes.

Abbie's Mac: If you weren't having coffee with me, Coach, what would you be doing?

Cameron's Mac: Running, playing basketball while talking shit about the Packers with my friend Max who thinks that Bears belong in the woods, not the NFL.

Abbie's Mac: I hate the woods. Football fan too?

Cameron's Mac: Fan of all sports. I don't miss a Bears game. I have it running in a window on my screen.

Abbie's Mac: I don't know if I should be flattered or offended.

Cameron's Mac: Flattered, definitely.

Dimples. Kill me.

Cameron's Mac: What's wrong with the woods?

Abbie's Mac: Nothing good happens there.

Cameron's Mac: Too bad. I love the outdoors.

Abbie's Mac: Me too, as long as they are lined with cement and coffee shops.

Cameron's Mac: Cute. Can I say something without you getting offended?

Abbie's Mac: Maybe.

I got a smirk.

Cameron's Mac: I knew that would be your answer. I'm saying it anyway. I like your freckles and I was hoping to see them today.

Abbie's Mac: Really?

Cameron's Mac: Really. I kind of miss the caramel on your chin too.

I lifted my cup and smeared a little from the side of it onto my chin, only too happy to oblige. I realized after what an idiotic move it was, but Cameron grinned as if all was right with the world. Neon yellow leaves swayed in the tree behind him and began to flood the ground.

Abbie's Mac: I love the fall.

Cameron's eyes didn't stray from mine as he mouthed "Me too." He hesitated briefly before he typed.

Cameron's Mac: Want to go for a walk? Cement only, I promise.

Abbie's Mac: Not yet.

He dropped it and typed.

Cameron's Mac: What would you be doing if you weren't here with me?

Memorizing the patterns of serial killers.
God, it was no wonder I lived alone. How would he ever think that was normal. Surely, I couldn't be the only one fascinated by them. There were thousands of resources dedicated to the psychotic mind.
Fuck it.

Abbie's Mac: Watching Snapped, reading a book about

a serial killer, or buying another throw pillow for my place.

I hesitated before I hit send. But I did. While he read, his brows hit his hairline.

Cameron's Mac: Wasn't expecting that.

Abbie's Mac: Yeah, I'm just letting my full-on, witchy-sanitarium, innate crazy show today. You should tip the barista on your way out.

His chest pumped with his chuckle.

Cameron's Mac: It's cool. I mean, that shit is fascinating to some, but I don't know that it would be my Saturday ritual. What kind of witch is afraid of the woods?

I narrowed my eyes. He chuckled and was easily forgiven.

Cameron's Mac: I hope you realize this unhealthy hobby may be the reason we aren't going for a walk, or at that Bears game sipping a cold beer. It's probably also why I'm not going to get to cop a feel or hold your hand by the end of the day. You know, watching that stuff will make you paranoid.

Abbie's Mac: So I've been told. I've just been fascinated with it lately.

I kept my eyes down and Cameron seemed to read my posture. He didn't press. Desperate to change the subject, I threw my first flirt.

Abbie's Mac: What would you pretend to accidentally graze?

There was a challenge in my eyes, and his gaze heated in response.

Cameron's Mac: I have an extensive list of places I would love to graze. How about a short list?

I nodded.

Cameron's Mac: First, I'd figure out a way to brush my lips against your neck. You have a beautiful neck.

Abbie's Mac: And then?
He shook his head.

Cameron's Mac: Sorry, not giving away my tells this early in the game, pun intended.

Abbie's Mac: What's the score?

Cameron's Mac: I have no fucking idea.

I lowered my eyes and let the zing rattle through my chest.

6

Abbie

"Morning, Abbie," Mrs. Zingaro chimed as I locked my front door. She was perched on her cement bench in front of her decayed garden.

"Morning, Mrs. Zingaro. How are you?"

My mother taught me to be polite, but "How are you?" was a loaded question with my tenant. I already knew too much about her. *Far* too much, including her extensive list of medical conditions that seemed to lengthen daily.

"I can't eat dairy anymore, I think I'm allergic. I watched one of those shows about food allergies. And I'm having bunion surgery next month."

And so, it begins.

Tucking my scarf into my jacket, I pulled out my gloves as I walked down the steps. "I'm sorry to hear that."

"Well, I love milk. So, it's a shame."

"Sure is. I need to get to work. You better put a jacket on, it's pretty cold out here."

"I'll be fine. I'm waiting for my son. He's supposed to pick me up."

"Oh? Michael's coming?" I asked, pulling on my gloves. "Please tell him I said hello." Her son had been the one to rent the place for her and visited her every chance he got. He was a good man and probably one of the reasons I still had faith in them.

"You should wait on him," she said. "He'd be happy to see you."

"I can't miss my train," I insisted, avoiding her eyes. I was three steps in the clear when she spoke up behind me.

"You don't have to be ashamed around him. He never faulted you for what happened."

"I'll wait for him another time. I've got to get going."

"Okay, well, if you get a chance to come by when you get home, my washer is making a funny noise."

"I'll find time," I promised as I gripped my tote and waved to her before hauling ass past the park.

Fuck this day already.

There were days when the world couldn't touch you. Where everything slid off your shoulders. When PMS didn't play a factor in your mood and the swings were a rarity. But on that particular morning, Kat was making sure those days looked like holidays. "What the hell are you talking about, Jefferson? That's not true!" She paused as she paced behind her desk. "God, I can't believe you just said that. You. Are. Pathetic!"

I winced as I listened to Kat belittle her husband, *again*. In less than a minute, she'd gone from all business with me to snarling at him. Why she answered the phone each time he called, I had no clue. It was like she wanted an excuse to lash out. Her shrieking was unnerving, and I was already irritated. I'd missed my train and was forced to take a cab to work. And work was proving to be impossible due to Kat's ranting. Not to mention my only plans for the night were to listen to a washing machine that wasn't broken. The only solace was that it was Friday and I would see Cameron in less than twenty-four hours.

"Oh, you would go there," Kat snapped as I sat helplessly, put in the shittiest of positions. Clearly, the woman didn't give a damn about my perception of her, or anyone else's, for that matter.

I stood up from the chair opposite her desk. She covered the mouthpiece and caught me retreating.

"Where are you going?"

She had to be kidding. "To give you some privacy," I whispered.

"I'm sorry," she said and nodded toward the chair I'd abandoned. She snapped into the phone. "I'm going to call you back. I have a meeting." She hung up and threw her cell on her desk with a thwack.

It was then that I noticed Kat was sweating and her face was ghostly white.

"Are you okay?" I was still standing at her door as she looked over at me with wide eyes.

"Fine."

"I can come back, and we can go through this later," I assured.

"I don't have later. It's *my* job on the line, remember?"

I pressed my lips together to keep my temper at bay. I'd never met a woman so agreeable one minute and volatile the next. It was strange, but when Kat was happy, she had the same type of effect Bree had on me. And despite the constant hot and cold on her part, I genuinely liked her. I pushed all my presumptions away and decided to give her the benefit of the doubt because I'd never been in her situation. Her marriage was falling apart, and she obviously needed a friend or confidant, at the very least.

"I know I'm here in a professional capacity, but I just want you to know, if you need someone to talk to, I'm here."

She looked at me pensively before she spoke. "I'm sorry," she said softly. "I am." She slumped in her seat and sighed before smoothing down her perfectly placed hair. "Lately he's been a nightmare. Just so damned needy."

"You'll get through this. Are you sure you're okay?"

"I'm fine, I just haven't been sleeping well." She stared down at her ring finger and then smiled over at me. "Tell me how it's going with the coffee shop guy."

"We're taking it slow."

"Still not talking?"

"Nope, messages only, and it's working out fine."

"At some point, he'll get tired of it," she warned. "You know men."

"Yeah, well, I'm not opposed to taking it further, but at least for now I have the upper hand. I don't think he's in a hurry, either."

"Sounds like a good one," she said, motioning me to sit.

"I hope so."

She massaged her temples and stared down at her phone, which lit up with messages.

"Are you sure you don't want a few minutes?"

"Just a headache," she said, opening her purse, grabbing a few pills, and swallowing them before she tossed a weary glance my way. "Now, let's get these quarterlies over with and make the idiots upstairs happy. And then I'll buy you a drink."

After four martinis in front of the fireplace at 2Twenty2, Kat disappeared. I'd been staring into the flames, trying to shake the ill feeling I'd had all day working side-by-side with her. In a way, Kat reminded me of my ex. They were both alluring from a distance, but upon closer inspection, you learned there was more than meets the eye. I watched the flicker of the orange light as I sipped my drink and cringed at the memory of him. Luke was charming, attentive, the whole package. He'd swept me off my feet, and I'd given him my trust. And in the blink of an eye, everything changed.

He changed.

Luke had accosted me at my front door after I'd been out with Bree. Never in a million years did I think he was capable of the type of crazy he displayed that night. After the incident, I realized that we all possessed a false sense of security until something unthinkable happened. And when it happens, it changes your opinion about humanity and opens your eyes. How I wished I was still blissfully ignorant.

Luke was sick, and when I discovered it, I realized how naïve I'd been.

The cynic in me came front and center, and my ability to trust myself and my judgment were nearly destroyed. That was when I'd become fascinated with alter egos, sociopaths, and serial killers. It was a form of therapy for me in a way.

Luke wasn't a killer, but he had me fooled into believing he was someone he wasn't.

"Luke, I told you I needed some space." I moved past him, and he ripped my key from my hand and moved in, plastering me to my front door.

"How convenient for you. This outfit is a little bit inappropriate, don't you think?"

"Luke," I started as he refused to let me move. "Stop it. Get the hell away from me. Why are you doing this?"

"I don't like being lied to, Abbie," he sneered, inching forward.

"I didn't lie. I told you I was going out with Bree."

"I don't know if I believe anything you tell me anymore." I barely had time to blink before he was berating me again.

"After all I've done for you," he started as he slapped his palm against the door next to me. I jumped as he pressed in while my whole body shook with fear. The look in his eyes was deadly.

"That's it. I'm done. Luke, this is over. Leave and don't come back." I pointed a shaky finger behind him and reached for my keys. An ominous smile covered his features. I studied his profile, unable to believe it was the same man who approached me months ago.

"As usual, you're overreacting. You think Bree cares about you? That's pathetic. I'm the one who worries about you, not her. I'm the one who takes care of you, Abbie. What the hell were you thinking wearing this and dancing with her?"

"You watched me tonight?" I asked, as bile rose in my throat. A sick feeling swept over me as I realized just how much of a stranger he truly was. And I'd let him into my home and my bed. It was only when his suggestions of what he felt I needed to be doing started to gnaw at me that we'd begun to have problems. It sank in at that moment just how long and how much I'd been manipulated—since the beginning. "Luke, you need to leave, right now."

"I'm not going anywhere! You owe me an explanation!

What were you doing, trying to get fucked?!" He moved in further, crowding me against the door as he spat his accusations in my face.

"Give me my keys," I demanded with a shaky voice.

"I don't think so," he said in a tone that let me know he had leverage and he would be using it to his every advantage. "You're such a fucking liar, Abbie."

"Hey, what the hell are you doing?!" The voice didn't belong to Luke, and in an instant, he was pulled away from me and pushed to the side of the porch. Mrs. Zingaro's son stood glaring at him as Luke fought his hold.

"I'm having a conversation with my girlfriend," Luke said lividly as he glared over at me before he turned to Michael. "So why don't you mind your own fucking business."

"I'm sorry if we disturbed you," I said, trying to catch my breath as I addressed Michael. Mrs. Zingaro shuffled outside her door, looked at her son, and began to speak in rapid Italian.

"Luke was just leaving," I offered, trying to defuse the situation.

"The hell I am," Luke said as he ripped his arms from Michael's grasp and came flying toward me.

"You alone?"

I jumped in my seat, spilling my martini as a man spoke to me from the pastel chair opposite the couch I sat on. But he might as well have whispered in my ear. I was on edge, and it was painfully apparent. Across a table full of oversized Jenga pieces, he apologized.

"Sorry, I didn't mean to scare you. I'll get you another drink."

"No, it's fine," I said, wiping the droplets of olive-flavored alcohol off my skirt with my scarf. "I'm going to go look for my friend."

Annoyed with Kat's absence, I ditched my drink to find her in the bathroom. She was going through her purse.

"Hey, woman, did you forget about me?"

She smiled at my reflection as she pulled out her lipstick.

"Just got off the phone with my husband. I think I'll head home soon."

"That's good news, right?"

Through our four martinis, Kat had revealed little to nothing about that morning's blow up. I couldn't be sure, but I suspected she only invited me to save face. She'd spoken about her career as a gymnast and a few people at the firm but little else. I studied her as she primped in the mirror. The woman was such a mixed bag, and I was exhausted trying to balance on her unsteady beam. But it was the subtle sag in her demeanor, the hint of sadness in her eyes that kept me trying.

"Maybe things are looking up?"

"We'll see," she muttered absently, lining her lips while she gave me a withering stare.

"Sorry, you don't have to tell me. I'm known for being a buttinski. My brother nicknamed me Miss Fix-It."

She turned to me and nodded. "Sorry to make you wait."

Kat seemed relaxed, but I was still crawling out of my skin. I had made so many strides for the better since Luke, but at that moment, I wanted nothing to do with being sociable. In the first few months after our breakup, I'd only felt safe around Bree or my mother, who was still in the dark about what happened.

"No problem. I think I'll head home too. I'm going to grab a taxi. Thanks for the drinks. I'll see you tomorrow."

"Sure you're headed home?" She gave me a conspiratorial wink.

She assumed I was off to see Cameron, so I took the easy route. "You busted me."

"Have fun. Before you know it, you'll be married and fighting about who's the worst driver."

At home that night, after a quick promise to Mrs. Zingaro that I would be by the following morning to check on her washer, I undressed and started a hot shower. Swallowing two sleeping pills before I stepped in, I let the water run over my back and shoulders in an attempt to relax. No matter how hard I tried, I would never forget the look on Luke's face when he came at me seconds before Michael's fist connected with his nose. Luke had the audacity to look shocked as he spat the blood pouring from his mouth at my feet, purposely spraying me with it, and inching closer as he threatened all of us.

Before he left, he looked at me one last time and smiled with blood-laced teeth, a haunting look in his eyes. *"It's funny you think this is over."* Michael had managed to scare him off and Mrs. Zingaro had already called the police, who had shown up seconds after Luke had fled. I filed a restraining order the next morning.

Shivering in my recliner, I clutched my phone while Bree talked me down. I never heard from Luke again, but the damage was done.

"I was on edge tonight just having drinks and I hated it. When in the hell is this going to go away?"

"I don't know. Your ex-boyfriend was a freak show, even I didn't see it. But you have got to stop watching shows and reading books about crazy people."

"I'm just trying to understand."

"First of all, Luke wasn't a serial killer. He was a borderline sociopath. And he lives in Washington now. He's moved on to manipulate someone else. You're safe."

After our breakup, Bree had monitored Luke's social media accounts. Less than a month after we'd broken up, he'd changed his status to *in a relationship* and latched onto someone else, claiming he was in love. I knew better. So did Bree.

"It just freaks me out. I let him into my life. I don't understand how I will be able to do that with another man."

"But you are dating again. It was a close call, and, yeah, it took some time, but you're dating. And that just proves how strong you are. Cameron seems nice. You just have to learn how to trust your gut."

"I hate this," I whispered.

"I know. Listen, I hate to cut this short, but I have to go check on my patients."

"Okay, thanks for calling me, *again*." I was sure she could hear the guilt in my voice and answered back in true Bree fashion.

"Shut up. Keep going on your dates. It's working. You can't shut up about him. Don't let one bad day ruin everything you have going. Promise me you'll show up tomorrow."

"I promise," I said as unexpected butterflies surfaced at the thought of seeing Cameron.

"Now, turn off the fucking TV. Take a bath or use that birthday present I bought you."

The present she was referring to was a sex toy called The Anaconda. No further explanation needed.

I sighed, grabbed my remote, and clicked off *Mindhunter*. "It's off. And I'm *never* using that present. One four three."

"Love you too."

Abbie

When I stepped off the elevator, I could see Kat pacing in her office, talking on the phone. I set down my tote and decided to make us a quick cup of coffee. It was only when I got to her office door that I realized it wasn't a business call.

"Jefferson, I'm at work. Don't you dare threaten to come here and make a scene. I said fine! Fine!" Kat hung up the phone and looked out of her office window. Frozen at her door, she caught my reflection in my attempt to retreat.

"Abbie, I need to get away. I need a few days off." Kat turned to me, and it was then I saw one of her eyes was bloodshot.

Steaming mugs in hand, I walked toward her, cringing at the sight of it. "Oh my God. Kat, does it hurt?"

"My blood pressure is off. I need to relax. Is there any way you can cover for me? I know it's a lot to ask with all that's going on, but I need a few days. Just a few days."

"Of course," I offered as I set down the cups. "Take the rest of the week. Where will you go?"

She opened her desk drawer and began packing her purse. "I'll go visit my dad, or maybe just get away. He owns a few vacation spots. One I love in Florida. Maybe I'll get some sun."

So, it was her father who was wealthy. I knew the woman grew up privileged. It showed in her demeanor, in the way she spoke, and in her bite.

"Kat, if you want to talk about it—"

She shook her head. "I appreciate your concern. I do. But I need to get out of this city and away from him."

"Are you . . . in danger?"

"What?" she asked incredulously, as if the idea was preposterous. "Of course not, no. And please don't say a word to anyone else about this. I hope you can keep this in confidence."

There wasn't a person within earshot of her office that wasn't aware of what was going on in her marriage, but I played agreeable.

"Of course," I assured as she picked up her purse and covered me with grateful yet weary eyes. "Thank you. I'll return the favor."

"No problem," I said as she walked past me and turned to face me at the door. It was the first time a conversation with her husband had rattled her that badly. I felt the tension radiate from her from only feet away. "Abbie, if anyone calls—"

"Go," I told her and waved my hands in a shooing motion for emphasis. "I've got this. I swear you're covered."

Squaring her shoulders, every bit of vulnerability disappeared from her as she faced the twenty-second floor that was rapidly filling with bustling employees. Slipping on her sunglasses, she bypassed the receptionist's desk and moved toward the elevator. The woman seemed to be a ticking time bomb, and I was sure I could get more work done without her at that point.

Just as I made the peaceful retreat to my own desk, my phone rattled in my pocket, and I rolled my eyes as I answered. "I'm surprised you remembered my phone number, dear brother."

Oliver was always quick to reply. "I didn't. Modern technology. I have no idea what your number is."

"That's the problem with the world. We rely on it for everything."

I could hear the smile in his voice. "What's my number?"

"I could rattle off anything and you wouldn't know your own."

"Someone is a little feisty today. What's eating you, little sister?"

I sat at my desk. "I have a crazy coworker."

"I love my coworkers."

"That's because you screw them all. If you are calling me to go in on Mom's birthday present, it's too late. She already got it."

"Shit."

"Yeah, shit. You'll have to go online and pick something out all on your own."

Oliver sighed. "Come on, help me out here. What does she need?"

"This woman gave birth to you. She needs a more in tune son. You can't think of one thing to get her?"

"Help me out," he begged. Oliver was shit at remembering anything. I was pretty sure electronics had alerted him to his own mother's birthday.

"You better show up tonight," I ordered.

"I can't make it."

"Richard Oliver Gorman, you aren't missing her party. This is an important day for her. I've planned this thing for months. All of her old field crew is going to be there."

"Then she won't miss me."

"You are a shit. You know that? Whoever she is you think is more important can wait on your beck and call list."

"It's not a woman."

"We're all busy, asshat. And I haven't seen you in months. You want to give her a gift? How about your presence at her birthday party?"

"Fine, I'll be there. You laid it on pretty heavy there, Miss Fix-It."

"The only reason I have that job is because you're the most irresponsible man ever born. How you got through med school is beyond me."

"You really need to get out more instead of hanging out with that creepy old lady you rent your basement to," Oliver chuckled.

"Don't you dare insult Mrs. Zingaro. And I'll have you know my social calendar is full at the moment."

"Oh yeah?" His tone changed instantly. Oliver had always been protective, but even more so in the last year. In a moment of weakness, I'd confessed about Luke and that confession had kicked in some overprotective man gene. Though we sparred, more often than not, he never swayed on that front. Since Luke, he'd only gotten worse.

"Don't worry, big brother. I'm being careful."

"I need to meet him," Oliver demanded.

"I just met him."

"Has Bree?"

"Yes."

"Fine, but if this lasts, I want an introduction."

"If this lasts? Says the man who has a little black book full of virtue to destroy."

"Black books are outdated too, sis. Gotta run. I'll see you at eight."

"The party starts at seven!" I said as he hung up on me.

Miss Fix-It. I hated that title, but as I sat back and looked at the skyline, I realized how true it was. I'd been that way my whole life. Always quick to try to figure out some solution, whether it be by numbers or something I could drum up to keep the peace. And the point was brought home as I powered through double my daily workload. That night on my walk home, I found myself searching the sea of faces on the streets of Wicker Park for the one I knew I could draw comfort from. It was inevitable that Cameron and I would run into each other eventually as neighbors. We'd be forced to break the rules, and the bounce in my step told me I was looking forward to it.

Abbie

Cup Twenty

I RAN MY FINGER DOWN THE DELICATE PETAL OF THE LILY that waited for me and mouthed a "thank you" to Cameron. He bit his lip and winked. My thoughts strayed as I entertained the idea of his teeth on my own lip.

Cameron's Mac: What are you thinking?

Abbie's Mac: What was it like growing up in Niagara Falls? I've never been.

Cameron's Mac: That is SO not what you were thinking.

I pressed my lips together.

Cameron's Mac: Uneventful. I actually grew up just outside, but it's easier just to tell people Niagara. Small town, everyone knows everyone type of thing. The falls themselves were pretty cool. I mean, you can only see it so many times before it becomes nothing special. And you don't want to ever overlook anything that beautiful. It was my own fault. I got my first job there when I was sixteen. I helped with events and worked at a gift shop. But I fucking hated it. I'm not a fan of thunderstorms or the rain because of it.

Abbie's Mac: That's criminal. I love the rain and thunderstorms.

Cameron's Mac: Yeah, well, everyone does if they're inside, dry and warm, not getting pounded by two different types of precipitation.

Abbie's Mac: I'm going to change your mind about that. I'll make you appreciate the rain again.

Cameron's Mac: Not possible.

Abbie's Mac: It's a promise.

Cameron's Mac: No promises you can't realistically keep, remember?

Abbie's Mac: It's good that you're paying attention, but I'm willing to bet I can sway you. What's the worst thing that has ever happened to you?

Cameron's eyes met mine briefly before he typed.

Cameron's Mac: My mother died almost five years ago.

She beat cancer years before and then it came back and ate her alive. It was too abrupt. I'm still not over it.

Abbie's Mac: I'm so sorry. I can't imagine losing my mother. That was kind of a deep question for cup one, wasn't it?

Cameron's Mac: It's fine. I love talking about her. She was so incredible. I was an only child and we were close. When I decided to move here, she uprooted my dad from New York just to be near me. I can't say I haven't lived a charmed life.

Abbie's Mac: Same here. My mom is my hero. She's an amazing photojournalist and still managed to be there when it mattered. My dad is so supportive of her. He never minded taking a backseat to her career. He was the one who was always taking me to school and cooking dinner when she traveled. He even tried to sew my costume together for a play once. It was a total disaster. It was called The Harvest Moon and my only job was to make the switch from a pumpkin to a jack o' lantern. All I had to do was twist my costume around on cue. I ended up flashing my strawberry-covered panties on stage to the entire fourth grade.

His deep chuckle had every hair on my body standing on end. We were the last two in the café and had been there for hours. I knew it was almost closing time but ignored the clock to savor every minute with him.

Cameron's Mac: I would love to have seen that.

Abbie's Mac: It was recorded. And you will never see it. It wasn't my dad's fault I did my first striptease in grade school. I love him for his efforts. How about you? Are you close with your dad?

Cameron's Mac: We have a decent relationship. He would have moved back home if we hadn't buried Mom here. I think he stays mostly because of that fact. I don't see him as much as I should. Christmas is weird now. It's like we're trying too hard to get back something we can't have.

Abbie's Mac: I'm sorry. But I'm glad you told me.

Cameron's Mac: I told you because I wanted to. Because I want you to know me.

Another long minute of staring. Dire need raced through me, and I could feel it emanating from him. It was equal amounts pleasure and torture, and I was sure he could see the longing in my eyes. But he didn't press. He never pressed, which was both fascinating and frustrating. I couldn't help but be happy he hadn't gone *there*. Yet, at the same time, I was hoping he would.

Cameron's Mac: I could have told you about the time I almost made out with a man.

My eyes bulged as he began typing.

Cameron's Mac: Yeah. I was drunk at a club and Max pulled me away by my collar and saved me years of therapy.

Abbie's Mac: You and Max seem close. He sounds like good people.

Cameron's Mac: He's the best. And I give him hell for it. Very few men would save me for a chance to have that type of leverage. He saved my ass a few too many times in college.

Abbie's Mac: College is where I met Bree. She was as wild as they come. Still is. Except she gets to live behind the nurse shield to justify the rest of her behavior.

Cameron's Mac: She seems like good people. A little loud, though.

I bobbed my head furiously and crossed my eyes.

Abbie's Mac: She's the best. And the loudest. I think I need to get her hearing checked. It would be terrible to find out all these years later that she's hard of hearing and I wasn't a good enough friend to figure it out. But I'm pretty sure it's just because she's from Georgia.

I laughed at that, and Cameron's eyes popped up to watch me.

Cameron's Mac: How's that *Black Like Your Soul* coffee?

Abbie's Mac: Delicious. And I must compliment you on your mug of choice today. It's not every day a man can admit that *Everything's a Dildo if You're Brave Enough*.

He let out a sharp laugh as I lifted my fingers, pressed them to my lips, and twisted them his way.

Did I just blow him a kiss?

I don't know why I did it. He stiffened and his eyes flared as he watched it happen. His fingers moved slowly over his keys while I waited with blood pounding in my ears.

Cameron's Mac: Did you just get embarrassed? Cute.

Abbie's Mac: Can we not talk about it?

Cameron's Mac: Well, I'm not accepting that as a first kiss. And, Abbie, there will be a first kiss.

Emerald eyes met mine while goosebumps covered me.

Abbie's Mac: I want that too.

Cameron's Mac: This experiment of yours has me thinking like a teenager again.

I gave him a deep frown.

Cameron's Mac: Hear me out before you start picturing porno flicks and sticky socks in my laundry hamper. I'm talking about the stuff in between. I really think about you. I wonder what you're doing because I can't text you to ask. I wonder what you'll think or what you'll say about something I'm reading. It's like I crave your opinion now and these conversations. Things can get so easily predictable when you first meet someone and all you are is mostly physical.

I wanted to pry for more, but I didn't. Those were the rules. *My* rules.

Abbie's Mac: How old are you?

Cameron's Mac: Thirty-four.

Abbie's Mac: I can't believe I hadn't asked that before. Aren't you going to ask me?

Cameron's Mac: Without sounding like a prick, I don't care. I know you have a thing for numbers, but whatever yours is, is fine with me. All I really want to know is if you want to have another cup of coffee with me?

The sincerity in his eyes showed me he meant every word. I nodded.

Abbie

"Mrs. Zingaro, I'm really late," I said as she greeted me just as I was shutting my door.

"Okay, honey, I was just coming up to offer some of my ziti. I know how much you love it. I'll put some aside for you." Guilt instantly wracked me as she looked me over. I'd been spending less and less time with her over the last month. "And for the hundredth time, please call me Jenny. You look snazzy. Did you get a new fella?"

"I think so," I answered.

"Good for you, Abigail."

"Thank you. I'm sorry. I didn't mean to be rude. I just don't want to be late."

"I understand. I've taken up a lot of your time," she said softly before she perked up. "I hope this one sticks."

"You and me both."

She lingered a moment longer. It was obvious she'd recently dyed her silver hair; her hairline was stained purple. I'd been the one to help her with it the last few times she'd colored it. This time, she hadn't even asked.

"Jenny, I really have to run. I'll come by and grab that ziti on my way home."

"Don't you worry. It will be waiting when you're ready." She carefully made her way down the steps as I watched her struggle with her footing. I didn't know how much longer she would be able to self-sustain. I would have to talk to her son about it in the near future. The thought of her leaving broke my heart. But instead of offering my company and making a promise for later, I kept my mouth shut. Miss Fix-It had a date.

Minutes later, after giving Bennie his twenty outside the café, I flew past Cameron with my borrowed *I Wish I Were Felicia. She's Always Going Somewhere* mug and opened my Mac.

Abbie's Mac: Hi. Sorry I'm late. I got cornered by my tenant again.

He'd been frowning at his screen while I got comfortable. His lips twitched with a small smile as he read my message then looked over at me.

Cameron's Mac: What did you have to pretend to fix this time?

Abbie's Mac: Nothing. Turns out she just wanted to feed me, and I was witchy to her before she even offered it. I've been spending a lot of time with her the

past year and I've been neglecting her lately. I feel like shit. But I have to stop before she asks me to join her knitting circle, ya know?

Cameron's Mac: I'm sure she understands. And I have to say, I'm fond of you for taking care of her like that. It's a good thing you care.

Though it was warmer today, he was bundled up in a hoodie and wearing a ball cap which was a first. He looked exhausted and for the first time ever, thrown together. Something was . . . *off*.

Abbie's Mac: Things looked serious over there when I got here. Everything okay? Are you getting sick?

He gave me a mustered wink as he did a slow perusal of me from the tip of my ankle boots to the top of my head. I didn't know how he did it with a look alone, but by the time he was done, I felt worshiped. We'd been having coffee every day for the last week and I had to admit I was growing tired of my own rules.

Cameron's Mac: And now you're worried about me? Everything's fine, nothing a little sleep can't fix. Besides, there's a lot more I'm interested in going on over there.
Abbie's Mac: I'll take that as a compliment.

Cameron's Mac: As you should. Fuck, you're beautiful.

Though the sky was gray, I felt covered in sun.

Abbie's Mac: Do you do that to every woman you woo?

Cameron's Mac: Do what?

Abbie's Mac: Say things like that?

Cameron's Mac: You get no history of woo. Your rules and woo? I mean I know what wooing is, but is that still a word fit for 2017?

Abbie's Mac: It's the best word. And I'd say you're bringing it back fucking nicely.

Cameron's Mac: Such a dirty mouth on a totally fucking wooable woman.

Though his eyes were lit with mischief and his tilted lips told me he was happy to see me, it was the weariness in his posture that prompted my next question.

Abbie's Mac: Tell me what's wrong.

He hovered over his keyboard and I saw him make the decision.

Cameron's Mac: Can't.

Abbie's Mac: You sure? Something I can help with?

Cameron's Mac: Not with this.

Abbie's Mac: That bad?

He shrugged.

Cameron's Mac: Just a shit day. I need a vacation.

Just as he said it, his phone rattled on the table. He ran a business and I knew more than anyone how taxing it could be. He silenced his phone without looking at it and put it in his pocket.

Abbie's Mac: Sure I can't help?

Cameron jerked his head as if the question annoyed him and I paused my hands over my keys. It was the first time I'd seen that side of him and I sat idle. Uncomfortable and ready to make an excuse, I began to type.

Cameron's Mac: I'm sorry. Don't even think about leaving me here. I've been looking forward to this all day.

When I remained quiet he spoke.
"Abbie, look at me."
I looked up over our Macs and saw his apology.
"I'm sorry."

Abbie's Mac: It's fine. I shouldn't have pushed.

Cameron's Mac: It's one of the things I like about you. I'm fond of Miss Fix-It. Okay? I'm sorry. I'm fucking stressed out and I'm tired and all I want to do is walk over there and ruin your lips.

I would have given anything to run my fingers through his

hair and kiss his thoughts away. I said a silent prayer he could deliver a kiss. It meant life or death to me.

> Abbie's Mac: Are you a good kisser?
>
> Cameron's Mac: I've had no complaints. But why don't you get that beautiful, jean-clad ass over here and find out?
>
> Abbie's Mac: You would kiss me for the first time in a coffee shop?
>
> Cameron's Mac: In front of God and everyone. At this point, I'd kiss you anywhere you let me. Are you ready for that, Abbie? Because once I get access to those lips, I'm going to suck them dry.
>
> Abbie's Mac: Sounds promising and painful.
>
> Cameron's Mac: A kiss can be an introduction, statement, and a promise. I plan to make all three when you let me.

I trembled inside at his words. He was coming on strong. But we'd been doing the coffee dates for over a month. I sometimes wondered if he was going to tap out. As if he could sense my thoughts, he sent another message.

> Cameron's Mac: I can wait. I will wait. Tell me about your day.
>
> Abbie's Mac: Much of the same. Nothing to report. Numbers don't lie—ever. It's so cut and dry, sometimes

I wonder what I was thinking with my career choice.

Cameron's Mac: Bored?

Abbie's Mac: I need a challenge. A puzzle I can't figure out. I need to be engaged, and the project I'm working on is ending soon. I just need that fire that comes with a new job.

Cameron's Mac: So, it's coming. You just have to be patient.

He smirked because he'd gathered through our earlier conversations that patience was something I lacked. Cameron read me well, and I loved that fact.

Abbie's Mac: My mother says I was the most restless and eager kid on the planet. And she claims I ruined every spelling bee, blurting the answers out of turn.

His brow lifted as he gave me another knowing twist of his lips.

Cameron's Mac: You totally ruined them.

Abbie's Mac: Yes, Cameron, I am I M P A T I E N T. I ruined the second-grade spelling bee and Steven Marcum's epic comeback. I was an asshole kid.

Cameron's Mac: Overachiever?

Abbie's Mac: No, but I wanted to be. So badly. My

mother's praise was all I craved.

I gave a light laugh while I typed.

Abbie's Mac: My mother's love made me an asshole.

Cameron's Mac: I love it when you crack yourself up. Laugh at your own shit. It's adorable.

Abbie's Mac: You do?

Cameron's Mac: Yeah, I do. And you're not even funny.

I shot him the bird. That earned me a chuckle.
I studied his Adam's apple while he laughed, itching to get my lips on it, that's when I saw the deep scratch next to it.

Abbie's Mac: What in the hell happened to your neck?

Cameron's Mac: Max's pit bull, Veronica. She gives shitty hickies.

Abbie's Mac: That looks awful.

Cameron's Mac: Doesn't hurt. And don't worry, she made sure to apologize by taking a shit in my Nikes.

He grinned and swept his tongue over his bottom lip. My breathing went shallow as I let my imagination get the best of me.

Cameron's Mac: Want to take a shot at a better hickey? I have the whole left side free.

Abbie's Mac: Hickies are for High Schoolers and now you're telling me I'm competing with a pit bull?

Cameron's Mac: You don't have to suck, I don't mind just your lips and tongue.

His smile turned devilish as he typed.

Cameron's Mac: And I've known Veronica longer, she's proven her loyalty.

Abbie's Mac: Ouch.

Cameron's Mac: Want me to come over there and attend to that? Just tell me where it hurts.

Warmth flushed my body as his eyes swept me.

Cameron's Mac: You're out of coffee.

Inwardly, I sighed as he stood and walked over to retrieve my cup. He leaned down and picked it up so we were eye level. It was the first time we'd been face-to-face since we'd met, and I felt myself sink into the seat as his heated green eyes scanned my face.

I felt it then, the undeniable pull, the buildup of attraction that flowed between us like a low lying electric current. It stunned me into clearing my throat. He picked up the cup and waited, for what I wasn't sure. Licking my lips, I concentrated on his mouth, my heart pounding as he leaned in a little further, and then a little more. One inch would have our mouths meeting.

My heart sputtered as blood flowed everywhere, circulating and collecting between my thighs. I wanted his kiss. I wanted it more than my next breath, the one he stole with his subtle inch forward. The sheer size of him was alluring on its own, never mind the intoxicating smell of leather and man that drifted into my nostrils. The man wore a cologne designed specifically to get me high.

At that moment, I needed to feel the full, pale cherry-colored lips that waited in the breath between us. Just as I started to close the space, he stood, dashing my hopes as he walked away with a wink.

He'd played me.

Face flushed with lusty thoughts of my lips, his skin, my heart, his cock, my teeth, and his tongue invaded my head as I tried to get myself together. I was in pieces, and all he'd done was toy with me.

Holy fucking shit.

Did abstaining from the physical make a relationship more meaningful? Maybe, but before long, it was inevitable you'd end up like Cameron and me, skirting around the elephant in the room that refused to be camouflaged. Our relationship wasn't based on sex, but we'd hit that crossroads. Our imaginations were taking over, and we were both thirsty.

Was it time to take a drink?

Take a drink, bitch.

"Thanks, Bree," I muttered.

Minutes later, Cameron set my cup down on the table, and I ogled his tight ass before he took his own seat, too far away. When he was comfortable, he glanced my way and read my posture. I was fully turned on, and he'd done next to nothing. But the heat in my cheeks told me I was flushed, and I was swallowing repeatedly. I wanted him, and it was evident.

Reflected in his eyes was a deadly combination of sex, desperate want, and intense need. Overwhelmed, I had no way to cope, and the only solution was to take a step in his direction. I wanted to lick the salt off his Adam's apple, to feel his weight on top of me. I was there.

Cameron's Mac: Penny for your thoughts.

Abbie's Mac: No way.

Cameron's phone rattled on his table and I nodded toward it.

Abbie's Mac: Want to get that? It's been buzzing for an hour.

I played with the petals of the pink peony he'd brought me and then sheepishly glanced his way. His jaw ticked as he watched me. He hadn't budged.

Cameron's Mac: Tell me, Abbie.

It was a demand on his part, and I couldn't blame him. I was equally as intrigued.

Abbie's Mac: You tell me.

Another staredown.

Cameron's Mac: You sure you want the blunt truth?

I slowly nodded.

Cameron's Mac: I want to make you come.

I closed my eyes as my whole body shivered at his admission.

Cameron's Mac: I want to taste you in every way a man can taste a woman, savor you on my tongue and swallow.

Cameron's Mac: I'm dying to know what you sound like moaning my name. I'm fucking dying, Abbie, just to kiss you.

Cameron's Mac: But I can wait. I will wait. I will wait as long as it takes for you to look at me and have a decision made.

Abbie's Mac: Why me?

Cameron's Mac: Why not you? I'm not interested in anyfuckingthing else. Nothing. But. You. This, you and me, is all I look forward to. And it already feels better than all the woos before you. Want some more truth?

Jesus, could I handle more? Hell yes I could. I nodded.

Cameron's Mac: Every night while I lay in bed, I stroke my cock thinking of you. And it's been every single night for the last two weeks. Ever since you started looking at me that way.

Abbie's Mac: What way?

Cameron's Mac: The way you're looking at me right now. Jesus, I'm hard, and I'm getting harder thinking about the kiss you almost gave me.

Abbie's Mac: You pulled away.

Cameron's Mac: I won't do it again. Your turn. And don't hold back.

Lips parted, my erratic pulse made me glad I was sitting. Every limb in my body thrummed with the possibilities.

Abbie's Mac: I had an orgasm for every letter of your name last night.

His eyes hooded as he read the words then looked over at me.

Cameron's Mac: When we leave here today, I want you to do the exact same thing. I want you to go home, slip your panties off, and touch yourself while thinking of me.

Abbie's Mac: Okay.

Cameron's Mac: Show me the finger you'll use.

I pressed my finger to my lips and sucked.

Cameron's Mac: Fuck. I need to go. Abbie, I have to go.

Abbie's Mac: Don't go.

Cameron's Mac: I can't stay a fucking minute longer and respect the rules.

He glanced over at me, his eyes pulling me under. I was sure I was in need of a panty change. And even more so, I was frustrated I couldn't bring myself to close my Mac and put us both out of our misery.

Cameron's Mac: I can't stay. But I'll keep waiting, Abbie. I promise. Meet me here tomorrow?

Abbie's Mac: Yes.

My shoulders slumped as he packed his bag. Pushing out my lips, I protested, but he shook his head adamantly. Were we really going to leave each other to touch ourselves in bed?

We were in a silent standoff. It was either pull the trigger and give into the physical or wait it out a little longer. Most of me told me to trust my gut, to try to trust him, but my head wasn't ready. I sighed and grabbed my purse and my Mac. Cameron stood stoically, patiently waiting for me to leave.

It was cruel to both of us, but we were still safe. All our good intentions toward the other kept intact. Our situation remained respectable, albeit the perverts that existed just under the surface were going to win the war that day.

I hauled ass home, my limbs burning with ache, my skin on fire, and heart pounding at the fact he knew I was racing home to come with his name on my lips. And he was going to do the same.

Abbie

Abbie's Mac: Hi. Sorry I'm late.

Cameron's Mac: You're still late. I can't see you.

Abbie's Mac: I'm here, but please don't look for me!

Cameron's Mac: What?

Abbie's Mac: Stay where you are. I'm here. Just don't come looking for me.

Cameron's Mac: Why?

Out of breath, I began frantically typing.

Abbie's Mac: I'm having an off day and I didn't have your number to let you know I couldn't make it. I didn't want to cancel.

Before I could hit send, his message came through.

Cameron's Mac: You're the most beautiful chipmunk I've ever seen.

Tears of pain and humiliation filled my eyes. I lowered my head, pulling my beanie down as he stood in all his man-splendor, peering down at me, dimples blazing. He placed his *Create, Hustle, Repeat* cup next to mine then opened his Mac on my table before taking the seat opposite me. I'd been hiding in the ivy plant section among the older, less used cups. He extended a soft pink buttercup toward me, and I took the flower. I moved to type a thank you, but he stilled my hands.

"Tank you, uh, Denbist," I pushed out between the bloody cotton.

"Dentist? Wisdom teeth?" he whispered, his voice full of concern.

Hastily, I nodded and typed in an attempt to silence him.

Abbie's Mac: I forgot I had an appointment. But we don't need to break our routine. Please. Things are going so well.

"Abbie," he pleaded, commanding my eyes before he slowly reached across the table, tugging my hand away from the keyboard. I closed my eyes as he laced our fingers, his touch jarring me. I knew I looked like death—pale, jaw pounding, and mouth overstuffed with bloody gauze. Chin wobbling, I was visibly shaking from the pain because the Novocain was wearing off by the second.

"You're hurting. Did you take anything for the pain?" I shook my head and tried to pull my hand away from the comfort of his so I could explain.

"No," he said, condemning me while stroking my skin with his fingers. "Not today. Give me your phone," he commanded. I pulled it out of my purse as he grabbed a napkin from the dispenser on the table next to us and wiped some drool from my mouth. I felt helpless against the pain-induced tear that trickled down my cheek.

"I dibn't have time to geb my perscibion filbed. I nind't wan to not show up and you tink de worst." I shook my head in frustration at my inability to finally talk to him. "Thib is cruel. Let's twype."

He chuckled as he gently wiped at the corners of my mouth.

"Abbie, there's the chink in our armor, okay? We need to loosen up the rules a bit." He grabbed my phone, held it out for me to unlock it, and when I did, he typed in his info. When he gave it back, I did my best to hide my grimace.

"Okay?"

"Otay," I said around a mouthful of disadvantage.

He reached for both hands and slid his fingers slowly through mine. My heart seized from his touch alone, but the look in his eyes was enough to have mine watering again, but for a different reason.

It was all there. I was his girl and I was hurting, and it hurt him to see me that way. That's what I saw, felt, and knew.

"Can I take you home?" he asked as he slid the pads of his thumbs over the top of my hands.

I shook my head. "I don't live faw. Bree is combing."

"I'll wait with you."

Minutes later, and driven by a need to get closer, I was comfortably resting in Cameron's arms in the booth surrounded by trickling ivy. It was a different world from the one we'd both grown comfortable in. His clean-scented cologne surrounded me as I sat nestled against his tall frame. I fit perfectly in his strong arms, with one hand resting on his chest, his head tilted down as he spoke softly to me.

He spared me from talking by telling me a little about his week. He had met a few of his favorite jocks, who were shooting a commercial for a new line of sportswear his stores carried. I wasn't much for sports, but I was one hundred percent for the man who spoke with childlike enthusiasm about his personal rock stars.

He also told me that he'd started watching *Mindhunter*—a show about two FBI agents delving into the psychology of murder. I knew my slow building, drool-filled smile looked goofy, but I couldn't, for the life of me, stop it. He'd taken an interest in something that fascinated me. He kept his tone low, and his deep baritone whisper was as soothing as the hand that covered mine on his chest. The timbre of his voice lulled me into a stupor as I tried to keep my aching and stretched mouth closed. Cameron stroked my fingers delicately as I peered up at him. Head tilted back, I memorized the fullness of his lips, noted a faint white scar at the edge of his temple, and the fan of his dark lashes. He was, without a doubt, the most attractive man I'd ever dated.

I found myself needing to make sure that was the case. I wanted more. I was ready. My gut, heart, and my mind, for the first time in a year, were in agreement. And I wanted him to know our relationship had turned into more. I didn't, for any reason, want it to be *less* than the beginning of something between us.

Want was quickly turning into need as he cradled me and paused his story to gauge my expression. He had to have seen it all there, but I decided to try to verbalize it anyway. "Cambron,"

I whispered.
Thank you for waiting.
You're so perfect.
I want you so bad.
Does this feel as good to you?
Gently cupping my jaw, he leaned down and spoke, a centimeter from my lips, and addressed my unspoken thoughts. "Me too." He rubbed his thumb across my lower lip. "I can't wait to take you away from here, anywhere." His deep green eyes scoured my features and landed longingly on my mouth as he slipped my beanie off and ran his fingers through the hair at the back of my neck. "And kiss these lips."

I knew I looked hideous, yet the man was treating me like I was his catnip.

"Okay."

He chuckled. "Okay." He leaned in and kissed my cheek then the corner of my mouth.

Content in his lap, my bliss was interrupted by the arrival of my escort home.

"Well, isn't *this* the shit. You two look cozy," Bree said as she approached our table with a warm smile. "Cameron, good to see you. I've heard nothing but good things." Her voice low, and in a playful warning, added, "Keep it that way."

Her eyes found mine and she winced as she looked at my swollen mouth. "Ouch, babe. Let's get you medicated and get you home." She pulled out the prescription I begged her to pick up for me and handed me two pills as she spoke to Cameron. "This stuff renders her unconscious in minutes. We'll have to make this quick."

Cameron stiffened beneath me as I popped the pills into my mouth and sipped the water bottle I had on my table. He warily eyed the bottle of pills as I put them in my purse.

Bree noticed his reaction.

"Just a few low dose Percocet to take the edge off," she assured him. "Let me grab a coffee and I'll get you home." I gave her a careless nod, still entranced in willing captivity of the man holding me. I sank further under his spell before waving her away.

All-knowing Bree looked between us as I tried to get myself together. I was sure I looked needy and desperate, like a lovesick teenager curled in his lap.

Zero shits were given as I imagined having lip access to every inch of his skin. I curled my fingers in his crisp shirt, tucking them beneath the seams to touch his skin. He let out a low groan as his amused eyes found mine when we were free of interruption. There was so much light in them. I hoped what I saw was a mirrored reflection of what he could feel from me.

At that moment, I was transparent, and I knew it. I wasn't doing anything to stop it. I had no fear. I wanted it, wanted us. To belong, not to just a man, but the man who held me. Warmth spread throughout my limbs as my body shuddered with sparked need. The pain was dull in comparison to the reaction of his touch, his words, the look in his eyes.

"I wish I knew what you were thinking," he said softly.

"Happy," I managed to say clearly while my heart pounded inches from his, in an attempt to communicate what it felt.

His eyes closed briefly, and when he graced me with them again, I saw a hint of vulnerability.

"Abbie," he whispered, his voice strained. My heart crashed against my chest as he bent and placed a barely-there kiss to my parted lips. Fearful of my breath, I shook my head, warning him away. I could taste the copper on my tongue, and I tried my best to clamp my mutilated mouth shut.

"Don't worry. I won't take that as our first kiss, either. And you are worth every second of the wait."

Far too soon, Bree was back with her coffee, and I was forced away from my Cameron cocoon. Reluctantly, he stood, keeping me close as he walked us to the door of the café. My mind was starting to cloud as the pills began to kick in. I was a lightweight when it came to the effects of any medication.

"I'll text you tonight," he whispered before he placed a kiss on my temple then gave a warm farewell to Bree.

Our fingers were the last things to separate.

11

Abbie

I woke to the sound of a garbage truck, feeling as if said garbage truck had backed up at top speed and dumped its load in my mouth. Flexing my angry jaw, I felt like I was still in a drug-induced haze. I was trying to convince myself to get my lazy ass out of bed when my phone buzzed on my nightstand.

Cameron would like to Facetime.

"Oh shit," I screeched as I pulled my comforter up to cover myself. My finger hovered before I decided to hell with it and unlocked the screen to answer it. Cameron appeared in what looked like his kitchen.

"Hey, beautiful, how are you feeling?"

"Like shit," I said truthfully. "I'm sorry I didn't answer last night. Those pills knocked me out."

He gave a sharp nod. "It's fine. I was sure they would."

I quickly ran my hands through my hair. I knew I must've

looked like a mess. "I probably look terrible."

"Not at all, you look comfortable," he said as his eyes scoured me, making my heart dance.

"So, that's your place?" I asked.

"Yeah, I'm home. I was just about to head out to meet Max and school him on the court."

"So, he's no competition?"

I felt disgusting from sleeping so long. I needed a shower and a toothbrush. Still, I did my best to seem casual, though the invasion of his face while I lay in my bed had me a little hot under the sheets. The man was chiseled glory, and I couldn't wait for my real first kiss. I was like a giddy teenager who got the call from the boy she'd been waiting for.

Except this was no boy. He was six-foot plus perfection.

"None. I ruin Max every time I win. I live to piss him off."

"I want to meet him one day," I said with a grin. "He'll give me the dirt on you."

"You'll never meet him now," he said playfully.

"Show me your place?" I asked, curious. I imagined Cameron's home to be a real bachelor pad of a grown-up nature. He had impeccable taste in clothing, so I assumed he had the same taste in furnishings.

And I was right. He had a large, open floor plan condo with a distant view of the park, which meant he only lived blocks away. I'd never asked him specifically where he lived. But seeing was believing, and, somehow, it made him seem more real to me. To my surprise, his place was scarcely furnished, but what I did see was a mix of dark wood and leather. There were a few boxes scattered around.

"When did you move in?" I asked.

"Too long ago to still have packed boxes. I just wasn't sure if I was staying here."

"Really? Why?"

He shrugged. "I just wasn't sure where I wanted to call home."

"And now?"

One side of his mouth lifted. "Now, I've got an incentive to stick around."

"You flatter me."

"You fucking floor me."

I sighed happily, no longer afraid to stretch in my bed as I snuggled deeper into the comfort of it and his words. He'd managed to touch me from the other side of the screen.

He nudged his chin toward me. "Show me your place. I want to see what you did to it."

"I'm not decent. I feel gross, I need a shower, and I'm too lazy at the moment."

He perked up. "You know we can continue Facetime while you're in the shower. It wouldn't bother me."

I laughed and then winced.

He stuck out his bottom lip in a pout. "Maybe when you're feeling better."

"*You* make me feel better."

His smile lit up my closed curtain bedroom.

"Thanks for yesterday. I haven't had anyone but Bree and my mother look out for me in a while."

"I didn't do anything," he dismissed.

I wanted to reach through the screen. I was itching to run my fingers through his musesd up, dark locks. He was wearing a hoodie, and I hated I couldn't see more.

"You were there for me, and you gave a damn. That's more than enough. I'll return the favor sometime."

Something dark crossed his features as he spoke. "It's such a basic thing, isn't it? Just wanting someone to be there through the growing pains. So many people have it and take it for granted."

I wanted to ask how long he'd been single, to ask what he'd been through that put that hint of sadness in his eyes. But asking meant telling.

"We won't take it for granted," I assured.

"No, we won't," he agreed.

It was surreal talking to him, seeing him in his element. I was sure he was thinking the same thing.

"I'll let you get to the court."

"I'd much rather be hanging out with you," he assured. "I'll call you tonight?"

I nodded. "Please."

12

Abbie

SNOW CRESTED ON THE WIND LIKE CLUMPS OF AIRY cotton as I made my way toward the café. My smile widened as the ground crunched beneath me. Chicago weather could be brutal. Case and point, it wasn't even a month into fall and Old Man Winter had already shown up to the party. But on rare days when the cold didn't have too harsh of a bite and the snow came down on the city like a soft blanket . . . well, I loved those days.

Excitement thrummed through my every limb at the thought of what was to come. Warmth spread as I got closer to the café, to Cameron. I hadn't seen him in over a week due to our conflicting schedules.

Over the weekend, I'd traveled for an interview for a job based in Milwaukee that would start after my contract at Preston Corp ended. The commission was the only reason I hadn't passed on the job, but I'd made it a point to find something with limited travel. Because, for the first time in what felt like forever, I had someone else to share my time with, and I didn't want to miss a minute.

It was the strangest feeling to become reliant on him as a part of my life. My thoughts of the future were swinging a little in his direction, but it was healthy in the way that made my new relationship a priority. Intimacy was our last real hurdle. We'd laid the foundation, and it was a beautiful thing to be a part of as it unfolded. It was scary and freeing at the same time. I trusted him to a point. I just had to give him the rest. And I'd decided before I walked out the door and left my Mac at home I would take a step forward with him. He'd been patient for just a date, a kiss.

And if I was lucky and he was receptive, he was about to reap the reward for it.

When I saw Cameron was waiting outside the café for me, I couldn't stop my smile. Dressed in dark blue jeans and a wool blend, collared trench, he looked GQ and irresistible as he stood with an air of confidence, blowing in his hands to warm them up. I paused my steps to watch him.

"All right, Abigail," I scorned myself in a whisper just as Cameron caught sight of me crossing the street. "Just because he looks like a sidewalk prince standing in the snowdrift staring at you with honest eyes and a beautiful smile doesn't mean he's the one." He rubbed his hands together and gave me his signature wink. "Okay, so he idolizes his mother, respects your opinion, and has a little bit of a dirty mouth. All good things, but that doesn't mean you have to walk over and hand him your heart."

His smile deepened as I sped up.

I'm so fucked.

I beamed at him as I closed the space between us, my eyes searching his. It was only when he whisked me away from the door, placed his hands on the side of my face, and leaned in that I realized he'd left his computer at home too.

And then his lips were on mine; his breath-stealing groan danced on my tongue as I gasped into his mouth. In order to reach him, I had to stand on the tips of my toes to compensate and wrap my arms around his neck. He accommodated by gripping my hips and lifting me easily so we connected.

And then he kissed me.

His kiss gave both life and death. The end of everything as I knew it and the beginning of a need, a craving for only him.

He opened my mouth with the swipe of his tongue, and I moaned in invitation as he dove deep, tasting me. Toes curling, our tongues dueled and slid against each other's, spurring us into a frenzy. He refused to let up as he gave and took, clutching me to him, feeding until we were both gasping for breath.

"Cameron," I sputtered as he broke away briefly and then went straight back for more. In the middle of Wicker Park, in front of my favorite café, I got the best kiss of my life. His tongue moved so languidly with mine that I was ravenous by the time he pulled away.

"I'm so strung out on you right now, woman," he groaned as he traced my lips with his finger. "You are so goddamn beautiful. It hurts to look at you." He bit his lip. "Did you dress up for me?"

"Of course."

He kept us nose to nose as he spoke low, our energy electric, and I was wired. I could feel the minute the decision was made. I was going to give Cameron my heart. I just hoped he'd ask for it.

"That makes me feel so good. It's been a long time since I've had that, Abbie. Had *this*. It's been . . . a long time."

"Preach it, brother, hallelujah," I said, and we both laughed.

"Cameron, I think about you all the time."

"Day and night," he rasped out in between kisses across my jaw. "I was going blind with the need to touch you. I want this more than anything." He pulled away and peered down at me. "What do you want?"

"You have to kiss me again to find out."

And he did. Again, and again, and again. I wanted to regret the wait. I wanted so much to hate myself for depriving us of what we both so clearly wanted, but I knew it was the right call. Because it was all there. All of it. There was nothing awkward about it, no second-guessing, and no hesitation. It was simply us, and most definitely an introduction, a declaration, and a promise.

When he pulled away, he trailed hot kisses to my ear. "Jesus, I never want to stop kissing you."

"I need you to kiss me exactly like you just did, every time you kiss me."

He grinned down at me, but I wasn't smiling.

"I'm dead serious."

"I know you are," he said with a smirk. "And now I've got leverage. You love my tongue."

"I do," I admitted, leaning in to suck on the bottom lip I'd been dreaming about for what seemed like forever. Now that I had his touch, I never wanted to be without it.

"Filthy girl," he said with a lift of his husky voice before our tongues dueled again.

When we reluctantly pulled away, I whispered to him as he rubbed his knuckles seductively down my sides. "Where in the *hell* have you been, Cameron?"

"Hard up in the desert of no man's land on the other side of a macaroni table."

He was exasperated because of our distance, and I was just as ready for the space to disappear. And in a matter of minutes, with his lips on mine, that space had disintegrated. Our reward was the other. Enamored, I stood beneath his watchful eyes as we feasted.

"But, Abbie, it was worth it," he whispered. "I would do it again. I would do it all over again."

"Me too."

We shared a smile as he jutted his chin toward the coffee shop. "You want to go in?"

"No way." I shook my head. "Take me anywhere."

He lifted a brow. "You sure about that?"

"Positive."

He took my hand and led us toward the unknown.

13

Abbie

CAMERON SLID HIS THUMB OVER THE TOP OF MY HAND before he squeezed it.
"Are you ready?"

"Hell no. No." I shook my head adamantly. "I'll just wait back here for you."

"Nope, we're doing it," he said. My whole body trembling with fear, he took the first step onto the glass.

"Oh, shit," I squeaked out as the line behind us laughed at my outburst. We stepped out onto the glass deck, 1,353 feet in the air, while I kept my eyes tightly shut.

"We're out," he said. "Open your eyes, Abbie."

I cracked one open and took a hesitant peek.

"Okay, that's good enough, right?" I said, anxious to retreat into the building.

"Nope," he said as he moved us further out onto the Skydeck, and I reluctantly followed.

We were at the top of the Willis Tower, which everyone still referred to as the Sears Tower. My erratic pulse only intensified as Cameron leaned forward, placing his forehead on the glass to hold all his weight.

"Oh, you're crazy," I said as I took a step back. He tugged me forward by our clasped hands.

"If you're going to do it, might as well do it all the way."

"I feel sick," I said, swallowing.

"Come on, witchy woman," he retorted, cruelly amused.

I braved another glance at the glass between my feet and saw the moving cars beneath us had been reduced to the size of ants from our bird's eye view.

Snickering ensued from behind us, and I glanced over at the two women who were practically swooning over Cameron and had been the whole time we waited for the elevator to bring us up. I couldn't blame them. He was beautiful. But at that moment, all I felt was the adrenaline rush of being encased in the glass that sat on the side of the famous skyscraper.

"You're really going to make me do this?"

"Yep," he said mercilessly.

I let out a little shriek as I placed my forehead against the glass and let my weight sink behind it. "If I faint," I said in warning, "it's on you. This building is moving, I swear it is."

"It is," he said without a trace of fear in his voice.

"Jesus."

"I can't believe you've lived in Chicago this long and never did this," he said as he smirked at the ground far, far beneath us.

"I avoided it, and for good reason," I bit out through chattering teeth.

"To be honest, I hadn't done it, either. My mother brought me up here the first time I came."

"Brave woman. Did she make you stand like this?"

"No," he said with a chuckle. "She did a handstand."

"She what?!" I said with wide eyes as I shook, scared shitless as I observed the sea of skyscrapers dwarfed below us.

"Yeah, I have a picture of it," he said, glancing over at me. "I was pretty freaked out my first time up here too." He looked down and let out a breath. "She brought me up here to tell me she was dying."

Heart sinking, I looked over at him. That time, I squeezed his hand.

"I thought it cruel at the time, but if you think about it, it's a pretty cool way to tell your kid you're dying, right? Suspended in a place where you are terrified so the gravity of it doesn't hit you as hard." He paused, swallowing evident pain, and I waited. "She said she wanted me to know what it was like."

"What being sick was like?" I asked softly, my heart breaking for him.

"No, what it was like to leave her son in a world she wasn't sure was safe. She said she wasn't afraid of dying. She was just afraid for me, to leave me. And this is what it felt like."

"Cameron, I'm so sorry."

He nodded, his beautiful eyes cast down, a shadow covering his features. "She taught yoga six days a week well into her sixties. She treated her body like a temple and it turned on her. I live with it every day, Abbie. Wondering if I could have done more for her. Different doctors or treatments. I didn't get involved because I was sure she and my dad had it covered. I was selfish with my pain. I was only thinking of me, of how much I needed her, that I couldn't see past my own fear to make sure we did everything." He swallowed again, then stopped talking.

"I'm sure they did everything they could."

We stayed silent for a moment, holding hands and looking at the world beneath us. "Hey, I'm sorry. I didn't mean to bring it up. I've been missing her a lot lately."

"Hey," I said as he glanced over at me. "I'm glad you told me."

He gave me a wink. "I'm glad I came back up here with you."

"Me too."

Cameron pulled out his cell phone and aimed it at the two of us from underneath. It was the worst angle imaginable.

"Don't you dare take that picture," I warned, forcing a smile anyway.

"Look down," he said as he aimed it at us. "Done."

He pushed away from the glass, and I followed suit, mildly distracted by his story but brought into the present as I took in the view of the city and the expanse of Lake Michigan.

He studied the picture as we walked off the deck. "It's a good one," he said, holding it out for me to look. I waved it away.

"I'll take your word for it."

He grinned. "Not a fan of having your picture taken?"

"Nope. I'm not photogenic, like at all. It's a curse. Every time I take one, my eyes are closed or close to it because my smile is so wide."

He inspected the picture, and I could tell that was the case when he chuckled.

"Yep, but it's still a good one."

Abbie

We ended up walking the streets of downtown, getting lost in conversation among the high-rises, talking about everything and nothing. When we sought brief refuge from the brutal wind between buildings, Cameron used the opportunity to warm us up. He kissed me every chance he got, without shame, and I loved every second of it.

I basked in the feel of him, in his tall frame as he surrounded me, the way his hands always seemed to be warm, and his smooth as silk voice—a voice I'd deprived myself of. Though we'd been dating for over a month, all of it was new.

Hovering on a bridge at the Riverwalk, he took another selfie of us, which I reluctantly smiled for. He pressed his lips together when he studied it, and I knew it was another disaster.

Due to the unrelenting wind cresting off the water, my eyes were streaming mascara. Cameron leaned in and cupped my face, wiping away the smudges with his thumbs.

"Come on, let's get you somewhere warm," he said after another stolen kiss.

Glued to his side, he shielded me from the cold. After a few minutes of walking in silence—that was anything but empty— we ended up nestled at a cocktail table at Howl at the Moon, a dueling piano bar on West Hubbard.

"Ever been here?" he asked as I shed my coat.

"Nope, another first," I replied with a smile.

When the waiter came by, Cameron ordered us a bucket of Moscow Mule to share as I perused the bar. Other than the pianos that sat on a spotlit stage, the neon-lit room was dark and intimate. "This is what I love about Chicago. You never know what's around the corner."

"Yeah," he agreed. "Most days I'm happy I got my first job coaching here after I graduated."

"And the other days?"

"The other days aren't summer, and I'm freezing my ass off," he said with a wink. "I've endured enough winters, so I'm used to it. I don't see myself living anywhere else."

"Me either," I agreed.

"You know, Max goes to Bears games in shorts. In fact, you can't get him to wear a pair of pants in subzero temperatures."

"That's just plain stupid," I said with an eye roll.

Cameron shrugged. "I used to think he was crazy and did it to show off, but it turns out he's comfortable that way. He's from Wisconsin, so . . ."

"That explains everything," I said as I gave him my own wink.

"Something in your eye, Abbie?"

I deadpanned, "That's the last time I throw flirt your way tonight, Coach."

"That was flirting?" he asked with a smirk.

I narrowed my eyes. "I'm going to the bathroom." I stood and was swept off my feet and into his lap. I had to keep my moan internal when he leaned in and brushed his lips against my neck.

"What was that for?" I asked, my voice raspy.

"An apology kiss is a perfect excuse to cop a feel," he whispered, reminding me of our earlier conversations at the café.

We were finally hurdling the physical and it felt so good, so natural. I couldn't believe what a difference a day could make. "What song do you want to hear?" His voice was damned near a groan.

We were bordering on indecent as he sucked on my skin, leaving a trail of goosebumps in the wake of his soft lips.

When I didn't answer, he asked again, this time with dimples on full display. "Abbie?"

"What was the question?"

He kissed me deeply, then ripped himself away just as I was about to forfeit clothes.

"Surprise me," I whispered back as he reluctantly let me go.

"I intend to," he said sincerely as we both licked a fresh promise from our lips.

A little after midnight, Cameron bid me goodnight at my front door. I was panting when he left me, his smile radiant as he closed my gate and glanced back to where I stood. I touched my lips as he crossed the street, his long strides taking him too far away from me.

"I said goddamn," I whispered before I shut the door and sighed. I instantly missed him. And before I could scold myself for it, I got a text.

Cameron: Any plans for today?

14

Abbie

"Tell me everything," Bree said as she slipped on her first dress.

"Nothing new to report since the last time we talked. He's brilliant and beautiful and good to me. Really good to me."

Cameron and I had been inseparable since the day he'd kissed me. I'd attended one of the home basketball games he coached, which started a string of fantasies that he starred in. I'd lusted over him as he stood on the sidelines in his silky black sweat suit with a dominating stance.

That night, though he coached basketball, I'd let him get to second base. He had drawn more moans out of me than I thought capable. He'd left me hoarse and needy at my front door, and I'd gone to bed with my fantasies on replay and his name on my lips.

The day after, we had our first dinner date. Again, we'd ended up on my porch, clinging to each other, an invitation on the tip of my tongue but never escaping my lips. And he'd never pressed. We'd left each other frustrated, but in the best way.

Last night, outside my door, and underneath the artificial yellow light, he'd whispered my name in a way that had me near orgasm just from the sound of it.

"Abbie," he rasped out as his fingertips traced the collar of my knit sweater. They edged around the soft fabric in a seductive caress while his green eyes held my blue. Wordless—though I could see a million of them on his waiting lips—he kissed me breathless, and then kissed me some more as I sank into him, our bodies locking like they belonged that way.

Swept away by the King of Woo, I still couldn't believe I was the lucky one on the receiving end of his attention. It was, without exaggeration, the most romantic courting of my life. No matter what we were doing, his affection seemed bottomless, and I lapped it up eagerly, starved for more.

I had it bad, and it felt so fucking good; I refused to overanalyze it.

Bree smiled at my dazed expression while my brain scrambled with racing thoughts of my new man. Trying to remain focused on my duties, I scrutinized the dress she was fastening.

"This isn't exactly your style," I said. "Neither is this place."

We were at a posh bridal boutique downtown. Anthony had insisted on giving her his AmEx and buying her dress. Bree was as independent as I was but seemed to have no issue with it.

I was proud of her for being so onboard with his plans. She was arranging the ceremony but agreed to leave the reception up to her fiancé. For a southern girl who came from a traditional family, it was completely atypical for a bride to give up so much say, but Bree was anything but typical.

I moved to free her from the tight confines of the dress

just as it pooled at her feet. "I'm not going to find it here." She sighed, slipping into another dress.

"No, you aren't, but it was a sweet gesture from him. There's a shop in Wicker that sells vintage gowns," I suggested. "We should check that out."

She beamed at me. "He's loving the whole thing, the planning and the details. It's so weird, right? He wants to be involved."

I shook my head. "Not weird, it's amazing. And you aren't the stressed-out bride at all."

She grinned. "We've been having a lot of sex."

Just as the words passed her lips, the woman who was assisting us brought in two more dresses. She cringed at Bree's comment and hung up her finds on the standing rack of silk and lace.

"Here are a few more that might be your style."

"Thanks," Bree said, picking through the rack before she eyed the attendant and walked over to me. "This place is so *Pretty Woman*," she said with a devilish grin. A grin I knew was trouble.

"Oh, *honey*," she spouted, pitching her voice before resting her booted foot on the sparkling white cushion next to me. "I think I've got a runner in my pantyhose," she said, running her hand down her bare leg.

The attendant eyed Bree in horror as she continued, adding her southern flair. "Oh me, oh my," she drawled. "I'm not *wearing* pantyhose," she deadpanned, as if it was the cue for the end of her scene.

Bree then went on about her business as she normally did when she'd embarrassed me. "Speaking of sex, when are you going to put the poor man out of his misery?"

The attendant scurried from the room as if she needed to

pray the evil away, and Bree kept her eyes on me. I buried my head in my hands. "Could you, for once, try *not* to humiliate me everywhere we go? I might be here for my own dress one day."

"Oh, come on. What exactly does she think happens to these dresses on the wedding night?"

"I don't know, but *she* probably didn't do anal to get her husband to propose."

Bree rolled her eyes. "You aren't a prude, and this isn't your first rodeo. Are you nervous?"

"No, I told you that we're taking it slow. He's a gentleman, and he's wooing me."

"You've become a little bit high maintenance," she said, slipping on her corduroy overalls.

"I have not," I said, averting my eyes.

"You have," she insisted as she thumbed through the dresses, unimpressed. "You have, and I'm proud of you for it. You've come a long way. Let's get out of here."

On the way to the bridal shop in Wicker Park, Bree stopped us in the street.

"Come on, it's been a while."

Realizing where we were, I looked up and found the sign hanging next to the dry cleaner marquee.

"Not again," I said, shaking my head. "This is a waste of your money."

She nudged me before she put her hand on the door. "You should get a reading. She's on point every time I come."

"And you believe her," I huffed. "No one can tell you your

future, Bree."

"Yes, they can, and she has. She predicted Anthony was coming," she said as she opened the glass door.

"There's always another man coming," I scoffed as I followed her up the stairs. "That's not a prediction. It's a normal progression when you're single."

Bree was the only woman I knew who got her palm read on a regular basis. I thought the whole thing was a crock of shit, but she believed otherwise. Bree thought certain people had the ability to look into your soul. I believed that certain people trained themselves to read mannerisms and clues to pinpoint background, signs of health, mental state, and took advantage of them emotionally.

"You're too cynical. You could just try it for fun," she proposed, taking the steps two at a time.

"I don't believe in this," I whispered as we neared the top of the stairs. "I believe in numbers. They're absolute. I can't believe in much else without explanation."

"You can't see love," she argued.

I shrugged. "True, but you know some scientists believe love is really just a manifestation of attraction, a chemical reaction that produces a rush of endorphins that gets you high. And eventually, the high dulls as the senses become immune due to exposure to the same person."

"But you're a romantic," she pointed out, her tone incredulous. "Like a diehard romantic."

"I am," I agreed. "I'm addicted to the high. I'm a fiend for it."

"You're breaking my heart," she said, glowering at me. "I've had the same chemical reaction with the same man for two years, and you're saying it will fade? You don't really believe that, do you?"

"I'm more of a scientist than believer at this point."

"So, you're saying my marriage is bound to fail because, eventually, I won't get high off him?"

"Hey, don't take my head off. It's just a theory. And I think Anthony *is* the one man who can make you consistently high. I'm not knocking love. I want it for myself."

"Well, *I* choose to believe that chemical reaction is *bullshit*."

"And for only fifty dollars, you can be reassured," I said, showing her all my teeth.

"*You* need a chemical reaction," she said, elbowing me hard in the side as we walked through the gate.

Marisela—who I was sure was born with a different name, like Mary or something less mystical—greeted us as we entered the living room that also served as a makeshift waiting room. "Hi, Bree," she said in a warm greeting. Marisela's apartment wasn't decorated with healing crystals and didn't reek of incense. It looked like a typically decorated living room. Marisela dressed in casual clothes, her appearance very girl next door. She was the opposite of what I'd expected when I first met her.

"How are you?" Marisela said, looking her over before she addressed me.

"And you? Are you finally ready to get your cards read?" she asked as Bree turned to me, both brows raised.

"I had a fortune cookie last night, so I'm good. Thank you."

Bree scowled at me while Marisela laughed. She had tried to lure me into her lair many times but was good-natured about the fact I didn't believe in it.

"I'm sorry," I said, apologizing as Bree shot daggers at me. "Not today, Marisela. Maybe some other time."

"It's fine. I hear those kinds of comments often. I get labeled as the crazy lady. It's nothing new." She looked me over and smiled. "Sometimes they even go so far as to call me a *witch*."

She studied my reaction. I couldn't help it. My jaw dropped as her eyes lit up in victory. "Come see me when you're ready. And tell your gypsy neighbor I said hello."

"*O-kay.*"

I had no idea who she was referring to, and the look on her face told me she knew that too. She turned her all-seeing eyes on my best friend.

"Ready, Bree?"

Bree followed Marisela past the French doors that led to her reading room. I was genuinely stunned as I took a seat on her couch. She couldn't have guessed Cameron's pet name for me. There was no conceivable way. I hadn't even told Bree.

Passing it off as coincidence, I picked up a copy of *Rolling Stone* from the coffee table and thumbed through an article about one of my favorite bands, The Dead Sergeants. I was drooling over a candid shot of the front man when Marisela's tiny, four-legged Q-tip approached me. I wasn't much of an animal lover. I wasn't born with the gene that made people capable of swapping saliva with a dog. And just as I wished I had it, the little shit mounted my new boot and began humping me.

"Oh no, don't do that." I shook my leg while beady eyes stared up at me. I could have sworn the little ball of fur was smiling. "Let's not do that. Shoo," I said, eyes narrowed on the French doors, wondering if Marisela knew what was happening.

Cameron: What are you up to?

I repeatedly shook my leg, to no avail.

There was no way I was talking to Cameron while being used as the perverted fluff bag's hump post.

Was this life's sick irony at my jab at love?

I needed to get out of that room. I stood, and the dog

remained steadfast as I stomped my foot.

I didn't want to leave Cameron waiting, so I crossed my arms and stared down at the violating beast. The act seemed criminal coming from a puppy so cute. It ignored my plea and kept at it, pink tongue hanging out. "Come on, let's wrap it up. You get no points for stamina."

After a few more minutes, I gave up and thumped its nose. I was surely going to hell for that. Resuming my seat, and in need of a cigarette and an apology for the dog who walked off like I meant nothing to him, I picked up my phone.

Me: You wouldn't believe me if I told you.

Cameron: Try me.

Me: I'm waiting on Bree who's getting her fortune read and a dog just made love to my boot. Didn't take it to dinner or anything, just fed his desires and left.

The bubbles started going, and I knew he was laughing because his answering emoji told me so.

Cameron: Poor boot. Are you getting your fortune told?

Me: Nope, don't believe in it.

While waiting for his reply, I glanced at the picture above the TV. It was an old movie poster with a prominent moon and stars in darkening blue above the title *The Man in the Moon*. I briefly thought of how astrology and astronomy were both based on numbers or the use of. I thought it ironic that if mathematicians had a religion, it would be either of those.

Cameron: There are numbers in the moon and stars.

I couldn't believe what I was reading. It was as if he were in the room.

Me: Wow.

Cameron: What?

Me: Just a lot of strange coincidences in the last few minutes.

Cameron: Are they coincidences? ;)

Me: Don't you start. I told Bree from a scientist's point of view that love was a chemical reaction and that people get off on the high of it and she got pissed.

Cameron: You make me high.

Maybe I was still a little cynical, but the man had an arsenal of woo and was tearing down any argument I held day by day. Whatever the science was behind the way I felt for him didn't matter. All that really mattered was that he made me high and in the most organic way. Time would tell if we would last, but I was enjoying the high.

Bree appeared from the room minutes later with a smile. "Ready?"

I smiled back. "I think I am."

15

Abbie

"Kat, you in here?" I asked as I walked into the bathroom. "I hate to bother you, but everyone is seated at the meeting."

"Yeah." Her voice was unsteady. "I'll be right there."

She opened the stall door, her face pale, her forehead covered in sweat.

"Are you okay?"

"It's the sushi I ate last night. I think I got a touch of food poisoning. And my head is killing me."

"Oh no. We can reschedule," I offered, knowing we would be hard-pressed to do so.

"Don't be ridiculous," she snapped, running the water and soaping her hands. "I'll be right there."

"Okay," I said, turning on my heel.

"Is there something you want to say to me?" she asked.

"Pardon?"

"I said"—she turned from the counter and crossed her arms in front of her—"it looks like there is something on your mind. Let's hear it."

She clearly had some sort of confrontation in mind as her dark blue gaze scoured my appearance like I was beneath her.

I shook my head. "Nope, just waiting to start this meeting."

"Sure? Because from where I'm standing, it seems like it."

"Kat, is there something I'm missing here?" I said, both annoyed and stunned at her uncalled-for aggression. "I don't have an issue here."

"Good," she said as she walked past me, the air around her filled with an unspoken insult.

"What. The. Hell," I mouthed, walking after her.

An hour into the meeting Kat was leading, I got a text.

King of Woo: Hey, beautiful.

Me: Hi.

King of Woo: How's your day going?

Me: Sucky. Full of suck. A suck fest.

King of Woo: Let me make it better. Plans tonight?

Me: I was just going to watch scary movies and pass out candy.

His answering text was the thumbs down emoji.

Me: You have a better plan?

King of Woo: Can you get together a last-minute costume? There's a pub party tonight. Nothing big, but I

would love it if you could come.

Me: I think I can dream something up.

King of Woo: I'll pick you up at eight.

Me: See you then.

"Abbie?" I met Kat's icy gaze that led the rest of the room to stare in my direction.

I was being called out like the distracted kid in class, which I was at the moment, but I'd covered her ass enough times to expect the same. I didn't work for her, and at some point, I might have to make that clearer.

Lucky for me, I was good at multitasking and met her challenge head-on. "We'll be implementing all of it next quarter along with the new software. It's clearly outlined," I reminded her, making her call-out redundant.

She continued the meeting I'd spent hours preparing for—prepping *her* for.

It was going to be one of those days.

Abbie

"Okay, woman, I'm here," Bree called from down the hall. "I don't have long. I have to get back to work and scan the ca—" her words stopped as she took in my costume.

"What do you think?" I asked, proud of myself for being able to throw together the perfect outfit on such short notice.

"What do I think? Are you serious?" she said, setting her

purse down, her scrubs tarnished with a blood stain that I didn't want the story behind.

Bree looked me over with wild eyes. "This is a *date*, not a costume contest. Where's the sexy?"

"Where's the *what*? I'm a witch," I answered, though it was clear with the black silk cape and matching hat I'd managed to swipe last minute from the drugstore.

The Goodwill down the street just so happened to have a pair of black wedge loafers with a buckle on top of them. I'd only paid four dollars for the perfect complement to my costume. I got lucky.

"That nose. Jesus."

"Hey," I defended, "it took me an hour to do my makeup. It's real latex like they use in the movies."

"Oh, you look like the Wicked Witch of the West," she said with a laugh.

"So, what's the problem?"

Bree shook her head in disbelief. "I don't know, babe. Look in the mirror and see if you find yourself irresistibly sexy."

"I'm a witch. Witches aren't sexy," I said slowly as if we were having a communication problem. Maybe I did need to get her hearing checked. I turned and studied the nose with a giant wart on the tip when it hit me. "Oh shit," I said, realizing what she meant.

"Yeah, you don't have to worry if tonight's the big night. You could wear an adult diaper and be safe."

"I wasn't even thinking along those lines," I said helplessly.

"I know, babe. But this *is* a date."

My face was rapidly paling beneath the green mask. Nowhere in my mind had I thought to seduce my new boyfriend with my costume. I could have picked any number of things and made it sexy, but I saw the witch hat and thought it a no-brainer. The dick nose I'd glued to my face with a giant wart attached would ensure I remained celibate. Had I done it on purpose?

"He's going to be here in twenty minutes! I don't have enough makeup to redo my face!"

"Damn, girl," she said, letting her laughter consume her. "It's fine. Just get it off and we'll go heavy on the eye makeup. Do you have something black and low cut in here?"

I heard the scrape of hangers on the rack as she went through my clothes while I tried to remove the nose. Tugging at it to no avail, I moved in closer to the mirror and saw a giant black hair hanging from the wart. Cursing my stupidity, even in my haste to find a last-minute costume, I began to panic when the nose wouldn't budge.

"Oh shit, Bree! It won't come off! I used too much adhesive!" The pain was becoming unbearable as I pulled and pulled on the nose, my eyes watering, and tears spilling over my cheeks. The side of the appendage was the only thing to give, but it still sat proudly erect on my face. "Shit! Shit! Shit!"

"What?" Bree said, emerging from my closet with a low cut black dress that showed tons of cleavage.

"I can't find the remover. I think that's why it was discounted. It was missing a tube!"

Bree began laughing hysterically as I went through every trash can in my bedroom.

"Nope, not in here," I said in a panic as she doubled over. "You bitch, stop laughing and help me!"

"I will," she said. "I will, swear to God, just give me a second." She composed her face. "Okay," she said, walking toward me before she broke down again.

"BREE!"

"Sorry," she said, trying to keep a straight face.

"God, I hate you right now," I said, my chin wobbling.

"Don't freak, we've got this."

Twenty minutes later, the doorbell sounded while Bree and I studied my reflection.

"This is insane. Just tell him I had a wardrobe malfunction and I'll meet him there."

"You look good," Bree said, smiling, but I could tell she was still on the verge of losing it.

I narrowed my eyes. "I've got an eerily realistic looking witch face and my tits are hanging out!"

"But you have amazing tits," she said. "You're fine. Own it."

"I don't even want to *borrow* it. This is too weird. Just please get the door and tell him I'll meet him there."

"No way," she said. "You look fine." She fastened the cape around my neck and fluffed up the collar. "See?"

I tilted my head, my nose in my peripheral. A surprising amount of hope surfaced. "Just get the door."

"Proud of you, hoochie."

"Go," I snapped, downing the rest of my wine. Taking a deep breath, I walked into my living room where Cameron and Bree chatted about her job.

"I'm scanning candy all night. Though I don't see the point. Most parents toss their kid's candy these days and replace it with stuff they buy from the store." Her eyes connected with mine. "There's our witchy slut."

His eyes bulged when he caught sight of me.

"Screw it, I'm not going," I said, turning on my heel.

"Hey, beautiful, where are you going?" Cameron's light

laughter echoed behind me as he caught up with me. "No, you don't," he said, turning me to face him. His eyes roamed over my costume. "You look perfect."

"You sure?" I asked as Cameron stared at my monstrous nose. "I can go shower now, but the nose won't come off."

"Leave it, I'm impressed," he said, scanning me. "You did this?"

"Right?" Bree spoke up behind me. "She nailed it. She looks awesome, sexy even," Bree said before she bit her lips. I mouthed an "I hate you" as she covered her mouth with her hand. "Well, I'm outta here. Candy to scan," she said. "One four three," she shouted toward me before she shut the door.

"One four three, asshole!" I shouted back and heard her laugh on the other side.

"One four three. That's I love you," Cameron said behind me as I grabbed my purse.

"Yeah, it's our thing." I sighed. I was humiliated and hated that the night was starting out on that foot. Even behind my mask, Cameron noticed.

"Hey, hey," Cameron said, forcing my eyes to his. "Why are you upset?"

"Because I look like a witch," I answered, making zero sense.

"You look like a witch on Halloween going to a *Halloween* party," he said, his perfect brows pressing together. "What's the problem?"

"It's not sexy," I whispered, widening my eyes as I pulled my cape tighter around me.

"Okay, so you won't be one of the thousands of women wearing a thong and fairy wings. Trust me, I'm good with that."

"Really?"

He leaned in, attempting to kiss me, and had to tilt his

head painfully to reach my lips. "Yeah, really, but I already hate this fucking nose." He gave me as much of a kiss as he could before he pulled away and smiled.

"You look so handsome," I said. Cameron was dressed in a black turtleneck, blazer, and slacks. "What are you?"

"Ted Bundy," he answered with a wink.

"You have got to be kidding me!"

"I am. I'm a warlock," he said with a chuckle as I rolled my eyes.

"Not funny."

"It's a little bit funny. And I thought serial killers were your heroes."

I cringed at that. "They aren't."

"Then it's a good thing I dressed as a warlock. I knew you would play witch tonight," he said, ushering me down the stairs. "We should catch a cab. It's too cold to walk."

"Okay," I said, taking him in, my little meltdown getting in the way of a more thorough appreciation when he'd arrived.

"Hey," he said, catching my lingering gaze and giving me a knowing wink.

"Hey," I said back.

My cape shifted a little, and his eyes did a slow perusal of my dress. "Definitely fucking gorgeous, 'sexy even.'"

"You're just saying that to make me feel better. I totally geeked out with my costume."

"You did, but I don't mind talking to these beautiful tits all night."

I slugged him with my purse as he pulled me to him with a curt laugh. "God, you're something."

"Something?"

"Yeah," he said, biting his lip. He leaned in and flipped up the edge of my nose to kiss me.

I flinched. "Ouch."

"Oh, man, this is really on there."

"Yeah," I agreed, deflated.

"I'll work around it," he promised before he gently took my lips.

"Mmm," I whispered as he pulled away.

His eyes glittered over me as he shook his head and gave me the smile I met him with.

"What?"

"You."

Hands clasped, my warlock led me into a black-lit pub and navigated us through a sea of brilliant white teeth. We were halfway to the bar when we heard Cameron's name shouted.

I watched as the man sauntered up wearing a chemical lab suit and a shit-eating grin.

"Who the hell are you supposed to be?" Cameron asked as they clasped hands.

"Who do you think I am, *bitch*?" he replied with a panty-dropping smirk.

"Ah," I said, giving him a nod as he held out his hand for me. "He's Jessie from *Breaking Bad*."

The man took my offered hand and kissed the back of it. "She's far wiser than you," he said to Cameron before smiling at me. "I'm Max."

Max was handsome in his own right, a little shorter than Cameron, but was just as massively built. Where Cameron was dark, Max was a bit lighter in hair and eye color. His were a beautiful light brown.

"Max, nice to finally meet you. I've heard a lot about you."

"Likewise, Abbie, love your costume. You went all out, didn't you?" Cameron nudged his side, and Max looked over at him with a "What?"

"It's fine," I whisper-yelled to Cameron over the high-octane house music. "Thank you, Max."

"Want some punch? It's killer. Or maybe some meth?" He pulled two bags of blue candy from his pockets.

"Nice," Cameron said, shaking his head with a grin. "And this man works for the government."

"CIA," Max said.

"Liar," Cameron said with an eye roll.

"Can't ever let me look good, can you, asshole?" Max groaned in jest.

"First of all, anyone who works for the CIA wouldn't openly admit it," Cameron said. "And there's really nothing intelligent about you. I should know, I lived with you for six years. The smartest thing you ever did was light that cesspool you called a bed on fire."

"That was an accident," Max retorted.

"I rest my case," Cameron said with a laugh.

They sparred like Bree and I did, and I felt comforted that Cameron had his own version of her.

Cameron leaned in and exchanged hushed words with him. Though I felt like I was intruding, he refused to let go of my hand. Max nodded and eyed me before he clapped Cameron on the shoulder. "Relax, man, it's a party. I'll get you two a drink. What are *you* supposed to be anyway?"

"A warlock," Cameron said as if it were obvious—which it was anything but.

"You look like Professor Hinkle," Max said as Cameron flipped him the bird.

"We both had Hinkle our first year at UChicago," Max explained. "Hinkle had a rare form of narcolepsy. Rumor had it, whenever he laughed too hard, he knocked out. I spent my whole first year trying to make it happen."

"You're such an asshole. That's probably why he failed you," Cameron mused.

"He didn't fail me. I got a better grade than you."

"Calm down, I believe you."

"You should, you were drunk that whole first year," Max said.

Cameron looked my way with an explanation. "I was homesick. I was coping."

"Yeah, coping. You coped all right," Max said, chuckling. "Living in a sea of shredded co-ed thongs."

With that, Cameron's grin was wiped from his face, yet my smile emerged.

"Really?" I arched a brow as Cameron glared at Max, who cleared his throat.

"Yep, this guy was a momma's boy through and through. I thought he was going to cry when she left him at the dorm our first day." He put his hand on Cameron's shoulder. "But I loved that woman. Emma was one of a kind."

Unspoken words passed between them, and I knew then Max was my new favorite person. Anyone could read between the lines that underneath the jokes and playful ridicule lay respect and genuine affection.

"I thought you were going to get us drinks," Cameron said.

"I'm on it." Max wandered off through the crowd while Cameron managed to grab us an empty two-seater booth at the corner of the dance floor. He sat down and tugged me into his lap.

"So," he said, tracing the hem of my neckline with his

finger before flicking his eyes to mine. Do you have a curfew tonight?"

"Nope." Leaning in, I took a whiff of his cologne, which was incredible, a mix of all things man.

"Good to know," he said as he circled my wrist with his fingers. A low pulse began to beat as I leaned into him. His eyes zeroed in on my cleavage. "This dress is cruel," he murmured. "Would it be totally inappropriate if I motorboated you?"

"Yes," I said, running my hands through the hair at the back of his neck. "I like Max," I said, nodding my head toward him just as he looked our way and grinned. "What does he do for the government?"

"He's a contractor, like you."

"He's probably having more fun than I am at the moment. I can't wait to start my new job. The one I have now is becoming a pain in the ass, and I have a love/hate relationship with the staff I'm working with."

"It's a good thing you're moving on then."

"My eyes are up here, Coach."

Cameron leaned in, attempting to make good on his motorboat threat, and I pushed his face away.

"What is it about boobs?"

"Do you want an intelligent Freud type of answer or the truth as I know it?"

"Is there an intelligent response, Professor Hinkle?"

He gave me a side eye. "I knew it was trouble putting you two together."

I glanced at Max. "I told you I'd get the dirt. Player, huh?"

Cameron winced.

"I plead the fifth," he said, looking up at me through thick black lashes. "Those are the rules."

I wrinkled my four-inch nose, and he pulled me closer. "Is

it bothering you?"

"No. Of course not. I always assumed it, honestly."

He frowned. "And why is that?"

"The way you look. And a man doesn't get as confident as you are by not having a collection of sexcapades."

He flashed me his pearly whites. "Sexcapades?"

"Were you the frat guy?"

"Maybe," he said as he turned us around and leaned in. "Abbie, it was a long time ago."

"I know. I'm cool with it. Just curious."

He tried to read me for jealousy that wasn't there, but I told him anyway.

"I'm not really the jealous type. I had a moment or two when I was younger, but I grew out of it. I think once you reach a certain age, you realize how pointless it is."

"Well, if it helps my case, I stopped thinking with my dick a long, long time ago."

"I'm sure. But I'm guessing when you were a player, you were still a gentleman."

"I was," he said with the twitch of his lips.

"Let me guess, you mopped up their tears with their ripped thongs after the 'it's not you, it's me' speech before you made them breakfast."

"I make good waffles," he assured with a wry grin.

"I love waffles," I said with a sigh.

It was clear we were both in the mood for waffles.

I stared down at him as he tugged off my pointy hat and ran his hands through my hair. His attentive fingers slid through my strands as he simultaneously rubbed my back.

"You're really good at that."

"At what?"

"Making me feel good."

"Abbie, you are not a thong girl."

"I know, and I'm proud of that fact. But I can't say I haven't been there. You know, chances are you were just a phase to them too."

Surprise covered his features. "You're taking up for them?"

"Absolutely. Maybe they used *you* for a night. We aren't all shrinking violets. I'm willing to bet when most of them pulled on that thong, they weren't thinking about their Sunday school lessons. They knew exactly what they were doing. It brought you to your knees, didn't it?"

He pulled me tighter to him. "Yeah, it did."

Max returned with two pints of punch and set one down in front of me. "Thank you," I said as I turned to Cameron, who took a sip of his and shook his head before he took the glass out of my hand. "Uh, don't touch that fucking glass. What is in this, Max?"

"It's called the Kitchen Sink," Max yelled. "Fuck if I know. After the first glass, it goes down like water."

"You don't say." Cameron looked at me pointedly. "Don't drink that."

"Loosen the reins, Coach. We aren't driving." I took the punch from his hand and swore I exhaled fire.

"Whoa," I said with wide eyes.

"Maybe just sip it?"

I nodded.

Max was oblivious as he scanned the crowd. "I asked Rachel to come. I'm going to look for her. She's supposed to be dressed as a little devil."

"She won't show. You've been trying to get her for a year," Cameron said.

"Oh, ye of little faith," Max said, leaning in to make sure I heard him. "Don't listen to him. She loves me."

"I have no doubt," I said honestly.

Cameron and Max had the watchful eye and attention of every long legged, big breasted woman in the bar. I caught a couple of them staring and smiled when I noticed a few of them had on thong leotards and wings. I squeezed Cameron a little tighter to me, and though he didn't know why, he returned the affection and squeezed back. Jealous type or not, he didn't want *that,* and I fell a little more for him because of it.

Max leaned in with a menacing expression. "I should warn you now, when this man drinks, he tends to love *everyone.*"

"Are you alluding to the time he almost kissed a man?" I asked.

Max's jaw dropped an inch. "He told you?" he yelled over to Cameron. "You told her?!"

"Yep," Cameron said as he looked at me with a mix of pride and amusement.

"Fuck, man, you threatened my life to keep a lid on that." Max turned to me. "Oh, he must like you."

"I'm not as wicked as I look." Cameron's fingers pressed into my hip.

"Cute," Max said. "I'm off. If you see a pint-sized devil with an amazing ass, lasso her over this way if you don't mind."

"Will do," Cameron and I both said in unison.

Max wandered off, and I questioned Cameron. "Why won't she show?"

"Max is her boss," he said. "She won't cross the line."

"He clearly isn't in it just for sex," I said, scanning the crowd for his little devil.

"How do you know?"

"If he's been waiting for a year, he's obviously in love with her," I said with a shrug.

"I think so too. It's a shitty situation. He can't exactly fire her so he can date her."

"That sucks. My brother can give him pointers. He's slept with his whole surgical team," I said dryly.

"And how's that working out for him?" Cameron asked, taking a sip of his punch.

"He's still breathing."

"Are you two close?"

"He's a good brother as far as brothers go. A little overprotective. I'm sure at one point he'll try to threaten you. We still fight like we did when we were kids, and he still embarrasses the hell out of me."

"In that case, I can't wait to meet him."

We shared a smile, and that was becoming routine for us.

"I'll spare you that for now, while I still like you."

I studied his face. "You've got a little green around your mouth."

I wiped it away as he stared up at me. "When I met you, your face was a little lighter shade than this."

"You noticed that?" Damned nightly facial mask. "Well, it was slob day."

"Slob day?"

"Yeah, no makeup, no dieting. Just roll out of bed and brush your teeth kind of day."

"Where do I sign up?"

"You could never be a slob, Cameron. You're too pretty."

"Yeah, but does this blazer make me look fat?"

"Har har," I said as he stood with me still in his hold.

"Dance with me, witchy woman," he said as he led me to the floor.

We barely fit in the small space. Cameron subtly moved his hips and I followed along.

After a few minutes of silence, he pulled me close and

whispered in my ear. "You might not be the jealous type, but I hate the fucking thought of anyone else touching you."

A few hours later, my body was buzzing along with the music. Despite Cameron's protest, I drank two pints of the Kitchen Sink and was feeling no pain. I kept my wits about me as the party cranked up, and so did the heat from the number of bodies in the pub. Cameron stayed glued to my side, ever attentive, making sure I was happy and comfortable. He even waited outside the bathroom for me like a true gentleman.

By the end of the night, Max and I were chummy, and Cameron and I were worked up for each other from hours of grinding our bodies on the dance floor. I wasn't much of a dancer, but I could fake my way through it. The man loved to dance. Not only that, he had rhythm—a hell of a lot of it. He wasn't a show-off, but he was good at it.

I caught a few more women eyeing him, which made my chest swell with pride, but he kept his eyes trained on my hideous nose. After working up a sweat, I was finally able to get the latex off and it sat at one of the empty pint glasses at our table.

The bar was sweltering when I exited the bathroom after thoroughly washing my face. My hair was slightly tangled, and I'd done my best to comb through it with my hands. I looked a wreck, but my date didn't seem to give a damn as he greeted me.

"There's my girl," he whispered, cupping my chin before he placed a kiss on my nose. "You ready to go?"

"Sure."

"Hungry?"

"Starving, actually."

"Let's go." Cameron led us through the bar as we searched for Max to say goodbye. He was in a deep conversation with a little devil and gave us a half wave.

"I guess we'll meet her some other time," Cameron said with a look over his shoulder.

"You think he's okay?" I asked, looking Rachel over before he pulled me out the door. She was beautiful, and from what I could tell, she appeared upset. Max looked like he was on the verge of tears.

"That didn't look good. I hope everything's okay."

"I'll check on him later." And I knew he would. Cameron was the type.

"Maybe we should go back." I stopped my feet, haunted by the amount of pain in Max's eyes when he had been all smiles moments earlier.

"You can't fix that. They have to work it out, Abbie."

"I know, it's just . . . he told me more about them when you were getting our drinks. She has a son, and Max loves him. I just wish we could help."

Cameron's eyes glittered over me.

"What?"

"I love the way you care about people. It's such a good thing. It's like your heart is too big for you."

"So, I'm not a witchy woman?"

"Of course you are," he said with a smirk. "You ripped my head off when I woke you up Saturday."

"It was early."

"It was noon, you big poser. When we first met, you were all dolled up early for our coffee dates," he said with a laugh as we walked outside to discover it was sleeting. The brisk air hit us, and we both sighed in welcome.

"Wait here, I'll get us a cab."

"Okay, good, because I'm melting, *melting!*" Cameron rolled his eyes and jogged to the street, successfully flagging down a taxi. Once he gave me the signal, I burst into a sprint to meet him there.

Cameron grinned as I met him at the door. "That was cute."

"What was cute?" I asked as I slid into the seat to make room for him.

"That little dance you just did."

I bit my lip as he shut the door, his hair covered in glistening water.

"Oh."

"Oh?" he said, confused. He spoke to the driver, "Hollywood Grill."

We took off like a shot away from the curb as I spoke under my breath. "I wasn't dancing."

"What?" Cameron asked. "What were you doing?"

Meh. Next subject.

"I love Hollywood Grill. They have good chicken fried steak, though Bree said it's shit, but that's like the state dinner of Georgia I think." I snorted at my own joke.

"Don't change the subject. What was that back there?"

I grimaced. Damn Kitchen Sink punch. "I was running."

"You were what?"

"I was running."

Despite my warning look, his laughter didn't stop until we got to the diner.

Hollywood Grill was a '50s style eatery and the best place to soak up a night of drinks in Wicker Park. When Bree and I moved to the neighborhood, we used to frequent the diner often after our late nights. It had been years since I'd been there. I missed my good-time girl and shot off a text to her telling her so as I sat with my good-time guy, who was still grinning at me.

"So that was running?"

"Would you drop it?" I scorned. "I think we've had enough fun tonight at my expense."

"We have, but there isn't a chance in hell I'm dropping it."

"I have a running affliction," I said, sipping my water.

"A . . . running affliction," he parroted, his expression showing he wasn't buying it.

"Yes, a running *affliction*," I reiterated, hiding behind my menu.

Cameron faced the wall in an attempt to hold in his laugh, and I kicked him under the table with my pointy shoe.

"Ouch," he said, giving me a wary glance.

"You deserved it."

"So, tell me, how long have people been calling an ambulance when that happens?"

"Cameron," I warned as he burst into another fit of laughter. "You're such an ass. I've been made fun of for the way I run my whole life."

"I'm sorry," he said, sobering. "Well, have no fear, beautiful. Running just so happens to be one of the things I'm good at."

"So you've told me," I said, pretending to scan my menu. "Some of us aren't that graceful."

"No one is when they start," he said sincerely.

"I'm a little bowlegged. It's always been hard for me," I

admitted, my face flaming.

A beat of silence. I didn't look at him.

"You know with running, there is a posture to it. We can retrain your body."

That piqued my interest, and I looked up from my menu. "Really?"

"Yes," he said, taking off his blazer. "If you want, I'll guide you through it. I'll coach you."

The little girl inside me who watched relay races from the sidelines and vied to get picked as someone's partner or just once for Red Rover perked up.

"I don't know. I'm pretty lazy in the morning."

"I can change that too. You can run your first marathon by spring."

I looked at him skeptically. "I doubt that."

"Then let this be my promise to you. Okay?"

"Okay."

───

Both of my hands pinned above my head, Cameron dipped and sipped my neck before he captured my mouth, thrusting his tongue deep, kissing me within an inch of my life. His solid body rocked against mine as he coiled me tightly beneath him.

Everything inside me was screaming for relief as he ground his hips and pressed his erection to my stomach. "Abbie," he murmured, trailing his palm from the side of my face, down my chest, cupping my breast as he kept his eyes on mine. I could see my breath as it hit his full lips. It was coming out in fast spurts. His hand drifted further, and he paused, his eyes flitting to mine for permission that I gave with silence before he cupped my sex through my leggings.

Moaning out my welcome, he brushed his fingers along the fabric, and I tilted my head back.

"Are you wet for me?" he murmured to my throat as we got indecent on my porch. Reaching between us, I gripped his dick through his pants and heard a grunt while he worked his fingers against me, adding pressure. "Should I make you come right here on your porch so every time you're at your door you think of me?"

"Cameron," I prayed.

"That's not an answer," he admonished as he made quick work of dipping into my leggings and swiping a finger against the edge of my panties. I twisted my hips before he skimmed a lone finger over the silk covering my drenched middle. He worked it back and forth slowly, toying with me as I ground into him, desperate for friction.

"Jesus, you're soaked," he said as he rubbed the finger over the barrier then tucked it beneath. He cursed as he buried his nose in my hair and bit down on my shoulder before he thrust his fingers inside me and began to work them. Gasping at the feeling, I was already *there* as he began to pump them while I clutched his shoulders. "Someone will see," I managed to get out, jerking myself against him to chase my release as he pressed in deeper.

"I'm going to come," I announced as if he couldn't feel my body start to tremble.

"Let go," he ordered as he worked me over. I succumbed to the wave of heat that swept over me. He straightened, looking down at me as I convulsed with lips parted, wordless as ecstasy coursed through my veins. Looking at his face only heightened it—his eyes blazing while his jaw pulsed. The strain in his features looked like a mix of pleasure and pain while he watched me crack under his touch.

"Watching you come . . . it's better than anything I imagined," he whispered as he slowed his digits and softly kissed me before he straightened my dress. My craving for him was only mildly tempered by the orgasm he gifted me. I wanted more, and I wanted it then. I gripped his blazer and threw myself into a kiss, which he returned just as feverishly. He lifted me so he could slowly grind his rock-hard dick between my thighs. I was already on the verge again while his tongue teased mine.

"We should probably not have sex on my porch," I said as he worried my lip with his teeth.

I was too turned on to be embarrassed about our little indiscretion, and by the look on his face, he didn't give a damn, either. But my porch wasn't the place and the words "come in" refused to come out.

Reluctantly, he pulled away slowly, setting me to my feet before he gave me a tight smile.

"It's late," he whispered. "I should go." He leaned in and searched my eyes. Once he drew a conclusion, he backed away.

I was already mourning the loss of him, my body aching for more.

"Tonight was amazing," I said. "Thank you."

"I'll see you tomorrow?"

I nodded.

I was about to speak when he beat me to it.

"'Night, beautiful."

Abbie

At six a.m. the next morning, there was a pounding on my door. I opened it to find a drop-dead gorgeous coach smiling at me. I promptly slammed it in his face. I heard his laugh before I slowly opened it again. This time, he held two boxes.

"Okay, we've only been asleep five hours. Can training wait until tomorrow?"

"No time like the present."

"When I said yes, I didn't mean today," I said, making a quick excuse.

"So, you want to start tomorrow?" he asked.

"That would be awesome. I can get new running clothes and everything."

"I had a feeling that might be your excuse. I've got you covered."

I groaned. Of course he did.

"New Nikes, size seven. These will be good for your affliction," he said sweetly. I didn't take offense as I pulled out the shoes.

"These are awesome," I said, "and expensive. Cameron, you didn't have to do this."

"I wanted to. There's some clothes in the next box. I like pink on you."

It took everything I had not to mount him in my entryway.

"Wow," I said as I pulled out the hot pink pants and matching shirt. There were a few more outfits as well as a sports bra. I was speechless.

"When did you get this stuff?"

"Last night when I left you, I went and robbed my own store," he said. "Go try that on, and then we'll stretch."

"Okay," I said, booking it down the hall, a strange excitement seeping into me. After brushing my teeth, I tied my hair up and washed my face. Everything he got fit perfectly, and I loved the look of it.

I walked out to meet him in my entryway.

"Sexy," he said, biting his lip.

"Thank you," I said, leaning in to kiss him. "Is it weird I'm kind of excited?"

"Not at all. I'm happy you are, especially at this time of day. And you're going to love this, once you find your stride."

I wanted to confess to him then I'd been trying to find my stride my whole life, both literally and figuratively. I was still fighting the emotion from his gesture. He would never know how much it meant to me. "Okay, let's do this."

Cameron led me through a list of stretches. He told me because of my gait, we had to do a few extra to make sure my inner thighs were taken care of. Apparently, he'd been studying up. I did as well and had watched a few videos on the art of running before I'd passed out. I'd laid in bed, dreaming about being one of those women that I envied who could run gracefully, confident. I wanted it more than I had led him to believe.

"We'll aim for a mile today," Cameron said as we hit the sidewalk. "But we'll start slow."

"A mile." I nodded. One didn't seem so bad. Mentally rehearsing everything I'd learned, I psyched myself up as Cameron gave me a few more pointers.

"Remember to breathe. Don't hold it. Steady in and out."

"Got it."

"Keep your own pace, not mine. If you get tired, try to press through with your breathing, and if it starts to hurt, stop."

"Okay."

"Let's go." We set off as I tried to push off on the pads of my feet, arms close, hands loosely fisted, and breaths even. Cameron had a long stride and looked graceful in his jogging suit.

I mimicked what I could. But less than five minutes later, everything I learned went straight to hell. I was panting and close to seeing black. Cameron looked back at me as I lagged, and my arms went full T-Rex. He stopped in his tracks, seeing me struggle, and chuckled.

Something about it set me off. My cheeks flamed, a burning knot formed in my throat. Maybe it was the years of criticism I'd endured or the fact that I'd told him about it last night, but it hurt to watch him laugh at me. My heart plummeted as his dimples appeared.

"Hey, I'm just going to go back to my house."

His smile was replaced with confusion.

"What?"

"Yeah, thanks."

"Abbie—"

"Text me later or something," I called over my shoulder as I headed in the direction of my house. Seconds later, I was caught by the waist and set on my feet as Cameron smiled down at me, but it disappeared when he read my face.

Hands on my hips, I glared up at him.

"This is what you call helping me? You laughing?"

Cameron surveyed my face. "You're really pissed?"

"Just forget it." I moved past him, and he stopped me.

"Abbie—"

"It's fine, okay," I snapped. "You know, whatever, I'm used to it."

I walked off, determined to make it back to my house without shedding a tear, when I heard him bark behind me.

"Hey, lady!"

Something in his tone made me stop in my tracks and turn back his way. Long strides had him in front of me in seconds, and he looked . . . pissed. He loomed over me as I crossed my arms.

"Abbie, for the past two months that I've conversed with you, I'd like to think I've learned a lot, and one of the things I've learned is that you can dish it out just as good as you can take it. So, what's going on?"

"You've seen too much."

"I assure you I haven't."

"It's like I'm a joke to you."

"I assure you, you're not."

"So, when you were laughing at me just then, it meant nothing, right? And what's with the six a.m. wake up call to exploit my weakness?"

"Exploit your weakness? Abbie, you can't be serious," he said, his brows pressing together.

"Like I said, I'm used to it. Everyone I love or am close to makes fun of me."

His eyes lit fire and his jaw ticked as he studied me.

"Just forget it. I'll text you later." I moved to walk around him and was caught by the wrist.

"Wait a damn minute. If I was laughing it was because I find some of your antics hysterical, which they *are*. You are funny most of the time, and sometimes you aren't, which is, oddly, still funny. I was at your house at six a.m. because I couldn't sleep. And I couldn't sleep because I couldn't stop thinking about being next to you again and I needed any excuse to see you. I respect the boundaries you're so insistent on keeping because I *do* care about you.

"As for running, I saw the way you lit up last night when I talked about it. So, instead of rubbing myself raw with thoughts of you and the need to touch you, I thought I would kill two birds and exercise them out with you by my side. I'm having a horrible time controlling myself at this point because you're the sexiest goddamn woman I've ever met. And in case it's not clear by now when it comes to weakness, you're becoming mine. So, if yelling at me on the street is making you feel better, I'm all for it, but I'd rather be doing much, much more, and by the look on your face, so would you."

I stood stunned. He closed in as my heart went hummingbird.

"I'm not out to get you, Abbie. I'm falling in love with you."

The sun chose that moment to creep over the horizon, hitting us both. I threw myself at him, climbing him like a tree until our mouths touched. Cameron guided me with his hands, cradling my ass before he moved in, touching my lips softly with his as I sank into him, my legs shaking. He slid his desire-filled tongue along the seam of my mouth, and I opened for him. I gasped as he pressed in, and he kissed me breathless. I felt my knees beginning to give out as he pulled away. "I'm so sorry, baby—"

"No, I'm sorry—"

"I swear to God, I would never intentionally hurt you—"

"I was just embarrassed—"

"You don't have to be, Abbie, never with me—"

"You were just trying to be good to me, and you are so good to me, Cameron," I murmured as I took in his features and clasped my hands around his neck, sliding my thumbs through the hair at the nape of it.

Our mouths fused again, all doubts erased. His need matched my own. Chest to chest, our racing hearts met and molded. Give and take, we were relentless in our craving for the other. All that I felt I expressed with my kiss, and his was far too much to handle. We only pulled away when we heard a car approaching but kept our foreheads together.

"This is so much better than—"

"I can't believe this," I said at the same time as we pulled away.

He leaned in again, and that next kiss stopped time, rebuked our pasts, led us crashing forward, and lasted a heart rendering eternity. The world was a blur as we stayed content in our cloud. He was all I saw, all I felt, and it was incredible.

I was flying high as he pulled his lips away but kept us close.

"I need this. I needed this so much," he declared before he shut his eyes tight. When they opened, they were full of emotion. "Tell me I can have this, tell me I can be this happy. Tell me I can have you."

"Yes," I whispered. "I'm nervous," I said honestly.

"I'm not. I want this, Abbie."

Normally those words would scare me, and in the past, have scared me, but his words were right. They weren't selfish. He was giving and taking. A gift. And I realized I never wanted anything so much in my life. I was gone, no longer just me but hopefully a part of a we.

And I would never be the same woman without him.

I realized I had everything to lose as I pulled him tighter to me.

"This is the best I've ever felt. Take me home, Cameron."

He pulled away and shook his head. "No, Abbie, that's not what . . . I shouldn't have said that, and I won't push you."

"I needed it, Cameron, don't you see? I needed you."

Brushing a wistful tear from my cheek with his thumb, he dipped in again, and again, sliding his warm hands around my waist beneath my sweatshirt and pulling me impossibly closer.

With that kiss, we sealed ourselves together, our fate, in Wicker Park.

"Take me home."

"Okay," he said before he placed a reverent kiss on my forehead.

I tugged at his hand leading the way and he followed, his brilliant smile magnified by the rising sun behind him. At a loss for words, we just stared at each other with matching intensity as we walked toward my three-flat.

We took longer strides as we neared home, and then we went into a full-on sprint once inside the gate. On my porch, he nailed me to my front door and kissed me within an inch of my life. Backing up, he placed his hands on either side of my head as he looked down at me, his lust-filled eyes full of warning.

"I can leave now, Abbie. But I won't be able to if I make it through that door."

He leaned in as he sucked my bottom lip into his mouth before he pressed his erection into my stomach.

"Stay," I moaned as he trailed his kiss down my neck and then pulled away to nail me with his stare. I reached down and cupped his cock, sliding my fingers along the hard outline. My whole body tensed as I gauged the size of him.

Hallelujah.

My mouth watered with the need to feed off him. I was starving, and he was the only one I was hungry for. The star of every daydream I'd had since our eyes connected in that café. It was happening. I didn't care we had so much left to discover, that he didn't know all my truths, and I didn't know much at all about his personal past. None of it could touch us. We'd spiraled from nothing into everything within a few months. It wasn't just attraction. It was far more, both unspoken and admitted. And just as sure as I was standing on that porch, I wanted him to know.

"I want this. I want you."

Once inside, he pushed me flat to the back of the door and slipped my Nikes off before slowly taking off my pants. He knelt and trailed his fingers inside my thighs.

"If we do this, it's only you and me. I want to make that clear." I clutched his head as he slid my panties down before pushing a finger through my sex while he looked up at me. "This is mine from this minute on."

"Yesss," I hissed as he rubbed a finger through my folds.

Grinding against his hand, I pumped my hips eagerly. He hooked my leg over his shoulder, his breath hitting my clit.

"I don't know how slow I can take this," he whispered before darting out his tongue and licking me smoothly from bottom to top. My moan echoed in my entryway as he spread me wide and devoured me. My legs buckled as his fiery green gaze met mine. He groaned as he swirled his tongue. Bucking into his mouth, I held onto him for support as he tore into me.

He might have been the one on his knees, but I was the one at his mercy.

Cameron's grip was the only thing keeping me standing as he darted his wicked tongue over my clit only to come back for seconds with slow, leisurely licks. Gasping as the orgasm hit, I gripped his hair, riding it out until I went completely lax against the door. He stood, peeling off his shirt until it hit the floor. He paused his fingers as he drank me in, naked and needy for him.

"Fuck, I'll never forget the way you look right now," he whispered.

I felt beautiful and worshiped, the new normal that only he could make me feel.

"I don't want anyone else."

"I'll keep it that way," he assured as he tore off his undershirt. Wide, defined shoulders led to an even more demarcated chest, and no part of him was undefined down to a trim torso. His pants clung to him, a nuisance accentuating the beautiful V I knew he worked hard for. The man took care of himself, and it showed on every inch of defined skin. Coarse dark hair trailed down past the waistband of his briefs, and I wet my lips in anticipation. Sexy, full lips twisted before he thumbed off his pants and briefs, just enough so they drifted to the floor. He stepped out, magnificently naked, and we stood in lust and appreciation. He watched me as I reached out with confident hands and spread them over his chest before bringing my eyes to his.

"Tell me what you're thinking," he said, moving both hands to my back, capturing my hair against my skin and massaging up and down.

"I'd rather show you." I grabbed his hand and pulled him down the hallway to my bedroom. We stopped at the foot of my bed. The scent of the fresh white roses he'd sent me lingered in the air as I placed tongue-filled kisses along the crest of his chest. His beautiful cock bounced between us, and I gripped it firm in my hand. I stroked him, sliding my finger across the silky head of his crown. With greedy hands, he explored my naked flesh, caressing my belly, my sides, cupping my breasts, and rubbing his thumb over my nipples. My center pulsed as his eyes roamed, taking in every detail. A hint of a smile twitched his lips before he cupped my face.

"Nice place."

He hadn't, not once, taken his eyes off me. I let out a nervous laugh as we kissed again. He pulled away, but I stayed surrounded by his warmth.

"Don't be nervous," he whispered. "You give me a new

reason to want you every single day."

"Cameron, I don't need this to be perfect. I don't. I just need you," I whispered.

He took control then as he lifted me to wrap around him. My head fell back at the feel of his thickness against my center. Once on my bed, he leaned over me, his words hitting soft blows to my core. "You and I don't deal in absolutes and perfection, remember? We're too smart for that."

"Okay," I agreed as I kissed his jaw.

"Nothing more than what we are," he whispered as he tugged my lobe into his mouth.

"And no more waiting."

"No more waiting," he repeated.

"I mean now. Right now," I moaned as he spread me out on my bed. His soft chuckle only amplified my agitation. I wanted him too much. He looked down at me with so much longing, I felt my eyes water.

"I would watch you every day of forever for the chance to touch you like this." He flicked his tongue over my lips as his fingers spread me and he slipped them inside. My back bowed off the bed.

"Jesus," he rasped out as his eyes raked down my body and he watched his fingers sink into me. "But if we ever decide to look for perfect, I would say this is as close as it gets."

He pushed in again, sliding his fingers in and out, and invading the deepest part of me, stretching me. He pumped in again and again before his head dipped and he curled his arms around my thighs.

Anxious for him, I looked down, and he anchored me in his hold. Unwilling to release me from his stare, he bent and watched me react to the swipe of his tongue. I seized at his touch, my body firing and igniting. He drank me in with slow, precise swipes while I drew his thick hair in my fingers and twisted beneath him. I yanked at the silky strands while he groaned, his arousal peaking with the urgency. He gripped my thighs, lifting my body to match the movements of his tongue. Lick. Suck. Lick. Suck. And then it went blurry as white-hot heat struck me and my whole body tensed.

"Cameron," I cried out hoarsely with an arousal-soaked voice.

Twisting his fingers inside, his tongue flicked along the ball of nerves, and I detonated again. He lifted to his knees, watching my body shake with my release. Our stare impenetrable, I gave him my every reaction, unabashed and completely vulnerable.

His length jerked at my response to his touch as he slowed his fingers and came up to take my mouth. I knew he was satisfied, his kiss told me so. I'd never been more ready.

Wordlessly, he hovered above me then leaned down to touch his mouth to mine. A slow kiss, and then another, and then another had me dizzy.

Enveloped completely by his warmth, he positioned himself at my entrance, and I locked my legs around his waist in invitation.

"No more waiting," I whispered as he brushed the hair away from my face with gentle hands. Eyes connected, he pushed inside me slowly, inch by steel pulsing inch, and stretched me full. My mouth opened in a silent O as his beautiful jaw went slack at the feeling of our connection.

The only sound was our mingled breaths when need took over and he moved back and pressed in *hard*.

I whimpered.

"Fuck, Abbie, Jesus Christ."

And then we were gone, our bodies took over as he filled

me to the brink. Chests glistening, our hands clasped over my head, he rocked into me so I felt every inch before he swiveled his hips and did it again. He hit me deep with every stroke, making sure to touch every place I needed.

My body his slave, I came apart as his name pushed out past my lips. It was his name that wrote itself across my heart; it was his eyes that spoke to my soul. It was Cameron.

I lost myself, trusting him with every minute. His sex was my undoing. His flesh burned as he pushed himself into the deepest part of me.

"Abbie," he grunted out, his voice needful as I nodded more permission he didn't need. He let go of my hands and pulled us to sit so that I straddled his lap. On instinct, I began to rock against him as he thrust up, one of his arms wrapped around me like a lifeline, and the other fisted in my hair, tightening so he controlled my gaze.

Lust-filled eyes connected, I bared my teeth as he struck deep and jerked me down. Biting his lip, I felt the onslaught as I watched his features twist with his release, eyes full of heat and ecstasy.

He thrust up again as he came, and I fell over the edge while he spilled into me. We were drunk on need, shrouded in pleasure, exhausted by the feeling of each other as I collapsed in his hold, chest heaving.

The last of the sunlight filtered through my room when Cameron moved us to lay down as our breathing evened out. In my silent bedroom, only our hearts sounded as he kept me pinned to him. Wrapping my thigh around his waist, I basked in his hold, a smile against his skin.

Minutes later, the fog clearing, I ran my fingers over the divots of his chest.

"Wow," I murmured bracing myself over him with

appreciation. His body was rock solid, not a single flaw, and I was sure if there were any, I wouldn't see them.

Wordlessly, he looked up at me as if he couldn't believe what he was seeing. All I saw was need, want, lust, and I prayed I didn't mistake what looked like love. Because in my greed, I wanted that too.

Please let this be love.

Goosebumps erupted on my skin as he lazily stroked my back with the pads of his fingers. I leaned in and kissed him, my mind reeling as our breaths synced.

We didn't need any more words. We'd said enough. Content, we laid surrounded by the sunrise, neither of us moving as he put me in a sleepy lull with his touch, his warmth pulling me as close as I could get.

Many hours later, but only seconds after we broke apart, Cameron's fingers traced the lines of my body while I glanced out the window at the snowfall. In a comfortable silence, I ran my fingers through his soaked hair while he kept his affection on my skin. It was a new kind of heaven.

"Abbie?" I heard shouted from my front door and shot out of bed. The only two people that had a key to my place were Bree and . . .

"Mrs. Zingaro!" I squeaked as Cameron shot out of bed too. We searched the carpet in vain. Our clothes were still in the entryway.

"Oh, good, honey. I was worried. I know you told me to use this key only for emergencies, but I heard some very loud noises. Oh, oh, dear. I see you aren't alone. Yes, these are men's clothes. I'm sorry."

The door shut with a thud as Cameron and I stood naked on opposite sides of the bed. My chin trembled before we both burst out laughing. But it was cut short when I thought of Mrs. Zingaro.

"Shit, shit. I always worry when it snows and she takes the stairs." I ran to my closet and threw on a sweater dress.

"I've got it," Cameron called from outside the closet.

"She'll beat you to death before you get near her. Trust me."

"I think I can take her."

"You sure?" I asked, peeking over at him, pausing to take him in, naked and in my bedroom.

Hallelujah.

"Like what you see?"

"Meh," I said as he charged me.

"What's that?"

I grabbed the growing muscle between his thighs. "I said meh."

"But you didn't mean it." He bit my lip and my eyes bulged at the pain.

"Ow."

"I'll go make sure she got in okay."

"Okay."

Fifteen minutes later, I was dressed and walking outside. I heard Cameron's deep baritone on the other side of Mrs. Zingaro's door. Poor baby. He'd been roped in.

I knocked and, seconds later, the door was opened by a grinning Cameron. "Heeey," I said with false enthusiasm, my eyes wide. "You need saving?" I whispered conspiratorially.

"Not at all," he said, opening the door. Jenny was in her kitchen cooking.

"She's making dinner for us."

"Great," I said, showing him all my teeth.

He chuckled and kissed my forehead. "It's fine."

I looked up at him. "Are you sure?"

"Yeah, I'm sure. I just want to hang out with you. This is what you two Golden Girls do, right?"

"Very funny," I said, nudging him in the gut with my elbow before I walked in.

Jenny's place was completely renovated and modern, save the décor. I couldn't help but laugh inwardly at the way she'd taken a completely post-century pad and rewound time. Her furniture was old, and she had a plant on every available surface.

I shook off the cold and walked toward her with Cameron on my heels. In her quilted robe and slippers, Mrs. Zingaro was holding a spatula over a boiling stovetop and appeared to be stuck in one of her crippled, dead states.

I nudged Cameron. "Why don't you go ask her if she needs any help."

Cameron obliged and walked into the kitchen casually. When he approached her and spoke, she startled and slapped him in the chest with a spoonful of tomato sauce.

I howled as he looked over at me and narrowed his eyes while Jenny apologized profusely. Cameron told her not to fuss as she reached under her kitchen cabinet and took out a bottle of 409, instead of the clearly marked stain remover, and began to spray his chest with it.

Cameron looked over at me, helpless.

"Yep, this is how we do it."

"This is delicious," Cameron said as he piled more spaghetti onto his plate.

"I loved to cook for my Roberto."

"Italian?" Cameron asked.

"Yes. I was raised here, but Roberto was raised in Italy. I learned to speak Italian for our son, Michael. Roberto was a true Italian man, loved the language and the culture. Kept many of his ways even when he moved to America. He never wanted anything but the same staples for dinner. His mother taught me all of his favorite recipes before she passed," she said, pausing to do the Holy Trinity. "I have to admit, I used to sneak in hot dogs and French fries during our marriage."

Reluctantly, Cameron posed the question. "When did Roberto pass?"

Jenny sighed, the light blue in her eyes dimming a little. "Twelve years ago. We spent sixty together. Can you believe it? I can't."

Cameron's eyes softened as he looked over at her. Her hair was thin and tied up in a knot on top of her head. She looked a little paler when she spoke of her deceased husband.

"He was on security detail the day Kennedy got shot," I told Cameron. "He was one of the men walking alongside the car."

"Really?" Cameron said. "Wow."

"Yeah, not so wow," Jenny said. "It ruined his life for a number of years. He ducked out after that and moved us from DC to Chicago. His next profession was a lot less desirable," she mumbled.

"What was it?"

"Laundry," I said with a wink toward Cameron, who was wearing a knit sweater two sizes too small that read "Ho Ho Ho".

I sat, picking at my food, thinking about the taste of his skin and the feel of him inside me. He seemed to be thinking along the same lines as he winked at me before he took a bite of his pasta.

"I have some videos of my Roberto," Jenny offered. "Maybe we can watch one after dinner."

"Sounds perfect," Cameron said as he turned my way. "Okay?"

I shrugged contentedly as I cut into my pasta, hungry, tired, sated, and happier than I could ever remember being.

Half an hour later, we were sitting on the couch when Bree texted.

Bree: What the hell is going on? You didn't call me when you got in last night. Are you still mad at me?

Me: Nope.

Bree: Okay, are you working?

Me: Nope.

Bree: Okay, fuck, I give up. What?

Me: ;)

Bree: Judas Priest! Oh, girl. I'm so happy. Holy shit! So, how was it? Is he any good? Please don't tell me that man can't work his penis.

My phone was plucked from my fingers and Cameron began typing away, and I sat mortified. Poor Jenny was explaining a video neither of us was watching—but in my defense, I'd seen it a dozen times—as I sat waiting for certain death.

Cameron handed my phone back and sank into the couch with his arm around me. Horrified, I looked down to see what he'd typed.

Me: I just had seven orgasms. I'll call you tomorrow.

"Seven?" I whispered in shock. I knew the count was high but had no idea how many.

"C-A-M-E-R-O-N," he leaned in and whispered, his eyes still on the video before they flicked to mine and he smirked. My cheeks heated as he pulled me closer to him while Jenny rattled on.

We ended up watching three more videos until Jenny fell asleep in her recliner, her mouth wide open. Cameron and I washed the dishes then crept back upstairs.

He spelled his last name that night, in a way I would never forget it.

B-L-E-D-S-O-E.

16

Abbie

The following week, Cameron and I had only managed to meet for a run in the mornings and kept our days full of texts, but missed every opportunity to meet after due to my workload and his coaching schedule.

I was inching closer to finishing my job at Preston Corp, but last-minute meetings had made my days twice as long. Kat came back from Florida a little less on edge, or at least she'd appeared to be. We were getting along famously, but I was fraying on both ends.

I was desperate for a break and knew the schedule would only get more grueling if I was going to finish out my contract on time. The only consolation was that I had cleared my weekend in hopes to spend it with Cameron. I was at the coffee shop trying to finish up when I got his text.

King of Woo: Hey, beautiful. Where are you?

Me: At our place.

King of Woo: What's your Monday looking like?

I sighed and closed my Mac, pushing it into my tote. Great. He's tied up until Monday. The weekend wasn't shaping up to be shit, either.

Me: The worst day of the week.

King of Woo: Not this time. Hurry up and get outside. I'm picking you up today.

Following orders, I dropped my cup off at the counter and slid on my coat as I pushed out of the door with my tote in hand.

Outside the café, Cameron waited in a navy suit, and looked gorgeous standing in front of a blacked-out Audi SUV, his hands in his pockets and two cups of coffee on the hood. He was dressed to impress and had a wicked gleam in his eyes.

"What's this?"

"This is us coffee-ing the fuck out of town?" he said with a hopeful lift in his voice. "I would prefer you in a bikini in Mexico, but this is all I could swing last-minute with little imagination other than seeing you naked every possible minute. Get that beautiful ass over here."

I pranced over to him, swinging my hips a little as he gave me that come-hither finger. In seconds, I was wrapped in his warmth while he took my mouth in a possessive kiss.

When we parted, I did my best to control myself and my thundering heart. "Cameron, I want nothing more than to disappear with you, but I have to work Monday."

"Is your Mac in that bag?"

"Yes, but—"

"You can work remotely, right?"

"Yes, but—"

"Take it with you. We'll have a little fiesta around it."

Elated and opting to just go with it, I still had reservations but only named a few. "I have no clothes, no toothbrush, and where will we go?"

"Too many objections," he said, grabbing my tote and packing it in the idling SUV.

Dear God, he was a temptation. Especially when he towered over me with his sparkling green eyes.

"Don't say no."

"Okay."

"Is that a yes?"

"Well, I can't say no."

"I want you out of this city. Okay?"

"Okay."

Minutes later, we were on our way to said fiesta, navigating easily through Saturday traffic. He'd refused to stop at my three-flat to let me grab anything, which I gave him hell for. I texted Kat to tell her I would be taking Monday off. She must have been on her phone because she texted back right away.

Kat: No problem. I owe you. ☺ Have fun.

I hadn't talked to Kat about "coffee shop guy" since she'd returned. She'd been a bit more distant and our workload had only increased. Though I wanted to share my new-found happiness with her, she was going through enough as it was with her marriage.

Cameron had a lead foot as he steered us toward freedom from it all. I put in one last call to Michael, who assured me he'd be checking in on his mother.

The Audi was cozy, and I glanced at the man next to me as I pulled my gloves from my hands and found his over the console. He swiftly pulled my offered skin to his mouth and kissed it with soft lips and a little tongue. That act alone had my stomach fluttering in anticipation.

"Take me away anywhere," I said as I kicked off my Uggs and rested my feet on the dash. "Is this yours?"

"Yep," he said with a breaking smile as he glanced at my posture. "Just got it. Do you drive?"

"Nope, I run," I said with pride as I looked over at him. "I hit two miles without breaking this morning, but I missed my coach."

He squeezed my fingers and brought them to his lips for another kiss. "Proud of you. I missed you too. Are you comfortable?"

"Yeah," I said, feeling whatever weight I harbored lift from me easily as we exchanged smiles.

Cameron let go of my hand, and I felt his warm fingers on my back as he rode them up to my spine and had my bra unfastened in seconds.

"Holy shit," I said, stunned as the girls lay free and heavy on my chest.

"That's better," he said in a sexy whisper.

"Seriously, that's an awe-inspiring skill. And it's kind of scary you're so good at that."

"Basketball camp. We used to wrap them around balls and practice. Yep, it's a talent."

I quirked a brow. "Any others I should know about?"

"All in due time," he promised as he lifted the front of my sweater and brushed his fingers along my stomach. I mourned the loss of his hand when he pulled it away to grip the wheel.

Cameron tapped his fingers to Kings of Leon "The Face" as we slowed to a stop at a light.

"God, I love this song. I swear Caleb's voice is sex." I began to sing along as Cameron drove on. The L train rumbled overhead as I got swept up in the moment and began jamming in my seat. I turned the music up loud and nodded my head.

It was only when I heard Cameron's rumbling laughter over the music that I turned to look his way.

I paused the workings of my hands, that I realized were playing air guitar, as he drove on, openly laughing at me.

"What?"

He made quick work of pulling over. Once we were stopped—in a grocery store parking lot—I looked out the window in confusion. I was about to ask what he was doing when I was swept from the passenger seat and onto his lap.

I let out a squeak as he looked at me with a new smile. One I'd never seen.

"What in the world are you doing, Coach Bledsoe?"

"Me? *What am I doing*? Jesus, woman, you have got to be the sexiest thing I've ever seen." With no more explanation than that, he took my mouth so possessively that I had to push at his chest to get some air.

"That was some kiss," I said with a smile.

"That was some *show*. Tell me, witchy woman, do you always rock out that hard in the car?"

Embarrassed I must have really gotten into it, I looked at him through my lashes. "I went geek on you, didn't I?"

"Little bit, and it was fucking awesome." His voice was low as he pushed my sweater down over my shoulder and drew my nipple into his mouth. I tilted my head back on a moan.

"Cameron," I breathed as he sucked my nipple until I was pulsing with need. "Hey, we're kind of in a parking lot."

He ignored my protest and sucked harder. "Cameron, what if someone sees?"

"Hold on, baby." He reached behind my seat and pulled out a sun reflector to shield us from prying eyes. "They would have to look really," he said, pushing his hips up against my clit, "hard."

The music, the man, the anticipation. It was all so fucking perfect.

Seconds later, I was staring at Cameron's straining cock as he freed it. I could see his arousal dripping over the tip, his breath heavy as he fucked my mouth with his tongue. His kiss went deep as he gripped my neck with one hand and yanked my sweater tights down with the other.

Once free, I saw him react, his eyes turning into liquid pools at the silk panties that lay underneath. I could see their fate and beat him to it as I looked around and quickly slipped them down my legs.

His voice was sexy gravel. "God, I'd give anything to feast on you right now."

I gripped him firm in my hand and hovered before I slowly sank down onto him. We both exploded in movement.

"Fuck yes, just like that," he said as he bit his lip.

I was gone, driven by need, and dazed by his words as he gave me more—more of him, more of us, more of everything that mattered.

"You're so fucking hot. Ride my cock, baby."

"Yessss," I hissed as he invaded me with his eyes and conquered me with his body.

His eyes lit fire as he palmed my breasts and watched me pump and flex on top of him. I was full and frenzied as I raced toward my climax. We were a tangled mess of searching mouths and limbs before he thrust up and gripped my face while I balanced myself with one hand on the door and the other on the console. I rolled my hips and watched his eyes darken further.

"Fuck, fuck, Abbie, you feel so fucking incredible." He nipped at my skin, unable to control his hard grip. Needy for more, I rode him faster while he pistoned his hips, holding me so close, I had no choice but to take all of him.

Our fucking was carnal but remained intimate as he grunted and murmured words of praise and worship. I was muttering nonsense, his pace maddening but rhythmic. My center slid along the edge of his cock as he filled me and *over*filled me, his words spurring me on.

"Don't stop," I begged as I tilted my head back and bounced along his thighs, grinding myself as hard as I could, choking on the fullness of him. I spread myself wider on his lap and we both inhaled sharply as we hit another crescendo.

"Give it to me," he ordered as he looked down to where we connected. His eyes flared as he watched me fuck him. With one hard thrust up, I tipped over and washed away on his lap, riding it out as far as I could take it as he grunted and finished inside me.

"This is going to be a good weekend," I said breathlessly against the hollow of his neck before I slid my tongue along his cologne-scented skin and curled in his lap like a cat.

"Yeah, if we make it out of Chicago," he murmured with a kiss to my temple.

"We'll get there. We've got a good pace."

"Yeah, we do," he whispered, caressing the small of my back with his fingers.

We stayed in our high for as long as we could before I moved back to my seat and took his offered Kleenex. I slid my leggings up and he tucked himself back into his pants. We were a hot mess, both winded with matching smiles. Mine faded when I saw concern start to darken his features.

"We haven't used anything, Abbie. We haven't even talked about it. I don't know what I was thinking."

"I'm covered in the multiplication department," I assured. "And I got the all clear a year ago and haven't slept with anyone since."

"It's been a really long time for me. A *really* long time," he admitted while my jaw went slack.

"Really? For you?"

"Really," he whispered, cupping my chin and bringing his lips to mine. "I feel possessed," he said as he pulled on my lip. "And I've never had sex in a parking lot." He shook his head and bit my lip before he sucked it into his mouth. "Damn, baby, you make me crazy."

"Crazy enough to do it again?" I waggled my brows.

One side of his mouth lifted as his eyes told me he accepted my challenge. "I'll do anything with *you* twice. So, I guess it's going to be that kind of weekend?"

"You're not the only one who's starved. I think we can manage a postcard-perfect weekend, with a side of porn-worthy," I assured as I rubbed my nose against his.

"You'll hear no complaints from me," he murmured into my hair as he wrapped me in his hold and took my lips in a seductive kiss. I clutched him tight as he slowly explored before pulling away.

"What are you doing to me?" he whispered. "Strike that, I know what's happening here."

I let myself ask the question. I had to know. "Do you want it to happen?"

"More than anything. I hope you believe me."

"I'll believe you if that's what you want."

"Good. Because I want you."

"You have me."

"Then I'm falling in the right direction," he said, running his fingers through my hair. In the crowded parking lot, I felt like we were in our own world as he rubbed some of my locks through his fingertips. "Someone told me once to picture something I can't live without and then decide what trumps that, so I know the truth of what matters to me the most."

"What trumps me?" I asked as his crystal green eyes pierced me. He tilted his head back in thought as I puffed out an indignant chest. "You better not say a Bears game."

He twisted his rearview so I could see our reflection. We both looked winded and a little disheveled and . . . happy.

"The only thing that could trump you today, Abbie, is you *tomorrow*. And I don't want to be without you tomorrow."

Our fiesta ended up taking place in a private cabin in Rockford, about ninety minutes outside of the city. The problem was, we couldn't find it. And as the night started to creep in, we were worse for wear when the cell phone service went spotty in the middle of a blizzard.

"So, you haven't been here?" I asked as I looked out the windshield of the SUV. We were getting close to zero visibility, and the only thing keeping me calm was that Cameron was calm.

"No, but the GPS said we weren't far. Well," he said with a laugh, "when it was working."

"Shit," I said, twisting in my seat, trying to get some signal.

"Don't worry, we'll find it," Cameron assured as he gripped

my thigh and squeezed.

"It's getting scary, you know?"

"Is this where your serial killer paranoia comes in?"

"Yes," I said pointedly.

"Hang in there."

"I can't believe you decided to take me to the woods."

"Surprise?" he said with a laugh.

It was the first time I wanted to grab his junk as a disciplinary action.

Cameron slowed down when he spotted a driveway. "This is probably it."

"Thank God. I need a hot shower."

"Does that come with an invitation?" he asked, glancing at me as we followed the small driveway through the trees and hit a dead end with no cabin in sight.

"What in the hell?" He got out of the car while the windshield wipers roared. The snow was blinding at that point and I could barely make out his frame when I began to get twitchy. I was about to blow the horn when he opened the door and jumped in while I jumped out of my skin.

He gauged my reaction and shook his head.

"Okay, so this isn't it. In fact, it's nothing. A driveway. Nothing else."

"Let's go, Cameron," I said as calmly as possible.

"I'm getting you out of here, baby."

I melted at his term of endearment as he put the car in reverse, gassed it . . . and we didn't move.

"Shit," he muttered under his breath as I told myself not to panic.

He slowly eased on the gas again and the SUV jolted as if it were free and then, spun tires.

"You don't have snow tires?!" I asked in calm observation.

"Abbie, baby, don't yell. It's okay."

"I'm not yelling!" I yelled.

"You're panicking."

"I'm not panicking!" I panicked.

"We're okay, Abbie."

"I'm fine!"

I was close to hyperventilating. I had to trust Cameron. He was a manly man. He could definitely give the woods a run for its money.

"Why did you bring me here?"

Cameron sighed as he hit the gas again and lodged us where we sat. He slammed his palms against the steering wheel. "FUCK!"

"We're stuck?" I asked as he hung his head and slowly nodded.

"I've got some stuff in the back," he said, glancing over at me. "I'll get us out."

"Okay, can I help?"

I was already shaking as he leaned over.

"Abbie, don't freak out, okay? It's a test, and we're going to pass it. Matter of fact, I'll wager with you right here and now that within an hour, I'm going to cook you the best steak of your life and we're going to laugh about this in that hot shower you want so badly. We'll wear matching flannel pajamas—you top me bottom—while we watch movies and then wear no pajamas while I watch you come. That's how tonight is going to go, okay?"

I nodded.

"Trust me?"

"Yes," I said with a sigh. "Just hurry up and get me out of here."

"How do you like your steak?"

Before I could answer, he was out of the SUV and lifting the lid of the trunk. All I could hear was the howl of the storm and the metal clacking behind me.

I pitched my voice back at him in warning. "If you're thinking about making any jokes right now at my expense, like merely fucking around that you may be hurt or in trouble in any way, I'm warning you, I will make you cry and you will lose a testicle."

"That's my witchy woman." He chuckled as I heard the clatter of iron and a few grunts.

Manly grunts.

Because Cameron was all man. But it did little to ease my nerves as he circled the SUV.

A few minutes later, confidence high, Cameron got back into the SUV and put the truck into gear. I clasped my hands together in silent prayer as he hit the gas.

"Man, it's really coming down," Cameron said as I glared at the side of his head. We'd been in the truck for hours and the snow wasn't stopping. He'd avoided my eyes for the last hour as we sat in the pitch dark, stuck in the dead-end driveway in the middle of a snowstorm, *in the woods*.

My back plastered to my seat, I continually looked out the windows, checking and double checking the locks to make sure no one could open the door. I should've felt safe with Cameron, but even if he'd multiplied by ten and surrounded the vehicle with heavy artillery, I would have been on edge.

"Abbie—"

"Don't you even say it. Don't you even think about leaving

me here. It's not happening."

"Abbie, listen—"

"If we die, we die together."

Cameron chuckled. "I know you have to use the bathroom. I've gone twice."

"I'm fine."

"Abbie."

I turned to him with what I was sure were laser beams coming out of my retinas.

"Why? Why did you bring me to the woods?"

"I don't feel safe enough at the moment to answer that question."

"Why?"

"I don't know. I guess because I thought somehow I could get you to like it if we—"

"If we what?"

"If we made good memories here." He shrugged.

I bit my lips in an attempt to keep the smart mouthed reply idle on my tongue.

"I'm sorry," he said sincerely.

"It was a nice gesture," I ground out. "Misplaced, but nice."

"Are you mad?"

I turned to look at him and saw the disappointment in his features. I climbed onto his lap for the second time that day. He smiled as he palmed my ass.

"No. I mean, yes, it's my worst nightmare come to life. But, hey, fears are meant to be conquered, right? Please, do tell me what your worst fear is so I can return the favor and make it just as romantic for you someday." I bat my eyelashes and his body shook with his laugh.

"Point taken."

"I do have to pee."

"I know."

"Once we do this," I warned, "there's no going back. All the sweet etiquette of our new union will be erased. You will have seen me squat."

"I'll turn my back. But I can live with it."

"I don't think I can."

"Come on." He moved to open the door.

"WAIT!" I shrieked.

"Okay," he said, taking his hand off the handle.

"Just give me a mental moment. Tell me something. Anything."

"The Bears won."

"Something else."

"We're still sitting on three-quarters of a tank of gas."

"Wonderful."

"We won't freeze to death."

"That's reassuring in a terrifying way," I said, swallowing.

"It's a real possibility if we don't get the hell out of here."

"Cameron, please don't try to leave me here alone."

He nodded. "We can't be far from the cabin. Check your phone for a signal."

I pulled my phone out of my pocket and saw I still had zero bars.

"Nothing. Yours?"

He pulled his phone out and shook his head.

"How in the hell was I supposed to work out here?"

"I was told there was WIFI. Abbie, if I can make it to the main road—"

"You aren't going out in a blizzard with zero visibility. It's not happening. I'm not that bossy of a girlfriend, I promise, but I'm not swaying on this shit."

"Okay," he said with a chuckle.

"Okay."

He pressed his full lips together, trying to stifle a laugh. "How mad are you?"

"On a scale of one to ten?"

"Yes."

I looked out the window and shook my head. "I'm really not. I just want us to get through this and have our weekend. I could use a steak."

"I'm sorry."

"No more apologizing. If I must be stuck here, I'd rather it be with you. You know that."

"I do now."

"Cameron," I said with a sigh.

"Yeah?"

"This was really sweet. Even if you are going to indirectly kill me in the woods."

He reached out a hand and brushed some hair away from my face. "I won't let anything happen to you. I swear it."

"I believe you believe that."

"You don't think it's true?"

"I think you'd do everything you can to make it true. But you can't promise me anything bad won't happen. It's not in your power."

"You're right."

"I don't want to be," I said in a whisper, "but I know better."

"Well, I can promise you this," he whispered back. "I can promise you I will never bring you to the woods again as a surprise and end up stuck in a fucking creepy dead-end driveway in a snowstorm."

I laughed and pulled him to me. "Good enough."

"God, you smell so fucking good. What is that?"

"My shampoo, I think. I don't know. I have an entire

bathroom counter of girly crap on."

"It's fucking tasty."

"Tasty?"

"Yes, you smell good enough to eat."

My stomach rumbled.

"And you're hungry," he said, gripping the wheel and rocking back and forth in aggravation, jostling me in his lap.

"Look at you," I said with a laugh. "Getting all moody. I bet you're sexy pissed off."

"I just feel like I could be doing more. What in the hell was I thinking? I live in Chicago and forgot to get snow tires! In my defense, I bought this out of state."

I laughed as he looked at me, exasperated.

"I'm telling you, Coach, people have no business outside of civilization. Nothing good ever happens in the woods. This is where the crazies come to congregate, multiply, and plot."

"You don't really believe that, do you?" Cameron asked. "You think that concrete jungle we call home is safer?"

"I think that if we were in Chicago right now we wouldn't be sitting targets in the middle of the woods."

"Even so, Chicago is the most dangerous city in the US. Talk about safety in numbers being an illusion."

I shrugged. "I have mace."

"Well, that changes everything." He rolled his eyes.

"You aren't safe anywhere, with anyone," I said with a bite. "The BTK killer was married. Like happily married and no one knew what a psycho he was for over a decade. Bind, Torture, Kill, and go home and eat meatloaf before you read the kids a bedtime story. Doesn't that baffle you? Like, how do you ever really know someone?"

"You have to trust them."

"Trusting doesn't mean knowing, two distinct definitions,"

I said with a little more bite.

"Abbie?"

I shook my head. "Sorry, I shouldn't have brought it up."

"But you did, so tell me."

"No," I said, feigning a smile.

"That smile was fake. This is on your mind. Talk to me about it."

"That's not part of our deal," I said, moving to my seat before I began nervously messing with the vents.

"How long are we going to do this?" he asked, turning in his seat to face me. "Why can't I know?"

"We agreed."

"That was then," he pressed. "This isn't a game."

"It's never been a game to me," I defended. "And I told you that."

"Fine, an experiment," he relented. "I won't fight with you. It's the last thing I want."

"Then let's table this. Okay?" I'd been creeped out enough for one day. The last thing I wanted to talk about was Luke.

"Okay."

The air had changed between us, regardless of our truce. I hated it. Loathed it. It was always when things got heavy that everything changed. That's why I would fight as long as I could to keep the old hurts and resentment away. It had no place between us.

"Want to play a game?" I asked as he rubbed a knuckle along the steering wheel. He looked over at me and read my expression. I was pleading with him to help me fix the strangling air between us.

"I brought some booze. Want me to get it?" he offered.

"Why in the hell didn't you say anything before now?!"

He grinned as he jumped out of the vehicle and opened

the trunk. Seconds later, he was back in the driver's seat with my choice of Tito's vodka or Maker's Mark.

"Perfect!" I said, grabbing the vodka. "Let's do this."

"That. Is. Insane," Cameron roared hysterically. "I can't believe we've been drinking coffee all this time when all I had to do was give you vodka!"

I grinned over at him and rolled my eyes. "You act like I never told you this."

"Seeing is believing, baby," he said as he tilted the bottle of vodka and took a healthy sip. We'd drank a good bit of it and were both feeling the effects.

"Wow, wow," he said as he watched me unfasten his tie and free my hands.

Minutes before, I'd stripped him of his maroon tie and told him to fasten my hands behind my back. Apparently, for Cameron, the fact that I was double jointed was the most fascinating thing he'd ever seen.

I had the ability to roll my bound hands over my head, but I'd decided to make it more interesting by having him use his tie on me. Basically, if I wanted to take my act on the road, I could be the Houdini of handcuffs.

"That's fucking wild," he said as he shook his head.

"Yeah, my mom screamed the first time I did it in front of her."

"What else can you do?"

"Wouldn't you like to know," I said, waggling my brows.

"I'm so fucking turned on."

I shook my head. "Of course you are."

"Hey, don't take that tone with me. You are the one putting ideas in my head."

"You pig."

"*Oink*," he said, pulling me into his lap. "You little weirdo."

"Hey, I don't see you performing any party tricks," I defended as he brushed his nose against mine.

"True, I'm lacking talent in that department. Why don't you let me make up for it with enthusiasm?" He pushed his hips up, and I bounced on his thighs.

"Hmmm, you've got a little making up to do before you get all of this." I motioned to myself. "And I can't believe you watched me pee in the snow. Reason one million why I hate the woods."

"I didn't watch. You screamed, and I had no choice but to look," he said, bordering on a slur.

"Well, I felt something."

"Sure you did," he said, amused.

I traced his jaw with my finger. "I bet you were popular in high school. Did you play football?"

"Yes, Ms. Random. And soccer too, but when I was younger."

"Date a cheerleader?"

"Yep."

"Prom king?"

He bit his lip.

"*Really*? Prom king too?"

A sharp nod.

"Wow."

"What?"

"I never even danced at my prom. My date was a dick. He only wanted to go to the after parties and get my dress off."

"Did he succeed?"

"Noooo. He was a dick. I'm no killjoy. But I was around when the fake yawn, arm stretch around the shoulder move still existed, and now it's not even a thing anymore. And I never got a second look from the king."

"I would have looked at you, Abbie."

"You're just saying that because you've seen my party tricks. Trust me, back then I wasn't your type, and you probably weren't mine."

"Oh, really?" he said with a smirk. Clutching his fists at his chest, he opened his mouth wide before stretching his arms out beside him and curling them around me.

He executed it perfectly, and I leaned in and kissed him.

"Dance with me," he asked softly. "Now, here in the real world where none of that shit ever mattered. Where all that really matters is what you think of me *now*."

"Let's address that when we aren't stranded in the woods," I said, feathering my fingers through the soft hair at the back of his neck.

"Fine, dance with me."

"You want me to dance with you? In the woods?"

"Yeah," he prompted, pressing his fingers into my hips.

"Uhhh, no."

"Come on, you're the one who said romance is dead. I'm willing to try to prove that theory wrong." With no effort, he deposited me back in my seat and picked up his phone.

"Cameron, I'm not dancing with you in the woods."

"Are you really afraid?" he asked with a hint of a smile as he flipped through his music. I looked around us and thanked the vodka for the brass balls I'd grown in the last few hours.

"No, thanks to Tito, and his vodka, I'm feeling pretty relaxed."

"Okay then," he said as he chose a song and set his phone

on the console. The heavy bass and whining guitar of "Witchy Woman" by the Eagles started to play.

"Funny," I said as his dimples shone through the dim light of the cabin. The interior light lit up the rest of his shit-eating grin as he opened his door and walked past the headlights to get to mine.

"I'm not even close to finished wooing you," he whispered as he led me to stand in front of the high beams.

My hands in his, he kissed each of my wrists before he pulled them around his neck and began to move with me plastered to his body. I followed his lead with ease while he swayed his hips. With no space between us and far too many clothes, I burrowed into his warmth.

Spotlighted by his high beams in the middle of nowhere, he slid his hands up and down the inside of my jacket, caressing me and lighting me up with need. Languid, we floated on a subzero cloud, fully immersed in the other. We were a little drunk, but more consumed by our connection.

Cameron began a slow grind as we drunk-danced in the snow. Twisting my hips, I put on a little show as he watched my movements, and his grin let me know he liked what he was seeing.

One thing I knew without him saying was that Cameron loved to dance. I loved that about him. I loved that he was so confident and had a way of making me feel comfortable when I was out of my element.

We laughed as we stumbled a little in our footing, our bodies bouncing in rhythm. I pushed out my lips as I shimmied up to him, and he turned me around so my back was to his chest.

Party of two, we were getting down in the woods, dancing and giddy. I felt free, I felt important, and I felt loved.

That moment was one of the happiest of my life.

When the song ended, I moved to head toward the SUV, but he pulled me back to him.

"One more dance," he said as "Hand Me Down" by Matchbox Twenty filtered through the speakers. Cameron began to sing to me, his vodka-laced breath covering my neck, the words of the song touching me deeply.

I followed his lead while he subtly moved, more intent on singing than dancing. Every second of that dance cemented itself in my heart.

If there was ever a definition of woo, it was the fine-ass man singing to me about what I deserved.

I had to fight back tears when his lips took my trembling mouth. I hoped he thought it was from the cold, but the truth was, I was raw. I wanted what we had to be *it*. I wanted him to be the last man I kissed, the last man I gave my heart and body to. And I didn't want my heart to be a liar. And only he had to power to make it true.

He said we didn't deal in absolutes, but my heart was starting to disagree as it beat for him. Cameron was making me a believer.

I was falling.

And falling *hard*.

I didn't need anything more from him than what he was giving. But what he was giving was so much more than I'd expected. I pressed into him, doing everything I could to show him how much he moved me.

Because Cameron moved me.

Don't let me be wrong. Please, God, don't let me be wrong again.

I looked up into jade eyes and took a mental picture at the expression on his face.

"Don't make me a fool," I whispered to him in a plea.

He paused his steps and looked down at me with a mix of emotion.

I shook my head with a smile. "But you can't promise you won't."

He tightened his hold on me. "It's really not so hard to believe in me, is it? I mean, you are dancing in the woods."

I smiled. "I am, aren't I?"

"You are," he said as the wind picked up and we kissed words away.

Only words made liars out of people.

Cameron said kisses were unspoken promises, and so he kissed me until I understood his.

Our mouths became urgent, and I used his kiss as assurance. Now that I had him, I was too afraid of the other shoe dropping. If I wasn't careful, I would ruin the here and now with the threat of the unknown.

I had to let go.

I had to let life happen.

And so, for myself, and for Cameron, I let go.

And he was still there, kissing me, touching me, being mine.

If karma and fate truly existed, I would make the exception and believe in them for the sake of *us*.

"I want you," I whispered as I clutched him tighter to me. Desperation laced my voice as I pressed my body to his. "Fuck me, prom king."

His answering groan rumbled through his chest as his hands gripped my ass.

The sound of crunching snow and moving headlights had us jumping apart like a bunch of guilty teenagers. I shrieked as a large truck approached, and Cameron made quick work of depositing me in the Audi.

I yelled for him to get in too as he closed the door. I was being irrational, and I knew it, but I couldn't help the full-fledged panic that raced through me as Cameron ducked to converse with the driver.

Instead of the relief I should have felt, I had more concern for him and our bubble that had been popped by the intruder. When Cameron pulled back from the truck, he smiled in my direction and jogged toward me.

"We're rescued. This guy is with the management company who rents the cabin. When we didn't check in, they came looking for us. He said it happens all the time. Hey, hey, what's wrong?"

"I . . . I . . ."

You're irrational, you're crazy, and you're in love with him. Crazy in love with him.

"Hey," he said, leaning over. "I'm okay. We're okay."

I nodded, my mind fuzzy from the booze, my heart pounding with residual worry. Relief finally made its presence known as I realized we wouldn't be making any headlines.

It was a good thing too. I would've been one pissed off woman at the pearly gates. Things were just getting good.

"Sorry, I guess I'm still a little on edge," I whispered sheepishly.

"Come on," he said, motioning with his chin toward the truck. "They're going to send a tow when the storm breaks. Let's go get you that steak."

A little after midnight, we finally made it to the cabin and it was nothing short of postcard-perfect. The roof and porch were covered with a blanket of fresh snow, the surrounding grounds immaculate and dusted with winter.

We collectively thanked the driver as we climbed out of the truck and made our way down the short walk that led to the porch.

"It's beautiful," I said in appreciation as he took my hand and led me up the steps. "How did you set this up?"

"A buddy of mine owns it. But it's normally rented this time of year. We got lucky."

"I wish you would have given me more notice or let me pack a bag. I don't even have a toothbrush."

"I packed an extra for you."

"I'm not playing Scrabble naked," I scorned as he opened the door.

"It's slob weekend," he declared. "I'm going to make sure of it," he said as he ushered me through the door.

The cabin had an open floor plan, and at the heart of it was a stone fireplace. The furniture looked new but homey.

The walls were free of expected taxidermy, and the place had the hint of a woman's touch. Comfortable, soft blankets and multi-colored pillows were scattered throughout.

Cameron unloaded his bags on the kitchen counter next to a cozy dining nook and opened the fridge, pulling out a beer.

"What's your flavor?" he asked as I spotted a washer dryer combo in the pantry of the kitchen, relieved at the very least I could wash what I had on.

It was obvious Cameron wasn't well versed in what a woman considered necessary for survival.

"A shower."

He quirked a brow. "Want some company?"

"No," I said, dousing his hopes. I had some intimate cleaning to do, and regardless of how sexy he thought it would be, I knew differently. Shower sex wasn't my favorite. Someone always ended up freezing their ass off.

"I had a shower sex incident," I explained. "It started with soap and quickly escalated to burning in places I don't ever want to burn. It's not in the cards," I said as his lips twitched. "Besides, I'm just not that into you yet to risk it."

"You'll pay for that," he said without taking an ounce of offense before pulling on his beer.

"As long as it's not in the shower."

He shrugged his coat off with a smirk. "Sure, it won't happen in the shower."

"Cameronnn," I whimpered, my eyes rolling back as his chest flexed and he thrust back in, hitting me so deeply my whole body quaked. "I'm coming," I rasped out as he closed his mouth around my nipple while the water cascaded down his back.

"Abbie, I can't get enough," he grunted out as he held me in place in the stall before he drove his point home. He pressed his forehead against mine, lips parted before he jerked inside of me with a growl.

Shower sex is the shit!

Spent, I stood lax against the wall as Cameron turned off the water, before toweling off my body and then his. I watched his muscles flex as he rubbed the droplets away from his ripped stomach and had to physically stop myself from taking a bite of his bubble ass.

If there was an award for asses, Cameron would rightfully claim it.

His knowing smirk at my inability to keep from having

shower sex showed on his face as he glanced at me. I gladly gave him the win as my imagination went wild with the possibilities for the rest of the weekend.

"For the record," I said with a voice full of lust, "I don't have table sex, couch sex, patio sex, hot tub sex, or counter sex, either."

"Noted," he said as his dimples appeared.

Later that morning, and without shame, I watched Cameron sleep. A lock of his dark hair lay in a slight wave across his forehead and his full lips taunted me. The fact that he looked so perfect without effort, well . . . it pissed me off. Tousled hair, flawless skin, he looked freshly fucked, but in a way that made him movie scene worthy, and I just looked . . . *fucked*. It was totally unfair.

I'd never been the girl to apply makeup in the morning to deceive some poor unsuspecting guy with a false future reality. But when I woke, I made damned sure to sneak in a run with the toothbrush and rinse with some Listerine I found in his leather travel bag.

After I dampened my three-million-watt hair to tame it, I used a squirt of his manly gel and ran my fingers through.

My lips were chapped from the cold and bruised from his kiss, so I put on some designer Chapstick that may have looked a little like tinted lip gloss.

In an attempt to keep things clean, I may have rolled on some of the deodorant I kept in my tote.

There was a chance I went through his suitcase and found a fresh button-down flannel shirt and slid it on. On a technicality, he did say he brought one for me. Cuffing the sleeves, I glanced back to him as he slept.

The man was a demigod, cut, etched, and completely at ease as he dreamed godlike dreams. He'd told me he'd lived a charmed life, and I believed it. As wrong as the thought was, I was sure his looks gave him a sort of advantage in his years.

And from what I'd gathered, he'd used that advantage, especially with women. But there was a difference between a man who was good looking and arrogant to a man who was good looking and had substance, and that difference was Cameron.

I loved that he didn't ramble on about his hey-days, though I was sure he was a bit of a bad ass. It was smirk implied.

Those ramblings would only have turned me off, stories of a cocky and insecure man, but Cameron had shed those years and grown into a gentle giant. His beauty went further than skin deep and behind it, he was all heart.

Enamored, I stood staring for a stalker minute while his body rose and fell, taking and expelling even breaths. Even in his sleep, he was too much to take in.

The attraction I felt for him only grew stronger when I thought of how his full lips felt on mine, and how his eyes shone when he looked at me. I couldn't get over it, no matter how hard I tried to play it cool. Everything about him appealed to me—his size, his strength, his beauty, *him*.

While I waited for Cameron to wake up, I decided to clean out my bag, and it was then that I brushed on a little blush along my cheekbones to make sure I still liked the shade.

Because I was in my tote, I grabbed my lotion bar to scent my wrists, what could it hurt to make a little bit of effort?

And then I got to digging in that bag and found some old diamond stud earrings that I loved in a hidden pocket. They were nothing special.

I may have played around with my phone, twisting my head at odd angles to make sure he didn't wake up seeing my unpredictable and opportunistic double chin. In my defense, that secondary chin tended to flare out like a lizard's neck without warning. I didn't want to scare the poor man.

When I'd finished polishing my nails and toes with a shade I'd bought months ago and forgotten about, I decided that Cameron was going to sleep forever, so I may have borrowed his razor and shaved my legs a little.

By the time I was finished *not* getting ready for Cameron to open his eyes, I was exhausted and even more disturbed by the slow smile that covered his face when I made myself comfortable back in bed.

"You are not human," I whispered, praying when he woke I'd see a hint of spinach in his teeth from last night's feast. He cooked a mean steak and spinach salad.

Come on, give me one flaw!

"Are you all dressed up for me?" he asked, his sexy voice filled with sleep.

I snorted. *Snorted* and ruined every chance I had of looking like a sexy sophisticate.

"No, this is how I always look in the morning." That was my story and I was sticking to it.

"Sooooo, you didn't brush your teeth, fix your hair, put some shit on your face, use my razor to shave your legs, and pose for twenty pictures you didn't take?"

I touched my forehead to his, my eyes wide and searching.

"What are you doing?" He chuckled as I climbed on top of him and peered at him closely.

I was sure I looked like a cartoon character as I pressed in. "I'm looking for your third eyelid, you *lizard!*"

He laughed and with the swipe of his arm, pinned me beneath him. It was then that I noticed his only flaw was a faint bruise on his chin.

"What happened?" I asked as I lifted to press my lips against it.

"Max caught me with an elbow on the court," he said pulling away from my lips, "and don't change the subject."

"Fine. I can't get away with shit when you're around," I grumbled while my cheeks flamed.

"I was forced to watch you for too long before I got to touch you. I've gotten good at it. And don't get too comfortable with your I don'ts, either. I do seem to recall shower sex being a definite no."

"Dick persuasion will not work on me, sir. That was a fluke."

His beautiful lips twitched. "A . . . fluke."

"Your job is to woo, not sway opinions," I reminded.

"Well, after all the effort you just put in to dress up for me, I *will* woo, madam."

Still slightly embarrassed, I shook my head and stared at the ceiling.

He trailed his lips from my neck to my ear. "I love that you did all of this for me. I loved watching you doll yourself up for my benefit. I got hard when you blew on your nails. Abbie, you are beautiful without all that effort, but it makes me feel so good that you do it for me."

Pulling me to sit, he plucked one of the freshly cut roses from the small glass vase beside the bed and handed it to me. I knew the arrangements of pale pink stems placed strategically throughout the cabin weren't a coincidence. Cameron had sent a few dozen roses in the same shade to my house in the last few weeks. I constantly filled my nose with their sweet scent.

"Thank you," I said before I pressed the flower to my nose and inhaled. "I meant to ask you, of all the flowers you left at my table, why did you decide to send roses?"

He rubbed one of the delicate petals between his fingers. "It was the only flower you picked up first, instead of an afterthought, before you left the coffee shop. I knew then they were your favorite."

"*I* didn't even know they were my favorite." I sighed as he traced my neck with his lips. "You really are the king of woo."

"King of woo?" he repeated in question, a small smile playing on his lips.

"Yeah," I said softly, "you earned it. So, what's on the docket today?"

"Well, first I'm going to ruin all your hard work," he said, reaching for the buttons on my shirt and freeing them before he slowly pushed the fabric away so it slid off of my shoulders. Eyes intent on mine, my nipple peaked under the careful trace of his finger.

"King of woo," he said softly, his tickled grin showcasing the divots at the corners of his mouth. "I like it."

I said his name on a prayer when he took the stiff peak in his mouth.

Wordless, he gently pushed me beneath him and sank between my thighs. I locked my legs around him while he lined himself up at my entrance and held his weight above me. His sculpted chest on display, my greedy fingers explored.

Pushing in slightly, he watched my reaction to him as the buzz between us increased.

"Damn," he grunted as I tightened around him. His lips parted as he thrust in further.

"I knew it."

"Knew what?" I rasped out as he pressed me into the

mattress, making sure I felt every inch of him.

"Maybe I didn't know, but I had a feeling," he whispered before his mouth took mine and he buried himself. No further explanation needed.

17

Abbie

I WAS DOING IT. I WAS RUNNING IN THE WOODS, AND IT wasn't because I was being pursued by a mass murderer, which was a definite bonus. Cameron had dressed me that morning in one of his thick sweaters that hung down past my knees. I also had my leggings, coat, scarf, gloves, and snow boots on. I looked ridiculous, but I was warm, and getting warmer as we ran through the woods.

After only a week, with Cameron's encouragement, I was getting to the point that I could keep his pace despite his longer stride, though I was sure he made allowances. But I'd been speed walking around Chicago for a little over ten years, so I already had a fair amount of stamina. And it helped. I was becoming a runner, and the knowledge of that had me blissful as he glanced back at me with a smile.

We didn't venture far. Cameron told me he wasn't pushing his luck. But he did bring me to a break in the trees the led to a breathtaking view of a large pond. Surrounded in a winter wonderland, I appreciated everything about the silence that engulfed us. It was a picture-perfect storybook type of isolation with the only person in the world I would want to share it with.

"Not so bad, is it?" he asked, looking back at me as I scoured the sight in front of us.

"It's beautiful," I answered, catching my breath before walking toward a small dock.

"There's a little boat out in the shed next to the house. I saw it last night when I was grilling. I'll bring you back here this summer and you can read me poetry or Jane Austen, while I row you around."

"Let's not get too carried away, Casanova."

"Too late," he said as his eyes swept over me. "Too fucking late." He tugged at my hand, pulling me to him. "You can't run too much in those boots. It's not good for you."

"I know. I just don't want to break the routine."

"I'm proud of you. You don't even look like you want to kick my ass when I show up at your door in the morning."

"Oh, but I still do," I said as we shared a grin.

"And it's just the beginning. Wait until you run your first 5K," he said with a wink.

A rush of emotion swept over me as I looked up at him.

"What are you thinking?"

I swallowed.

"Okay," he said playfully, "now I have to know."

"I don't know how to say this without geeking out."

"Abbie, you can tell me anything."

"It's just..." I frowned to keep my chin from wobbling, but the tears sprang up anyway.

"Baby, what is it?" he asked, his hands cupping my face.

"It's like when people say they can't swim, I have a hard time believing them because it came so naturally to me. Some people are terrified of the water, and treading it seems simplistic. I mean, it's not exactly swimming, but it serves the purpose. For most, it's like a natural reflex. But treading water isn't swimming."

"Okay," he said, biting his lip.

"Okay, so, shit." A tear fell, and before I could wipe it away, he leaned in and took it with his lips as my heart swelled.

"I feel like before I met you, I was treading water and . . . God, am I making any sense right now?"

"Perfect sense," he said softly.

"It's not just running, Cameron. It's *us* too."

"I feel the same, more than I can explain. More than you could ever know." He searched my eyes. "Why couldn't I have met you ten years ago?" he added, taking me by surprise. "What were you doing when you were twenty-three, Abbie?"

"College, then work—so much work. I worked too hard."

"Same here. I can't say I did one significant thing in my life then, besides becoming a coach. And seeing your face right now is such a high. I love watching it happen. You thank me, but you are the one who did all the hard work."

I shook my head. "No, you don't get it. I gave up. Without you, I wouldn't have given running a second thought again. I never thought I could be that woman. *This* woman. It seems simplistic, but it's anything but for me. Running has been my Achilles heel my whole life. My *whole* life," I said as my chin wobbled and more tears threatened. "So, thank you."

"This," he said softly. "This right here is why I do it. The look on your face. I love pushing people past what they think they can handle, past what they think they're capable of. As your boyfriend, I think you're getting good at it, and I'm proud of you. But as your coach, I can't wait to see where you go with it next."

"You really love it, don't you? Being a coach."

"Yeah. I do. It's everything to me. Don't get me wrong, I'm glad I ventured out into something different with the stores. Coaching part-time at a private school doesn't pay much, but coaching has always been my dream."

"Not to play professionally?"

"No. I mean, I guess it could have been, but it was training that appealed to me more. I like the tactics of it. And I got lucky with a lot of my coaches. I had one in high school, Coach Bryant. He was a mentor. I had so much respect for him and for the way he spoke to people. He would lose his shit, like any other man passionate about the game, but he always had this dignity about him. An air about him that seemed unfit for modern society. You didn't fuck with him, no one really did. He was damn good at his job. I kind of aspired to be just like him."

"What makes you think you aren't?"

Cameron shook his head. "I could never be him."

"How do you know?"

"Life told me so." His face darkened briefly and then it was gone. I should have pressed him for more at that moment. I could have told him he exuded all of those qualities in droves. It was on the tip of my tongue to tell him so, but instead, I showed him by letting him grab my gloved hand and lead me through the trees.

"Shit!" Cameron exclaimed from the porch just as I emerged from the bedroom, freshly showered. I slid open the glass door and saw the grill was covered in flames.

"Oh shit!" I said as he tried to slap them out with his iron spatula. "What do you need?"

"A do-over," he said with a laugh as he shut the lid to suffocate the fire then turned the gas off. When he opened it back up, the chicken was black. He stabbed the burned meat with a large fork and held it toward me. "Dinner is ready," he announced.

I wrinkled my nose. "I think I'll pass. I saw some things in the cabinet. I've got dinner covered."

"You deem this unfit for consumption, woman?!"

I kissed his cheek. "You don't have to do all the cooking. I can earn my keep. Give me half an hour."

"Okay, but you're missing out."

My mother was an amazing cook. She could take anything in the cabinets and turn it into a king's feast in a matter of minutes. My skills were subpar at best. I never really took the time to watch and learn from her. But I was sure I could muster up something more edible than charred chicken. After five minutes of studying the cabinets, I decided to send out an SOS and call my mom while Cameron sat in the living room watching soccer.

"Mom, I need your help," I said in a whisper once she answered.

"What's wrong, honey? You didn't answer last night when I called."

"I know, I'm sorry. I'm with someone."

"Oh?" she asked.

"Long story short, we've been seeing each other for a while now. He's amazing, and I'll tell you all about him soon, but I need some cooking advice."

"Okay, step back and walk away."

"Not funny," I said with a hand on my hip she couldn't see.

"I think it is," she said with a light laugh. "Take your hand off your hip, brat. I'll help you."

"We aren't in the position to get to the store, and this place is stocked with everything, but I can't think of a single thing to make."

"Okay, give me the run down."

I listed off everything in the cabinets, fridge, and freezer.

"Why are you whispering?"

"Because I don't want him to think I can't cook."

"You can't cook. I bet you wish you would have helped in the kitchen more rather than whined."

"Mom, I'm glad you think this is funny, but I really, *really* like him. Okay?"

"Why haven't I heard about him before now?"

"Because I wasn't sure, and parents don't need to know every hit or miss of their daughter's dating life. Don't be hurt. I wanted to make sure it was something before I told you. So, will you help me?"

"Sure, you can bring him to dinner next week."

"No way. Too soon."

"But we are negotiating," she said with a playful lift.

"No, we're not. Mom. Help me, okay? I don't have time to look up recipes and I kind of want to impress him," I whispered.

"Does this man have a name?"

"For you? Not yet."

"Fine, but I want dinner with you. Next week."

"Done," I gritted out. "And I would have come anyway."

"I'll text you a recipe."

"Thanks, Mom. I love you."

"And, Abbie?"

"Yeah?" I whispered as I looked back at Cameron, who was sitting on the edge of the couch, his eyes fixed on the TV. I briefly daydreamed about a future where getaways became our ritual.

"If all else fails, add more butter."

"Okay."

More minutes than my promised half hour later, I had my mother's creamy rosemary chicken on a bed of pasta and a tossed salad on the table. I was happy with the execution, and Cameron seemed to be as well as he closed his eyes with his first bite.

"This is incredible."

"Thank you," I boasted as he inhaled a mouthful of pasta.

"So, I think it's time you had me over for dinner," he said with a wink.

"Do you?" I said in a slight panic. I could have Mrs. Zingaro give me her recipe for ziti. That would buy me a week.

Cameron's next words cut through my thoughts. "How is your mother?"

"She's fi—" I deadpanned. "You're an ass, you know that? And how could you have possibly heard that conversation?"

"You get good picking it up being a high school coach. And, Abbie," he said around a mouthful of garlic toast, "it's good to know you really, *really* like me."

My face flamed as he devoured the chicken on his plate and forked another piece out of the cast iron skillet. I stood from the table to get the bottle of wine. He circled my waist with his arm and pulled me onto his waiting lap.

"Where are you going?"

"To get some wine. Want some?" I asked as he moved my hair away from my shoulder and rested his chin on my neck.

"Nope." He twisted his fork, gaining a bite of pasta and brought it to my mouth. I opened and took it, chewing as he repeated the motion. "I have a plate of my own, Coach."

"Yeah," he said, moving his free hand underneath my borrowed flannel before trailing lazy fingers along my stomach. "But I'm not finished wooing."

"Back to reality," I said, mourning the end of our long weekend as Cameron closed the door to the cabin. We'd spent every second in bed that morning until we had no choice but to clean up and head out. My heart was sinking at the loss of it.

He gripped me in his strong embrace. "Okay, so this isn't our every day," he said, commanding my eyes, "but there will be plenty of this in our future for as long as you want it."

I kissed him soundly on the mouth. "Consider that my RSVP. I can't believe I'm saying this, but I'll miss the woods."

"We'll be back. This isn't the last time, okay?"

"Okay." *You are ridiculous, Abbie.*

He placed a gentle kiss on my forehead and led me down the steps, his duffle bag in hand as I took one last look at the cabin. We'd played house for a weekend and it was more than nice. It was heaven.

"What are you thinking?" he asked as he opened the passenger side door and I climbed into the Audi.

"Just that I'm glad we waited. And now I'm glad we've stopped waiting."

I clicked my seatbelt.

His hands rested on either side of the doorframe. "It was hell not being able to touch you, but I wouldn't change a thing."

When I was comfortable, he closed the door and walked in front of the hood as I dreaded the empty house waiting for me.

We sat in the idling SUV for a moment longer before Cameron placed his hand on my headrest and twisted his body for a clear view to exit the driveway. While the scent of his cologne and his proximity knocked me senseless, I pressed my lips to his Adam's apple and kept them there. He stopped the truck at the edge of the driveway, put it in park, and stared at me long and hard before he spoke.

"I know something happened. Something that you don't want to tell me about yet. It's painfully obvious, but I want you to know this is not over between us, not by a longshot."

"I know."

He leaned over. "Are you sure? Because I get the feeling you aren't."

"I'm sorry I make you feel that way." I sank into my seat, hating the fact that I needed so much reassurance. But he'd been consistent every step of the way. I had no reason to doubt him. I averted my eyes, my heart pounding.

"Look at me," he whispered. "I'm *with* you."

I couldn't help but remember Bree declaring her and Anthony were on another level in Scotland. It rang true for Cameron and me as I looked into his earnest eyes.

He took my hand and pressed it to his chest before he leaned in and took my lips. His kiss was slow, thorough, and I "hmmed" happily and smiled as he pulled away.

"You're an excellent coach."

18

Abbie

"Happy Thanksgiving," Cameron said as I sat at my mother's kitchen table, looking at him on my screen.

"Happy Thanksgiving," I said as I stood to make my way upstairs to my old bedroom for some privacy. I'd asked Cameron to come with me to Naperville, but he wanted to be with his dad despite how heavy it felt in the house without his mother there.

I wasn't one to neglect family and friends due to a new boyfriend. It was one of my new life rules, no matter how perfect said boyfriend was. When you accidentally date a sociopath, you learn your lesson about things like that. Luke was constantly making me break plans with Bree and my family to manipulate my time, manipulate me.

No matter how happy I was being a part of a we with Cameron, I made time for Bree and my parents, even if the relationship was by far the healthiest of my adult life.

But I had to admit, the man smiling at me on the screen

made it extremely hard to be without him. I'd grown used to waking up roasting with his arm thrown over me.

Spending Saturdays watching him battle Max on the court before we used up the rest of the day roaming the city or Wicker Park. When weather permitted, we ran every morning, and when it didn't, we made up for it in my bedroom. I was up to three miles per day and it was beginning to show. I was in the best shape of my life.

Cameron was most definitely a good-time guy. There was rarely a dull moment. Even quiet nights at home, which we mostly spent with Mrs. Zingaro, were blissful.

I closed my door and plopped myself on my old bed.

"How is it going over there?" I asked.

"Awkward and fucking lonely. I hate this. I don't know what to do. It's like he stopped living when my mother did. We already had a damned communication problem."

"All you can do is try to talk to him," I offered. "You know Mrs. Zingaro was the same with me for a little while. She was kind of stand-offish when we first met. I know it's not the same thing, but you can't get to know him if all you are is polite. It might have backfired for me a little, but I can't say she isn't worth it. Talk to him, *really* try to talk to him."

"I'll try," he said softly.

"Talk about your mom. He might be hesitant at first, and maybe that's his way, but it couldn't hurt."

"I will."

"Promise?" I asked. It was the only one I'd ever asked for. I hated the guilt and the pain that covered his features, so I was selfish with my request, but I saw it more often than I wanted to. Even though they weren't close as father and son, I knew Cameron longed for it.

I saw his hesitance and apologized. "I'm sorry, it's not my

place to ask for that."

"I promise," Cameron said. "And it is your place. You can ask me for anything, Abbie. I mean that."

My heart galloped. It was so obvious we were more than coffee. I was having a horrible time not verbalizing how I felt every time I looked at him. We were still new, and patience had gone a long way for us. I was fine with waiting.

"So, what's on the menu at the Bledsoe house?"

"I'm going to burn a turkey," he said with a grin.

"Sounds delicious."

"And you?"

"I doubt we'll eat until later. Oliver won't show up until he feels like it, so we have to wait for his highness to arrive."

"His highness is here, punk," Oliver spouted as he walked into my bedroom. "Who are you talking to?"

I gave Cameron wide eyes. "Busted," he said from the screen.

"None of your business," I said as my brother plopped onto my bed beside me.

Cameron looked at Oliver and gave him the man nod. "Hey, man."

Oliver looked at me. "Who's this?"

"This is my boyfriend, Cameron."

"Same one?" I was going to kill him.

"Bledsoe, nice to meet you," Cameron added.

"I haven't heard anything about you," Oliver said, barely glancing at the screen.

"Abbie likes to keep me a secret," Cameron retorted without missing a beat. "But I think I'm her only boyfriend. I think it's safe to say one and the same."

"You are," I chimed in, pledging my allegiance.

"You don't say," Oliver said, leaning back on my pillow

before tossing a piece of croissant in his mouth.

My brother and I looked a lot alike, except he had my father's curly blond hair, which he cropped off shorter and shorter as he got older. We had the same mouth and eyes.

"Cameron, this is my brother, Dr. Dick."

Oliver rolled his eyes before he pressed my head down with his palm, making it look like we were playing an abusive version of Duck, Duck, Goose. I slapped at his wrist as he lifted the tip of my nose, giving me a pig face, before he palmed it, twisting my features in a free for all. I struggled with Oliver as Cameron's laughter rang out of my phone.

"Damn you, act your age, idiot," I fumed as I dropped the phone and landed two solid punches to Oliver's arm. He "oofed" with a chuckle.

Retrieving my phone, I pointed at the door then righted myself and the phone so I could see Cameron as my face flamed.

Oliver walked out of the room with a "Later, Cameron."

"Later, man," Cameron answered as I put my attention back on him with no dignity intact. "He's such a shit."

"I'll take your word for it."

"The man is a thirty-five-year-old toddler."

"He seems like a lot of fun."

"He's a dick. Enough about my brother, I miss you." God, I was so gone. I waggled my brows. "All of me misses you."

"I'll be at your door the minute you get home. And next Thanksgiving," Cameron added, melancholy, "we spend together. Okay? I feel like we're teenagers sneaking around."

"Okay."

Heart overflowing, I twisted the new gold bracelet on my wrist. An early Christmas gift Cameron gave me before I left for my parents' house.

"I love my bracelet."

Cameron grinned. "It's engraved. I was waiting for you to notice but you didn't."

I snapped it off and peered inside. It read: *You've bewitched me body and soul.*

It was a quote from *Pride and Prejudice*. My eyes glistened with happy tears.

"Now I love it even more. What do you want for Christmas?"

Cameron's eyes closed briefly. "I'd say Santa came through early this year. I got what I wanted a few months ago."

"Oh, and what's that?"

"I'm looking at her."

My eyes watered as he leaned into the phone, his eyes filled with affection. "Abbie—"

"Hey, Jezebel!" Oliver called from the top of the stairs. "You think you can ditch the new boy toy long enough to help Mom in the kitchen so we can eat today?"

I glared in my brother's direction as Cameron chuckled. "Are your hands broken?"

I rolled my eyes and looked on at Cameron. "I'm sorry."

"It's fine, go feed Dr. Dick. I'll see you tomorrow."

19

Abbie

King of Woo: Hey, beautiful, are you almost ready?

Me: Yes, I'll be ready in five.

King of Woo: I'll be there in four.

He was chaperoning the winter formal at the high school he coached for and had invited me as his date. I had to admit, I went a little overboard when I went shopping for my dress.

But the butterflies that raced through me weren't one of a high school girl. These belonged to a woman who had kissed far too many gutter frogs and had finally met her sidewalk prince.

All of my fears were being put to rest daily. I was no longer a woman afraid. I was a woman in love.

I had that inexplicable connection with someone that had nothing to do with work, friendship, or family. The connection that makes your heart pound and keeps your throat dry in anticipation. I finally had the man you dressed up for.

I applied a coat of lipstick then stood back and admired my dress. I'd picked a floor-length, shimmering pale pink gown—his favorite on me—and curled my crimson hair in ribbons before I pinned them up.

True to his word, my doorbell rang four minutes later. On the other side, Cameron stood in a tuxedo—far too ostentatious for a school dance—his dark hair swept back, holding a delicate rose corsage for my wrist.

His eyes drifted from my heel-clad feet to the top of my twisted hair.

"Abbie . . ." He didn't have to say any more than that. I felt touched inside and out.

"Thank you," I whispered.

"Give me your hand," he said, opening the clear box and sliding the small spray of roses onto my wrist.

"Do they even do corsages anymore?"

"We do," he answered, guiding me into my coat.

I couldn't help but think my invitation to the dance was due to the conversation we had on our weekend getaway.

When I saw the limousine parked at my curb, I glanced his way.

"You went to too much trouble," I gently scolded as the driver opened the door for us.

After we were safely inside, he gave me a wicked grin, along with his 'come-hither' finger. His lap had become my favorite chair, and he seemed to think it appropriate for any occasion. I sat cradled in his arms, my glittering dress cascading down his long legs.

Though I'd told him he'd gone to too much trouble, I'd spent the day getting pampered at the spa a few streets over. I'd had every treatment available, and Bree had spent a few hours getting a massage while we caught up about all things wedding and I filled her in on the last few weeks with Cameron.

The minute we pulled away from the curb, Cameron's eyes dipped to my exposed cleavage while he leaned in and pressed a soft kiss to my neck.

"And how was your day?" I asked with a light laugh as his fingers roamed beneath my coat. He remained wordless as he kissed every inch of skin the fabric didn't cover. Lips, tongue, fingers, he massaged my calf as he nibbled at the spot behind my ear.

"I missed you too," I murmured as he continued his sweet assault, turning me into a puddle on his lap.

"Hey, Coach," I said in an attempt to get his attention. In the rearview, I could see the crinkle form in the corner of the driver's eyes as I softly tugged on Cameron's jacket.

"That good, huh?"

My breaths came out heavier as his lips roamed.

Dangerous arousal spiked between us as his kiss drifted along with his hand to slide up my thigh while simultaneously pushing the button for the partition between us and the driver.

"You do this to me, Abbie," he whispered tracing my jaw with his lips. "You look so beautiful," he murmured, as he lifted his hips showcasing his erection. "You get me so fucking high."

He cupped my face and kissed me so deeply I thought I would drown in it. Pulling away he pressed his forehead to mine.

"What do you want, Abbie Gorman? Ask me for anything."

"You," I said easily. "I want you. I'm not jaded anymore, Cameron."

"I feel the same," he whispered softly. "You've changed everything for me."

The tender lift of his voice had me searching his eyes which conveyed so much. I felt the shift on his part, I felt the words he wasn't saying. The car came to a stop and unfortunately for us, so had the moment. Cameron sighed as I made my way off his lap and searched my clutch to fix my lipstick.

My hand in Cameron's, we walked down the halls of the high school and I noticed several banners that read *All in All Sports*.

"You sponsored the dance?"

He squeezed my hand, a pride-filled smile whispering on his lips.

No man could ever be so perfect.

"What did you do, Coach Bledsoe?"

Music drifted from behind a set of double doors as a group of students passed us.

Cameron glanced around us and then peered down at me. "I can't kiss you in there, but just know that I want to."

"I have a feeling you'll make it up to me. Are you going to answer my question?"

I got my answer when he ushered me into the intricately decorated hall and I realized the lengths he'd gone to. Floating roses were draped from the ceiling, along with large globe lighting. The tables were all covered with enchanted roses that hung suspended in glass. Large storybooks were stacked in all four corners of the square hall.

"The theme is timeless romance," Cameron said, standing next to me. My eyes drifted to his and he turned to me with a proud smirk. "It's not dead, Abbie."

"Cameron," I said softly as I noted the endless detail that filled the four corners of the room, "how long have you been planning this?"

He squeezed my hand.

"How long?" I demanded.

"A while," he said, his answering look unwavering.

He wanted me to know but didn't boast about it. While I stood in a daze due to his gesture, he shed our coats.

A while.

Months, it had to have been. The truth was in the details, and there were so many.

Even though I was sure it took a village, he'd been specific about those details. I couldn't stop my wandering eyes as he took my hand and led me to the dance floor.

"You aren't chaperoning?"

"Yes," he said as he ignored the snickers of a few of the students. "But it was just an excuse to get you here."

"Looking good, Coach," one of the guys said as we passed them on the floor.

"Thanks, Rafferty," he said without looking his way.

We danced alongside an oversized stack of classics—*Romeo and Juliet*, *Great Expectations*, and *Pride and Prejudice*.

Though the school was elite, I was sure they didn't have the budget to pull it off. I was certain Cameron had funded damn near all of it.

It struck me then that I'd never had a man go so far to make a believer out of me. No one had ever come close.

Weightless, I clung to him. I felt like I was floating as we moved across the floor. It took every bit of strength I had not to tear up.

"Cameron," I said, unable to put into words what I was feeling. Instead, I buried my head in his shoulder. "Where in the hell have you been?"

"Anywhere but where I needed to be," he whispered softly.

The Killers "Be Still" rang out as he pulled me to him and began to move. Cameron nodded toward the DJ.

"This is a beautiful song," I said, looking over his shoulder and meeting a woman's eyes that zeroed in on us.

"It's the senior song of 2018," Cameron said with a grin.

"Oh God, I feel so old," I said with wide eyes.

"Not me. I would never want to go through what they're about to go through *again*," he said dismissively. "I'm good."

"True," I said, mulling it over. "For a second, I forgot how hard it was."

"Right? Fuck that," Cameron said, trying to keep respectable space between us. "I hated school."

"Typical jock," I cooed. "I loved it."

"I have no doubts. Let me guess, you graduated Magna Cum Laude at Northwestern?"

"Yep. But I wasn't high school valedictorian."

"Second in line?" he said, his eyes telling me he knew that to be the truth.

"Yeah, Michelle Chen. I got felt up at a party while she studied. I considered it an even trade."

Cameron's brow lifted.

"I never said I wasn't popular. And I told you I got asked to prom. I skirted the line. I didn't spend my Friday nights working on a science fair project. I studied hard and then snuck out and partied harder. You just assumed because I geek out *now* that I was then."

"I don't assume anything when it comes to you, Abbie. I know better."

"So, this isn't like a prom do-over for me?"

"No," he said softly. "It's for me. Because if we could go back, I would've been your date."

I paused my steps and we stumbled a little. Cameron swept me back up in his hold and made us both look good.

"You just . . ." I shook my head. "Happy," I whispered.

"Would it scare you if I told you I want to keep surprising

you as long as you let me?"

I shook my head. "Not at all."

"Good," he said, gripping my hip tighter.

My eyes drifted over his shoulder again and I tensed.

"I think you have an admirer," I said. "Three o'clock. She looks dejected."

I subtly nodded toward the woman who was burning holes through us. She looked at Cameron like he hung the moon, and then looked at me like I'd lassoed it away.

"That's Bianca," he said without glancing her way. "I've been throwing away her baked goods for the past year. She's under the impression I'm a widow. I don't correct her because I wanted her to think I was still grieving. I guess the jig is up now."

"Heartbreaker," I said with a frown. Her anguish was visible in her posture. "She's crushed. I feel terrible."

"Look at me," he commanded. "For once in your life, Miss Fix-It, you aren't going to worry about anyone else but yourself. I never led her on, not for one single minute. The only woman I've been interested in since I started at this school is the one I'm looking at. We don't have that many songs to dance to until I have to abandon you for my post, so keep those beautiful blues on me while I think about the ways I'm going to ruin your virtue when I get you home."

"That's quite an assumption," I said, quirking a brow. "Being so reckless with my virtue."

"I'm going to get so much shit for this from every single one of the boys I coach. Trust me, I'll earn it."

"You already have," I said, caressing the back of his neck with my palm.

The urge to kiss him was overwhelming, but we just swayed along the floor instead. "I'm hoping this covers the '90s rom-com portion of woo," he said with a chuckle.

"I guess I was a little unreasonable in my demands," I said sheepishly.

"If you think you don't deserve this, you're wrong," he said as he rubbed his thumb along my waist. "Whoever had you before me didn't know what the fuck they had."

"So, this isn't the grand finale?"

"Never," he said as he pulled me tighter to him and led me around the dance floor. "Besides, I figure if we set a good enough example for the millennials, maybe they'll follow suit.

"Well, they're definitely watching," I said, sliding my thumb along his jaw.

"Good, then they can see what it looks like when two people coffee."

I laughed. "I wonder what they would think if they knew what you did to your date on the way here."

"Don't remind me. If I get hard now, I'll never be able to coach again. Damn it, woman," he said as he closed his eyes tightly. "Two a day football practices, Trent Marcum picks his nose, Sloppy Joes."

"Sloppy Joes?" I laughed again as he spun me around. "Those disgust you?"

"You have no idea. There's a story behind it."

"There always is."

"It would make this night less romantic if I told you."

"Some other time," I said as the song ended, and Cameron led me off the floor.

"My turn, Coach," a young guy that looked to be around sixteen said as he eyed me inappropriately.

"Not a chance, Marshall," he said as he walked us toward the refreshment table and the jaded baker—who was murdering me with her stare—to get the rundown.

Though Cameron urged me to be selfish, I couldn't help but pray she would get a chance to dance with her own prince someday.

Later that night, after a few hours of watching Cameron chaperone a room of teenage angst, break up two fights, and give a pep talk to one of the players who had cost them last week's game, we strode out of the high school arm in arm.

"I loved watching you in that role. You're a great mentor. You should see the way those kids look at you."

Cameron remained quiet as we got into the limo.

"What's wrong?"

"Nothing," he said, staring out the window as we sat in light traffic.

"Horseshit," I said, grabbing his hand. "Sorry, that was the Bree coming out of me."

Cameron nodded.

"Okay, you didn't laugh, and I *am* funny," I argued. "Spill it."

Pulling away from my hand, he unfastened his tie and loosened his top button.

"Don't get me wrong, I wouldn't trade this for anything, but I hate that the older I get the closer I am to all business, less coaching. I don't . . . I know things could be worse. I could not be coaching at all. At least my stores are doing well, right?"

"Hey," I said as he turned to look at me. "You can coach as long as you want to. If it's your thing, there's nothing wrong with it, right? Just because it didn't happen on the level you wanted it to doesn't mean it couldn't still happen. Just don't give up and there will always be the possibility."

"Tonight isn't about me," he said. "I shouldn't have brought it up."

"I beg to differ, Coach." Pulling his tie free, I straddled his lap and undid a few more buttons.

"I'm going to make the rest of this night *all about you*," I whispered, leaning into him as I pushed the button for the partition before I sank to my knees between his legs.

One of his perfectly sculpted brows lifted as I rubbed his cock through his pants. His reaction was immediate as I unzipped him and gripped him firmly in my hand.

"Sloppy Joes," I whispered with a grin and his dick jumped. Leaning in, I licked the tip of him. His eyes closed, and he let out a string of curses.

"I can just see you now on the sidelines in a suit, salt and pepper hair, keeping your sexy poker face," I said as I pumped his thick dick and kept his watchful gaze before I took the whole of him in my mouth.

Cameron hissed as I pulled my lips away with a pop and pumped him vigorously with my hand. He grinned down at me. "Is this your fantasy or mine?"

I grinned back. "Maybe a little of both?"

He grunted as I put my lips back on him and took him to the back of my throat. "You aren't such a bad coach yourself," he murmured, fisting my hair.

Abbie

Abbie's Mac: Why exactly did you call this meeting here, sir?

Cameron sat comfortably on his side of the table as I surveyed his dress. He looked gorgeous in a cream sweater with a cuffed collar, dark jeans, and light brown boots.
I swear to God the man looked camera-ready no matter the day.
His hair had grown a bit longer and it suited him.

Cameron's Mac: Because we've been spending a lot of time in bed. I need you at a safe distance.

Tilting my head, I gave him an incredulous look.

Abbie's Mac: Are you really cockblocking yourself right now? I think I can control myself, Cameron Bledsoe.

Cameron's Mac: Well, I can't. How 'bout them apples.

And did you just first and last name me, witchy woman?

Abbie's Mac: Did you just Good Will Hunting me, Coach Bledsoe?

We both typed at the same time.

Cameron's Mac: Maybe.

Abbie's Mac: Maybe.

Cameron twisted his lips and then licked them. I could tell he was just as ready to eat up the annoying distance between us. Whatever reason he had us on opposite sides of the fence was apparent in his frown.

Maybe we had been spending a lot of time in body worship, but we were only making up for endless days of staring at each other and trying to live out our fantasies.

And those had added up. Two of our months together had been behind our Macs.

As of late, I was spending a lot of time at the office running the day to day while Kat prepped the staff in endless meetings to implement our changes. We were down to the wire and had barely been able to share a cup of coffee since the New Year.

Cameron was wrapping up basketball season.

Though we slept in the same bed, we didn't see each other as often as we wanted, which only made us hungrier. I didn't see the harm and told him as much in a message.

Abbie's Mac: Are we having an argument right now about how much we love having sex?

Cameron's Mac: I'm more attracted to you than any woman I've ever been with, than any woman *ever*. I'm addicted to your taste, your smell, the sounds you make when I'm touching you. But that's not how we came to be us. I don't want the physical outweighing our connection.

I studied him then narrowed my eyes.
Is this where the other shoe drops? Is he letting me down gently?

Cameron's Mac: No reason to be suspicious. I mean it. I want to keep us grounded. I don't want to lose what we have.

Abbie's Mac: What is it we have?

Cameron's Mac: Nothing I'm willing to proclaim in lieu of telling you privately. But it rhymes with fucking incredible.

I smiled at that.

Abbie's Mac: Okay, Cameron. I'm all yours.

I nodded, and I saw a little relief in his eyes.

Cameron's Mac: Good, that's exactly what I wanted to hear. I'm all yours too. But you know at some point we need to talk about what we don't talk about. I'm ready. I've been ready.

I shook my head and mouthed a "no."

He mouthed "yes."

It was at that moment I realized I didn't want anything coming between us. I was too addicted to the happiness I felt with him. It was a dangerous game because I didn't know how exchanging our forgotten baggage would affect us or how he would view mine with Luke—which seemed to be less of a task to admit the longer we stayed together.

I typed my words slowly, not ready for the answer.

Abbie's Mac: Will it change things between us?

Cameron's expression was more solemn than I'd ever seen it.

Abbie's Mac: Then no.

Cameron's Mac: Things have changed.

Abbie's Mac: But they don't have to.

Cameron's Mac: I meant for the better.

My fingers hovered over the keys.

I knew he loved me.

Isn't saying you're falling the same thing? Can you really stop yourself once you've started? I've never found that possible, especially not with the man sitting across from me.

I knew no matter what his bags held I was in love with him and that wouldn't change. I opted for safe and prayed whatever his held didn't come with a price I couldn't pay.

I stared at him long and hard. Cameron wasn't the type of

man to harbor sick tendencies. But I'd thought the same thing of Luke.

Whatever it was he was trying to confess, I thought it was more major in his mind than it would be in mine. Then again, I was too much of a coward to find out.

He was everything I wanted. Honest to a fault, highly intelligent, self-reliant, successful, thoughtful, and highly sexual, which I didn't know I needed until I found him.

If we could keep going a little longer without our scars weighing us down, I knew the strength of our relationship would grow. It had only been months. Mere months with him and my whole life had changed. I'd been flipped upside down, hit hard with a love I knew I would feel for a lifetime.

Still, I couldn't help but type out the words.

Abbie's Mac: Tell me.

I deleted each letter one by one and sent the coward's response.

Abbie's Mac: Not yet. Please.

His posture told me he was just as wary of the exchange, but he was calling it, and I still wasn't ready to show my cards. I wasn't ashamed of what happened. I wasn't even afraid to talk about it, but I didn't *want* to.

Our relationship was too perfect. Too right.

Fuck Luke. He had no place in our lives. We were happy. That was our present and future; the past could only disrupt it.

Abbie's Mac: Not tonight.

Cameron's Mac: Okay.

Abbie's Mac: Okay?

He gave me a small smile, despite his worry etched features.

Cameron's Mac: Love your cup.
I lifted the mug up that read *You are the luckiest guy in the world. I would love to be dating me.* and gave him a wistful grin.

Abbie's Mac: Don't blame me for all the bedding. You know I've never been this horny in my adult life. You've changed me.

Cameron's Mac: I'm proud my new girlfriend is insatiable. Who knew you were such a pervert?

Abbie's Mac: Your wicked tongue drew it out of me. I have to say I'm just as surprised as you are.

Cameron's Mac: Spread your legs a little, baby.

My lips parted at his candor, but I didn't hesitate to show him my lacy, bright pink panties.

Cameron's Mac: Nice.

Abbie's Mac: They'd look better on my floor.

Cameron scanned the café. We were mostly alone in our section. And those sitting in it had their heads buried in their devices.

Cameron's Mac: Move them to the side.

Abbie's Mac: What happened to getting back to the basics of us?

Cameron's eyes stayed heated as he adjusted his cock and began to type.

My movement stopped as he kept his eyes glued to my hand that slipped beneath the table before I pushed my panties to the side.

Cameron's Mac: Fuuuuuuck.

I was tempted to type with one hand.

Abbie's Mac: Say the word and we can be at my place in minutes.

Cameron's Mac: Abbie . . .

Abbie's Mac: I keep thinking about the night in the back of the limo. I want a repeat.

I licked my lips to show which part of said indiscretion I was talking about.

Cameron's Mac: Jesus. You will be my undoing. Behave yourself.

Abbie's Mac: Too bad.

Since the winter formal, we'd done nothing but feast on

the other, and even on Super Bowl Sunday—a day Cameron donned a holiday—it took a back seat to our thirst.

We'd managed to catch the end of the game at Pint—a local pub on Milwaukee Ave and Cameron's favorite—with Bree and Anthony. But upon our disheveled arrival, they both knew what we'd been up to.

With my family, Super Bowl Sunday together was tradition due to my dad's fandom, and my brother was more than peeved when I told him my whereabouts.

"All that guilt about keeping with the family and you ditch Gorman tradition to slum it where?"

"Pint, it's a little pub in Wicker. Cameron's favorite."

"You are so on my shit list," Oliver whined.

"Hey, for once I get to be the bad kid. I'm cool with that."

"I heard that," my mother yelled in the background.

"Have fun, kiddo," my father yelled after. My dad was always the encouraging one.

"Get me off speaker phone, Dr. Dick."

"Bring him here," Oliver said with authority.

"Not yet. Soon."

"Yeah, that's what you said last time," he warned.

"Don't do that, Oliver. You need to trust me. I've had a hard enough time doing it myself."

"Fine. Bree likes him?"

"Yes," I said with a grin as I watched Bree and Cameron go back and forth as I stood in a quieter spot in the corner of the pub. I was dressed in the oversized jersey Cameron had gifted me hours earlier. Only, as I got dressed, he'd decided to peel it back off.

"Then I guess I'll give you a pass. But, Abbie . . . just be careful."

"He's not Luke. Not by a longshot."

"I believe you."

"Good."

"I'll pick up your slack this time, but you owe me."

"I owe you nothing, Oliver, and I'm all too happy to recount the days and dates of the reasons why."

"Whatever," he said with a chuckle.

"Love you, bye."

Right at the moment I ended the call, Cameron looked around the bar in search of me, and when his eyes found mine, he gave me his 'come-hither' finger. I loved that finger, and the hand, and the man attached to it.

We spent the second half of the game downing beers and catching each other's eyes. I knew all too well it was the honeymoon phase of our relationship. I was no fool, and I was going to eat up every minute of it.

And sitting across from him in the café, all I could think of was the way he felt when he was closer, so much closer.

I knew Cameron was thinking the same as he engaged me while I ran my finger along the edge of my cup, then sucked the caramel off, inching my legs further apart.

His gaze hot on my hand, need ate up his features. I felt powerful.

"I couldn't help but notice you sitting over here all alone."

I nearly jumped out of my skin at the voice to the left of me. I clamped my legs shut and glared at Cameron, who was so entranced by the movement below he had failed to give me the heads up above.

Confused eyes turned icy as he stared holes through the man who spoke to me in a low beckon.

"I would love to buy you a cup of coffee," he said as I twisted my head in the politest reception I could muster.

Cameron's eyes blazed as I gave attention to the

interloper, who was oblivious to the tension in the air.

"I'm Patrick," he said, taking the seat next to mine. "I was just admiring you and wanted to see if you would be interested in more coffee or maybe some lunch?"

I gave him a sincere smile. He seemed like a nice enough guy. And four months ago, I might have considered it.

He was the light to Cameron's dark features—blond hair, blue eyes, and pale skin like mine.

But he wasn't Cameron, so that made him not my type.

"Thank you so much for the offer, but I'm seeing someone."

"Does this guy have any idea how beautiful you are?"

Cameron's Mac: I will strangle that fucking douche bag with his own necktie. Tell him to fuck off, Abbie.

"He's told me once or twice," I told Patrick with a shrug.

Cameron's Mac: I told you last night before I stuck my tongue between your legs and you called me Jesus.

I bit my lips to keep from laughing.

Cameron's eyes fired, and his nostrils flared. He'd never been so possessive, but he'd never had reason to be.

Cameron's Mac: Don't play games, get rid of him. My cock is so hard right now, I can't stand, but I will, woman. I'll show the whole coffeehouse my hard-on. You want that on your conscience?

"So, are you two serious? Because I would hate to catch him slipping," Patrick said carefully. I let his arrogance slide past me as the man opposite me began to white-knuckle his table.

"You know, I'm not sure. We were just talking about it. He seems to think we're just sexual."

Cameron's Mac: Nice twist full of bullshit, Abigail. I will club you on the head Neanderthal style with this cock and drag you out of the coffee shop if you push me an inch further.

I let out a loud laugh and threw my head back. Cameron's eyes flared again while he scrutinized Patrick and then kicked back in his seat in challenge.

He closed his laptop and packed it in his leather bag. He was done asking. It was a power play and clear alpha move on his part. I found it sexy as hell, albeit redundant.

But he wanted me. He made it clear. And in no way did I want to ruin that with any sort of game.

"I'm in love with him," I said to Patrick as I spoke directly to Cameron. "I've never been in so deep with anyone. I couldn't even entertain your invitation for a second. So, again, thank you, Patrick, but it's very serious."

Cameron stood then. Our jig was up as Patrick looked between us, read our posture, sheepishly apologized, and was ignored by us both as he walked away.

Cameron's eyes nailed me where I sat as he made quick work of grabbing his bag and getting to my table.

"Let's go," he said as I gathered my things. I tried to read his expression and came up empty.

I couldn't tell if he was still angry while he followed me out, his hand possessively on my lower back, guiding me. When we stepped outside the café, he gripped my hand and began to walk toward my house.

He took long strides, and I struggled to keep up. His steps purposeful and his silence agony, I stumbled behind him in a plea.

"Cameron? What's wrong?"

He ignored me and kept moving while the chill, both in the air and in his demeanor, sobered me up.

Was I wrong? Had I misjudged his feelings, his words? He'd all but confessed his love and intentions for us.

"Cameron, please say something," I begged as I took two steps to his one. He raced us through my gate and pounded up my steps.

"I'm sorry if—"

"Open the door, Abbie," he ordered as I fumbled with my keys, my heart heavy.

Stupid, stupid. I should have never confessed how I felt first. But did I?

It didn't seem possible with all that had happened between us.

He kicked the door shut while I rushed through my living room toward my kitchen. Reeling from the change in his behavior, I opened my fridge and grabbed a water, gulping it down as he stood on the other side of the counter, hands in his pockets.

My blue eyes were engulfed by the intense green blaze and I swallowed while the sweat dried on my forehead.

"Say it again."

"Cameron," I pleaded, terrified by the tone of his voice. "The moment has passed, don't you think?"

"No," he argued quickly and shook his head. "Not at all. Say it."

"Maybe I don't want to," I said with a shaky voice. "Clearly,

I got the wrong impression."

"Clearly, you don't know the lengths I would go to hear you say those words to me again, Abbie. Say them."

"No," I said with contempt. "Maybe you think I'm taking our relationship lightly, but I'm not. This isn't a game for me. I got a little carried away back there, but in no way should you punish me for saying how I felt in that moment."

"I'm not punishing you."

"Feels like it," I said, my pulse pounding in my ears.

"And how do you feel now?"

I crossed my arms in front of me and spoke low. "The same."

He audibly exhaled. "Then say those words to me."

I scowled at him. "What kind of head trip are you on?"

"Why can't you just do it?"

"Because I *meant* it, okay? And you're acting a little too . . . you're scaring me."

I was shaking, and he could see it. He moved toward me as he spoke and gripped my shoulders.

"You're scared?"

"Yes," I whispered."

"Good, because with you I'm a lot of fucking things. I'm a lot crazy about you, I'm a lot terrified, I'm a lot possessive, and that's new to me. I'm dangerously in love with you, so much so that I'm going to lose my fucking mind if you don't tell me again that you feel the same. Because I *love you*, Abbie. I have since before I confessed I was falling, and I kept it to myself for so long that it's been agony waiting for you. So please. Say it."

My lips parted, and the words fell easily.

"I love you. I do, so much," I said as he closed the space between us and smashed his mouth to mine.

Captive in his hold, he kissed me mercilessly, his tongue

flicking over mine in long, languid strokes. His seduction was on the back burner of his emotion-filled kiss. I felt the hesitance in his touch only next to insistence that I believe his earnest heart over the bulge in his pants. Our connection only turned to fire when I pulled away on a breath.

"Please touch me, Cameron. It's much too late to keep us from getting burned," I begged as I gripped the back of his head and raked my fingers through the hair there.

"I love you," he murmured as he trailed a soft kiss down my jaw. "Fuck, I need you." He lifted my hands above my head and held them there. "I just don't want to screw this up."

"You won't do that by touching me," I promised as he lifted my sweater over my head before his impatient lips found mine. Mouths fused, I unzipped his slacks while he pulled my leggings down mid-thigh before he turned me to face the counter.

He pressed my head down, flattening my breasts as he pressed himself fully inside me. We both sank a little once connected.

"It's yours, Cameron. It's all yours."

"Fuck yes, it is," he said as he reached around and pressed a finger to my clit while I hung on the tips of my toes. Impaled, I loved every second of it as he pulled back and pushed in deeper than he'd ever gone.

I felt myself fold then, my body convulsing as he sped up his thrusts, his powerful thighs anchoring me while he pressed in and hit me so deeply I grappled with the stars I saw.

"Yes," he hissed out aggressively as if he were angry I hadn't waited for him.

"Please more, please," I begged as he sank in deep and then pulled back, pressing me down again and pushing in just . . . so. My orgasm shot through me in waves, my legs shaking from his deep penetration.

"Oh my God!" I screamed as my body detonated from the inside out.

"That's possession, baby. That's the part that I need to own aside from what beats in your chest. I'm taking the rest," he whispered before he licked the skin of my back while he feathered his lips across what he left wet.

I was still trembling with my release when he reared back, pressed his finger to my clit, and hit me again. My legs gave out beneath me, and Cameron caught me by the hips while I gripped my counter for leverage.

I couldn't stop my body's response. I just kept falling apart with every other strong stroke, and he refused to let up.

"Cameron," I begged as he slid in precisely, letting me know he knew exactly what he was doing, and his intent to claim me. He'd always known.

"I can't. I can't."

"Come," he commanded as he swiveled back in, finishing me again. My mind blown, I realized it was his last card to play, and he'd waited to use it because I meant more to him than the act of sex.

And he could've so easily used this side of him for leverage. Our sex had always been intimate, hot, incredible, but something about the way he took me that night was primal, animalistic. He'd been an expert at this card and refused to use it to get what he wanted from me, but by playing it, he claimed all of me.

"I love you," I breathed out through clenched teeth as he took me again and again, breaking my hold on reality as I lost myself in his love and his body.

I was owned from that moment forward, irrevocably his.

We sank onto my kitchen floor after endless minutes of mind-blowing sex, and I curled into his lap, our clothes still partially on as we caught our breath.

His face was still intent as he looked down at me cradled in his hold.

"Abbie, I had no idea what this would be. You have to believe I didn't know it was you I was looking for. This, us, it means everything to me. I didn't expect this."

"Me either."

He held me tightly to him and kissed me again, sweeping me away.

21

Abbie

"Cameron, your phone," I said with a groan. I heard the shower running as I looked on the nightstand.

"Cameron," I said a little louder.

I looked over at it to see twenty missed calls from the same number flashing along with a few notification texts, so I carried it into the bathroom.

"Cameron," I repeated, annoyed, as he opened the shower door, his beautiful body distracting me.

"It's early," he said. "What are you doing up?"

"Your phone is ringing off the hook again. Put the damn thing on silent like normal people."

"I normally do, sorry." He eyed the phone while it rang in my hand.

"It's a local area code," I said. "Do you want it?"

He turned off the shower and began toweling off. "I'll call them back."

"What are you doing awake? It's—" I looked at the clock

on his phone "—four o'clock in the morning."

"I have a seven o'clock meeting," he said, pressing a kiss to my lips before retrieving his phone. "Get back in bed."

"We just went to sleep," I said, grumbling before I made my way to bed and pulled my comforter over me.

Cameron walked out a few minutes later, straightening his tie. I loved watching him dress for work. I reveled in the package he presented to the world and the fact that I was the only woman who got to open it every night.

"You must be so tired," I said, feeling my own exhaustion set in.

"I'm good," he said, leaning over me, giving me a whiff of his heavenly scent before he pressed a kiss to my forehead. "I've got meetings all day, but I'll be back tonight. Dinner?"

"Sure," I said.

"I'm telling you now, tonight, we talk."

That time I didn't object. I nodded.

"Okay."

"I love you, Abbie, so fucking much," he murmured as he brought his lips to mine.

He left me a sated believer.

I woke up later that morning with a stretch and lazy smile. We'd done nothing the night before but make serious love in every sense of the word. And in the middle of the night, in a snooze filled recoup, we reached for each other with the need to stay connected. He'd taken me again and again as we tangled my sheets, drenched.

I was physically spent but had the promise of so much

more to get me through my morning routine. Between the sheets, Cameron had much more to offer than I could have dreamt of, but the evidence of his appetite stung between my legs as I gripped the pillow full of his clean scent and inhaled.

I clung to those promises. They told me I had a new life to look forward to, one filled with we instead of I. A happy tear trickled down my cheek as I thought of dancing with Cameron at Bree's wedding.

Futuristic visions flooded my mind of repeats of opening gifts together on Christmas morning at his father's house, of more gluttonous dinners at Mrs. Zingaro's, of another New Year's kiss.

I already had those memories with Cameron but vied for more. And we hadn't missed a day together since the beginning of the year.

I knew without a shadow of a doubt, the next week when cupid came to taunt the single thirty-somethings of Wicker Park, I would finally be spared.

For the first time since we started dating, I dared myself to dream of bigger milestones. At that moment, I didn't care if marriage was in the cards, I wasn't dreaming of our future children. *Yet.* It had only been months and that didn't matter in comparison to how desperately in love we were.

But I knew, without a doubt, any life with him as my best friend and lover would suffice no matter what we turned out to be. One day I would want more, dream of more, but for the moment I was content with the hope of us and how it felt to be with him.

I wanted to make him smile, make him happy. That was my only want. And needing him was a given.

I needed Cameron and he needed me right back. He'd been just as starved to give his heart away, and it was only until we were both certain about the other that we took the leap with faith and trust on both our parts.

Sometimes I think I placed too much importance on having what I thought I was missing. Again, my mother was right. For the first time in my life I wanted what I had.

Sweet relief.

I found him.

Well technically, he found me.

But I wasn't keeping score.

I smiled at my reflection as I went through my morning ritual, brushed my teeth, and hesitantly washed the smell of him off my skin.

On the train to work, I relived every minute of our time together.

Walking down the street toward Preston Corp, I swayed my hips as "Closer" by the Chainsmokers serenaded my trek, though the idea of the big reveal happening that night put a slight damper on my mood. But if he was sure we could work through whatever we unpacked, I had faith.

When I exited the elevator, Kat looked over at me from her office and read my face. I didn't hide it.

"Oh, wow, *wow*," she remarked as I beamed at her behind her desk.

"Yeah, I'm totally fucking in love."

"I'm so happy for you," she said with a genuine smile. "A little jealous, but happy."

"That used to be my line," I said as I dropped my purse at my desk and walked into her office.

"So, what happened?"

"We just confessed. I mean, it's been there for a while, but we kind of just opened the gates and it was everything. He's so perfect."

She shook her head. "That's great, Abbie. You deserve it."

"Damned right I do. No more dateless weddings."

"Maybe you have your own to look forward to," she said softly. I saw it then, the fatigue.

"Don't worry about today, okay? I've got it handled. Look at it like just another meeting."

She nodded solemnly. "I need a change. If they let me go, maybe it's a sign."

"Don't think that way. You love it here. I can tell. We'll get this handled. You've seen the reports. Piece of cake, okay?"

She nodded before handing me a cup of coffee, just the way I liked it.

"So, tell me what's been going on."

Before I got the chance, several executives walked out of the elevator. Kat visibly cringed at their arrival and whispered to me.

"This really is it, isn't it? Are you done after today?"

I followed her toward the conference room. "I'll be done here, yes, but I'll still have a few things to tie up from home."

She threw her shoulders back and looked at me earnestly. "I just want this to be over."

"I've got you," I swore, every bit as confident as I was the day we'd met.

Nine hours later, we walked out of that meeting with matching smiles.

"I can't believe it. Not only did you save my job, you made me look good. You're a miracle worker, Abbie."

"I told you. You are capable of running the division. It was just a matter of time."

"Walk me down?" she asked as she grabbed her purse.

"Sure," I said, checking my phone for a text from Cameron. He'd been quiet that afternoon, but he knew it was an important day for me at the office. I sent a text of my own.

I hope your day was as good as mine, Coach. XO

"I really can't thank you enough," Kat said as we walked out of the elevator.

When we pressed through the heavy set of double doors into the freezing cold, I looked over at her. "Maybe we could get together sometime?"

"Absolutely," she said, though I was sure her response was plastic.

I'd had one too many office friendships that only lasted the duration of my time on the job. Our relationship had been far too one-sided for me to pursue it any further.

"Damn it, there's my husband."

"You didn't drive today?"

"No, I wanted to pick up some things I ordered, that's why I told him to come and get me, but of course he can't even get that right and shows up in my car! Gah, the man's incompetence knows no bounds. So, I'll call you?" She asked as she stepped toward the curb toward a flashy sedan.

"Of course," I said as she thought better of leaving me with a promise of a phone call then hugged me. I hugged her back in surprise as she spoke.

"Thanks for, well . . . everything. I'll text you. I swear I will."

"Sounds great. Good luck," I said. "With everything. And try not to kill him."

She laughed and took a step back before opening the door and lashing out. "Jefferson, I *told* you to bring the *SUV*."

Curious, I peeked in the car, a nervous smile on my face for the poor man who was probably humiliated by being talked to like an infant.

Somewhere in my imagination, I expected to see a prematurely balding man or something less desirable and was pleasantly surprised when I took in his wool trench coat, well-fitted suit, but froze when I met his ocean green eyes.

No.

My eyes traced the five o'clock shadow that hours prior had left fresh marks on my breasts, between my thighs, and on my neck.

The man stared back at me, stunned, as his wife got into the car and berated him while my heart shattered on the sidewalk.

No.

My throat burned as my soul tore away and threatened departure.

"What are you waiting for?" she snapped, following his gaze to meet mine. "Oh, yeah, Abbie, this is my husband, Jefferson. Jefferson, Abbie."

Eyes locked, I coughed out a sob as my chest screamed with ache.

Neither of us said a word as she shut the door after muttering an, "I'll call you, okay? Thanks again, Abbie."

I could hear her incessant but muffled bitching as Cameron sat behind the wheel, his eyes still fixed on mine.

No.

No.

That's not him. That's not the man I love.

This can't be wrong. This can't be wrong. I wasn't wrong.

Another sob I couldn't hold back escaped as I let myself

break on the cement. There was no saving me, nothing to catch me as I toppled over, helpless, and splintered into millions of tiny pieces.

And every single one of those pieces loved him.

I dropped my bag and looked down at my hands, expecting them to be filthy. What had I done? What had he done to me? Why!? A scream lay idle on my tongue.

I shook my head feverishly, refusing to believe that the man in the car was mine. Because he wasn't. He had never been.

The blood left my face as the driver door opened and he stood to face me over the hood of the car.

"Abbie, look at me."

Helpless, I looked to my love and best friend for help. But it was all wrong because he was the one responsible for the bleeding.

I gave myself another selfish second on the street to try to make sense of it.

"What did you do?" I asked in a whisper. "Oh, my God, what did you do?" I said as I fisted my hands on my chest. "What did you do?!"

Cameron moved to shut the door, and my eyes snapped to the passenger side as Kat yelled at him. "Jefferson, what in the hell do you think you're doing? You're embarrassing me! Get in the car!"

She couldn't see his face, and I just wanted her shrieking to stop. I had to get away.

I grabbed my bag and let my instinct to run kick in.

"Abbie!"

Jefferson. I didn't even know his real name. I knew nothing real about him.

It was all a lie.

One.

Huge.

Lie.

He was never mine. Not made for me. Not my soul mate, not my other half. Not my missing piece. He was someone else's husband.

A liar, a cheat, a goddamned figment of my overactive imagination.

And I'd never be the same woman without him.

22

Cameron

I SAW HER END US. I SAW IT HAPPEN. I DID MY BEST TO straighten my face and got back into the car. It took seconds to undo months of the trust we built. In those seconds all hope for my newly paved road had been obliterated by the tinderbox that was my wife.

"What in the hell do you think you're doing?" Kat spat out while I stared in the direction Abbie fled as Kat ranted. There was only one reason I picked her up and explaining myself to her wasn't a part of it.

Abbie was gone in every sense of the word. There was no use trying to catch up with her. She would never forgive me. And I couldn't blame her. I was selfish to make us happen.

Months of indecision to come forward and do the right fucking thing had ruined everything. Despite her pleas to keep things as they were I should have manned up and demanded we exchange truths.

Still, I knew the one I harbored would be far more of a game changer than hers. I would never be able to make her understand. And seeing Kat and me in that capacity, as a couple, even though it was a lie—Kat's lie—would do the most damage.

"Jefferson, I told you to bring the SUV. I told you I needed to pick up some things." I wiped an open palm down my face.

I'd been so close to the unattainable, the impossible. Of breathing life again, of having her. All I had to do was be honest, but honesty could never have saved me. She'd judged me standing there on the sidewalk. She snapped our connection and erected a wall leaving us both standing on opposite sides with no way through. I was shut out the minute she saw me, but that meant nothing to my heart.

I would fight with every ounce of my being to get her back. I would make her understand, no matter how much pride it cost me, no matter what I had to reveal to her.

Even with that mindset, even as I tried to convince myself that I could tell Abbie anything, I knew the whole truth would be the hardest thing for me to give her.

"Once again you've tuned me out. Just forget it. Jesus, you're useless. Just take me home," Kat snapped. "I'm so sick of this."

I ignored her, while I looked for any sign of Abbie. When Kat's shrieking could no longer be overlooked, I took a deep breath and tried to compose myself.

"Today you're going to sign those papers, Kat. I'm tired of asking. I'm telling," I said calmly. She waved me away with her hand and opened her purse. I snatched the pill bottle from her hand and tossed it to the back of the car out of reach.

"Stop this car right now," she snapped. "Jefferson!" She shrieked.

I didn't answer to that name anymore. That was a nickname a woman gave to a man whom she loved when he was on her shit list. My middle name, a name I never wanted to hear again. A name that had been muddled by wrath, addiction, and hate. The joke hadn't been funny in years.

"I don't know who the hell you think you are," Kat snapped as she twisted in her seat in an attempt to reach the bottle and I grabbed her coat by the pocket and pulled her back to sit.

I looked for bitterness in my words and found resolution instead. "I'm no one. I was your husband for a few years, and your punching bag for another few. I'm done. I left you a year ago. Your denial is over. We're doing this."

She scoffed. "I'm not in denial. It's you who needs a reality check."

"I want my goddamn life back, Kat. It's time you sobered up."

"Oh, fuck you," she hissed. "And what was that back there, huh? How do you know Abbie?"

"Don't ask questions you don't want the answer to," I warned. "I'm moving on and I'm not going to come the next time you call or any other time after for that matter. The only reason I picked you up tonight was to watch you sign those papers."

Kat was still inching toward the back seat when I scared her with the aggression in my voice. Slowing to a stop at the light, I studied her hostile profile. "Look at me, damn it."

Her blue eyes snapped to mine and then narrowed.

"Kat, I'm done."

"I don't know what's gotten into you, but you need to get your shit together."

I couldn't muster an ironic laugh as I smashed the gas and took off like a shot. She was the perfect picture of denial, hauntingly beautiful without a soul to sell.

"You will grant my divorce *today*. Write in whatever

contingency you want, Kat. Rob me blind. Take it all, you have the house, take the rest. Take half my stores. Take everything you think you're entitled to, but you don't get the rest of my life."

Her eyes clouded with anger, not fear, or regret, feelings I'd hoped and prayed to manifest in the endless months I tried to save my wife and my marriage. "You don't mean that. You're just . . . tense."

For the first time in years, I exploded. "I'M FUCKING DONE WITH YOU! You're a drug addict and you've emasculated me at every turn since the night you got hurt. I don't love you anymore. Our marriage is over. You've turned us into something too riddled to fucking figure out. I can't do this anymore. I won't."

"Oh, I did this?" She said with an accusing tone. "Me?"

"Jesus Christ, not the blame game again."

"You are the one who jarred my back!"

"Fine it's my fault, but your career was already over. You had therapy and a multitude of ways to get healthier since I jarred your back. But you are the one who denied recovery and turned yourself into this fucking mess."

My words had barely made the air between us as her fist connected with my jaw and I jerked back in my seat scanning the road to get my bearings. I was halfway aware of where we were on the road when she landed her second blow.

"Kat, I'm driving. Stop!" But she didn't.

The hits just kept coming and I had to force us off the busy street cutting off two cars in an attempt to get her under control. Throwing the car in park, I was blindsided when she connected with my temple.

"Jesus, Kat stop!" I growled as she came at me full force. All of her anger front and center. She struck a few more times before I gripped her hard and shook her. "Goddammit stop! It's over just . . . stop!" She glared at me, her eyes full of hate.

It was never me she was angry at. It was never me she wanted to hurt, but it was me who dealt with both after she lost the last of her hopes to age and addiction rather than injury which had turned into the perfect excuse.

When I met Kat, she was full of vitality even at thirty-four and had the world at her fingertips. She was a retired gymnast with big dreams of opening a chain of gyms. She wore her future in her smile. We had similar dreams and insatiable appetites for life and more than enough lust between the two of us.

Two years into our marriage she injured her back after she got sloppy drunk and claimed I dropped her while we were having sex on Max's boat. The truth was she'd lost all mobility by the time she got to me half naked and I wasn't sober or alert enough to catch her when she flew at me. I shouldered the blame, giving her an out to shield her from embarrassment. We'd even made a joke about it in the hospital, while she waited connected to a morphine drip before she got the news the surgery was inevitable.

She'd blamed me ever since for the agony she endured afterward. In a year of unimaginable hell, I helped her through it all, the surgery, the pain she dealt with daily and the rehab, but the rehab she truly needed never came.

Kat barely let me touch her after the 'accident', surgery and recovery. And once her anger surfaced, it was over for us. She'd taken to pills to numb herself and I'd tried to be there until self-preservation kicked in.

The therapist I kept appointments with—that Kat never bothered to show for—said she was in a mental state of paralysis. That her mind couldn't accept her body's limitations, so she abused the pills to make herself feel capable again without the pain. Months after her surgery, Kat gave up on her life-long dream of mentoring other gymnasts due to those limitations. She turned up her nose at my every solution.

And still she blamed me, and I let her, but nothing helped. Her misplaced anger only grew, and my resentment began.

All she saw when she looked at me was someone to guilt and all I saw when I looked at her was a woman who had to get off on narcotics to function. And the scary part was that she *was* functioning, picture perfect to anyone who didn't get close enough to see the cracks. But those cracks only got magnified by her wrath and I was the chosen one on the receiving end of it all.

I was finished pretending that our marriage hadn't ended the first time she took one of those pills to get high and escape the reality of her life with me. I was done pretending I wanted things to stay the same, to sink into her pit of despair with her and stop living. I selfishly let myself live while she drowned, hoping I could do it for both of us. But I was empty. So utterly empty.

Three years into my marriage I realized my wife was a spoiled, entitled, wreck of a woman who needed things fixed by everyone else, to feel safe. I couldn't fix her, so she broke me first with her words and then with her fists.

And Abbie . . . Abbie was much-needed evidence life was still worth living. I wanted to tell her about Kat before we got physical, but I got caught up in our whirlwind and I never wanted out. Being with Abbie gave me clarity. I brought nothing of my life with Kat into the new relationship, and it wasn't in vain.

I discovered more of who I was without the battle scars of my marriage blurring my vision. And I felt better, though I could never deny my life before Abbie, and I had every intention of sharing that part of it with her. But without that burden of truth, I felt free to be the man I wanted to be with her, where I'd been paralyzed for years with Kat.

I'd already separated myself from my wife in every way. Kat's denial was toxic, so much so that my final attempt at finishing what I started when I left her backfired into a loss I would never recover from.

I lost Abbie.

Goddammit!

Kat imploded in the seat beside me as I stopped her again from retrieving the bottle from the back seat.

"Can you," I muttered as I wiped some blood from the fresh cut on my lip and studied the dark purple polka dot next to my eye in the rearview—no doubt a result of the connection from her wedding ring, "for one fucking minute, talk to me like an adult. I've been good to you, Kat, even when I shouldn't have. Doesn't that mean anything to you?"

"I hate you," she screamed as she did her best to get a rise out of me.

Defeated, I stayed mute until I pulled over to the shell of the home we used to share before she jumped out. I whispered the truth under my breath. "I hate you too."

I dialed her father's number as she ranted and smashed her palms against the passenger window. "Unlock the fucking car!"

It was no use. If I didn't give the pills to her she would be roaming some shady neighborhood to get a fix in a matter of minutes. Kat slammed the car door after retrieving her bottle and made a beeline for the house.

When she opened the door, she would see the petition for divorce on the counter. I had no doubt the divorce papers would be looked over the way they had been for months. She would take a few pills and make herself busy until she took two

Xanax downing them with a glass of blanc to pass out. In the morning, she would take two more pills before her feet hit the floor, and two more with her ten o'clock cup of coffee.

With Kat safely inside, I got out of the car as her father answered. "Cameron?"

"Billy."

"You ended it," he said with a sigh.

"It's been over. I don't know what she's told you, but I left her a year ago. I can't do this anymore. I won't do this anymore. She's an addict. She needs your help. And I think tonight is going to be bad."

"Can you just sit tight until—"

"Listen to me," I yelled. "I'm done. I've bled enough over this shit, Billy. I'm done chasing her around the streets. I'm not taking her phone calls anymore. I'm done. If you give a damn about your daughter at all, get her help. Get her clean."

"I'm sorry, Cameron. I'm leaving the office now."

Walking over to the mailbox I tossed Kat's keys inside before I hopped into my SUV. My plan had been simple. Pick her up without any way of escape and make her face reality. But my plans were as delusional as Kat remained. Tomorrow she would call me without giving it a second thought. It wasn't that phone call I was afraid of avoiding. It was the one I would avoid that could save her life.

I coughed out my emotion as four years of my life was laid to rest and guilty tears soaked my face, for Kat, for Abbie and for the abomination that had become my life, my marriage, and my new quest for happiness.

Every light on the house went on as Kat moved around in another pill-induced rage. I could hear her screaming at me from inside of the house, daring me to set foot inside.

I wiped the clotted blood from my lip and held it in front

of me before I glanced back at the house remembering the day we moved in. So much had changed, except for the number outside of the mailbox on the porch.

The first few years of our marriage that number meant life and the rest of mine. The number was now the bane of my existence. It mocked me and told me I was a fool though a certain level of relief passed over me when I knew I would never have to see it again.

No matter what happened to Kat from that moment on, I wouldn't be there to witness it. I couldn't.

And I had to let the fear go and I tried my best as I drove away.

I thought I'd hit rock bottom the first time Kat hit me. I was wrong.

Cameron

Shivering in my jacket, I watched her approach. She stopped when she spotted me from her gate.

"Abbie," I said, moving to stand on her porch, my breath blowing in visible clouds of regret in front of me. It was well after midnight, and I hated that I was itching to find out where she'd been. I hated the hypocrite I was, but with her, I couldn't rationalize anything I felt.

It seemed such a surreal predicament. I'd never felt so out of control in loving someone. I was terrified, and when I confessed as much, and she confirmed I wasn't alone, it was the most beautiful thing I'd ever felt. At that moment, I felt cursed, like I'd lost every right to know anything at all about her.

It was enough to make me lunge for her, to grasp onto her, and beg her for any breath she gave me. In the memory of that feeling, a split second, I went from a man with an apology to a man begging for his ability to breathe. She did that to me. I had to make her understand I would suffocate without her. That I'd been breathing all wrong before we'd met.

I wiped my eyes of the emotion that threatened as she attempted to push past me, and I gently gripped her shoulders and forced her to face me. The skin of her cheeks was splotched red, and tear soaked.

"Abbie, please. I was going to tell you everything tonight. I tried. I swear to God, I just needed to be with you first. Fuck, this is coming out all wrong."

I swallowed hard, praying the right words would come. Tears clouded her vision and she did nothing to hide her hurt. Every hitched breath, every anguished cry seeped into my chest. I was ruined by her evident pain. So fucking ruined. And I had no way of getting through to her without permission she would never give. No amount of begging would do it, but I pressed on anyway with the glimmer of hope that was us. Everything we'd built. Everything we knew about the other.

"Please."

The look in her eye leveled me as her hurt morphed into anger and my fear set in.

"There's nothing you can say," she cried. "*Nothing.*"

Her voice was raw when she spoke, inches away but it might as well have been a universe. "Leave and don't come back. I don't ever want to hear from you again. Please respect that. Please just leave me alone."

"Just let me talk to you. Let me explain."

"Whatever excuse you have, no matter what it is will never be good enough. It's over. It's so over." She choked on her words as my chest sank with the weight of them.

"That's not us, Abbie. We don't deal in absolutes. That's not what we're about."

Her lips parted, her eyes incredulous. "Was that always going to be your excuse? This is different, and you know it."

"It's not." If I had any chance of getting through to her, I had to remind her of us. "This is exactly what it's about. I need you to forget every conclusion you've drawn for one second and remember why we started this. Everything about what's happening right now is *then*. I left her and filed for divorce eight months before I met you. It's only been prolonged due to her mental health. Abbie, she's a drug addict and a liar. I know that sounds like a cop-out but it's the truth. And I can almost guarantee anything she may have told you about me is a lie. I made a huge mistake by not telling you sooner, but I swear to God it's over between us. It has been over for *years*. Kat refused to acknowledge it, and that's why I picked her up tonight. I wanted our divorce final. So we, you and me, could be free to be what we are. For our future. That's the *only* reason. Please believe me. I'm not that kind of man, and you don't believe it, or you don't want to. I *know* you don't want to believe it. I can prove every word I'm saying is true. I can take those doubts away from you. I can make you believe me, believe in me again."

I didn't know if it was the truth, and I hated myself for telling her things that may border on more lies, but I wanted to believe it because she made me believe. Her love made me feel like a king, a god, even if I was the Judas of our story.

I stared into her bloodshot eyes. She loved me, without a doubt, but it was the pain in them that I feared. I knew what it was capable of. It was always the pain that twisted love into a tragedy. Expectations ruined the rest.

"The phone calls," she said in realization, "this morning, that was her?" Without admission, she jerked away from me, the look in her eyes eating away at me by the second. It was too familiar to me and foreign with her.

She was tearing me apart piece by piece with her anger and it could only destroy us. I knew all too well. I'd lived it.

"I was trying to give you what you wanted. You didn't want to know." She couldn't hear me, she couldn't hear a single word I was saying. I'd never felt so helpless. Even after all I'd been through with Kat.

"I don't know you," she whispered between us. "I don't know you."

"That's not true, you know that's not true."

"Of all the questions I should have asked," she said faintly as a tear trickled down her cheek, the light from her porch highlighting the sight of it as it sliced my chest. "The question I should have asked . . ." she said with a humorless laugh. Her eyes seared into mine, icy blue steel. "Tell me you're not married, Cameron. Please tell me you're not married."

"Abbie, I wanted to tell you, I tried to tell you."

"You hid behind our arrangement. It's the same damn thing as lying, and you lied to me this morning! You lied to me and you told me you loved me!"

I swallowed hard, my back pressed against the rock that was my heart and the hard place I'd forced myself into.

"Tell me you're not married, Cameron."

"I'm married." I only let that truth rest a half a second. "Separated—"

It was the sting of her hand and the sound of it connecting that distorted everything. The feel of it altered every intention I had by showing up at her door. The defiant look on her face and challenge in her eyes brought forth some part of me I didn't identify with and took over at that moment. The shock filtered and remained the only thing I focused on until the anger set in.

The pieces of myself I was most proud of slipped out of my reach as I splintered.

And then I snapped.

"Don't you ever lay a goddamned hand on me in anger ever again! Keep your fucking hands to yourself, do you hear me!?" I caught her retreating hand by the wrist. "Never again!"

Abbie shrieked in surprise and cowered in fear as she watched me stand to my full height while I seethed with outrage. The pain that radiated from her palm streamlined to the inner workings of my chest, seeped and dripped like acid burning a hole straight through me.

I felt like the monster her eyes accused me of being. Anger blistered me from all sides as my love for her spilled over my face and the incredulity at what she'd just done. Salt dripped into the cut in my lip as my wrath came out, along with years of unchecked anger.

She stammered out an apology. "C-Cameron, I shouldn't have done that," she said as she looked up at me as if I were a stranger.

I shut my eyes tightly as she whimpered in fear. When I opened them, I was no more. Fist clenched at my sides, I lashed out. "Fuck it, fuck it! To hell with you! Believe whatever the fuck you want to believe about me. I've done nothing but love you since the minute I fucking met you!"

I stormed off, my eyes cloudy and my heart erased as she sobbed out my name behind me to . . . what . . . stop me? I would never know because I sealed the door on us the rest of the way, for her, for us both. I thought I was done with being miserable, but with one strike of her hand, I was done with it all.

Staring out the window I could pinpoint the street where she slept. The address where I'd made some of the best memories of my life. It was only fitting that I watched from afar. I welcomed the pitch black I stood in while I sipped the bottle and the burn crept in with the warmth that covered me.

But it was a false substitution.

I didn't care. I wanted to be free of the gnawing in my chest.

I had four months of something bordering the perfection I swore didn't exist with a woman who fit me. She was the epitome of everything I'd ever craved. And just as easily as she came in and stole the biggest part of me, she took it with her. All I wanted when I met her was a little bit of peace. I still wanted it, but I only seemed to find it with her.

With things as they were, I knew peace was lost. And my soul wasn't going to rest without her. I'd never been so exhausted in my life. She'd unknowingly pushed me past what I was capable of. I had nothing left, where I had so much inside before. For her. Because she brought me back from the brink and made love beautiful and simple. And I jumped at the chance at something so pure with her.

Maybe we were better off as strangers. She should hate me. I was guilty in an unrepairable way. I hated so much of what I saw in my reflection off the glass I stared through. I could still feel the sting of her hand, but it wasn't my face that ached.

On Christmas morning I woke up in her arms, her fingers on the back of my neck, her healing touch my new addiction, her smile erasing the days I spent without her. The last few years of my life bearable by the minutes with her.

Why were the best fucking things in life always so short lived? Good one minute, and then stripped away in a blink. It always seemed the case, especially when it came to the women in my life.

My mother's friendship and sudden absence, the truth of who my wife was, and the loss of the woman I was meant to love had the same type of effect. A common bond they all shared to let me know I wasn't ever in control.

All I did was fight for the happiness I wanted to deserve. When the fuck was it going to be my time? And hadn't I given enough flesh? I could have sworn I paid for my sins, apparently, I hadn't shed enough. But life could take it all if I could have her back. The irony was, there was no deal to be made, no one to barter with and I knew the why.

This time, I did it to myself.

"Fuck you," I muttered to the bastard that watched me swig the bottle. Posing was how I kept it together. It was in my posture, the way I dressed, the way I pretended not to care, not to need, when it was all I'd ever done. I was just as much of a hypocrite as my wife. She was the queen of liars, and I her loyal subject. No matter how much of her I'd thought I'd shaken off in the last year, she had mutated me to the point of keeping up appearances.

When my mom died, I kept busy, using small talk to tune out the pain. I did the same thing when Kat and I started having problems. It was easier to cope when you were busy asking questions about someone else's life. A way to escape your own. I had a constant need to connect. Abbie had that same need. Nothing alike but hearts in common.

'Sticks and stones' was never my motto. The phrase had never been a part of my vocabulary. It meant nothing to me growing up. I'd never dealt with the kind of things I'd had to in the past few years with Kat. I was the golden boy, the poster child. I resembled a carefree man most of my life. I had no issue getting the vote, the friends, or the women.

But I only excelled because I worked hard for it, sometimes twice as hard. And I rewarded those who pushed me by pushing back and doing better. I made few enemies and I was never afraid of shadows because I cast my own.

I might have been labeled perfect, but I never fucking asked for it. I was the son of an unimpressed father and doting mother. Early on I accepted it and vied for her affection because she made up for the lack of his. Failure was my enemy. I excelled to spite him though I never hated him. I only wanted to save myself the embarrassment of failing in front of him. And now I could never admit where he truly succeeded, and I had failed.

My father had the unconditional and unwavering love of the woman I loved most in the world . . . until Abbie. But even at his worst, my mother remained loving and loyal. I foolishly thought I could have the same thing. I loved Abbie's flaws, quirks, and her imperfections. More so, her willingness to admit them without disguising them in sex and perfume. It's what drew me to her.

She'd let me need her. She'd let me love her, and it was reciprocated. I stopped caring who was watching with her. I needed her love over everything.

Maybe I didn't deserve her as the man I was.

But I deserved her now.

Didn't I?

I'd played her way, by her rules. I left my baggage at the door because it worked for me on the same level that it did for her.

I was the man she needed me to be, but it was effortless because it was who I was. The man I'd grown into despite my past. And being free of that burden was a God send when all I wanted to do was forget.

Bottle in hand I moved to my bathroom and studied the cut on my lip and the purple and green bruise on my jaw. I was, once again, covered in Kat's wrath.

Cupping water over my face, I stared at the evidence that wouldn't be washed away. A day or two and there wouldn't be a trace of her physically, but the anger that brewed was what fucked with me. It wasn't hopeless, at least not in the way it used to feel, trapped.

Anger surfaces as I thought of how I had given Kat my life, my time and attention. She'd wasted it, wasted us both. I ran my finger over the faded scar at my temple, a gift from Kat, an everyday reminder she happened.

"Babe, haven't you had enough of those today?"

"I'm hurting," she muttered, absently recapping the pills.

"Your therapist said we should do as much activity as possible. Let's get out today."

"I don't feel like it," she replied low, her resentful eyes meeting mine in the mirror.

"Okay, let's stay in."

She sat at the vanity, running a brush through her hair while I lay in bed watching her. The first time she did her morning ritual, I thought it was odd, like out of some old movie where handmaidens would eventually come in to dress her. She'd been raised regal, and over the years I found it a comforting routine, and oddly sexy. I watched her as she combed through her dark strands, her hair cascading down her frame, her porcelain skin covered in silk.

"I know a few things we can do indoors," I rasped out as I pushed off the covers and walked over to her table to kiss her bare shoulder.

"Don't feel like that, either."

"I miss you," I said softly to her in the mirror.

"Don't be ridiculous. I'm right here."

"Are you?" I pushed a breath out and knelt in front of my wife, stilling her hands.

"Kat, you haven't let me touch you in months. I'm hurting too." I slid my arms around her.

She pushed at my shoulders as I kept hold. "Jesus Christ, Jefferson, is your dick all you care about?"

"No, but it would be nice if my wife gave a damn," I said as evenly as I could manage. Her eyes flared, and I shook my head. "Forget it, I'm sorry. Let's just do something today, anything you want."

"I've got work to do."

"Kat," I reasoned. "It's Sunday. The office can wait."

She pushed my arms away and I hung my head.

She resumed with her brush as I sat on my heels. "You're only thinking of you. What do you expect from me? I'm hurting!"

"Well, that's surprising considering you've taken half a bottle of pills."

She tilted her head and shot daggers at me. "Who in the hell are you to tell me when I'm not in pain!"

"You don't sleep, you barely eat, our marriage is suffering."

"You mean your dick," she scoffed.

"I mean our marriage! I can't get a few words past you without you twisting them and throwing them back. You're always on the defensive. We need to talk about this," I said, snatching the bottle of Vicodin off the vanity. "This fucking shit is wrecking your brain. You aren't yourself."

"Give them back, Cameron. Don't you dare hang those over my head."

I shook my head. "I want to talk about this."

"You're fucking pathetic, you know that?! The only problem here is you."

"Oh, I'm pathetic? I'm the problem? When did that happen? I'm not the one numbing myself to the point of being frigid." Her body went stone still as I reeled it in, because her words hurt, and I could see something in my wife's eyes for the first time that looked like hate. But that couldn't be true. Kat didn't hate . . . anyone.

"Stop," I said, reaching for her, "let's stop."

It was the shock that registered first, not the pain. But I didn't get a chance to recover because she swung the steel-plated brush again and caught me in the temple. She stood, hovering above me, and landed another blow. I felt the rush of nausea as blood trickled down my temple.

"Get the fuck away from me! Don't touch me! It's your fault! I fucking hate you every day I wake up feeling like this! This, all of this, it's your fault!"

Blinded by pain and boiling with rage, I stood so abruptly I knocked her back in her seat. I cupped my jaw where the last blow landed before I ripped the brush from her hand, cracking it in half and tossing it to the floor.

"What the fuck, Kat!"

"Don't act like you didn't deserve it," she hissed. "What? You can't take a punch, Jefferson All-Star!? Eight months I've been in pain because you let me fall. Eight months!" she screamed at my retreating back as I walked to the bathroom with my heartbeat ringing in my ears. Until then I never knew words had the ability to ruin flesh and bone worse than a hand or fist. How those syllables could rip apart visions of a future while they left invisible scars. Throbbing everywhere, I glanced in the mirror and saw my jaw was swelling and a large gash across my temple was bleeding freely. I watched it trail a path down my jaw and drip to the carpet. I threw out half of her cabinet to get to the antiseptic as she slammed the bedroom door. Intent on seeing it through, I turned on my heel and snatched the bottle off the floor before she came back into the room, her pills her focus, the pills her afterthought, not her husband. I shook my head as she moved toward me.

"This has got to stop."

"Give them to me," she said, holding out her hand.

"Jesus Christ, Kat, look at me! You need to think about what you're doing!"

"What I'm doing? You're ruining my life!"

"I'm pointing out the fucking obvious. This shit is changing you."

"Give them to me!" Her face was porcelain perfection and her eyes stung the deepest part of me. They were laced with hate, and it was all for me.

"No."

She flew at me then, the blows coming more rapidly, her nails scratching my skin, my face, her eyes wild. It was as if a switch had flipped. I moved to stop her, and it only fueled her. She landed every blow, determined to draw as much from me as she could, and I backed away before I snapped. The second I loosened my grip, she snatched the bottle away. Head pulsing from the fresh hits, I watched her open her bottle and palm a pill, swallowing it to spite me.

"What the fuck did you just do, Kat?"

"Stay away from me, Cameron," she warned, tears pouring out of her as if I'd somehow hurt her. "You don't know what it's like to need this, you don't know what it's like to need it to breathe! You don't love me. There's no way you love me!"

"How can you say that? We went through this together!"

"I hate you," she heaved out through a sob. "I hate you."

"Cameron." Max's voice sounded on the other side of my door before he rapped his knuckles against it.

"What are you doing here, Max? It's late."

"Door was unlocked. Why in the hell is it so fucking dark in here?"

Fuck.

I closed my eyes. "Not feeling great, man. I'll call you tomorrow."

"You and me both. I think I got dumped."

"Dumped?" I answered, searching my cabinets for some way to cover the bruises and finding nothing.

"Yeah, if you can call it that. She let me in then kicked me out. Look, man, why am I talking through a door? Got anything stronger than beer?"

Gripping the bottle in offering, I opened the door to see he was shitfaced. There was no way I could ask him to leave. I ducked my head as I walked past him. He was on my heels as I moved toward the kitchen. "So how did it go with Kat?"

"Same old shit. I think I might be divorced soon."

"I'll drink to that," he said, snatching my bottle from my grip before taking a healthy sip.

"What's with the stalker lighting? Why are you sitting in the dark?"

"Just got home."

He flipped the switch in the kitchen and I cringed. "Where's Abbie?" He peered over at me. "The fuck happened to you?"

"My goddamned life," I said bluntly and instantly regretted it.

Max sobered. "What happened?"

"Nope," I said, shaking my head. "Like I said, I'm not in the mood."

"I didn't come over to make love. Kat did that to you?"

Whatever lie I told him, I already knew he wouldn't believe.

He took my silence as confirmation. "Then why the hell aren't you on the phone with your lawyer? She can't touch you now."

I stared down at the bottle. "First, because it's two o'clock in the morning. And second, because it's not worth it."

"Jesus Christ, man," he said, moving toward me as I took a step back. "Kat's done this before?"

"I didn't say that."

"You didn't have to," he said, taking another step forward.

I shook my head, my voice stone. "Back off. Leave it alone."

"How long?"

Something foreign crept up my spine. The same part of me that lashed out at Abbie. I couldn't control my bite. "I don't want to talk about it, fucking ever. We're never going to have this conversation."

I gritted my teeth as he watched me too closely. "Let it go, Max. She's gone."

"Okay," he admonished. "Where's Abbie?"

"Gone too," I said, snatching the bottle from his grip and finishing it off before I spoke. "Turns out they were working together."

Max stood speechless, a first for him.

"I know," I said with a dry laugh, pulling two beers from my fridge.

"You have the worst luck of any pretty boy I've ever met."

"Yeah," I said, tossing the beer caps into my sink and handing one of the bottles to him. "I thought my luck was turning."

"Apparently, you need Jesus," he said, taking a swig.

"Trust me, he won't listen, either." Max eyed my chin.

"Damn, we're a mess. It's like we're back in college again, screwed up little boys instead of grown men." I didn't have an ounce of argument until his eyes trailed over my face.

"Stop looking at me that way, man. If it was anyone else, you would have asked me how he looked."

"But it wasn't a he, it was your wife."

"I'm telling you now to let it go."

"I always hated her. She was such a pretentious bitch. Just tell me why you let her do it."

"Why I let her?" I sneered. "I never *let* her do shit," I said, taking a long sip. "And I'm not talking about it."

"So, what now?"

"Am I'm supposed to have a plan for this? It's over," I said, hating the words, wishing them back and away from me. But it felt over. It felt more than over.

"She loves you. It's so obvious."

"I don't want a pep talk, all right? This is so much more than that. There's no fix. I fucked it up permanently. And don't bother to say I told you so."

He took a sip of his beer. "I wouldn't."

"Then you can stay." Max stared at me from across the island.

I took a sip of beer, careful to avoid the cut on my lip. "Tell me about Rachel."

Max shook his head. "Sorry, but I'm calling bullshit. I can't let this go, man. I know that's what you want, but I'm pretty fucking pissed off. Give me one good reason why I shouldn't call someone and report this shit right now."

My retort was instant. "Because you'll end our friendship."

"It will save you from a messy divorce. Cameron, you can't let her get away with this."

"Let it go. It's over."

Max ran his hands through his hair as he weighed my words. "She took advantage of the fact you wouldn't hit her back. I know you, Cameron, but this isn't chivalry. This isn't you being the bigger man."

"If you give a damn about me, you'll listen to what I'm about to say. I left her. Our relationship is over. She's no longer a part of my life. Drop it and never mention this again."

Max nodded. I walked over to my closet and pulled out a pillow and blanket tossing them on the couch before I slammed my bedroom door behind me.

I didn't sleep. Instead, I stared at the ceiling until the sun lit my bedroom. Half the night, I tried to figure out how I would move on after what we had, the other half I had to resist the urge to go to her.

We were never strangers. The largest piece of me had recognized her as home. But even if I'd made it to her door, I had zero defense. And part of me was furious she'd touched me in a way I never expected. In a way I couldn't press past.

"Cameron," Max said at my door.

"Yeah, man," I said, sitting up, my head splitting in half as I moved to sit on the edge of the bed.

Max stared at the floor. "I'm still fucking pissed off and you look like shit."

I grinned. "I love you too, man."

"I'm heading out."

"Where are you going?"

"I'm not playing ball today. I'm too hungover and I have work to do."

"By work, do you mean Rachel?"

"Hell yes, I'm not going to end up like you. Mid-thirties, ugly, and alone. But I'll be back later."

"What in the hell for?"

"Someone has to keep you drunk."

"Some would argue that that's not being a friend but an enabler."

"Some would say I know better for you and others can suck my cock." He grinned spitefully and shut the door behind him with a thud.

I was still kicking myself for admitting it to him. The Band-Aid had been pulled off, but I never told a soul about Kat's abuse. Even when I was going through it, I was in a constant state of denial that she meant to hurt me. I knew the woman attacking me wasn't the woman I married. That was my frame of mind at the time.

It was the day I realized it *was* Kat that I left. And a few months after that to fully leave her emotionally. The rest of the time I was trying to make sure she didn't hurt herself or anyone else. And damn near every time I went to help her, she attacked me verbally or otherwise. It was a vicious cycle, but I could never bring myself to report it, to report her and it was mostly because I didn't want to admit it to anyone, let alone a lawyer or any fucking judge. I'm six-foot-three with an athlete's build. I dwarfed Kat in size. It was a ridiculous notion that she could do so much damage.

But women *can* scar, they can *always* scar, if you let them.

And Max was right. She took advantage of the fact I wouldn't hit her back.

It was a nightmare on a consistent and predictable spin cycle.

Foolishly I checked my phone and saw that I had nothing to look forward to. Instead, I stared at the screen saver, a picture of us on Abbie's front porch on New Year's Day, the day she reached her goal of five miles. It was my favorite picture and had the opposite effect it had the day before. Raw inside, I gave into temptation and flipped through more pictures while my heart hammered as a reminder that in no way was it over for me. Even as angry as I was with her refusal to listen, or that she slapped me, I couldn't believe we were done. But I needed peace. It was the only thing keeping me sane. And I needed a distraction because Abbie was far too angry, and I had too many fresh bruises.

For the first time when it came to her, I didn't trust my judgment to make any call.

I had games to coach. My only saving grace.

I'd barely toweled off from my shower when there was a knock on my door. My hopes of who was behind it dashed when I opened it and took a step back.

"Dad?"

"Hey son," he said casually, a smile briefly touching his lips. "I know it's early. Hoped you might be up."

He'd lost a few pounds since Christmas. He seemed smaller in stature, his hair in need of a cut. He looked lost, as if he was uncomfortable standing there.

"Can I come in?"

"Sorry, yeah," I said, opening the door wider to let him in.

"Nice place."

"Thanks," I said holding the knob as I watched him walk around. He looked completely out of place in my living room.

"I would have come sooner but I wasn't invited," he said dryly as he studied the picture of me, my mom, and Max that sat on one of my end tables.

Ignoring his sarcasm, I shut the door. "Everything okay?"

"I'm fine. What happened to your face?"

I shrugged. "Got rough on the court."

He eyed me warily and I moved toward the kitchen his

sarcastic timber unmistakable. "I don't recall basketball being that hands on."

"Shit happens," I said with a shrug. "Want some water?"

"Sure."

Pushing the dispenser on the fridge I stalled, reluctant to let him get a good look at me. Walking over to him, I handed him a glass and made a quick excuse. "I'm just going to go throw some clothes on."

My father nodded as he continued to inspect my apartment.

Minutes later and freshly dressed in sweats and a hat that I felt confident would cover the bruise next to my eyes, I walked out to join him in the living room. Leaving the ball in his court, I waited as he looked out the window watching the passing traffic. "You like living here?"

"Sure."

He absently smirked at my answer while he kept his attention outside.

"Dad, what's up?"

"Are you still seeing Abbie?" When I remained quiet he turned my way. "No?"

I shook my head and he didn't miss it. He scrutinized me far too closely than I was comfortable with. "That's a shame. I really liked her. I liked when you brought her home for Christmas. It was . . . nice, different."

Abbie had made it work for the three of us. She'd spent all day in my mother's kitchen cooking. My father was right next to her, helping, laughing, telling her stories I'd never heard. As much as I hated it, she was the perfect buffer between us. Just like my mother had been.

"Yes, it was nice," I agreed.

His eyes zeroed in on my face. "What happened?"

I shrugged, unsure if he was addressing my face or Abbie.

I chose to go with the latter. "Didn't work out."

"Something you did?"

I nodded sliding my hands into my pockets.

He smirked. "Some days it's clear that you're my son. I fucked up with your Mom and often."

I furrowed my brows. His visit was shock enough, him getting personal was . . . never.

"So, do you need anything?"

His whole body tensed as he looked at me with contempt. "No, I guess not." Anger radiated off him as he shook his head in a way that said he should have known better.

"I see you're getting pissed, which is normal, but do you want to help me out here? I'm confused."

"What confuses you?" He spoke up quickly. "I'm sixty-five years old. I have shit to look forward to. I'm here to check on my son."

"Because you promised her you would," I shot back.

"Because I miss my family," he countered with just as much contempt before he fisted his hands at his sides and spoke low. "I miss her Cameron. And it's not getting easier."

"You aren't happy here," I admitted. "You've never been happy here. You resent me for being here. But it wasn't my decision."

"I'm not going to be happy anywhere," he said gruffly. "It wasn't just her decision, you know. We decided together to move closer to remain a part of your life."

"Right," I said dryly.

"I'm not leaving you, no matter how hard it is for us."

"What?"

"You heard me," he said walking toward the front door.

"Dad, I'm sorry. This is coming out of nowhere. I don't know what you want me to say." He expelled a breath and paused his retreat.

"I didn't do a lot of things right. But Christmas with you and Abbie was the first time I felt like things might be okay. It was the first time I felt that way since she died. We had forty years together. I know I won't move on from that. But I don't want to miss any more of *your* life. Because no matter what you think, I was always aware of what was going on with you. Always. I know everything you told her. She was your best friend, but she was mine too. I was a shit father, but she let me off the hook. I don't deserve the same grace from you and I understand that, but I still want to know."

"You weren't a shit father," I said sucking back the emotion that threatened.

"Let's not start with lies," he said softly. "All I have to think about now are regrets. I was an ornament at your wedding and I knew which parent you truly wanted there. I had no idea you were divorcing Kat. I missed your whole marriage. I wasn't there when I should have been. And I'm sorry. I'll never be her. But it's not her promise I'm trying to keep anymore. I miss my son. I want to know. But only when you're ready and if you want to." He took one last look at me. "Put some ice on that eye."

I stood stunned as he shut the door behind him.

Abbie

I waited a long time for runner's high. I'd run endless miles for the moment when I felt that adrenaline rush. Confident in my stride it surprised me when my focus became singular and my body fluid in motion, no longer forced, but flying. The feeling was cut short by the realization I couldn't share it with the one person I wanted to.

Three weeks had passed since Cameron stood outside my door and every day of those weeks had been agony. Not one of those days did I breathe evenly, not one of those nights had I slept more than a few hours. Every step I ran in any direction felt like a step away from Cameron. I wanted to ignore the truth. I wanted to forget whatever it was keeping us apart and be ignorantly blissful again.

But I couldn't, so my heart bled freely and I ran.

And life wasn't done with me yet.

No, life was a villainous vampire who refused to let up until I was an empty shell. I spent my days with the dead weight of my heart, holding it tightly to me while I exhausted myself running through Chicago. Every step crushing me while my every racing thought was amplified by the loss of him.

I wandered aimlessly, ignoring my needs, thirsty for only him. I'd convinced myself it was inevitable. I just wasn't ready for it. And no matter how I tried to cover the wound, it emulated through my whole body. Lost and unable to believe in recovery, I ran, searching for some semblance of order. There were no numbers I could make sense of, no calculations for easy resolve, but numbers never lied.

After a record-breaking six miles downtown, I rode the train without direction, got lost in the reality of others, watching those who I passed and then sinking into myself when I could no longer fathom having a new reality of my own.

The first notes of Hand Me Down by *Matchbox Twenty* began to filter through my earbuds as I exited the L for another night alone with my tortured thoughts. I hadn't reached out to Bree, only texting the bare minimum to keep her at bay. I hadn't reached out to anyone. I wasn't living, I wasn't existing, I was paralyzed to those minutes at the foot of my porch.

Forever a fool, I'd thought it was finally my time. I somehow thought I could be the woman to have earned the life of my choosing. But love was a cruel charade of mismatched hearts, and I'd played it long enough. All that was left was the big empty. I welcomed it back like an old friend I secretly despised. At least there, I was safe. At least in that place, I knew where I stood.

The words of the song hit me hard as my face flooded with ironic tears. The rip was too far inside, I couldn't reach the hemorrhage. It tore wider as I passed Sunny Side. Unable to tamp down my emotion, I was openly crying in the street with my chin tucked in my jacket shouldering the cold and welcoming the numbing chill that kept me running.

A man paused next to me in wait at the crosswalk and I wiped a stray tear away and braved a glance in his direction. Rude as it may have been I nodded as he spoke without a clue as to what he was saying, my earbuds full of the serenade of my demise—Cameron and Abbie's greatest hits. Desperate to start running, to mask my pain, I took the cue to walk when the man next to me began to move. Out of habit, I looked up and had a previous prayer answered.

You're a cruel bitch life.

Cameron stood on the other side of the street, his dry-cleaning hooked on his finger at his shoulder, a basketball at his opposite hip, his emerald eyes on me. Blinking furiously, I tried to wash the illusion away and froze mid-step in the middle of the street. Cameron flinched as a cabbie laid on his horn, while the man next to me pounded on the hood screaming that we had the right of way. Knees weak and heart hammering, I began walking again in Cameron's direction while he stood in wait, his expression solemn.

You wanted to know if that soul altering love still existed, Abbie. Here's your proof.

Only a man can make you feel like you have the world one minute and take it away the next. And they only have that power because we give it to them.

Intent on walking past, he reached out and grabbed my coat sleeve in an attempt to stop me, and I rang out a sharp, "no." His hand instantly retreated, and I met his eyes briefly and my heart plummeted. Unshed tears glistened in his depths and I shook my head.

Tearing myself away—destroyed—I sobbed openly as I sped home. But even behind the safety of my door I was flooded with fresh memories and sank into a puddle behind it. Seconds later Bree appeared from my living room, scorn written all over her features due to my shitty communication. I saw it disappear as she read my face and squat in front of me.

She pulled my earbuds out and gripped the hands resting on top of my knee.

"Abbie, what happened?"

I shook my head, unable to talk. I was too raw, even after so many days of going black. I didn't have the luxury of being numb.

"Oh, God," I cried, before she pulled me into her arms and cried with me.

24

Abbie

"You look beautiful," I said to Bree as she traipsed around the hotel dressing room in her vintage wedding dress. A golden butterfly clasp in her hair—a gift from her groom—held up most of her blond locks as the rest flowed in loose curls at the V of her back. It was perfect and perfectly suited for her, just like her groom.

"I'm going to live this bride thing up," she said as she turned to face me with her hands on her hips. "It's like prom, but I'm not scared of losing my virginity this time." She waggled her eyebrows.

"That's one way of looking at the best day of your life. And you weren't a virgin at your prom."

"I was at the one I went to my freshman year, Ms. You're Judging Me. And I love Anthony. He's got the best bedside manner of any guy I've ever met, a big dick, and today I'm marrying them both. The possibilities are endless."

I laughed my first full laugh in weeks.

"God, I'm so glad you're staying in Chicago. I don't know

what I would do if you left."

She fastened a teardrop diamond earring and spoke to my reflection. "He passed up that job in New York, which would have meant early retirement for me, but I love our life here. He got the shit end of the deal, but he doesn't care. He's even living with me in Wicker so I can stay close to you. Thank you for giving him to me."

I shook my head. "I didn't *give* him to you. I introduced you."

"Same thing. He's gorgeous and so naughty and perfect. Why didn't you try for him yourself?"

I plucked a loose rose petal off her bouquet and sniffed it, my eyes threatening to water.

Smell dredges up memory, moron.

"And all I could think of when I met him and spoke to him for the first time was *you* and how you would get a kick out of his jokes and the fact that he loves to travel. All of the things *you* would adore about him. It's weird, right? It was intuition."

"Well, I'd say it paid off," she said, turning to look in the mirror.

Not for me.

Intuition was one thing. Confusion still had me reeling. Everything from the moment I stood on that curb at Preston Corp, to the moment I slapped him, and the anger and hurt in Cameron's features. It was like I'd shot him. Any explanation I could have gotten, I'd screwed myself out of with my anger. And I was still doing it.

"He'll come back."

Bree eyed me from the mirror, and I shook my head. "I told you it's over. There's no way we're coming back from that. Any of it."

"Why can't you come back?" she challenged. "Why?

Because he's not perfect? He told you he wasn't. He also told you he wasn't divorced because of her mental state and kept it from you because he wanted to start fresh with you, not on the end of his horrible marriage. They were your rules."

"He. Was. Married."

"She is an *addict*. And you told me that she did act skittish when you started working for her and throughout. You just got used to her. I work on and *with* drug addicts every day. Most hide it like professionals. And in case you didn't know it, there's an epidemic going on. I've called time of death on soccer moms who have had their pain prescriptions taken away and started to shoot up heroin instead. It's not a fucking joke."

"I know Kat. I believe that part of it." I adjusted my dress and whirled on her. "Nope, nuh-uh, we aren't talking about this today. This is your wedding day," I reminded.

"And I intend to get married. And it will be perfect, but right now I'm being cruel and distracting myself with your issues so I don't get nervous. Now, before I go get married, let's fix you."

"I don't want to be fixed."

"Before you move to finish the final stages of grieving," she said, turning to look at me, "I only think it's fair I point out now that this is your man, Abbie."

Stunned, I looked at her.

"I knew it from the beginning and I am still certain of it, just as I'm sure you're going to let him go, and it's going to be the biggest mistake of your life."

"He was fucking married, Bree. And he was when he slept with me. Am I next?"

Bree walked over the plush gold carpet and stood in front of me.

"Sixty seconds of truth. I mean it, no holding back."

"Bree, please, I don't want to be upset." I'd just gotten to the point where I could function. Work was my refuge, and as much as I hated to admit it, I'd gone right back into spending my nights with Mrs. Zingaro. Nothing had changed. It was as if he had never existed, except he did. His tux was still hanging in my closet. I could still smell a hint of his cologne, a haunting reminder.

"We're doing it. Right now. Sixty seconds."

I shook my head. "Don't. Or I swear to God, I'm going to ruin your wedding photos. I'll photoshop a dildo in every single one."

"I'll marry Anthony again next year and take new pictures."

"I hate you," I said as she gripped my hands.

Prompting brown eyes commanded mine. "Sixty seconds starts now."

"No."

"Do you love him?"

We were both short in stature, but she may as well have stood ten feet tall. We used the same technique in college to get to the bottom of things. But it usually had to do with whether or not I ate her nana's baked goods. What can I say? The woman was a goddess in the kitchen.

"Stay with me," she said, jerking me into the moment. "Do you love him?"

"Yes, so much. You know I do."

"Do you want it to be over?"

"No. God, no."

"Do you think he's a cheating pig?"

I cringed at her words. "No."

"Do you think he was telling the truth?"

"Yes."

"Why?"

"Because he's not that type of man."

"Will you give him a chance?"

"No."

"Are you ruining your own chances of happiness with that answer?"

"Yes."

"Why?"

"Times up."

She gripped my shoulders and squeezed. "Why?"

"Because I'm scared I'll be wrong again."

"You aren't. Not this time. Not about him. Listen to me. This. Is. Your. Man."

I crumbled in her hold as she spoke on, ignoring my tears. "Luke was an evil bastard who took your innocence and made you feel guilty afterward. You'll never get that back, and you'll never be as naïve. You were cautious this time, and with good reason, but you know better with Cameron because this guy just wants to love you. Exchange your baggage and you two will be better for it. Don't miss your man on some principle that he was wrong. Hear him out before you make a decision. Or even better, *don't* ask questions for once. Trust yourself and reap the reward. You don't have to know every sordid detail about someone to truly love them. Life changes people in a matter of seconds. We both know that. Who he was a year ago is not who he is today. Maybe *you* changed him for the better and are hurting him for the worse. You know who you love. You know who Cameron is. You don't have to know who he was before you loved him. Don't be so black and white about all of this."

"I'll think about it," I said with a wobbling chin.

"Hurry up, Abbie. It's not over for you and you're only hurting your chances by playing it safe."

"I'm scared."

"I know," she said. "*Now* it's time for me to get married."

"Bree," I said with an emotion-filled voice.

"I know. You love me, you're happy for me. Blah blah, save it for the toast."

"Okay. But I do love you."

"You better." She took a deep breath and grabbed her bouquet. "Roses are so traditional, don't you think? I can't believe I bought into all this hoopla. I expected better of myself."

"They're my favorite too. I didn't know it, though."

"Oh?" she said, taking a whiff of the heavenly scented stems. "Cameron?"

I nodded, picking up my own bouquet. "Where's the honeymoon again?"

"I still don't know because Anthony planned it. He said he's taking me somewhere I've never been."

A knock at the door had both of our eyes widening.

"Showtime," I said with a wink.

"I'm coming for you Big Dick!" Bree yelled before I pulled her into a hug.

My mother's laughter rang out from the other side of the door.

○

"Keep the blindfold on, baby." Anthony led his wife through the doorway as we all stood silently in wait.

"What is going on!" Bree asked excitedly. "The jig's up, husband. The car ride wasn't long enough to make it to O'Hare and we didn't even cut the cake! Everyone is going to be so pissed off we missed our own reception." Anthony guided her outside as we all held in our chuckles.

"Do you trust me?"

"Are things about to get freaky? If so, babe, you need to let me limber up—"

"Hold that thought," Anthony said, cupping her mouth as his face turned crimson. A chuckle was heard, and Bree paused her footing. "I just heard my nana laugh. Anthony, what is happening?"

When he had her centered where he needed her, he took a step back. "Okay, babe, now." She removed her blindfold as we all watched.

She looked into the faces of her small wedding party and handpicked guests and tilted her head. "Uh, hi . . ." she said with a weak smile before she looked back at her groom. "Anthony?"

"I told you I was taking you someplace you'd never been before."

Bree, true to form, looked back at him with irritation. "This is my backyard."

He chuckled as he twisted her to the right and the crowd parted.

Her gasp was audible. Her eyes filled with tears as the photographer took a few snaps and then smiled at them. "It's our place," she said as she moved toward the cascading waterfall and down the intricately placed path that resembled the legendary stone wake with aqua water flowing in the center.

"The fairy pools," Anthony said as he slid his arms around her waist and kissed her neck. "It's beautiful." The crowd parted again on the left side of the backyard and Bree's eyes bulged. "Oh my God, Japan!"

Anthony guided her over to the wood walk and fawned over the intricately laid Zen garden. It was stunning. Japan was my favorite. She leaned down and trailed her fingers along the empty koi pond and looked at him in question.

"April is too cold for fish. The ground barely thawed enough for us to get this done." Her eyes filled with tears as the photographer took a few snaps and then wiped a tear from her own eye. Anthony admired his design as the cluster of guests watched on while Bree turned to her love.

"Baby, how did you pull this off?"

"Like I said, you've never been to your backyard."

Everyone chuckled as she palmed her forehead. It was no secret Bree wasn't much of a housekeeper, let alone a gardener. Her idea of weed eating was winter. But I had to admit it was a genius idea, even as Anthony spoke the words.

"We may not always be able to go on these amazing trips. Life might get in the way. We'll have a baby, maybe two," he added pointedly, hopeful. "But we'll have this to help us remember."

"Anthony," Bree said, completely stunned. "I'm . . ."

He leaned in and kissed her ring finger. "I just wanted you to know it's adventure enough just to be your husband. And I'm *never* going back to Thailand."

Everyone laughed as she flew into his waiting arms. "I love you so much," she whispered before she pressed a fiery kiss to his mouth. "This is perfect. I don't need anything else."

"So, I can cancel our trip to Spain?"

"Hell no, when do we leave?"

Oh my God, I'm at another wedding reception in a bridesmaid dress eating another third piece of cake. Fuck you, life! Seriously, FUCK YOU!

"Would you care to dance?"

"No," I said without glancing the man's way. He'd been

eyeing me all day. I knew it was coming. I think his name was Berry or Harry or Larry, some -arry that I didn't even want to attempt to get to know.

After endless weeks of crying my eyes out and five very well-shaken martinis, the cynic was back and in full effect. "I absolutely do not want to dance with you."

"Wow," Berry Harry Larry remarked of my nasty candor.

"Yeah, wow, I would apologize but this is my behavior pattern now. It's never going to end. Cut your losses and run, man, fucking run for your life!" I whisper-yelled sarcastically.

His amusement at my sarcasm rubbed me the wrong way. It wasn't Cameron's, and still, Berry Harry Larry, stood there smirking until I finally glanced up at him. Cute, clean cut, decent smile. I narrowed my eyes.

I've got your number, asshole. "Please, and I mean this in the nicest way possible, *fuck off.*"

My mother scowled at me in the distance, ever the scorekeeper, and I gave her two sarcastic thumbs up.

I was on a roll.

"Jesus," the guy said, giving me the *you're a bitch* look I deserved before he took off, justly mortified. I looked around quickly in a *did I just ruin Bree's wedding* panic? The answer was no, everyone was smiling, dancing, or eating cake. And most of these people would probably have sex tonight.

"Not me," I muttered as I shoved cake into my face while I prayed for lightning to strike me and end my misery.

All I wanted was to be part of a we. Was that so hard?

Why in the hell does everyone else seem to be able to do this but me?

Pity party, table of one, let the fucking frosting licking commence.

I downed every glass of passed champagne offered as I ate

my way through the reception, furious at my predicament.

I *did* have it. I did find a man to love and he was *married*. Married, a little jaded, and a whole lot stupid with his omission, but I had him. A real man with a good heart who gave so much of himself it didn't matter what he got back, who'd met my crazy, embraced it, and found it endearing. A man who'd braved my oral surgery dragon breath and told me I was beautiful, a man who was worthy in every way of my time and attention. A man who knew the clitoris wasn't a fictional character but a best friend he conversed with like an expert linguist. A man who dedicated his life to the happiness of others.

Okay, maybe that was too much of a stretch, but he dedicated himself to making *me* happy. And I slapped him for it. I slapped him without letting him explain himself or getting answers I deserved to the questions I didn't ask.

Was Bree, right? Was our love made in the gray area? And did we have enough of it left to see it for what it truly was when it came into the light?

In the grand scheme of *us*, his baggage didn't fit in. He'd checked it at the door and tried to keep it there as I had mine.

Maybe it wasn't real, or I wanted it so much I turned a blind eye to everything else, every clue he gave me that he wasn't a surreal creature in some mystical fairy tale where nothing bad happened. But whatever we created turned into something that became the truth of who we were *together*.

We never denied who we were in the moment as we vowed. We didn't change ourselves to suit our relationship. Our relationship evolved out of the truest version of us. We created our own little universe where we could be exactly who we wanted with each other.

We had it. And we lost it.

To dull the bitter taste of defeat I tossed back more vodka

and champagne and stuffed a puff pastry in my mouth.

"Oh, baby. You're going to puke," my mother whispered as she took a seat next to me. "Have you called him yet?"

"No," I said, chewing on the sweet steak and onion gravy. She was right. At some point, I was going to puke. I shoved another pastry in.

"It's time to talk to him. It's past time."

"I'm just delaying it. Okay. Delay of game. Timeout. I'm still so screwed up and pissed off I don't know what to say."

"Say what you feel," she said, grabbing the champagne out of my hand before I could take another drink. I had my mother's eyes and mouth and my father's red hair and temper. My mother was always reasonable, a trait I really wished I'd genetically inherited, especially at times like these.

I shoved another beef-filled pastry in my mouth. "Atta girl," my mom said as we leaned in together and I smiled for the camera with a mouthful of meat.

"You are being a horrible shit. And you're too old to throw these tantrums."

"I know, Mom. I should be more refined at weddings when I have a pony barrette in my hair," I sassed.

Clean up on aisle five, bitter old maid in a bridesmaid dress.

"Hey," Anthony said, insulted about the barrette comment as he pulled his wife to his side, who thumped me on the head.

"Sorry," I said sheepishly in an attempt to save face. "I was being a shit to my mom. Not knocking the barrette. It's beautiful."

"Thank you," Anthony said, leaning down to kiss my cheek. "I mean it, thank you for today."

"My pleasure. I love you both so much," I said in an attempt to sway my mood in a better direction.

Bree gripped my mother's hand. "Nancy, dance with me?"

"I'd be honored," she said, taking leave of her chair as Anthony sat next to me. "Where's your brother?"

I rolled my eyes. "I think I saw him tackle a bridesmaid with a favor kit."

He chuckled. "What's a wedding without a little love tackle kit."

"I can't believe you let her get away with mini bottles of lube and condoms as wedding favors."

Anthony was handsome in his tux—dark olive skin, kind brown eyes, and a perfect match for Bree. "I would let her get away with a whole lot worse, but don't tell her I said so."

"I'll keep it under wraps." I tapped my temple.

His eyes focused on me as I fiddled with one of the starched napkins. "Are you okay?"

"Nope, not at all, not even a little bit. I'm not even going to say with time or tomorrow after a good night's sleep. You get no timeline. I may be that sloppy drunk a year from now who tells too many 'you remember when' stories like my prime has already passed, cries to her cats, and makes love to couch cushions."

"That's the saddest thing I've ever heard," Anthony said with a frown.

"Those poor cushions," I said, catching a tear of both irony and sadness. I'd come full circle and I was officially drunk.

"You are sleeping here tonight," he said firmly.

"My mom has me. HA! That's even sadder!" I proclaimed as a few heads turned in our direction.

"Sadder," Anthony agreed with an amused grin.

"The saddest."

Anthony winced.

"Okay, I can see the groom light dying in your eyes. Let's cheer you up."

"I'm sorry, Abbie," he said sincerely. "I really liked him."

I paused my snarky reply. "Don't do that. Don't be sincere and all adorable about my broken heart. I'll be okay."

"Really?"

"No, I'm devastated beyond repair," I said dryly.

We stared at each other for a full ten seconds with straight faces before we burst into laughter.

"I thought you were serious."

"I am, come dance with me."

Anthony looked at me cautiously. "You're nuts."

"I *was* born in a sanitarium," I pointed out without hesitation.

Oh, Cameron, how you freed me.

"Explains a lot," he said. "The prettiest women are often the craziest."

I pushed another stray tear from my eye. "That explains why your wife is a nut job."

"Pretty much."

I felt Bree's elbow dig into my ribs and let out a ticklish laugh as she passed us on the carefully laid dance floor in the middle of her yard, my mother in her arms. My mother, though unamused with my behavior, egged me on. "I love her more than you at the moment."

"You two can go straight to hell," I said with a smile plastered on my face.

Anthony led me to the dance floor with a chuckle. "I really love the three of you together."

"Meh, we only let my mom in because she's a good cook. Oof," I said as my mother elbowed me. "Kidding, Mom. Shit, I need that to breathe."

"Would you please try to act like a lady tonight?" she hissed my way as we all danced in the tight space.

I refused to let it go. "Your adopted daughter is passing out lube and French ticklers as wedding gifts." My mother's eyes widened as she smiled at Bree with delight. "Oh, remind me to grab one of those before I leave."

"It's always the blonds that get away with shit in this family!" I said with an eye roll.

"Watch your mouth," my mother scolded as Bree stuck out her tongue.

"You have gotten a little worse, sailor," Anthony commented.

"I know," I said, remembering how Cameron loved my filthy mouth. "It's unattractive, right?"

"Nah, I just wanted to give you shit too, but it seems to be backfiring on me tonight."

"Hey, I should be consoling you. Have you seen the feet on your bride? Jesus."

I felt two asses simultaneously bump into mine as "Shake Your Groove Thing" began to play. My mother looked like an old lady trying to dance, and I couldn't help but notice her age as she did her best to get me to move with her. Taking off my heels, I gave in and joined my two favorite women in the world while my heart was still slipping away from me piece by piece, filtering in the air above me, calling like a siren to its owner who had disappeared like he'd never existed.

Cameron

ASK A HUNDRED PEOPLE WHAT LOVE MEANS TO THEM and you'll get a hundred different answers. I suspect most of them will say it has something to do with comfort or safety. But that's false.

That's what God is for.

Maybe in the afterlife of firsts; first look, first kiss, first year, comfort and safety come into play, but the initial feeling should make you scared and more than uncomfortable. It should terrify you to lose it.

Most people don't know that. In fact, I bet only a handful of those hundred have ever felt it. And that makes those who haven't had it envious, but that can be dangerous too.

A lot of people covet freedom but have no idea what to do with it once it's earned and then find they were better off without it.

I think the same thing applies to love. The kind that can change you and twist you into a better person all for the affection of someone else. It's both a gift and a curse and it has the power to elate you as well as leave you destitute within seconds. Because nothing that feels so good could ever, should ever, start feeling so bad. But, that's the way of it. It's the most powerful of emotions, therefore those who are gifted it should have the most powerful of consequences if it's left unattended or taken for granted.

And I did.

I was guilty. I had too much faith in our relationship and I ignored the threatening undercurrent in time to save us both from being swept away.

I needed her. I needed to believe there was more for me. For us both.

I was living with the consequences with every breath I took while my days blurred with the loss of her.

And still I'll tell you she was worth it.

Because she was.

Every second, every minute I stole with her was worth the hell I was tossed back into without her.

She slapped me. Most men wouldn't think anything of it, but with her it was my breaking point and it was no secret why. At least for me. Abbie was still in the dark.

I scared her with my reluctance to tell her the why, when all I wanted to do was erase the wall before it erected between us.

How much I'd fucked up.

When I tried everything in my power to save my marriage it still collapsed, and so had my shot of happiness with Abbie's refusal to believe I was a worthy man. A man better than just some philandering asshole who didn't think one woman was enough. But Abbie was enough.

She was overabundance.

In the entirety of my life, all I knew was that I wanted to be seen as a worthy man. That had been my only goal, in my marriage, in my business, in my friendships as a coach and in my relationship with Abbie. It was instilled in me by my mother, it was my foundation.

From the time I was young enough to know better to the day she left us. I needed her, and she wasn't there. I needed her when my marriage fell apart, when my life spiraled out of control because of it. And I needed her then, as I stood at her grave, looking down at the granite etched letters of the name of my best friend and compass. I'd relived the last day I was with her too many times and yet not enough to figure out what to do when there were no more words. No more direction. I wondered how many other cancer orphans wandered around aimlessly seeking answers to questions they forgot to ask.

"You can't be here son. We agreed," my father said softly as I approached her bedroom door. In that moment, I hated him for trying to take her from me. But when I looked at him, all I saw was a man defeated. He was losing her too, and it showed in the lines covering the face mine mirrored. But I had her eyes and I knew it was painful to look at me. I was a product of her and I think, in a way, that fact hurt him too. Mark Bledsoe was a man's man, full of pride and quick to anger. The only tenderness he revealed was when it came to his wife. Despite the fact that I mostly played every sport in some search for misplaced approval, she was what we had in common. It was our love of the games that kept us civil, but it was always her that held us together. What would we be without her?

"I'll never forgive you for this," I said through gritted teeth. "If you do this I'll never forgive you."

"It doesn't matter."

"Of course it doesn't."

His jaw set as he studied me. "This isn't about us."

"I know."

"Then respect her wishes."

"She's still here," I said choking on my words. "Jesus, Dad, don't take this away from me. Please."

"You need to go."

"Mark," we heard her call from behind the door. "Let him in."

He let out a harsh breath and studied me before he opened the door. The hospice nurse hung another bag of fluids and made quick leave and my Dad shut the door behind her. My mother sat in the middle of her bedroom which seemed unbelievably bare with only a hospital bed centered in the middle of it. Everything about it seemed wrong.

She was wearing a yellow knit cap that her sister had made for her and her favorite robe. Her body was void of life, her thin frame withering beneath the thin sheet draped over her. My eyes stung as she held out her hand, her fingers skeleton. I bit back every sound threatening to escape.

"Come here, Cam," she said low as I took the seat next to her and took her cold hand which was covered in bandages, bruised from the needles full of medicine that didn't help her, and couldn't save her. All the hell she went through, for nothing. She was leaving, and my chest caved knowing it was the last time I would ever lay eyes on her.

"Look at me," she said sternly. I gave her my eyes and through all the strength I saw in hers, I faltered.

"This is why I didn't want you to see."

I took in a sharp breath that burned my throat. "Mom, stop trying to protect me. I'm too old for that."

"Never. It's my right and it's been the best privilege of my life. Over everything else you were the one thing I'm most proud of and I know you believe that. You know how much I love you.

I made sure of it. Because that's what you do when you live for someone else. When you have your own, you'll understand."

I nodded, studying her fingers, unable to speak.

"Cameron, we agreed. I don't want you to see this. I won't let you."

"Mom-"

"Just be a good man," she whispered as my father cried openly at her side. She squeezed my hand faintly before she let go. I felt the loss of her warmth and it ripped my chest wide open. She was determined. Even in her final days she kept so much authority. Over me, over us both.

"I don't know how to let go," I whispered. Knowing she was terrified, I was selfish. I needed her comfort. She taught me how to tie my shoes, stand my ground, and take care of myself. She taught me how to love, she never taught me how to let go.

"I don't have anything else for you Cameron. It's not that I don't want you here, it's that I can't handle it myself. Please," she whispered as her own tears got the best of her. "I don't know how to do this either. I don't think I'll take my last breath and be okay knowing you're here and I won't be." She turned to my dad. "Mark give us a minute." He nodded before he left the room and the door clicked softly behind him.

I surveyed the space. She'd painted her walls sky blue when she got sick. She said it would make her feel more out in the open on days where the chemo refused to let her leave. But somehow, even with filtered sun streaming through the windows, the room felt ominous. I inhaled the scent of her lotion next to her bedside table, a scent I knew I would never forget, it was of no comfort and damn near brought me to my knees.

Cancer had stripped her, taking her skin, her hair, her joy and using her body as a punching bag. She'd survived it once. I didn't know why God thought she deserved more, but I asked him. I asked him every day. And every day she got weaker until I had no choice but to accept her fate.

I could no longer demand answers but pray anyway, even if God was cruel. She hurt, and I prayed. And when praying proved to be pointless, I watched her wilt, I watched her choke on breath, I watched her cry out in pain, helpless, hopeless, it was the first time I felt forsaken and humbled to the point I no longer had an ego.

God broke us both and my father watched.

I looked at my mother, a floating vessel in a shell that refused to house her. So much life was left in her eyes, but she was stuck in a body that wouldn't cooperate. I knew in that moment she was right. Seeing her like that altered me. It took a piece of me. She looked back at me as she weighed her words like she often did, before she spoke while I prayed one last time.

No more pain. God, hear me. You take her, but no more pain.

"Cameron, your father and I started this life together, and I want to end things with him that way. I know that seems selfish, but I need him with me. He's my strength, son. No matter how you see it. He's mine. It's a gift if you think about it. I get to devastate him and then I'm free. But he won't be. You two need to figure out how to do this on your own. Promise me you'll try."

"I will," I said burying my face in her blanket. I gave myself three seconds of anguish before I faced her. Three seconds to breathe in the hell fire, breath that I could take freely, and she would suffocate for. I felt her fingers on my neck as I braved another look at her. And in her eyes, I saw the woman who gave me the best of herself. I saw a woman capable of so much more than being Mark's wife or my mother. I saw her for the first time, a woman who was able to choose any other life than belonging to us. But we were her choice and I was grateful. And so, for my *mother's sacrifice, I made mine.*

"Okay." *Grabbing her hand, I leaned in and kissed her fingers before I moved to press my lips to her forehead. Her hat slipped off and I heard her gasp. I didn't flinch as I pulled the soft fabric down cradling her head. Every step away from that bed became laid brick in my chest. But it was when I looked back at her from the door that I realized I was her strength too. So, I gave her the only thing I could.* "You are the best friend I have ever had. Even if you grounded me every day."

She laughed lightly and made quick work of pulling up her sheet, averting her eyes so I couldn't see her pain. I couldn't lie. I couldn't tell her that I would be okay without her because I wasn't sure. I couldn't tell her that my life would be full without her because I knew that wasn't true. I would miss her, every second of every day for the rest of my life. I would never be ready to lose her.

So, I looked at the woman who gave me breath, and I told her the truth. "I see you, Emma." *She paused her hands and looked up at me.* "I see everything now. I just wish I would have seen it sooner. I would have done so much more. Thank you, mom."

I gasped at the memory of her face in that moment as I closed the door. She died a week after I left her in that bed with my father at her side. My chest stretched unbearably, and I coughed at the stab. And for the first time since she died, I spoke to her like she could still hear me.

"I'm coaching again. I know you were pissed when I quit after I met Kat. It's because you knew it would make me miserable," I swallowed, "maybe you knew she wasn't the right one, or maybe she had us both fooled." I stood and shoved my hands in my pockets as the wind picked up. "I met the right one. She reminds me a little of you. She's so beautiful in every way, so unassuming. She just wanted to make me happy. And she was good at it. She's so smart it scares me, but in a good way. The way that lets you know you're out of your league and lucky they haven't realized it. But I went and showed her. I fucked up, mom. I don't think I can come back from this the man you want me to be. God, I tried so hard with her. I thought, if I could get it right, just once, then maybe I could feel a little safer again, a little freer, with Abbie. With her, I could just be him. Your son, *myself*. And that was enough. But I didn't put her first. I didn't do it. I don't know if I'll ever be that man."

Even if my marriage wasn't falling apart I couldn't help but ask myself if I would've wanted Abbie anyway. Would I have strayed? Would I have thrown my marriage away for just a chance to get near her?

Everything inside me told me I would have if it meant I could feel a tenth of what I felt when I was with her.

Maybe I *was* that fucking guy. Because I knew in my soul I would sell, trade, kill or steal for another ten minutes of feeling like that and regret nothing. But even without more words, my compass showed me the truth. Love wasn't just about being there, it was about sacrifice. It was the one thing love required that could make me the man I needed to be. What I needed would come second. It's where I went wrong. It's where I've always been wrong.

Sacrifice would be my penance for taking her trust and muting it to hear my own heartbeat.

"Hey," Kat whispered faintly behind me. I sighed as I wiped my face of debris and prepared myself for the worst.

"Please, please don't, Kat. Not now, not *here*."

"I'm so sorry, but you keep avoiding my calls and I had to talk to you."

I turned to face her and was surprised to see her father at her side, holding her hand. Kat's mother had died before we met, and it had been our common bond when mom got sick while we were dating and then passed away five years to the day we stood as strangers at her grave. She knew I would show up.

"Hi Billy," I said with a nod.

"You look good Cameron," he said politely.

"You're a horrible liar," I said offering my hand. We shared a barely-there smile. Kat favored her father and he looked like he'd aged a decade since the last time I saw him. Some small part of me felt guilty about that because I knew the cause. But she was no longer my burden to shoulder.

"I can't believe it's been five years," Kat said softly looking down at where my mother rested. I couldn't bring myself to acknowledge her sincere empathy. I was too numb to her. I'd been through too much when it came to her. Still, I couldn't forget there was a time that I loved her, that I would have done anything for Kat.

She turned to her father. "Daddy, can you give us a minute?"

"Sure." Billy kissed her temple, ever the doting father as the wind gusted over us and left her shivering. I took off my coat and handed it to her.

She bit her lip as she cast her eyes down at my mother's picture. "She was so beautiful."

"She was."

"I really loved her, you know? I felt so close to her."

I nodded. "You two were thick as thieves."

"I bet she would hate me now," she sniffed.

I kept my jaw clamped tight. "My dad . . . he's been," she swallowed, "well we've been talking and I'm thinking about getting help. There's a place I checked out in Florida a few months ago. I think it might be good for me."

"I hope you go, and I hope it sticks," I said carefully in an attempt to keep the peace. "I really do, Kat."

"I'm high now," she said with a shrug. "I don't know if I'll ever be able to get clean. You were right to leave."

I stayed mute. I resented her for being there. I resented everything about the conversation that I'd begged for that seemed to flow so easily at that moment.

"And after what I've done to you," she swallowed hard. "The guilt is worse than anything I've ever felt. I want you to know that's one of the reason's I haven't stopped using. I know what I've done. I know what I've done to us, mostly to you. I'm sorry Cameron, with my whole heart, I'm sorry. You deserved so much better."

My whole body jerked at her admission. I swallowed the emotion down and the anger that threatened. "What do you want, Kat?"

"I wanted to tell you I'm sorry."

I couldn't help the suspicion, it fit.

"That's all?"

"No catch," she said before biting her lip. "I know it's hard to believe. But I don't want to be this person anymore."

"Why couldn't you say that to me then? All I wanted was for you to say you were still there."

"I wasn't," she said solemnly, "I'm still not, Cameron. I've been posing for pictures nobody's taking for so long, I have no idea who in the hell I am anymore."

A long moment of silent resolution passed between us.

"I don't think I was ever the woman you thought you married," she admitted, her voice low.

Her hair whipped around her pale face as her blue eyes implored mine for anything I would offer. Kat was startlingly beautiful, had always been. Even in her sickness, it hadn't faded, which made her beauty deceptive in a way that made me feel sick. And her admitting to that deception only made me feel worse.

It made me a fool. It made me feel taken. And for the first time since I left her, I saw she never wanted it to work out between us. And maybe that was the truth for me too. Ours was a marriage of convenience and I'd paid hell for it while she played numb and indifferent.

"Can you ever forgive me?" Her eyes were cloudy as I swallowed my bite and sighed. "I don't want to know you anymore, Kat. I know that sounds cruel. But it's the truth. I'm sorry."

She nodded as tears streamed down her cheeks. "I deserve that."

"I just can't," I told her. "But I will remember I loved you once. And I want you to be well. I'll hope for that, for you."

She cried quietly as I tamped down any human need to console her, and it wasn't difficult. I'd hardened myself to the point where I couldn't care. I couldn't afford to. What was left of my heart, my loyalty, resided with a woman in Wicker Park.

Kat broke the uncomfortable silence. "I won't contest the divorce. I'll accept your terms, it's the least I can do."

"Thank you."

"And Abbie?" She said as a question and I confirmed it with my silence. "What a fucked up and small world we live in."

"Please don't talk about her—"

She shook her head to cut me off. "I like her. Isn't that a crazy thing to say? And I like her for you."

"She didn't know about you. Don't . . . don't fault her." It was the last conversation I wanted to be having with Kat. She nodded as more understanding passed between us.

"I have no right to ask Jeffers—Cameron, but will you reach out to my father once in a while and let him know how you are?"

"I'll think about it."

Kat swallowed and shrugged off my jacket before handing it back to me. "Thank you, Cameron." I didn't know what it was for, but I nodded in response. She looked up at me with a forced smile. One that I knew was first nature after years of hiding. "Be happy. You deserve it. And maybe one day I will too."

"Take care, Kat. Good Luck."

She made her way down the narrow hill stumbling in her footing and her father was at her side in seconds. He embraced her, and I could see her crumbling in his arms. She'd never let me be her comfort. She never wanted me to see that far inside of her. A part of me was relieved she was finally letting someone else see her. I had to let go of the anger. She was never my puzzle to solve.

I looked back to my mother's headstone wondering what she would think of me, of how I've behaved. Of what I've done. Kneeling down, I pressed my fingers to my lips and then to her grave. "I miss you."

Half an hour later, I was pacing outside the front door. Nothing was working. Nothing helped. I felt hollow and completely alone. I had nothing to lose, I'd already lost everything that mattered.

Exhausted from battling demons, Kat's and my own, all that was left was the new throb of Abbie's loss. Even with Kat's confession, I got no relief. Mixed up in a way I couldn't navigate, I stared at the front door.

Thunder rang in the distance as droplets of rain began to fall on the porch, pinging off the empty plant stand. Thinking better of it, I took the first few steps away from the door when it opened.

"Cameron?"

I stopped my retreat and turned to see my father in the doorway, his eyes searching mine. "Son?" He took a step forward and put his hand on my shoulder as I faltered.

"Hey Dad," I croaked out as I crumbled on his doorstep. For the first time in my life, I let him see that I needed him. "How . . . how about now?"

26

Cameron

That night I sat at the bar staring through a hockey game. My conversation with my father on replay. I left out the details about Kat, but I was sure he knew. He spared my pride by keeping it to himself as I talked, and he listened. He was, for the first time in his life, careful with his words when it came to me. He didn't lecture, he didn't judge, he just listened.

And when all was said and done we were better off for it. It was a start. After he closed the door, I realized that he had the same need to connect as I did.

"Looks like they're getting their asses kicked." The voice came from the newly occupied seat next to me.

I mumbled a "yeah," without a clue to what team he was referring to and motioned for the bartender for my check when I got a text from Max.

> Max: Damn it, man. We're all here. Where are you? Don't do this again.

"You a fan of hockey?" The guy asked, indifferent to my vibe.

"Sure," I said as I pulled out my wallet and turned to address him.

The resemblance was unmistakable.

"Oliver," I said as my heart drilled out beats.

"Yep," he said coolly, rolling a toothpick on the side of his mouth. He was wearing a tux and his tie was hanging loose on his collar.

Panic crept in. "Is she okay? Abbie—"

"Thank you," he said as a beer was set out in front of him, he swallowed half of it before he brought his menacing gaze to mine.

"How did you know I was here?".

"I asked someone where an asshole would go to get a beer around here."

"Cute," I said as he glared at me with clear accusation.

Oliver shouldered off his jacket and hung it behind him as he spoke. "I just wanted to see the face of the asshole who destroyed my sister."

Irritated, I stood and placed a few bills on the bar.

"Are you here to take a shot at me? Go ahead but I can assure you it won't fucking touch the blow she landed."

"Why don't you tell her that?" He said unaffected.

"Why am I explaining myself to you?" I said through gritted teeth.

"That's a good point, why aren't you explaining yourself to *her*?"

"I tried. She knows how much I love her, I made sure of it. And she knows me. She knows me better than anyone else on this earth. And she's the only one."

"But that's not true, is it? If you're hiding behind a *wife*."

"Obviously you've never married the wrong woman. And I'm not hiding behind *shit*. And you don't *know* shit, so say your obligatory *shit* and fuck off."

Oliver released his cufflinks and began to roll up his sleeves.

"There are only a few things in this world I give a damn about and my sister is the first, so you will be explaining yourself to *me*, asshole." He scowled at me with eyes the color of hers as he spoke. "Abbie's a good woman. A little naive, a little bit crazy, but she's never intentionally hurt anyone in her life and she doesn't know her worth. I'm guessing you were the only one smart enough to figure it out and show her as much and then dumb enough to walk away."

"Again, you don't know anything about us, Oliver."

He started to roll up his other sleeve, his voice ice. "Another thing I care about are my hands. They're insured for millions, so, we can either talk this out like adults or I can play big brother and kick your ass to make myself feel better."

I had him by at least a few inches and fifty pounds. Still, I knew I'd let him land any punch he wanted. It was the caveman in me that spoke. "By all means, if you're a betting man and want to give in to that delusion, Dr. *Dick*."

Crystal blue eyes the color of hers raked over me unfazed as I held my breath until the pain passed. "I need these answers Bledsoe, so I can try to figure out how to get her to lift her head."

Razorblades sliced my chest as he spoke his plea.

"She's barely breathing, man."

I coughed out my emotion and ran a hand through my hair. "Want another beer?"

27

Abbie

"Okay Abbie, you need this. It's time to join the land of the living. No time like the present, yadda, yadda, yadda. Baby steps." My phone rattled in my pocket and I checked the screen. It was another picture text from Cameron. I silenced it, unwilling to look at it until I was safely behind closed doors. They'd started a week ago in lieu of the texts and calls I wasn't replying to. It was his way of letting me know he was still there. It had only been a few days since Bree's wedding and I still couldn't shake the anger so I found a distraction.

Rushing down the street toward the pub, I faintly heard my name called. Bennie sat next to the cigar shop entrance and waved at me from his seat on the sidewalk. Wrapped in a filthy black coat, he had several blankets piled on his lap. Guilty tears threatened as I made my way toward him and crouched down to greet him.

"Bennie, hi. How are you?"

"I'm keeping on, Abbie. I've been missing you."

He looked terrible. It was obvious winter had done a number on him. His face was cracked, and his lips were peeling. My heart plummeted as I thought of how many weeks I'd missed seeing him at the café.

"Oh, Bennie, I'm so sorry," I said digging through my purse for my wallet and grabbing every bill I had. He stilled my hands.

"I said I've been missing you, Abbie, not your money."

"I know," I said with a wobbling chin. "I know Bennie." I held out several bills toward him. "Please take it."

"I only take what I need, and you know that ain't much. I've been okay. Staying at the church most cold nights. That Cameron man comes to see me every week. Gives me food and blankets and plenty of money for dates."

My throat filled as my eyes watered. I'd forgotten Bennie. In my heartbreak, I'd completely abandoned him, but Cameron hadn't.

"He looks as sad as you. I think he's on the sauce."

"The sauce?"

"Drinking a little bit. I see him all the time."

"You do?"

"Yeah. Saw him not too long ago today."

"Really?" I cleared the burn in my throat and looked over Bennie. "Please just take a little money," I insisted, folding a couple of twenties and pushing them into his calloused hand.

"Thank you, Abbie."

"Bennie, I'll be there this week. I promise."

"Abbie," he said sternly. "Nothing to feel guilty for. You don't have to promise me anything. I'm always going to be alright."

"Are you still taking your meds?"

Bennie lowered his eyes as I challenged him. "Bennie?"

"I'll go see Bree first thing tomorrow."

"You need those meds, Bennie."

"I know. I know."

Bennie had HIV. He confessed to me weeks after I met him. He met and married his wife a few years prior to finding out. She miraculously hadn't been infected, but upon hearing his diagnosis she cleaned out his life, kicked him out of his home and left him to fend for himself.

The problem was he was too sick to help himself at the time and ended up selling everything he had to try to survive. Eventually, he was left with nothing.

Bree had taken it upon herself to get him enrolled in a program to keep him supplied with the HIV cocktail. He wasn't religious about taking it and it was clear by the way he was wasting away beneath the blankets. Everything about his situation shocked me to my core. And I hated that he had given up.

"Bennie, I'm going to get you a cab. I'll pay for it. You get to Bree. She's at work right now. I'll text her and tell her you're on your way, okay?"

"Abbie, I'm fine."

"Bennie, please?" He stayed silent, his eyes weary. "Please?"

"Okay."

Bennie gathered his things as I hailed a cab and spoke to the driver. I stood at the door while he piled into the cab and the driver gave me a side eye. I ignored it as Bennie grabbed the handle and looked up at me with his signature toothless grin.

"Abbie, you are good people."

"Bennie, you go right to the hospital, promise me."

"I promise."

"See you Saturday." I shut the door and the cab driver sped away.

After shooting off a quick text to Bree, I rushed into the pub and wandered through the small happy hour crowd until I heard my name. "Abbie?"

"Terry?"

"Yes," we both said in unison. We shook hands before I joined him at the cocktail table where he stood. He was handsome—in a silver fox sort of way—and had soft brown eyes.

"Sorry I'm late. I missed the train and had to take a cab," I offered knowing I was making a shitty first impression.

"It's fine, it's good to finally meet you," he said taking my coat and hanging it on the chair behind me as I took a seat. "I'm glad you could make it on such short notice."

"Me too. I've been anxious to meet you as well."

I swore I heard a mottled scoff behind me. "I'm not sure about this place. I haven't been here in years, it was the first bar I could think of in the neighborhood when you called me." That was a lie, but I wasn't about to take him anywhere near the bars Cameron and I frequented on Milwaukee.

"It's fine. I used to live in this neighborhood years ago."

"Really?"

"Yes. I had a place just down the street. Are you new to the area?"

"No, I've been here a since I graduated from Northwestern. I live just down the street in a three-flat right across from Wicker, the dog park side."

"What a coincidence I was of the park as well."

"Small world," I said.

"Yes, it is," he agreed.

"Are you going to ask her sign next?"

Neither Terry nor I had said it and in searching for the source, I looked behind me and saw a set of stairs. My phone buzzed on the table and I hit ignore before I spoke.

"Anyway, it's great to finally meet you. I've been reading up, and I have to say I'm impressed with your bio."

Terry grinned. "Thanks. I'm just going to admit now, I'm kind of nervous about this whole thing, I wanted you to know you're my first. You'll have to guide me through this."

I sat up straight on my stool. "I'm an old pro at this point, I'll take care of you. I promise."

"Good to hear, I've been anxious to have a more in-depth conversation other than online and phone calls. Let me buy you a drink." He motioned for the bartender and that was when I saw Cameron appear from a table just behind the small staircase.

"And old pro huh? Funny, I got a different impression." A slight slur accompanied his words as he came into full view.

My chest screamed as I got a whiff of his cologne. He was dressed in his well-fitted suit and wool trench coat. My lips parted when he glanced my way, his eyes full of fire and accusation. I went pale as he slid out a free chair at our table and leaned in on it. Terry drew confused brows as I stood, momentarily speechless.

I couldn't take my eyes off Cameron who was slightly disheveled, his tie loose at his collar. His hair looked like he'd been running fingers through it and hadn't shaved in days. A shadow coasted along his features as I sank back in my seat, my insides coming apart at his nearness.

Cameron went on, his gaze lingering on me before he addressed Terry. "I couldn't help overhearing and I'm sorry for the interruption." He spoke that time with a definite slur. "But I'm in need of an opinion."

"Please don't," I said leaning in on a whisper. My whole body jerked when his green eyes flew to mine. "Hi."

It took every bit of my willpower not to cry.

"Humor me, please," he asked, his attention back on Terry. He was intimidating as he loomed over the table, his jaw ticking, his posture stone. "For the sake of argument, I would love to run a scenario by you and then I'll let you continue your time with this stinging woman."

"You mean stunning?" Terry said seeming to clue himself in on the situation by the amount of a tension in the air. Though I was mortified he seemed oddly amused as his eyes flicked between Cameron and me. "So, what do you say . . . ?"

"Terry," he offered.

"Terry, thank you Terry, nice to meet you," he said as he nearly tripped over the leg of the chair making himself at home before extending his hand. Terry took it and they shook across the space.

"Cameron," I said on a bark, "this isn't an appropriate time."

He ignored me completely. "Just hear me out," he said to Terry.

"Let's hear him out Abbie," Terry said with a wink my way. I cringed. Cameron's eyes flared, but he went on.

"Let's say you met this *stunning* woman, and you agree to take things slow, but there are rules."

"I'm following," Terry said crossing his arms.

"Nice suit," Cameron remarked.

"Armani," Terry said.

"Of course," Cameron said dryly. "Anyway, the rules are that you both have to leave your baggage at the door. No personal history, no ex talks whatsoever."

"Okay," Terry said.

"And let's say this woman was so beautiful, so engaging that you couldn't resist giving into her demands, that you would channel the patience of fucking Job for a chance to get to know her, because trust me, you'd need the patience of God's forsaken to get to her."

"Cameron," I grit out.

"But maybe in this scenario," he said taking a long pull of his drink, "you're in a type of prison."

"Prison?" Terry asked as I white-knuckled the edge of the table.

"Yes, a living hell, one you can't see your way out of. And then this woman smiles at you, and you think to yourself, 'maybe I'm not one of God's forsaken'. Maybe, just maybe, life's worth living."

"That good?" Terry asked.

"Better than you can ever imagine," Cameron said tossing back a piece of ice from his glass and crunching it obnoxiously. "Infinitely better."

I pressed my lips together to keep my chin from wobbling.

"Okay," Terry said. "But you can't tell her that?"

"About the prison? Oh, no," Cameron said as a cross smile graced his face and he shook his head at Terry with wide eyes. "*Her* rules."

"Terry, we should go," I said standing.

"I'm almost finished," Cameron said his voice so raw I couldn't look away. He continued to speak with our eyes locked.

"And maybe you fall in love with her, and she's the closest goddamn thing to perfect you've ever known. Your secrets are killing you, but your happiness is finally there, it's finally there to the point you can touch it, taste it, you can see life differently with her."

"Is this woman happy too?" Terry asked looking pointedly at me. I pressed my lips together.

"Oh definitely. Things are so good, neither of you can imagine life without the other." His voice cracked slightly with his words.

"Please," I pleaded softly, and neither of them heard over the noise of the crowd. Cameron had sent a picture every day.

The first was a shot of us on the Skydeck and the ones that followed devastated me. The two of us after a run in the woods, in the limo before the dance, for some reason that one hurt the most. I was kissing his cheek, eyes closed as he smiled for the camera.

I'd saved them all but couldn't bring myself to text back. He'd documented almost every one of our days together and was tearing me apart with the reminders of just how good things were.

"But the rules," Terry said following Cameron's lead, snapping us both out of our daze.

"Yes," Cameron lifted his glass. "The goddamned rules. The thing is, you realize later that those rules were there for her, not you. But you followed them, because you knew she needed it, just as much as you needed her."

Terry played along. "And this prison? Do you get out?"

Cameron tossed back the rest of his drink. "Let's say she freed you the minute you touched her."

Tears finally escaped as I tore my eyes away from Cameron to silently plead with Terry. He glanced my way before he spoke.

"She's upset, Cameron. Have you made your point?"

"I'm not sure, but tell me, Terry, just look at her. When you found her on Match.com did you ever dream you'd find such a *stunning* woman?"

"Stop," I said pleading with him. "Please stop."

Cameron leaned in. "She's one of the good ones, inside and out. A real game changer. Have you ever been the bad guy, Terry? I have, I *am* and it's a sick feeling."

"Can't say I didn't have a bit of a heyday when I was younger."

Cameron smirked, his eyes emerald and ice. "Yes, definitely a heyday as you're what, now, sixty?"

"Damn it, Cameron," I snapped.

"Forty-eight," Terry chuckled taking zero offense.

"Playing it safe aren't you Abbie?" He said, his voice cracking as he turned to me.

"Terry," I pleaded. "I took the liberty of making us dinner reservations. I hope you don't mind."

"Not at all," he answered.

"We should probably go," I said just as Cameron smacked his palm on the table commanding our attention.

An ill feeling crept over me as my mind wandered back to Luke.

"Romance is dead, she thinks it's dead, did you know that, *Terry*?"

"And what do you think?" he replied.

"I think," Cameron swallowed, "I think people are afraid of it, but I have proof it still exists."

"Really?" Terry said, more concerned for me than amused at that point.

"Nothing beats a picture," Cameron said softly

I spoke up then. "My mother takes pictures. She says that there's always more to the story."

"Oh, there's more," Cameron said as his hard eyes swept me. "So much more," he rasped out, his features softening. Can you sleep?" He croaked. "Baby, I'm not sleeping."

Terry stood. "I'll get us a cab."

I nodded. "Please."

"Of course, I've taken enough of your time," Cameron said keeping his eyes glued to mine.

"It's nice to meet you, Cameron," Terry said. "Good luck to you. Abbie, I'm going to step outside."

"Thank you," I said as Terry grabbed his coat draping it over his arm and wordlessly asking my permission to leave me alone with him. I nodded and turned to Cameron as a thousand emotions ran through his features.

"Do we mean anything to you at all?"

"Don't act like I wasn't there," I said defensively "I was there."

"Are you going to fuck him?" He snapped, his fists clenching on the table. I moved to leave, and he caught me by the hand. "I'm sorry, but I can't handle knowing he might want to and you might let him. Jesus, Abbie, are you going to let him touch you?" He broke then as I watched, paralyzed by it. "What are you doing with him?" he asked, the desperation in his voice breaking me. "I *love* you."

"I'm not with him, Cameron, I'm not with *anyone*."

"I'm still there, where we were," he whispered softly. "You're in my veins, Abbie. You should know that. I'll never stop loving you."

Through the large window, I watched Terry hail a cab.

"Look at me," he whispered. "This is me at my worst. Please don't do this to us."

"I didn't do this."

"You're right. I did. Love me anyway."

I do.

"Cameron, where is Max?"

"He's here," he said motioning over his shoulder. I spotted Max ordering a drink at the bar, his eyes on our table. I hadn't even noticed him walk in.

"Abbie," Cameron pleaded, "please talk to me."

I looked at the love of my life and got lost in the beautiful plains of his face, the angle of his jaw, the jade of his eyes. He was the same man I fell for, but nothing made sense. We'd been torn apart by truth and lies. "I have to go."

He reached out to touch me, and I flinched.

"I'm still angry, Cameron." In a shaky voice, I let a little of it take over. It was the only thing saving me from fraying. "I worked with her, your *wife*. You made me an adulterer. You didn't even give me the choice." I shook my head at the memory of it. "And I told her," I swallowed, "I told her private things about *us*. Kat knew about you when we met, she knew the day you told me you loved me." I let him see my anger, my pain. I let him see the betrayal I still felt. "I trusted you and you made damn sure of it. I begged you not to and you made a fucking fool out of me."

His face twisted unbearably.

"I have to go."

Max looked between us as Cameron took a step forward, "Abbie, I know you still love me, I know you do—"

My eyes drifted over to Max who stopped him. "Let her go, man."

Cameron's eyes turned to ice, his jaw ticking as Max did his best to keep him at bay. "Let her go."

"Is that what you want?" Cameron said, his voice gravel as Max kept us separated. "You want me to let you go?"

"Get him home?" I asked Max and he nodded.

"Don't do that," Cameron snapped, his eyes volleying between us. "Abbie, I'm right fucking here, talk to me."

"Thanks, Max," I said grabbing my coat.

"Abbie," Cameron tried again. I ripped my eyes away and walked out of the bar, splintered.

Outside, Terry opened the door as I glanced in the window of the pub and saw Cameron was still standing where I left him, his eyes penetrating through the glass between us as Max rapidly spoke to him. I saw it then, the break in him and nothing about it satisfied me.

Terry met me at the curb. "Abbie, if you need to stay we can reschedule." I shook my head and slid into the car as he opened the door. Swallowing several times in attempt not to sob, I apologized on a shaky breath. "I'm so sorry."

"You couldn't help that any more than he could," he said with reassurance. "I have to say, I'm curious about the prison."

I looked over at him. "He was married. *Is* married. Separated."

"Ah," he said as the cab sped away from the curb, my soul freshly ripped, I spent several minutes inwardly gasping before I turned back to Terry.

"I'm mortified."

"Again, Abbie, don't be. I hope you two can work it out."

"I'll understand if you want to find someone else to fill the position. I can recommend several others well qualified that may be able to take the contract on short notice."

"Totally unnecessary. I have no intention of replacing you. This meeting was just a formality since I was out of the office when my assistant hired you. This has no bearing on your employment."

"Thank you." It was all I could manage.

A few minutes later I was still at a loss for words, my chest screaming as I finally bled out.

"You know Abbie, when I met my wife, I was in the middle of my own divorce," he said carefully. "I'd been married eight years to my college sweetheart," he explained as I looked over at him. "It was different."

"How was it different?"

He thought about it for a moment. "It was like I was two

different men. I'm a bit of a believer we can't evolve with those we start relationships with when we aren't full bloom unless you are capable of growing together. It's too hard to sustain a relationship when you're changing and embracing it and your partner is intimidated by it. My ex-wife was. It's what ended us. Sometimes you just have to accept defeat to figure out it's the only way you can really get anywhere personally."

Another strangling beat of silence as I pressed my fingers to my forehead, Cameron's words ripping at my resolve.

Love me anyway.

"What will you do, Abbie?"

"I don't know."

"Well, I hope it works out. I remember feeling that helpless over a woman once."

"What did you do?"

"I married her. We celebrate our fifteenth anniversary on Sunday."

28

Abbie

I closed my laptop, relieved to be out of the virtual meeting. I finally understood the meaning of the coffee cup that read *I survived another meeting that should have been an email.* I walked down the stairs of my three-flat, nervous for the first time in months. I'd shot off a text to Cameron earlier that morning and asked him to meet me. He'd replied instantly letting me know he would be there. I was finally ready for the answers. The ache of missing him, the need to know, was too much. I wasn't sure if we had a future, but I needed clarity. Some sort of justification for the pain. He'd stopped texting me a week ago due to my refusal to acknowledge him. I couldn't bring myself to answer any of his calls. I needed, no, I *deserved* the one on one. It was anger that kept me away. But it was also the anger that kept me lost.

Due to the meeting, I was already running late and did a last-minute change into black slacks and a cuffed purple blouse. In a rush, I grabbed my purse and paused when I opened my front door.

She stood in a long black designer trench coat, perfectly put together and I cringed at the guilt that must have surfaced on my face the minute my eyes met hers.

"Kat."

I was fumbling for words that would never come. She had bared witness to the beginning of my relationship with her husband and heard about it as it evolved.

It was too fucked up to decipher. It struck me then she'd never once asked his name. She really was a bit narcissistic in that sense, and in all probability, feigning interest while calling Cameron 'coffee shop guy'.

Even so, I'd given her first-hand accounts no woman should have to endure. I felt responsible and angrier than ever as she looked over to me. It was enough to make me second guess my decision to reach out.

But it wasn't only Cameron's deception that irked me. I didn't know the truth from a lie where Kat was concerned. And though I was blissfully ignorant of the truth on her end of things, I felt a sense of relief seeing her at my house. But no words would come, so I let her take the lead.

"I've been standing here for twenty minutes trying to get the courage to knock." It was a rare sign of weakness on her part. "I'm sorry to show up like this unannounced. I didn't know if Cameron would be here."

"Is that why you're here?" I asked cautiously. If she wanted to stir the pot she had a leg to stand on at that point. I had no idea what was going on as far as Cameron was concerned, but I had every intention of finding out.

"No. I'm here to see you."

"Okay," I said carefully taking a step forward. "Kat, I didn't know."

She nodded. "He told me."

"So, you have to know I told you what I told you out of friendship and confidence, not out of cruelty," I said with a trembling voice. I'd felt so justified in loving him moments earlier. I needed that strength back, but looking at the ghostly thin woman in front of me, I was on shaky ground. Was she high? I would never know the truth, but I did want the truth that I could see building on the tip of her tongue.

"Did he leave you?"

She nodded. "Almost a year ago."

Relief for myself and anguish for my friend ran the gauntlet.

"I don't understand. Why would you act like you were still married?"

"Because I was," she said harshly.

I felt that blow to my toes.

"That's not why I'm here. It's not," she back peddled.

"So, you were never trying to work things out?"

"I was raised to keep up appearances," she said in a hushed tone. "I was an Olympic hopeful. I never took Cameron's name when we married. I was a golden child, remember? I didn't want to admit my husband left me."

I nodded, though the irony wasn't lost on me that she looked nothing like a doting wife with her treatment of him. She'd saved *nothing* as far as appearance went. Her addiction made her nothing short of a monster.

She seemed to read my thoughts. "Not so much a golden adult. I've made so many mistakes."

"We all have, Kat. I could have been there for you."

She gave me a weary smile, "While my husband fell in love with you?"

"God, what the hell did I just say?" Mortified, I hung my head.

"It's okay, you know," she said descending the steps. She looked stoic in her stance from years of practice. I had little in the weight of posture. I was hanging off the ledge myself. "All of those times you spoke to him?"

"He was always talking divorce, begging me to set him free. But I wanted to punish him."

"For what?" I asked thinking of Cameron's beauty and wondering how she could treat him so vile.

"For being everything I wasn't," she said with a trembling voice. "I was angry. I was resentful. And I hurt him in ways no woman should ever hurt a man," she admitted. My eyes snapped to hers. "In every way you can imagine," she added, but didn't elaborate. But she didn't need to, I saw it all there. I felt sick.

I wasn't letting her go that easily.

"You *hurt* him?"

She swallowed casting her eyes down sweeping over it. "Yes. And he deserves someone like you Abbie, someone with tolerance who could never wound him the way I did. Who could never talk to him the way I did. I don't want you to hold it against him. The way I treated him," she swallowed again, "is unforgivable."

Anger rushed through my veins but all I could do was pity her. "Why are you telling me this?"

"Because maybe he won't, and he deserves a little understanding. And maybe it won't be easy for you to break through what I did, but if anyone can do it, you can."

"What is he, that you aren't?" I asked as she sniffed and wiped her nose. It was as if the weight of what she was telling me was getting to her and she stumbled a little in her heels. My hands shot out and I caught her.

"Kat! Are you okay?"

"I'm fine," she said weakly ripping away from my hands. "I have a headache and I haven't eaten today," she said dismissively. I didn't believe her for a second. "Kat, I can help."

Her eyes narrowed. "Take a number Miss Fix It," she snapped using things I told her in confidence against me. "Let's not go down this road," she warned with a clear hint of ice in her voice. She was definitely high and for the first time ever, I saw what Cameron saw. I bit my tongue and nodded. "Can I help get you home at least?"

"No," she said with the shake of her head. "This is not why I'm here. You need my help, I don't need *yours*."

"I wouldn't be so sure of that," I said with my own bite. "Kat, you look terrible." And beautiful. But she was a disaster and we both knew it. "If you're feeling sick, I can—"

"Damn it, listen to me. I'll figure my shit out. I'm here to talk about Cameron."

"Well I don't need your assurances, I know who I fell in love with. And really what gives you the right? You forget I heard the way you spoke to him. I heard it."

Something close to remorse covered her guilt-ridden features before she squared her shoulders. "Fine," she snapped before she pressed past me and walked toward my gate.

Unsatisfied I shook my head. "Wait, Kat, wait," I said catching up with her just as she made it through and shut the gate closed behind her.

"I appreciate you coming by, but I'm worried. And I'm ashamed and I don't know how to even approach this. Tell me how to do this Kat, tell me how to help."

"You can't." She looked over to me and gripped my hand tightly before she let go. "Just . . . love him like I couldn't. Take care, Abbie."

I stared at her retreating back as I walked up my steps and

sat on my stoop trying to process it all. The sun was slowly descending on another day without him.

"Hey Abbie," Mrs. Zingaro greeted as she checked the mailbox outside her door in her usual attire. She slowly flipped through the envelopes as I looked on after Kat. "Same old garbage," Jenny huffed.

In my headspace, I wondered how much of Cameron still existed and how much of Jefferson was left. I wondered if somehow the two had merged into the man I fell in love with. I didn't know Jefferson. And I was still reeling from the fact that the same man Kat made a mockery of was the same man I'd been in awe of. Maybe that was his bigger confession. Not that he had a failed marriage, but he lay victim to his ex-wife. Her treatment of him was vile, cruel, intolerable.

There was a fine line between keeping his dignity and our downfall. I couldn't bear the thought of him hiding. But I cringed at the way Kat smiled at me when she hung up the phone with him. It was a sardonic victory that I saw.

I wasn't a better woman because Luke left me terrified and guarded. I was different, sure, less trusting, that was a given. But I wasn't finished living. And from what I knew of the man I met, he wasn't either, despite his deeper issues. He had a shitty marriage, a marriage he kept hidden. There was nothing subtle about it. It was a glaring obstacle and he somehow expected me to forgive him despite the gravity of it. Maybe he never expected us to become a we. But then again, neither did I.

"Another bill collector spelled my name the wrong way," Jenny chimed in as I hummed in agreement.

Cameron and I had already hurdled our mountains before we met. Alone and in our own way, we fought the good fight and won to give ourselves a chance. And when the other shoe dropped, I ran from his scars instead of brushing over them with fingertips of admiration. That's the kind of love I expected, so why hadn't I given it? No matter what cross he'd bared it helped him evolve to the man who I loved and who loved me.

"Guess I don't have to pay them."

"Pardon?" I said looking over at her.

"They spelled my name wrong, I said I won't have to pay the bill."

"That's not exactly how it works, Jenny," I said absently.

"No, but to try to escape it on a technicality, it would represent the name well."

I frowned. "I'm not following."

"Zingaro is Italian for gypsy. I told you that when we met, remember, but I promised not to skip out on rent."

Say hello to your gypsy neighbor.

"You forgot. It's okay sweetheart it was a long time ago."

My jaw dropped.

"Abbie. Are you okay?"

I looked over at Jenny and nodded. I was so far from okay. Bree's words struck next.

It was like kismet or fate or destiny or that stuff you don't believe in.

Jenny studied me from where she stood. "Okay, well if you get hungry I have some stuffed shells in the freezer," she said before she shuffled back into her apartment and shut the door while I sat stunned.

How much proof did I need? How much more could he have shown me? He'd proven himself in every way. Before I found out about Kat, I had complete faith in Cameron. He'd earned my trust. I believed him, he made sure of it.

It's really not so hard to believe in me, is it?

My eyes flooded as my heart sank.

He didn't ask me for anything other than to love him back.

He never manipulated me or used my words against me. Why was I punishing us both for misconception when I never fucking asked? When I refused to let him confess. When no matter how cliché his truth was in women of jilted past—those who unknowingly entangled themselves with married men—I had refused to let his attempt at honesty be enough to cushion the blow. I erupted even as he begged me not too.

Abbie, I had no idea what this would be. You have to believe I didn't know it was you I was looking for. This, us, it means everything to me. I didn't expect this.

In hiding our paths and with Kat's confession I realized we'd triggered each other's biggest fears in seconds. He'd turned into someone I didn't recognize right before my eyes while I hurt him in the same way Kat had while he lay crippled in her wake.

We had hindered and hurt ourselves despite our warnings. Did that make us worse off, volatile, or just vulnerable?

It made us human.

"Jesus, Cameron, what have we done?" I said as I raced toward the train.

I had him. I found him, I had the love I envied in spades. And I lost it to my insecurity and fear and he did the same. Did he know that? Did he realize it? And why wasn't he here fighting for us, for me?

The answer was clear. He'd given up.

And I'd given him every reason to.

Utter panic ripped through me as for the first time, I ran for my life.

29

Cameron

Moving past one of the twin lion statues, I walked up the steps of The Art Institute. I didn't know the fate of the night, but what I did know was Abbie had reached out and I wasn't going to deny her the chance to say whatever she wanted to say to me. But she'd made it clear with her silence, after my shitty attempts to talk to her, that she wanted shit to do with me. And I didn't want her to be another casualty of my ex-wife. I wanted her as far removed as possible from the hurt I caused her with my deception. She deserved better. Kat had only just signed the divorce papers that morning. Billy had seen to the rest. I would soon be a free man.

Fuck you life.

At the ticket booth, I couldn't help my smile as the attendant asked me if I was there for the rain exhibit. I nodded with an ironic smirk and waited as she handed my credit card along with my ticket back to me. Helpless to her pull, I looked around for any sign of long, fire-kissed hair and brilliant blue eyes. I'd missed her so much my chest screamed, and my head pounded. It was just as physical as it was mental.

She'd become so much a part of my life, without her I stumbled in my footing as if life never existed before her. Even if our night was laced with a goodbye, I had to see her again. But my fear was that she wouldn't see the same man when she looked at me.

Water poured from the ceiling in every form as I walked through the glass door to the exhibit. My heart beats mimicking the rain trickling down the multiple installs that filled the space. A multi-colored waterfall fell at my feet as the scent of fresh water hit my nose. It was nostalgic and hurt at the same time. I wandered aimlessly around and was stopped short when I saw a large photograph with a rain install on either side and small spray cascading over the picture.

The title was "My House."
Photo taken by Nancy Gorman.
Abbie's mother.
I read the digital prompt.

In two thousand and four, a Tsunami stemming from a megathrust earthquake swept Thailand and thirteen other countries killing more than 230,000 people. Photographed here is a young boy bathing an elephant in the rain who was covered in the aftermath. When Nancy asked the boy where he lived, he proudly pointed to the five by five shack pictured next to the animal and said "My house." Nancy won the Pulitzer Prize for her humanitarian efforts to raise relief funds with this photograph. This picture is also featured in the Smithsonian museum of art. Copyright 2004 Nancy Gorman.

I was speechless as I stood staring at the photograph that looked like something out of the Jungle Book. Inexplicably drawn to it as I imagined most people were when they first saw it. The boy had barely made a dent in the mud covering the elephant's skin, as the rain thundered down on them both when the photo was captured.

It was in that moment that I felt convinced Abbie had done the same thing for me. She'd wiped years of debris away from me and cleansed me with her love and by doing so freed me from the disappointment and loss. And I rewarded her by betraying her trust.

But maybe, there was a way for us to just . . . move on. Maybe with the right perspective, we could remain free of what tainted us, of the lies we told ourselves and each other and just let it go. With Abbie, I could. I had. I knew it was possible. If she could just look at me the way she did before. And maybe, the power to do that was in an act as basic as washing it away from view. That was how we started.

For the first time in my adult life, I appreciated the rain because Abbie *was* my rain. She embodied hope for me.

"My mother is a genius behind the camera," she spoke up behind me. I clenched my fists trying to keep my emotions in check.

"Somehow she managed to capture that picture with a broken leg. She was fifty and had taken that trip for her birthday. It's ironic, isn't it? She survived one of the worst Tsunamis in history and was there at that exact moment to take this picture and share it with the world. She told me that when she saw this boy washing this elephant it helped a lot to erase all the horrible things she'd seen as a career photo-journalist. That it renewed her sense of humanity when she needed it most. She'd almost given up. She's insanely gifted and raised Oliver and I to believe we could be just as extraordinary as she is, but I'm not. I'm just not. Oliver's a brilliant doctor with a sub-par bedside manner. In short, he's a bit of a dick."

I couldn't agree more.

"He's good at being a doctor. That's true of him. But I've been looking for something to be good at my whole life. Cameron," she whispered, her voice on a plea, "please look at me."

Abbie

My body flushed with a mix of nerves and emotion when he didn't move. But I pressed on, too afraid to stop. It occurred to me then, that in all our conversations Cameron had never said a word to indicate his childhood was anything but typical, if not wholesome, and something resembling the norm. His mother was on a high pedestal, and he respected and loved his father.

We had that in common.

Never in my wildest dreams did addiction and abuse factor into the life Cameron had lived or the one we shared. It was so far removed from who we were as a couple. It was the kind of thing that happened to other people, much like what happened between Luke and me.

I felt sick as I studied his tall form and not for one second could I believe he was a battered husband, it was unfathomable. In the strength he showed, in how he cared for me, it was inconceivable. But the reality was, he was. I needed to somehow break through, to show him it was okay to be both men with me. The one who could show strength and weakness, and to let him know I would love him the same no matter what.

"I'm nothing special and I'm okay with that. It's like with Bree and all her talents. I've always tried to adapt to some of her ways to make myself more interesting, to be a little more adventurous. Learn to belly dance like her or go on one of her safari's, but that's Bree. That's part of her allure. Me, well I study crazy human behavior, eat dinner regularly with an eighty-six-year-old and count numbers for a living. My kind of exciting is so lame that I have a hard time explaining myself to others. But not you. I never had to explain myself to you." He stood statue-still as I spoke to his back.

"I can count." My voice cracked as I choked on a threatening sob. "I can tell you how many cups of coffee we've shared. Fifty-six. Or how many times you told me I was beautiful. Twenty-two times you've said that to me, twenty-two times that you've made me feel like heaven existed on earth. I can tell you how many times you've kissed me and taken my body, and I promise you, it wasn't nearly enough. Twice you told me you loved me," I was crying quietly at his back. "And both times I felt like I could be myself and nothing else and that was enough for you. It's the best thing I've ever felt in my life."

My tears fell freely as I stood with my heart bleeding and held it out to him. He gave me nothing, not a word or a single movement, but that didn't keep me from fighting.

"I've only made one promise to you, so I had to keep it. But I wanted to make it clear about what I aspire to be, and what I'm not. What I may never be. But I know special when I see it. And you have it. Whatever it is that makes a person . . . *more*. I won't win the Pulitzer and I can't belly dance, but I can do something so much better than any woman alive. I can love you." He flinched as my voice cracked. "And I can treat you the way you deserve to be treated. I'll show up for you. I'll be there every time you need me. I'll be your best friend. I can love you,

Cameron. You are the thing I'm good at. You. Being yours. And I swear to God I will never lay a hand on you in anger, ever again."

People began to filter through the exhibit, so I took a breath and collected myself. I barely heard him when he finally spoke.

"Who told you?"

"She did."

His shoulders fell, and he hung his head.

"You should know, she just left my house, I texted you to meet me before she came to my door. Me being here and asking you has little to do with her confession."

"Don't feel sorry for me, Abbie, that's not what I want."

"I don't. Okay, that's a lie, I do. But I can't stop those feelings. Any feelings when it comes to you. And I don't want to. Cameron, please look at me."

His voice was a whisper. "Forgive—"

"Yes, that's what I'm saying—"

"No," he turned around with unshed tears in his eyes. "Forgive *me*. How can you forgive me for fucking up something so perfect because I selfishly let it happen between us? But how could I . . . " he choked on his emotion.

"How could I tell you that I could be the man for you Abbie *and* the truth? I wasn't enough to save my marriage. I got selfish, I gave up. I stopped loving her and I started loving you and I don't regret it. But I let her destroy herself because I was tired of trying. I wanted to move on without her. I hated her, Abbie. I *still* hate her. How can you feel anything for me?"

"I feel *more* for you because of it. I want more for you. How can that be wrong? And if there's a little pity involved, then I'm sorry, you'll have to deal with being vulnerable like I have to deal with your dishonesty."

He looked around us and lowered his voice as a couple passed by sensing our tension. "I was going to tell you everything. That night."

"It was too late. And instead of believing the best in you, I hurt you in a way you may not be able to forgive me for. But even if some part of me thought the worst and acted, my heart won't ever let me forget I chose you and it's not because you're the perfect man."

Tumultuous oceans of green swept my face.

"But just so you know, you and me, *we are absolute.*"

He closed his eyes tightly and two thin tears streamed down his face and stole my breath. It was wrong, it looked all wrong on him. This wasn't the carefree man I fell in love with who had the strength of mountains that at that moment resided on his shoulders. The need to fly to him was unbearable as I kept where I was standing.

I took a step forward as he gazed down at me with desperation. "I just want us back, Cameron. I'm choosing to believe you. If that makes me a fool or susceptible to an outsider's eyes, then let me be those things. But I couldn't give a damn what anyone thinks. Stupid, naïve, whatever, I don't believe it of myself and I don't believe the secrets you hid taint you. I do know you, Cameron, maybe not every detail of your failed marriage or trivial things that really won't change our relationship one way or another, but I *know* you and I love you."

"Abbie—" His voice was thick, agony laced and matched the ache in my chest. I was shaking with need to touch him, to fly into his arms and erase the days without him. I hated myself in that moment for missing a single minute, but I wasn't solely responsible.

"I want us back. But I deserve the man who pursued me with good intentions and an open heart. I deserve him because that's the man I want to love. If there's any left of him inside you, that's the man I'm waiting for. He didn't want to give up and I don't want him to either, because he makes me happy, so incredibly happy. He makes my life so much better, he *knows* me. You ask me how I can forgive you? Ask my heart who refuses to let me hold this grudge. I love you too much. I choose happiness over bitterness, *now* over *then*, always with you. Always. I don't want to be without you, ever. We all die at zero, Cameron if we're alone, we all end up at zero. There is no point in keeping score."

"I'm sorry," he whispered.

"I know," I said my voice laced with ache. "Please," I said on a whisper, "please don't take too long."

I walked away then because it would be far too easy to fling myself at him and beg him to love me, because he would. He would take me into him and feed my need, because he loved me enough to do so.

But I wanted him to walk into the rest of our relationship with the open heart that he was when I met him. It was my own selfish condition.

With Cameron, I was playing for keeps.

Cameron

PEERING THROUGH MY REFLECTION OF THE COFFEE shop window, I saw her sitting at her table. Her dark-red locks swept over her shoulder as she sucked on her full bottom lip—a habit I loved—while she typed.

"Hey, Cameron," Bennie spoke up as I eyed her through the glass. "See something good in there?"

I mustered a grin. "Where did you come from?"

"I'm everywhere. Been seeing you a lot less lately. You finally done sucking on that bottle and if so why didn't you just bring it here to me?"

We grinned at each other. "I wasn't that bad."

"You smelled worse than me."

I pulled out my wallet and he waved me off. "I'm good."

"Abbie?"

"She took care of me. She's good people." Bennie stood. "I'll be seeing you around?"

I looked back into the coffee shop. "I hope so."

"I have a good feeling you two gonna be alright. You take

care of her."

"Thanks, Bennie, I will," I said absently, still focused on Abbie when the bell on the door rang out beside me. Swallowing my fears, I grabbed the handle before it closed and took a step inside.

Standing in front of a wall of cups, I took my time. I had so much to say, but I knew it couldn't be conveyed with a fucking Hallmark slogan. I needed her to know I was there as the man that met her. The man who wanted to merge my life with hers. Without a doubt, I wanted her to know she came first, not my pride or my selfish needs. And once I did tell her I wanted her to know I would respect her decision.

Everything that had happened between us up until the point our weaknesses collided had coincided with the needs of my heart. But regardless of the words she spoke at the museum, about not knowing about the truth, I wanted to tell her. Not because I wanted her sympathy, because I had it and I hated it. But because she deserved the truth. And I was a slave to my love.

It may have started out with me and my selfish haze, for my need to believe in something better for myself, but she would always come first.

I'd made a mistake with the original woman I'd promised forever to.

I'd damn near made the same mistake again with the rightful woman who deserved that promise.

I needed to grow the fuck up and it was time to break the pattern no matter the outcome.

I chose my cup and walked to the small booth across from the macaroni table. Abbie sat typing away, earphones in as she moved subtly with the beat of her music. I knew the second she became aware of me when she froze, and her eyes found mine while I took my seat and opened my Mac.

In her bright blue eyes, I saw a mix of relief and fear. I kept her gaze as I typed with my heart in my throat.

Cameron's Mac: Hi.

She bit her lip, her chin wobbling as she typed back.

Abbie's Mac: Hi.

Tears filled her eyes and fell, and it took everything in me not to go to her.

Cameron's Mac: Please don't cry.

Abbie's Mac: I'm sorry. I can't help it. I'm afraid.

Cameron's Mac: Don't be afraid. Please don't be afraid of me.

Abbie's Mac: I'm not afraid of you.

We held our gaze for a good minute as her tears fell.

Cameron's Mac: I love you. No matter what. You know that, right? Nothing can take the time we had away from us. Nothing could ever touch that. Okay?

Abbie's Mac: Okay.

There was no way to go into it lightly. This was the heavy we'd avoided for far too long. I wasn't wasting any more time.

Cameron's Mac: Kat was a gymnast when she was young. Did she tell you that?"

Abbie nodded, and I had to rip my eyes away to keep going.

Cameron's Mac: She had a bulging disk and for years she was in constant pain. After she finally had to have surgery, she got hooked on the pain meds and became an addict. Her addiction stemmed from nowhere. At least that's what I thought. Before the surgery we had a decent marriage and a good life. We wanted for nothing and were talking about having our first child. I can't say that our marriage was blissful because I know what that feels like now, with you. But at the time I wouldn't have second guessed it. Looking back, maybe she was unhappy because the drugs seemed to fill up something I couldn't. At first, she tried to hide it from me. And then when she stopped trying to conceal her addiction, everything changed.

Abbie nodded at me in encouragement.

Cameron's Mac: The first time I confronted her was the first time she lashed out.

Abbie nodded and wiped her face as she looked at her screen. I knew she was afraid I would see the pity in her eyes. But all I wanted was understanding.

Cameron's Mac: I tried everything I could. She did not want my help and made it clear she didn't want to get clean. I finally gave an ultimatum and kept it by leaving her. She never did anything to bridge the gap on her end. I didn't stop trying to help her when I left, and she didn't stop destroying herself. I would catch her seeking all over the worst parts of the city. I froze her credit cards, I kept tabs on her twenty-four seven. I damn near lost my business following my wife all over Chicago to get prescription drugs. She was a functioning addict, so no one was concerned, not even her father who I tried repeatedly to get through to. It was a fucking nightmare. One morning I woke up and all we had left in common was her addiction. We hadn't been physical in the whole year before I left.

Abbie's Mac: Did she do it a lot?

Cameron's Mac: Too often to talk about comfortably. I think I was mostly in shock. She was nothing like the woman I married and I'd never dealt with anything like that before. A few fights when I was younger. I went to see a therapist and Kat refused.

Abbie nodded as if she already knew. I had no idea what my ex-wife told her.

Cameron's Mac: I honestly don't know if it was all because of the drugs now that I look back. For the most part, she had a shitty temper but never lashed out like that. I think her father knows something more about that and they both never shared it with me. The night you found out, I handed her fate over to him. I wanted to be free of her, so I could be with you. Selfish, yes. Every single minute. I left my wife a drug addict to save my own life. To find another reason to be happy, to find you. I was tired of living in her nightmare. I sacrificed her well-being for my own.

Abbie's Mac: That's not true Cameron.

Cameron's Mac: It is. In sickness and in health. She got sick and I only spent a year trying to help her before I left. I can't say I wouldn't do it the same way again. That's the truth.

I swallowed.

Cameron's Mac: In a way I think I knew this, us, would blow up in my face. In some idiotic way I think I deserved it. I should have felt guilty for being as happy as I was with you when she still struggled with her addiction. I couldn't blame you now, if you couldn't trust me. And I don't know how to move forward from this. I never wanted you to know. I'm almost certain I would have kept that from you. Probably. I think. Fuck, I don't know if that's the truth. But I never should have lied to you about the fact I was still married.

Her breath left her as she read and re-read my words shaking her head.

Abbie's Mac: No.

Cameron's Mac: You had every right to be angry. I'm the bad guy, Abbie. In this scenario, I *am* the bad guy.

She shook her head refusing to believe me.

Cameron's Mac: This time I am. This round I was the one who was in denial and it paved my way into your heart and into your bed.

I saw her face pale as she shook her head adamantly.

Cameron's Mac: Yes. I hid behind your rules, so I had a shot with you. I did all of these things. But loving you was never a lie.

Abbie's Mac: You would never purposefully hurt me.

Cameron's Mac: I did hurt you, I scared you. That night, at your house I scared you.

Abbie's Mac: You would never hurt me.

Cameron's Mac: I did. And I did it by trying to save myself.

"This is bullshit," she said as she closed her Mac and shoved it in her tote. She wiped at her face with her hands stained with dark streaks I'd caused and met my gaze head on as she gathered her things and walked out of the coffee shop.

Stunned, I scrambled after her. "Abbie," I caught up with her a few steps out of the café. "Abbie! Damn it! This is happening. We're doing this." She walked forward and I caught her by the arm. "I mean it. I'm not going anywhere. Just tell me what you want."

She turned on me.

"Oh, this is happening? Really, Cameron? Are you sure about that?"

I stared at her in confusion as she looked up at me with contempt. "I don't think you know what *this* is."

"What are you saying?"

"You want to play villain instead of victim? Fine. But unless you can admit to being both we have *nowhere* to go."

Shock filtered through me as she challenged me. I stood slack-jawed as she called me out on my last lie. I couldn't look away from the woman I loved. Her commanding eyes washed me in their blue fire, and in a way, I felt cleansed. I'd never been more vulnerable in my life. Every card I had was laid bare at her feet, every emotion I felt reflected in her eyes. I had nowhere to go.

She pressed in, seeing it all. "No more secrets, Cameron and no more hiding. She's the goddamn bad guy. She hurt you physically and mentally and she doesn't get a pass for that. Especially not from you."

"What do you want?" I said as acid lit my veins.

"I want the truth."

"You want me to admit being a victim? Fine. I'm a victim, but it was never by choice, and I fought my way out of that hell by myself, so I think I'm entitled to a little discretion. No man in the world wants to admit to anything like that. No man in the world ever wants to talk about anything like that, Abbie."

I glanced around the sidewalk and found we were alone. "You think I wanted you to know, to *see* she hit me?"

"I did see. I saw it, I just didn't know what I was seeing! And I can tell you now, I will never be able to forget it. She hurt you. Do you think you're somehow less of a man because of it? *She* did this, that makes her a coward. You're still a man, Cameron. And you're still going to bleed no matter how strong you are. She's the fucking villain, not you. Just tell me you know that much."

My throat filled with acid and I slowly nodded.

"You didn't have to lie to me."

"I'm sorry. But I had my reasons. You saw them. They were written all over my face. I had to protect my happiness, but what I had with my mom I lost, and what I thought I had with Kat was beaten out of me. So, I'm sorry I fucking lied to you. I shouldn't have. But it was over with her a long time ago. You weren't the only one afraid of masks, Abbie. Not by a damn long shot."

She nodded and looked down at the cement below us. "My ex, Luke," she started.

"I know," I interrupted.

"What?" She said in a whisper.

"Your brother," I said connecting the dots. "I know."

She swallowed. "When?"

"The night of Bree's wedding. He tracked me down at the bar. Mrs. Zingaro, too. She slipped up one night after you went upstairs. She said he attacked you and her son stopped him."

"It wasn't their place," she said tightening her hold on her bag.

"I just wasn't sure if I'd ever hear it from you."

Residual anger stirred as I recalled the conversation with her brother.

"It seems so pointless now anyway," she said carefully.

"Don't do that, don't compare yours to mine. Don't do that," I said stuffing my hands in my coat. "Tell me, Abbie."

She shook her head. "I don't *want* to relive it. I don't *need* to. I've done enough of that. I got fixated and it wasn't healthy. If you know anything you know enough. He was controlling and manipulative and he scared the shit of me. But the thing is,

I got over it without you. And you helped me stomp the rest of my fears out. I don't want or need you to know every detail and I don't need to know yours unless you *want* to tell me. It's just some bad shit that happened to us on the way to each other. And if it keeps us apart, they win. I didn't want to admit my weakness for a man who used me any more than you wanted to tell me about Kat. And I know you tried. I knew we weren't invincible, Cameron. We have plenty of chinks in our armor. I know that, it's life, but with you I feel a hell of a lot stronger. That night I found out about Kat, I *was* afraid when you got upset, but in my heart, I know you would never hurt me. I won't believe that now or ever. You just aren't capable. And it's not that I'm glad this happened, but in loving you, I realized I could trust myself again. Luke's gone, you're here, that's all that matters. I just want you to be sure."

I swallowed her hard admission as she had mine and did my best not to ask any more questions, specifically those of an address. When Oliver left me at the bar that night, he was none the wiser, other than what doubt I could try to erase that I genuinely loved his sister.

And I was destroyed by the news she'd been treated that way. It only fed my head to the bullshit notion she was better off without me. But that's what it was, bullshit and she was calling me out on it.

If I wanted her to believe, I had to believe it myself.

"I miss you so much," I said studying her profile in the half-light casting shadows from the café. "Losing you is killing me. Just tell me what to do."

Her anger disappeared as she looked up at me.

"Tell me what *you* want, Cameron. Don't give me the answer you think I need, just tell me what *you* want."

"Jesus Christ," I choked out. "What I want? Abbie, all I

want, all I'll ever want again, is *you*."

And in that moment as I looked at her, I believed we were absolute.

A lifetime of promises raced through me as I stared down at her. "I will never keep anything from you again," I said softly as I took her face in my hands and made the first promise to shimmering blue eyes. "Ever. And I'll never let you go again without the fight you deserve. Everything you think you aren't, I can tell you right now you *are,* to me you are. And if loving me is what you're good at, I'll spend my whole life earning that affection. I want this, with you, until I'm not breathing. I need you to remember that when shit gets tough. Okay?"

"Okay," she agreed easily as if we were making simple plans for the day ahead instead of decisions on our future.

She'd just given me back my life, my happiness and I nodded and pressed a kiss to her forehead out of words as my heart stuttered in relief. "Okay."

Epilogue

Cameron

Chinese food in hand, I walked down Milwaukee Avenue as the sun set. I passed the graffiti walls and strode underneath the squeaking train as I made my way home. I'd taken the long route because Abbie liked her Lo Mein cold, the weirdo. I grinned as I thought of her text.

Me: Dinner tonight?

Witchy Woman: Will sucky suck for some sweet and sour soup and shrimp lo mein. Me love you long time.

Me: You're geeking out again, babe.

Witchy Woman: Fine, no sucky for you. Just get the food.

When I was growing up, I never really gave love a second thought. It was just something I was supposed to have.

A futuristic endeavor of . . . eventually or when the time was right. At the time of my choosing, I always assumed I'd have it when I wanted it.

I'd never been more fucking wrong.

Love in all its splendor is a damned nightmare if kept secluded to a timeline. You don't just stumble upon the love of your life and expect things to work out in your favor.

Love by its definition is a lie, its true definition is work and a fuck lot of it.

It also means so much more than that one syllable. It's a one-word representation of everything that can make or break a person. Love is only meant for the brave.

I didn't know when I was younger that I had love. I had the love of the first girl I bedded in high school. I remember feeling it and dismissing it for some other time. I had the love of my college sweetheart but never really returned her affections, always knowing in the back of my mind that she wasn't the one I would marry. That's a harsh truth. That makes me a bastard in a way. I'd abused her affections for my own personal gain and to pass the time.

The brutal truth about my ex-wife was that I'd married her because I loved her just enough and the timing was right. It was another bastard move on my part. And I still can't help but wonder if somewhere deep-down Kat knew it too, and that's what ruined us. I didn't love her like I should've.

In hindsight, I'd fucked it all up with my assumptions about something I'd never truly experienced. I honestly feel like I could have loved my high school sweetheart. But I'll never know, because that's how I taught myself how to love, by timing and convenience.

With Abbie, the timing was both right and wrong. I had no right and every right to fall in love with her. It didn't matter, because she was the one I was supposed to give my heart to.

But I got knocked on my ass—because of my arrogance and sense of entitlement—when loving her showed me different.

Hers was the love I craved all along. It was a gift. And *real* love is a fucking miracle. And if you're lucky enough to find it, you throw every one of your preconceived notions away and you hold onto it with every ounce of your being, because it's unforgiving in its wrath and if you're not careful it will let go of you as fast as it took hold.

Love broke us both and put us back together.

I was going to hold on to my love for Abbie, so tight that it hurt. And I would let it hurt as a reminder of how lucky I was to have her. I would never find another love like what I had with her, not in my lifetime.

And I was done bending to the timeline.

The day my divorce was final, I asked Abbie to be my wife.

I turned the key and walked into our three-flat.

"Abbie?" I called out as I looked around the living room. The TV was on and her purse and cell phone were on the coffee table along with a pharmacy bag. I went upstairs to find her in the bathroom.

"Abbie?" I knocked on the door. "You in there, baby? Did you freak yourself out watching Tru-Crime again? I told you to cut that shit out when I'm not home."

I could hear her light laugh behind the door. "Nooo, come in."

She stood in the middle of her bathroom with a pregnancy test in hand. I was sure she could see the surprise in my eyes as she held the test behind her back.

"So," she waggled her brows with animation. "How do you feel about kids?"

Mouth gaping, I took in her appearance. It was my favorite day—slob day—

and I loved it when she dressed down. Without a stitch of makeup on, I could see the faint line of freckles over her nose and everything God intended for me to see when he created the woman standing in front of me.

Every part of her a thing of beauty, every curve and nuance. From her flame-licked hair to the tips of her toes, I loved everything I saw. I couldn't help the subtle turn of my lips as I stuck my hands in my slacks and leaned against the door in an attempt to keep my poker face.

"I thought we were safe."

She frowned. "We have sex, so there's always a chance. We have lots of sex, so lots of chances. Don't stall or give me a rehearsed answer, tell me the truth."

Just as I suspected, she didn't let my silence stand as she commanded my attention, all five-foot-five of her. She didn't have to do much to earn it, she had it the minute I laid eyes on her.

"I love you," I said easily. The answer to the rest of my life in the palm of her hand, both literally and figuratively.

Her eyes watered as she stood on shaky ground. I knew whatever answer I gave had the ability to break her heart, but I gave her the truth anyway.

"You will come first, always and forever unless we have a piece of life we created together. Then he or she will have to come first. So, if you can handle being second I can handle being a dad. But I promise to always make you feel like first."

I could feel every bit of pent-up tension in her shoulders leave her as she spoke. "Good, I'm thinking you have several months to put a crib together."

She flew into my arms and kissed me soundly on the mouth. My heart ignited with a new kind of burn that told me I had everything in the world to lose. It scared the shit out of me and elated me at the same time. I kissed the ring that covered her dainty finger and then held her crystal blue eyes.

"Baby," I whispered.

"Baby," she whispered back as I pushed her sweatshirt off her shoulders and bared her breasts. She let out a moan as I dipped and captured a peaked nipple into my mouth.

"Cameron," she pleaded as I made quick work of freeing her clothes and lifted her to sit on the vanity.

"When did you suspect?" I asked as I pushed her knees apart and stood between them.

"Last week. My stomach started doing strange flips and I felt nauseous for a second. This morning, I got sick," she answered, her breath speeding up as I massaged her sides with my fingers.

I leaned in and kissed her deep and she moaned into my mouth before I pulled her closer. Bending, I bit the space between her shoulder as she clutched me. I loved the feel of her in my arms, the way she fit me. My hand trailed down to the silky skin of her abdomen and I dipped to cover it with my lips. Her head fell back against the mirror and I knelt in front of her.

"Abbie," I said as she tilted her head to look down at me, her beautiful blues full of love and promise.

"This is the best day of my life."

"Nothing can trump today?"

"I know you will. I know it will happen," I said spreading her thighs and pressing my lips to her creamy skin. Goosebumps erupted as she gripped my shoulders before I darted my tongue out.

"Oh God," she moaned as she ran a hand through my hair before she gripped it hard with my next lick. "I'm going to come."

"Already?" I said my attention drifting between her perfect peach nipples and her parted mouth, "I think I like you pregnant. Much easier to get you off," I murmured into her slit before I devoured it like a madman.

My baby was growing inside her, and in a month's time, she would be my wife. Everything about our progression felt natural, and the baby along with its mother had become my sole purpose in life.

Months ago, I was just a man searching for some sort of happiness when I met Abbie. With her, I would never need to look far. It was all there, my present, my future, my forever.

"I love you so much," I whispered as I licked and sucked her into screaming my name. Her legs shook with the weight of her orgasm as I slowed to a stop and grinned up at her.

"Who's your baby daddy?" I chuckled when she sank against me as I stood. I picked her up as she gave me a lazy smile, pulling me closer with every step I took. I saw it in her eyes the minute her mind kicked into overdrive.

"Are you really happy? I was religious with the pill. I promise. But I don't want this to be an 'oops' baby. I want you to want him or her."

"This could never be an 'oops' baby. Damn, woman, don't doubt it for a second," I said as I laid her across our bed. "I want whatever comes with being with you and *lots* of chances. And you, my future wife, are going to be full of surprises."

"Really? You're really happy?"

I frowned. "Is this pregnancy hormones or are you afraid I may really not want this baby?"

"I don't know," she said in a low voice as I stood up and slipped off my shoes.

Eyeing her naked and ready, I stripped my clothes anxiously to get closer, knowing even when I was buried as deep as I could go, I could never get close enough.

I loved her abundant for two lifetimes. Something I'd never had before and couldn't get enough of. I was addicted to her voice, her skin, her smile and her moans, her. In her, I discovered a new kind of love that came with a healthy addiction.

In a new world of second chances, I was the luckiest son of a bitch alive. I knew it. And I would never take it for granted. I vowed the day I put the ring on her finger never to lie to my future again, no matter how ugly my past, how distasteful my present thoughts may be.

All lying did in a relationship is delay the inevitable. Because no matter how hard you tried to be someone else with the person you loved, the truth revealed itself one way or another, either in anger, frustration or hurt. Good or bad she would get it all.

"I want this baby, I want you, I want our life. Every day. That won't change. Okay?"

"Okay," she said with a breathtaking smile. "Now, please don't take this the wrong way, but I want you to fuck me."

I couldn't hold in my chuckle. "As opposed to?"

"Making love. I want to be fucked."

Smirking I pushed in and buried my cock until she was milking it.

"God . . . yes," she groaned. I stopped my hips until her expectant eyes met mine.

"You just challenged my manhood woman, prepare to pay for that."

I didn't give her a chance to reply.

Abbie

"I'm a mom!" I announced to Bree on the phone. "I'm so knocked up! Two months! I didn't even know. I've had like fifteen glasses of wine. Are we okay?"

Her laugh across the line was hysterical.

"I had a feeling you were when you were scratching your nipples at dinner the other night.

"I was?"

"Yep, I thought it was your bra but then thought about it later."

"Why didn't you say anything?"

"And ruin the sound of your voice right now. No way. It's better that you found out organically and with Cameron. So much sweeter that way. And I watched you drink most of that wine. You'll be fine."

"Where are you?" I asked. "I want to celebrate."

"At your front door," she answered. Cameron's lips twisted when the bell rang.

He could hear every word, of course, because *Bree*. He'd been stroking the skin of my belly with his fingertips and winked at me as I sat up.

"You told her to come over?" He nodded and kissed his favorite freckle. "Yep, now I get to go play ball."

"You ass," I said as I smacked him on his mesh-covered butt. "You could've just gone."

"You guys decent?" Bree called from the hall.

"You may enter," I said as Cameron stood.

"That's what she said," both Cameron and Bree spoke at the same time as she ended our call. I rolled my eyes at the two of them.

Cameron had made it his mission to beat her to the punch. He was getting good at it. Annoyingly good.

"Congrats on your winning sperm!" Bree said to Cameron.

"Thank you," Cameron cooed back as he finished tying his Nikes and gave her a celebratory hug.

"We have dinner plans at eight," I reminded him as he pulled away from kissing me goodbye.

"Nag, nag. *Jeesh*," Cameron said with the wave of his hand. "I'll be back in time."

"Did you just say 'nag, nag' to *me*?" I shrieked.

Bree let out a belly laugh as she hugged me, and I glared at Cameron over her shoulder.

"I'll be here beautiful. It's not like I want to miss a date with that rounding ass of yours. From behind baby, it's perfection."

He kissed his fingers and let them go as if he were giving the best of Italian food compliments before he hauled ass out the door.

I stood stunned mouth gaping, but Bree read him easily. "Oh, he's so trying to push your buttons. Did you guys have hot angry preggo sex recently?"

"Did he just call me a fat ass?!"

"Noooo, he said your ass was getting bigger. A sure-fire way to land himself in a good fight."

"He better—"

"Forgot my keys," he called from the hallway, his eyes full of mischief as he gave me a once over, licked his lips and walked back out the door. I narrowed my eyes. "It would seem so."

"Yep," she said with a knowing smile. "Yeah, he's feeling the pregger sex, and the angry pregger sex. You will have no issue being worked over by that man. That's a good sign."

I was already in front of a mirror doing my best to look at my ass.

"God, what a punk. I'm going to kick *his* butt for saying that!" I winced. "I meant that figuratively."

"I know that, babe," she said looking on at me. "And so would he if he heard you."

"I still get worried I go too far sometimes," I said carefully. "I swear every time I hit him in jest, I realize what I did, and I end up crying in a closet. He busted me the other day and we had an argument about it."

"Because those aren't your mistakes to pay for," Bree pointed out.

"That's what he said."

"You're just being yourself. Cameron's man enough to realize that. It's not your fault. Don't beat yourself up for shit like that."

"I'm trying not to," I said with a sigh. "He went to therapy when his marriage fell apart, but I feel like I'm out of my element."

"Because he got the help he needed and if he says he's okay you have to trust that. There's nothing you can do but listen, and only if he wants to talk."

"He doesn't. I don't think he ever will. I told him I told you about Kat before he had a chance to stop me. It took him almost a day to talk to me after that. I don't think it will ever be something he'll be open about. He says he did his time in therapy and he's not going back. Not when it's about Kat. All I can do is read up and it's horrifying."

Bree nodded. "I stitched up a seventy-four-year-old man the other night whose wife hit him with a lamp. He begged me not to turn her in because she'd taken his social security check before he was admitted."

"Jesus," I whispered. "Did you report it?"

"The doctor did. It was the second time he's seen him. But

I would have. This stuff happens every day."

"How do you do that? How do you handle that, Bree?"

"Because that man needed someone to be there to stitch him up and to listen to him. It's not about me, it's about them."

"You're my hero," I said with a wobbling chin. "But you may have to talk me out of eye for an eye. I can't forget that she hurt him. He had bruises while we were dating because he was attempting to reason with her. At first, he told me they were from roughhousing with Max on the basketball court, but confessed later it was because he was trying to finalize the divorce without getting anyone else involved. He was protecting her, and she just kept hitting him!"

"He should have reported it," Bree said softly. "And he knows that, Abbie. He just didn't want it known. Some people are just too proud. It's his way. He worked through it the only way he felt he could while trying to keep his dignity."

"I know, but look at the cost," I said glancing out the window inwardly cringing about the signs I missed. "It makes me hate her in a violent way. My sweet man. How could she hit him?! How could she touch him like that?! I can't believe I had the nerve to be sorry for my part in all of it when she didn't even fucking deserve him! I swear to God I want to go all Scarface on her ass."

Bree's eyes widened. "Wow, mamma bear, not that you don't have a right to be pissed, but your hormones are raging already. You wouldn't hurt a fly."

I showed her my teeth and winced. "Oh no!" I hung my head. "You think that's why he ran away to play basketball?"

"You are a hot mess. Okay, yeah, we need to work some of this energy off and that big fat ass of yours."

"You are going to hell," I said as she tossed my Nikes at me.

"Female, mid-thirties, first baby, yeah your body isn't going to bounce back."

I crossed my arms indignant. "I got pregnant. I earned nine months of being fed chocolates while he rubs oil on my belly."

"You got laid and made another human you are going to have to push out of that virginal vag and chase around for the next four years."

I cringed.

"It's not so romantic now, is it? We need to get those hormones under control right now, so we don't scare the groom away a month before the wedding. And we need to get you in shape to be a late-blooming mommy."

"Fine, that's all I need is another coach in the family. I hate you already."

I strapped on my shoes and looked outside to see Cameron approaching Mrs. Zingaro, who was in one of her trances while watering her freshly planted flowers with the hose Cameron had just installed. I almost tapped on the window to warn him and thought better of it.

Three, two, one.

Cameron was soaked seconds later and caught me laughing in the window above. He narrowed his eyes at me while Jenny apologized.

I gave him my biggest smile before I disappeared and turned to Bree.

"Let me guess. Mrs. Zingaro?"

"Yep," I said as we walked out into the last of the spring sun.

The grass was a crisp green and the temperature was perfect. My mind flashed with the memory of the leaf I saw fall at Cameron's back after our first cup of coffee. So much changed after that day.

My whole body flooded with emotion as Bree stood at my

front door waiting for me to turn the lock. I looked in the direction Cameron fled from the crazy women his life.

"I love him so much," I said with a shaky voice.

"Oh . . . my . . . fuck," Bree exclaimed giving me a thorough once over.

I nodded my eyes widening. "Is this normal?"

"I would say that with you, it will be. Let's get this going, shall we?"

"Okay, I would do anything for Cameron," I professed.

She laughed and pulled me in for a hug as I did my best to suck it up. "I know girl, and he will for you too. That's what it's all about."

I married Cameron on a warm Summer night surrounded by candlelight in a little ceremony in Wicker Park. Most of our wedding day I'd suffered from morning sickness and by the time I got to his side, I was ghastly white. He didn't seem to mind. In fact, he told me I looked more beautiful than ever.

I'm sure my fairy godmother blinded him when I looked my worst. Which meant as I aged I would begin to look like a centerfold. That was good news.

What sucked is that I was sick for half of our honeymoon cruise and only managed to see the sparkling blue water of the toilet. I had two good days out at sea before we called it quits and flew home from Mexico only to end up on my couch watching Netflix and eating take out.

But my husband, *my husband, my husband* didn't seem to mind in the least. He assured me we'd do it again someday as long as we didn't have another 'oops' baby on the way. He teased me mercilessly as my pregnancy progressed and despite my fear, he never had an issue handling my hormones.

Once again, my mother was right, because after my lull,

my life picked up again and was not slowing down anytime in the immediate future.

So, I got joy out of the little things. And although I took fewer jobs to spend the first few months of my marriage as a wife, life was life, so I prioritized.

Almost seven months to the day I found out I was pregnant I made a much-needed date with my husband.

> **Cameron's Mac: Hi. Sorry I'm late. I had to pick up some supplies for my wife.**
>
> **Abbie's Mac: You're married?**

Cameron cringed and shot daggers from where he sat.

> **Abbie's Mac: Too soon?**

He glared at me while I burst out laughing.

> **Abbie's Mac: Come on! It was a little bit funny!**

Dead green eyes stared back at me before he typed.

> **Cameron's Mac: Not even a little.**
>
> **Abbie's Mac: Okay let's see the supplies.**

He pulled out two boxes of Milk Duds, my only pregnancy craving.

> **Abbie's Mac: Thank you. What else do you have over there?**

He pulled out some Ziti noodles and shrugged.

Cameron's Mac: I called Mrs. Zingaro while I was at the store to see if she needed anything.

My sweet man.

Abbie's Mac: You're so wonderful to her and I love you more for it. Anything else?

He pulled out a onesie that read *Future King of Woo*.

Abbie's Mac: Did you have that made?

He gave me a slow pride filled nod.

Abbie's Mac: God I love you. I'm such a shit. Okay, let's start over.

Cameron's Mac: Fine. Hi.

Abbie's Mac: You can't type Fine. Hi. Try again.

Cameron's body sagged. "Really?"

Abbie's Mac: Hey pal, we're only a few months into this marriage thing. You better give me more effort than that. And you better not ever be mean to me when I'm sick. I heard that's a thing with married people. And I demand that you have sex with me tonight. I was doing this to open you up to the possibility and try to mix things up, but now I'm just going to put it out there. I'm

a wife now, I can demand sex when I want it, right? We need to have sex. I need this baby out of me right now!

Cameron's full-blown laughter could have been heard for miles. I glared at him in the space between us. My macaroni table at my hip because I was too big to fit in the tight space despite my vigorous workouts. Our son already weighed eight pounds.

"God you're beautiful," he said across our tables. I lifted my hot cocoa in my cup of choice that read *MILF.*

Cameron laughed as I puffed out air and blew the bangs I cut in a hormone rage out of my eyes. I looked at the darkening sky outside as I tried to swallow my emotion.

With every day that passed, I was fighting the Olympics of tamping down my random rotation of emotions. I had hurdled the first few months of my pregnancy hormones, but the last few had proved just as hard on me.

"I don't want to cry, so don't be nice. Piss me off or something."

My chin wobbled, and Cameron caught it. The way he caught everything, because he was good at it.

"Baby, don't you get it yet?" He stared at me across the space. "I don't care what you say, as long as you're talking to me. I'd give in to any demand you made, as long as it was of *me*. All you have to do is reach for me and I'll give you what you need. I don't need to be courted by my wife, who I'm obsessed with by the way. I'll follow *your* lead, always."

And here come the waterworks.

I took in his five o'clock shadow and his longer hair—a new part of his appearance I'd grown to love. He'd made it a point to have his own slob days of the week and I loved every second of them.

I wiped a tear of fear away showing him the truth. "Promise? Because I'm kind of sad we didn't get more time alone and I know I said I was okay with being second, but maybe I'm a little jealous. I don't want us to change."

"Come on. I want to show you something." Cameron stood and walked over to me, pulled my hand and gathered our things before we made our way outside. The instant we set foot on the cement, snow began to drift down around us.

"I wish I could take credit for this," he whispered pulling me into his arms and pressing his lips to mine. His kiss became urgent, more frantic, reminding me of the first one we shared the previous winter, except this kiss wasn't mixed with fear and what if's. It was filled with certainty and a new kind of longing. It wasn't rehearsed, but it was comforting. When he pulled away I saw the life we lived unfold as snowflakes dotted his lashes.

"A year ago, I kissed you for the first time in this same spot."

Just as I thought it, he verbalized it.

"And it felt different then. It was new. Things change. But *we've* changed too, Abbie Bledsoe, and we can't stop it. And with you, I don't want to stop it. I want to go through all those changes. I'm not afraid of them," he assured as he rubbed my face with his palms.

"Let's go home, okay? I have a feeling my wife needs a little attention."

"Okay."

We walked home hand in hand as the snow drifted silently to the sidewalk. Cameron held me tightly to his side as I tried to make a quick excuse for my crazy.

"I blame the latest outburst on the penis growing inside me. Do you have any idea how weird that is?"

"I didn't even think about it that way, but now it's weird," he said with a chuckle. I nudged him as I wrapped as much of my arm around him as I could. "I was thinking about a name today."

"Oh, no," he looked at me full of objection and shaking his head. "I don't want to fight, okay? I think it's cool you want to name our kid something unique, but I will not be naming our baby a direction or something that's found in the produce aisle. Seriously, this new celebrity stalking is getting out of control. I never thought I'd see the day I wished to watch another serial killer documentary, but I do."

"Hey," I defended. "The only reason I started watching those celebrity miracle workers was to see how quick I could bounce back from pear-shaped to something a little more banana like. And then, I don't know . . . it was like a vortex and I got sucked in. I'll snap out of it eventually. I'm over the serial killer phase. Besides, I was thinking of a *word* that describes his father, not a direction *or* a fruit."

Cameron turned to me in the snow drift and looked down with curious eyes.

"Noble."

His brows drew together. "That's the word you would use to describe me?"

I reached up and wrapped my arms around his neck and pulled him to me while I ran my fingers through the thick hair at the base of it.

"Absolutely."

Stunned, I could see the emotion building in his eyes as he leaned in and took my lips in the gentlest kiss we'd ever shared. He pulled away, his eyes searching mine as he stroked my face.

Noble it is.

"Abbie, you make me feel so high," he said as he wrapped

me in his hold and pressed a kiss to my forehead. "Come on, I need to go stretch for the sex you demanded."

I playfully slapped his chest. It took me a few minutes of walking to realize I'd done it and neither of us was affected by it. I felt another lump form in my throat as I looked over to Cameron and squeezed his arm.

"Don't be a smartass but what word would you use to describe me?"

"I've got several," he said with a wink.

After a few seconds, I paused our walk. "Well, aren't you going to tell me?" I asked.

He gripped my freezing hands warming them up in his with his scorn.

"You forgot your gloves."

"Cameron," I said in warning. "You can't think of one word to describe me?"

"I have too many. Goddess, light, hope, heart, mother, wife, healer, menace, beautiful, life, sex, empath, sunshine . . . and rain."

"And rain?"

"Yep."

"But you hate the rain."

"Not anymore," he said as he twisted my wedding ring from inside my palm to right it on my finger before he kissed it.

"Anything else?"

"Real."

The End

Listen to *The Real* Playlist on Spotify

According to the NCADV-National Coalition Against Domestic Violence

On average, nearly 20 people per minute are physically abused by an intimate partner in the United States. During one year, this equates to more than 10 million women and men.

1 in 3 women and 1 in 4 men have been victims of [some form of] physical violence by an intimate partner within their lifetime.

1 in 4 women and 1 in 7 men have been victims of severe physical violence by an intimate partner in their lifetime.

1 in 7 women and 1 in 18 men have been stalked by an intimate partner during their lifetime to the point in which they felt very fearful or believed that they or someone close to them would be harmed or killed.

Read more about it here: ncadv.org/statistics

If you need help please call the National Domestic Violence Hotline

1-800-799-7233

Thank you to every reader who has given any of my books a chance. Because of you, all my dreams have come true. I'm forever grateful and I hold you in my heart.

I've got so much love for this community. I want to thank every blogger who spent their precious time reading and promoting my words. Thank you will never be enough for all you do. You're appreciated more than I could ever express.

There are two women who have worked with me since day one. This book would not be what it is without them.

A huge thank you to my sister, Angela Scott, who helped me from the starting line with the development of the story and who became so passionate about the project she texted me daily to point out some needed details. Your enthusiasm for this one made the process so much better. It was such a blast working with you! Thank you for those details, and for listening to me as I hashed this story out. I love you.

And Donna Cooksley Sanderson, I would be lost without you. Because you pushed me, this book is exactly what I hoped it would be. You refused to let me off easy and forced me to dig deep and I thank you so much for it. There are billions of people in the world and to have been paired with a person so perfectly suited for a coach, well, I'm convinced it's not a coincidence. I finished the marathon because of you and your endless support. You became such a vital part of this process and made my days so much better. Thank you for the endless hours on facetime, for sacrificing time with family, sleep, and your sanity to get me through. Your endless patience was such a blessing. I love you, dear friend.

A huge thank you to my betas, Kelly Collopy, Sophie Broughton, Sharon Dunn, Anne Christine, Kathy Sheffler, Stacy Hahn, Donna Sanderson, Maiwenn Blogs, Malene Dich, Patty Tennyson, Daisy Rock, and Christy Baldwin. Your feedback was invaluable and your support priceless. You ladies are amazing.

A huge thank you to Amy Queau for helping my vision for the cover come to life.

Thank you, Stacey Ryan Blake of Champagne Formats, for pulling these books together and polishing them so beautifully.

Autumn, you are amazing. Thank you for taking this writer on with no guarantees and nothing but faith. I'm so happy we found each other. I can't wait to see what's next. Thank you so much for all you do.

A huge and never-ending thank you to my wonderful and tolerant PA, Bex Kettner. Bex, you are the most amazing lady. Your strength, patience, and friendship, especially these last few months, has meant everything. I love you. Thank you being the stellar friend that you are. And thank you for all you do.

A huge thank you to Christy Baldwin, who continues to take the baton running and always shows up to the party. You are a true blessing and I adore you.

A special thank you to my dear friends, Emma Scott and Jewel E. Ann, for the bitch slaps and the hand holding. This one was rough, and I couldn't have done it without you. Thank you, Kennedy Ryan, for being there for message jam sessions and making me laugh. You are awesome!

Thank you to Jessica Florence who messages me with nothing but inspiration. I feel the hugs across the miles. You are a true and dear friend.

A huge and never-ending thank you to my ASSKICKERS! Wow, ladies, how we've grown and I'm so fortunate to have a safe-haven full of friends like you. Your bottomless support is astounding, and I'm so blessed to have you ladies in my life. Thank you, thank you, thank you!

Thank you to my girls in DHI-I love laughing and crying with you.

A collective thanks to my amazing family and dear friends spread out across the miles. Without your support, I know I wouldn't have been able to get far.

A huge thank you to my rock, Nick, my home, my forever. I love you.

About the Author

USA Today bestselling author and Texas native, Kate Stewart, lives in North Carolina with her husband, Nick. Nestled within the Blue Ridge Mountains, Kate pens messy, sexy, angst-filled contemporary romance, as well as romantic comedy and erotic suspense.

Kate's title, *Drive*, was named one of the best romances of 2017 by The New York Daily News and Huffington Post. *Drive* was also a finalist in the Goodreads Choice awards for best contemporary romance of 2017. The Ravenhood Trilogy, consisting of *Flock*, *Exodus*, and *The Finish Line*, has become an international bestseller and reader favorite. Her holiday release, *The Plight Before Christmas*, ranked #6 on Amazon's Top 100. Kate's works have been featured in *USA TODAY*, *BuzzFeed*, *The New York Daily News*, *Huffington Post* and translated into a dozen languages.

Kate is a lover of all things '80s and '90s, especially John Hughes films and rap. She dabbles a little in photography, can knit a simple stitch scarf for necessity, and on occasion, does very well at whiskey.

Let's stay in touch!

www.facebook.com/authorkatestewart

www.twitter.com/authorklstewart

www.instagram.com/authorkatestewart/?hl=en

www.facebook.com/groups/793483714004942

open.spotify.com/user/authorkatestewart

Sign up for the newsletter now and get a free eBook from Kate's Library!

www.katestewartwrites.com/contact-me.html

Other titles available now by Kate

Romantic Suspense

*The Ravenhood Series
Flock
Exodus
The Finish Line*

*Lust & Lies Series
Sexual Awakenings
Excess
Predator and Prey
The Lust & Lies Box set: Sexual Awakenings, Excess, Predator and Prey*

Contemporary Romance

In Reading Order

*Room 212
Never Me (Companion to Room 212 and The Reluctant Romantic Series)
The Reluctant Romantics Series
The Fall
The Mind
The Heart
The Reluctant Romantics Box Set: The Fall, The Heart, The Mind
Loving the White Liar*

The Bittersweet Symphony
Drive
Reverse

The Real
Someone Else's Ocean
Heartbreak Warfare
Method

Romantic Dramedy

Balls in Play Series
Anything but Minor
Major Love
Sweeping the Series Novella
Balls in play Box Set: Anything but Minor, Major Love, Sweeping the Series, The Golden Sombrero

The Underdogs Series
The Guy on the Right
The Guy on the Left
The Guy in the Middle
The Underdogs Box Set: The Guy on The Right, The Guy on the Left, The Guy in the Middle

The Plight Before Christmas

Printed in Great Britain
by Amazon